PRAISE FOR THE NOVELS OF KAREN ROSE

"From the first rousing chapter to the last, *Scream for Me* is intense, complex, and unforgettable."
—#1 *New York Times* bestselling author James Patterson

"Riveting. Emotional. Karen Rose at her best."
—#1 *New York Times* bestselling author Christine Feehan

"High-wire suspense that keeps you riveted."
—#1 *New York Times* bestselling author Lisa Gardner

"A high-octane thrill ride that kept me on the edge of my seat and up far too late at night!"
—#1 *New York Times* bestselling author Lisa Jackson

"Fierce suspense and compelling romance . . . pure alchemy."
—*New York Times* bestselling author Jayne Ann Krentz

"Takes off like a house afire. There's action and chills galore in this nonstop thriller."
—*New York Times* bestselling author Tess Gerritsen

"A fast-paced, high-intensity story that'll carry you along on an amazing journey."
—*New York Times* bestselling author Lori Foster

"Blistering, high-octane suspense that never lets up."
—*New York Times* bestselling author Karen Robards

"Suspenseful and engrossing."
—#1 *New York Times*

"Karen Rose has written anot
this book. You wo   be able t
—*New York Times* be

TITLES BY KAREN ROSE

DIRTY SECRETS
(enovella)

Baltimore Novels
YOU BELONG TO ME
NO ONE LEFT TO TELL
DID YOU MISS ME?
BROKEN SILENCE
(enovella)
WATCH YOUR BACK
MONSTER IN THE CLOSET
DEATH IS NOT ENOUGH

Cincinnati Novels
CLOSER THAN YOU THINK
ALONE IN THE DARK
EVERY DARK CORNER
EDGE OF DARKNESS
INTO THE DARK

Sacramento Novels
SAY YOU'RE SORRY
SAY NO MORE
SAY GOODBYE

New Orleans Novels
QUARTER TO MIDNIGHT
BENEATH DARK WATERS
BURIED TOO DEEP

San Diego Case Files
COLD-BLOODED LIAR
CHEATER

BURIED TOO DEEP

KAREN ROSE

BERKLEY
New York

BERKLEY
An imprint of Penguin Random House LLC
penguinrandomhouse.com

Book design by Alison Cnockaert

ISBN: 9780593638606

Berkley hardcover edition / August 2024
Berkley mass-market edition / January 2025

Printed in the United States of America
1   3   5   7   9   10   8   6   4   2

To the Starfish—
Christine, Sheila, Brian, Kathie, and Cheryl.
I love you all, especially your fiendish minds!

And, as always, to my precious Martin. I love you.

PROLOGUE

Merrydale, Louisiana
SATURDAY, OCTOBER 16, 4:45 A.M.
TWENTY-THREE YEARS AGO

THROUGH HIS BINOCULARS, Alan watched the man emerge from the house at the end of a private drive. It was a nice house with a dark green door and a tidy front yard. The man's hands had been full when he'd entered. Now they were empty, save for the satchel he now carried.

It's done.

The magnitude of Alan's actions hit him like a punch to the gut, a wave of shame that made him sick to his stomach. But it was too late to wonder if he'd done the right thing.

It's done.

The man he'd hired to do this terrible thing threw one last look over his shoulder at the house before putting the satchel into the trunk of a plain brown sedan.

Payment for a service rendered.

Then the man got into the sedan and drove toward the main road.

Setting the binoculars on the empty passenger seat, Alan flexed his fingers in the leather gloves he'd worn to keep from leaving fingerprints. There was no one with him tonight. No one to witness what he'd already done. Nor what he was about to do.

When the brown sedan turned onto the main highway, he followed the man. He needed to get far away from here to accomplish what he needed to do. Far away from that nice house with the green door and the tidy front yard.

For an hour he drove, biding his time. For an hour the brown sedan seemed not to know he was being followed, and that was . . . unsettling. The man should suspect. He should notice. He'd seemed much smarter than this when they'd spoken on the phone, even though the voice distortion device the man had used had made it hard to detect details.

The man's name was John Robertson. Or so he'd claimed. Alan didn't believe that, but it didn't really matter.

Finally, John turned the brown sedan into the nearly empty parking lot of a grocery store. The store was closed for the night and a few of the tall streetlights were burned out, creating pockets of darkness. John drove into one of those dark pockets, stopping next to a silver Lexus. He got out of the brown sedan and opened the door to the Lexus with his key.

John was switching from his job car to his actual car.

Alan had expected as much. He'd done something similar, after all.

Turning off his headlights, he let his own car glide to a stop on the other side of the brown sedan and got out. *Finally*, John looked up, surprise on his face before it changed to fear as he reached into his pocket.

Don't hesitate. Just do it.

Before he could change his mind, Alan lifted the gun in his hand and fired over the top of his car, thankful that he'd spent the extra money for the silencer. It wasn't silent, but it was quiet. And there was no one around to hear either the little pop or John's groan of pain.

He looked around and, still seeing no one, rounded the brown sedan to where John lay on the asphalt, blood spreading to soak the front of his shirt. Wide eyes stared up at him and Alan stared back, committing John's face to memory. It was the least he could do.

"Help me," John whispered. "Please. Help me."

"I'm sorry," Alan said softly, because he was. Sorry that any of this had happened. Sorry that he'd been forced to do such terrible things. "I'm so sorry."

"I have a family," John begged. "A wife. Babies. My son is sick. I have to get home to him. Take my money. Take my car. Just . . . help me."

But he couldn't. He simply couldn't.

Finish what you came here to do.

"I'm sorry." Drawing a breath, Alan pointed the gun at John's head and fired twice more.

He had to make sure John was dead. Had to make sure John couldn't live to tell.

Two men can keep a secret if one of them is dead.

It was a truth he'd have to live with for the rest of his life.

Leaning over John's body, he pressed the trunk release and retrieved the satchel. He would never spend the money, but he couldn't leave it. Couldn't leave anything that could trace back to him or what he had done.

Then he got back into his car and drove away, leaving John's body where it had fallen.

He drove the long way back to New Orleans, to the north of Lake Pontchartrain, exiting the interstate in Slidell to park the car he'd been driving on the side of a deserted road, keys left in the ignition. With any luck, someone would steal it before dawn.

Then he gathered the satchel, his binoculars, and his gun and walked a mile to where he'd parked his own car. He got in and drove home.

Forgive me, Lord. I didn't have a choice.

It was done. And God willing, he'd never have to do anything like that ever again.

1

1

The Quarter, New Orleans, Louisiana
TUESDAY, DECEMBER 13, 8:01 A.M.
TWENTY-THREE YEARS LATER

PHIN BISHOP STUMBLED to a stop, staring up at the building that was as close to a home as he'd known in a long time. It wasn't the building itself, of course, although it was beautiful with its cast iron balconies and its shutters thrown wide in welcome.

Even to me. He hoped.

Because the magic of the building wasn't in its bricks or balconies. It was in the people who worked within its walls. Burke Broussard and his people had become Phin's family.

But I deserted them. I ran.

No. He could hear the voice of his therapist in his mind. *You didn't "run." You have PTSD. You left to get better.*

But was he better?

Am I ready to be back?

A hand closed over his shoulder, warm and reassuring. "Phin?" Stone O'Bannion murmured. "We can come back tomorrow. Or we can get SodaPop. This is exactly what she's trained for. Helping you through situations just like this."

Swallowing hard, Phin turned to meet his best friend's eyes and saw understanding and compassion that Phin didn't think he deserved. Stone was right. Phin should

have brought his new service dog. But he hadn't, wanting
to stand on his own two feet.

Which had been wrong thinking. He knew that. Knew
that there was no shame in needing a service dog. No
shame in having PTSD. He'd accepted that. Accepted that
he'd have episodes. That he'd sometimes relapse.

SodaPop made it easier to stave off his episodes. Helped
him recover faster when he did relapse.

And you deserve that help. Those words were again in
his therapist's voice. Phin could accept that there was no
shame in needing his dog. But he hadn't been able to accept that he deserved the assistance. And that was the real
reason he'd left SodaPop behind this morning.

"That we could come back tomorrow is what you said
yesterday," Phin said. And yesterday, he'd jumped at the
chance to turn tail and run.

He'd been running most of his life.

"And I'll say it tomorrow and the next day." Stone gave
his shoulder a squeeze. Anchoring him. "What are you
afraid of? Be honest with me."

Phin forced the words out. "That they won't want me
back."

"If they don't, it'll hurt," Stone acknowledged, and Phin
was grateful that Stone hadn't brushed his concerns away.
"But I read their texts." Phin had given Stone permission to
read all the communication from his New Orleans friends.
"These people care about you. They will want you back."

"What if I flake again?" He hated losing control of his
own mind, hated the spiral that tugged him under.

Stone shrugged. "Then you leave, you heal, and you try
again."

Phin's chest hurt. "I'm so tired of leaving."

"Then stay. Take a step. Right now. There you go. Now
another. That's the way."

Phin forced his feet to move closer to the building that
housed Broussard Investigations. "I should have stopped
for beignets."

Stone chuckled, clearly not fooled by the lame procrastination attempt. "I'll get some for you. Once you're inside and talking to your friends."

The building grew closer and Phin's chest grew tighter. "Why are you still here? Babysitting me?" He was grateful. He was. But he didn't entirely understand why Stone put up with him. "You have better things to do."

"No, I don't. Right now, I'm exactly where I need to be, doing what I need to do. Because you need me. And because I've been where you are. Someone stuck by my side until I could walk alone." Phin knew Stone's story. His friend had been an addict, sober for years now. "So I'm paying it forward, doing it for you. Keep walking, Phin."

They were nearly at the front door. *Just another fifteen feet.*

Then the door burst open, banging into the wall behind it. Startled at the sound, Phin lurched back, once again grateful for Stone's steadying hand. When he'd righted himself, he got a glimpse of the woman who'd thrown the door open. She wore a gray hooded cloak that hid her face, but a wisp of black hair escaped the hood to whip in the wind. For a moment, Phin stood stock-still, staring as she rushed away, heading toward the center of the Quarter.

The only part of her body that was visible was her legs.

They were very nice legs. Her calves were perfectly defined, thanks to the three-inch heels she wore. How she was able to walk in heels that high—much less run—was a mystery.

She took an abrupt left at the next intersection and disappeared from view.

"Who was that?" Stone asked.

"I don't know." He'd never seen her before. He'd remember legs like that.

Importantly, her appearance had stopped the mental spiral of his anxiety. Sometimes a distraction was exactly what he needed to get his head on straight.

That's what SodaPop's supposed to do, you idiot.

Fine. Next time he'd bring her along.

"Did she come from your office?" Stone pressed. "From Broussard Investigations?"

Phin stilled. She hadn't been a woman with nice legs. She'd been a *fleeing* woman with nice legs. "Shit."

The sound of two gunshots, one right after the other, shoved his body into motion, and he started to run.

"Joy." *She'll be alone.* Because she was always the first in the office.

"Joy's the office manager?" Stone asked, running beside him. "The lady who uses a wheelchair?"

"Yes." Phin bypassed the ancient elevator and took the stairs. He'd told Stone about everyone in Burke's office. He cared about them all, but Joy was special. She'd accepted him from the beginning. Taken him under her wing. Mothered him. Trusted him. "Ex-cop. Got shot on the job. Paralyzed from the waist down. Tougher than she looks."

She'd be okay. Joy could take care of herself, he told himself, propelling himself up the last few stairs in a single leap.

They rushed from the stairwell into Burke's lobby. It was an open space with large windows along one wall that faced the street below. Joy's desk would be in the dead center of the room and she'd be sitting behind her computer, doing whatever it was she did every morning. She'd give him a look that was both chiding and welcoming.

Just like all the other times he'd returned from having run.

Except . . . she wasn't behind her desk.

"Oh no." Phin's heart went from a gallop to a dead stop.

Because Joy lay on the floor next to her desk, her wheelchair on its side. Her white blouse was rapidly becoming red with blood and she wasn't moving.

"*No,*" he gasped, racing to her side. "Call 911."

"Already on it," Stone said grimly.

Phin pressed his fingers to Joy's throat, searching for a pulse. She was a petite woman, barely five foot two. But she was strong, emotionally and physically. She could not be dead.

His shoulders sagged when he felt a faint pulse. But his relief was short lived when he saw the blood pooling beneath her head. Wounds to her head and heart.

"Fuck!" Stone snapped, and Phin spared him a glance. His friend had the big window open and was half hanging out of it. "Yes, I'm sure," he was snarling at the 911 operator. "There's a man running from this building. Dressed in black. Ski mask covering his face. He's headed north."

The same direction in which the woman had fled.

Later. Phin ripped off his coat, then pulled his T-shirt over his head and pressed it to her chest since that wound was bleeding more profusely. Her entire blouse was now soaked.

"Joy." He fought for calm. Took deep breaths, just as his therapist had taught him. "It's Phin. Stay with me."

The clatter of running feet had him looking up in time to see two uniformed cops rushing toward him. Guns drawn.

"Back away from her," one commanded.

"You, by the window," the other snarled, "put down the phone and put your hands in the air."

"I'm helping her," Phin insisted, and he could hear his panic. "If I let go, she'll bleed out."

"I'm talking to 911," Stone said, putting up his hands but holding on to his phone.

The second cop snatched the phone from Stone's hand and exchanged a few words with the operator before returning Stone's phone. "Just keep your hands where I can see them."

The first cop stalked toward Phin, gun still drawn. "You are?"

"Phin Bishop."

"What are you doing here?"

"I work here. I came in and found her this way. When will the medics be here?" The blood flow had slowed, but

Phin didn't know if it was because of the pressure he was applying or if she was bleeding out.

Please don't die.

He couldn't do this again. Couldn't have blood on his hands again. He'd barely survived the last time.

"They're on their way," the first cop said.

But Phin barely heard him, his ear hovering over Joy's mouth, listening for her next breath. Her chest had stopped rising and falling, and a new wave of panic washed over him. "She's not breathing. *Stone.*"

Ignoring the second cop's protest, Stone left his post by the window and joined Phin on the floor next to Joy. "I'm going to do mouth-to-mouth," he said. "You keep applying pressure."

Horrified, Phin kept both hands pressed to Joy's wound while Stone breathed for her.

"Let me go! Goddammit, let me go!" a male voice demanded, heavy with a Cajun drawl that could only belong to one man.

Burke Broussard was here. Phin's boss would know what to do.

Burke shook off the cop's grip, his bike helmet clutched in one hand. "Phin?" The bike helmet dropped to the floor as Burke stared, myriad emotions flickering over his face.

Fear. Surprise. Horror.

And there, for just a moment, accusation.

Burke thought that Phin had done this.

Phin stiffened. He didn't have to wonder about his welcome anymore. He now knew the answer. Burke thought he was capable of hurting Joy. "We found her," Phin said bitterly.

Another man raced into the lobby from one of the back offices, his clothes rumpled. Antoine Holmes, their IT specialist. "Phin? What the fuck?" His gaze pivoted to Stone, breathing into Joy's mouth. "Stone? What're you doing here? What the hell's going on?"

Burke and Antoine rushed over to where Joy lay. Burke

dropped to his knees next to Phin. "Tell me what happened."

Antoine knelt on the other side of Stone, looking helpless. But not accusatory.

At least there was that.

Phin lowered his gaze to his bloody hands pressed to Joy's even bloodier chest, to Stone still giving her mouth-to-mouth. "We found her" were the only words he could find to say.

Burke brushed his hand over Joy's close-cropped hair. "Joy, honey, I'm here." He spared Phin a quick glance. "I'm sorry, Phin. I panicked. I know you could never hurt her."

Stone looked up, glaring at Burke. "Asshole," he muttered, then went back to breathing for Joy. "Cameras?" he asked during his next mini break.

Burke looked over at Antoine. "Did you check the feed?"

"Yeah." Antoine scrubbed at his face with his palms. "I was asleep at my desk. Headphones on. Heard the shots but they were muffled. Didn't wake me up right away. I immediately checked the feed. It was a man, dressed in black. Joy shot him, then he and Joy fought over her gun. He shot her, then hit her head with the grip. Pushed her wheelchair over."

"I should have hired . . ." Burke winced, his voice trailing off.

"Night security," Phin muttered, because . . . yeah. "This is my fault."

Burke's voice hardened. "No, it's not." He stared at Stone. "Why are you here?"

"He came with me," Phin said. He knew that Burke knew who Stone was. It was Stone who'd asked Antoine to help Phin get a job in New Orleans. Antoine had asked Burke, who'd welcomed him into the group. "Escorted the prodigal son home," he added, hoping his words hurt Burke to hear as much as they hurt him to say.

He thought I did this.

Burke winced. "Dammit, Phin. At least wait to be angry

until after we get Joy taken care of. Was she conscious at all? Did she say anything?"

Burke was right. This was about Joy. *Not me.*

"No. She was unconscious when we found her. We saw a woman running from the building, heard the shots, then Stone saw a man running away. That's all I know."

Burke clasped Phin's shoulder much as Stone had done. Phin fought the urge to shake him off. "I'm glad you're home," Burke said quietly. "I swear it."

Phin wished he could believe that. "Where are the medics?" he shouted to the cops, who were just standing around, watching.

"On their way up," one of the cops said.

Thirty seconds later, two medics with a stretcher burst out of the elevator. Stone straightened, sitting back on his heels as they put an oxygen mask over Joy's mouth.

"Phin," Stone said quietly, tugging at his arm. "Let them get to her. You need to move."

Woodenly Phin rose and took a step back, his hands warm and wet with Joy's blood. Now that the medics were here, he focused on the blood dripping from his hands.

And remembered the last time.

The office dissolved, Phin's nightmares taking its place. Explosions. People screaming. Bodies falling.

Body parts everywhere. Just . . . everywhere.

And blood dripped from Phin's hands. So much blood.

Dry hands gripped Phin's face harshly. "Phin," Stone hissed. "Stay with us."

Phin blinked. Stone was staring at him, his expression too urgent to ignore.

"There you are," his friend said with relief. "Don't disappear on me." Stone spared an angry glance at Burke. "You're an asshole."

Burke was watching the medics work on Joy, his face pale under his tan. "I know."

Phin shuddered. "His reaction was fair."

"It wasn't," Burke said quietly. "I'm sorry."

"What the fuck happened? What did you do, Burke?" Antoine asked, but his voice was growing faint.

The whole room was growing faint as the buzzing in Phin's head grew louder.

Shit. Not now. Not again.

Phin leaned against the wall. His brain was going numb. He could feel it happening. Sliding to the floor, he watched the medics with the out-of-body detachedness that he hated so much.

He was disappearing. Again.

The Quarter, New Orleans, Louisiana
TUESDAY, DECEMBER 13, 8:25 A.M.

Cora Winslow darted around the pedestrians on Bourbon Street, trying not to look like she was fleeing for her life. Even though she was.

The throwaway phone was cutting into her hand, her grip on it punishing. *Call 911 again. Get help.*

But panic had overtaken her, her feet still rushing forward. *Get to Tandy's.*

Her best friend's art gallery was a safe place.

She glanced over her shoulder and nearly cried with relief. No sign of the man who'd stormed the private investigator's office.

Unless he'd removed the ski mask and his black jacket.

She had, after all. Not a ski mask, but she had taken off her cloak, bunching it up and carrying it under her arm like a football. The black wig she'd worn had come off as soon as she'd turned the first corner and had been flung into a dumpster outside a diner after she'd cut through the kitchen. The banging pots and pans and shouts of the staff had been muted by the pounding of her own heart in her ears as she'd darted out the back door.

And then she'd seen him a block away, running in her direction.

Run. She'd done exactly that, crisscrossing the back alleys of the Quarter that she knew so well.

Cora loved New Orleans. She never wanted to leave.

But she might have to. The city was no longer safe for her. This morning had proved that.

She turned onto Bienville, passing her favorite bakery without even stopping to look in the window. As usual, there was a line of people waiting for cupcakes, and she used them as a shield, mumbling apologies as she slipped through the line to get to the alley behind the bakery.

She was finally alone. She leaned against the bakery's delivery van, drawing her first full breath since the intruder had shoved past Joy into the boss's office, demanding to know where "the Winslow woman" was hiding.

Cora's throat closed. *I should have stayed with her.* But Joy had told her to run and Cora had suddenly been a teenager again, obeying the woman who'd been one of her mother's dearest friends. Joy had insisted that the man in her boss's office would soon realize that everything in there was locked down tight and abandon his search. That she was armed and could take care of herself.

Run before he comes out. He doesn't want me. He wants you. Run, girl. Now.

So Cora had run.

At least she'd called 911 before she'd taken off. The cops would come and help.

Drawing another deep breath, Cora shook out her cloak, draping it over her arm. She was sweating despite the morning chill.

Tandy would know something was wrong. They'd been best friends since the third grade. Nobody knew her better. Nobody that was still alive, anyway.

Move. Get to the gallery. Think of a reason you look like you ran through the city like you were being chased.

"Ma'am?"

Cora wheeled around to find a young man giving her a troubled look. "Yes?" Her voice was full of residual fear.

The young man worked at the bakery, if his Marica's T-shirt was any indication. He was tall and lanky, like he still needed to grow into his frame. But his blue eyes were kind. "Are you all right, ma'am?"

"I'm okay. Just . . ." She managed a smile. "Can't do crowds." It was a lie. She'd grown up in New Orleans and crowds were a fact of life.

He didn't look convinced. "Can I call somebody to help you?"

She must have looked as bad as she felt. "No, thank you. I'm really fine. Have a good day."

She set off at a brisk walk, ignoring his repeated offer to call someone for her.

Great. A witness. She looked around and sighed. There were cameras everywhere. Her flight from Broussard Investigations had undoubtedly been captured.

You didn't do anything wrong.

Except leave Joy behind.

She turned another corner into another alley, only pausing when she emerged onto Royal Street, Tandy's gallery now within sight. Her friend didn't open the front doors until ten, but she'd be there already, doing the books or inventory or whatever tasks needed to be done.

She'll know something's wrong. She hadn't told Tandy that she was going to see a private investigator because her best friend was a worrier. Then Tandy would tell her father and they'd both smother Cora with concern and Cora hated that. Their concern always made her feel helpless and she *wasn't* helpless, dammit. She'd been taking care of herself for a long, long time.

Besides, she hadn't even been sure she had a valid reason for her fear. Not until this morning.

Now . . . well, Tandy was going to be mad that Cora had kept this from her.

Slipping the burner phone into her pocket, Cora pulled the pins from her hair, releasing the braids she'd put up that morning so that she could wear the black wig.

Just in case whoever had been messing with her house was watching her.

Uneasy now, she looked around, searching for the man who'd chased her. All she saw were a few tourists, out early to gape at the sights.

Working the braids in her hair free, she knocked on the front door of Tandy's gallery, but it was dark inside and there was no sign of anyone. Cora frowned. Tandy was always in her office by eight a.m.

I need to get off the street.

Just because she didn't see the man who'd chased her didn't mean he wasn't out there.

She race-walked to the next alley and to the gallery's back door. Punching in the keypad code, she let herself into the storeroom that doubled as Tandy's office and disabled the alarm, then locked the door and reset the alarm. It was a security door and the windows were hurricane glass. Nobody was getting in.

She sank into Tandy's desk chair. *I'm safe.* And now she could think.

She'd run this morning, like a coward. She needed to make sure that Joy was all right. Setting the burner aside, she dialed Joy's cell from her personal phone, but it rang and rang. New dread made it hard to breathe once more.

"Answer your phone, Joy," she muttered, but it went to voicemail.

I shouldn't have run.

She had started to leave a message when another call came through. It was Tandy.

"Where are you?" Cora demanded, not even saying hello.

"In an Uber on my way to the hospital. Why are you in my office? Are you all right?"

Cora lurched to her feet and stared into the camera in the corner of the office. Tandy could see the live feeds on her phone. "Am *I* all right? Are *you* all right? Why are you going to the hospital?"

That they'd go after her friends hadn't occurred to her. *I should have told her everything.*

"I'm fine. It's Joy. She was shot."

Cora's knees buckled and she landed back in the chair. "What?" she croaked weakly.

"Joy was shot this morning. Her boss told Nala, and Nala sent out a group text. I'm going to sit with her. Why are you in my office, Cora? What's wrong?"

"I . . . I just wanted . . ." She didn't know how to finish that sentence. She quickly checked her messages and saw the text from Joy's daughter Nala. And the ten follow-up texts from Tandy. "Is Joy okay?"

"Nala doesn't know yet. She and Louisa are waiting on the doctor to tell them."

Cora's stomach rolled. *This is all my fault.*

"Cora, what is wrong with you? *Tell me.*"

"I need to go. I'll meet you at the hospital."

Cora ended the call, a wave of nausea washing over her. She would not be sick.

I shouldn't have run. It should have been me that was shot. Not Joy.

But even as she thought the words, she knew they weren't true. *No one should have been shot.* But especially not Joy.

Squaring her shoulders, Cora rose. She wasn't going to the hospital. She was going to the police station.

She'd make sure they listened to her this time.

The Quarter, New Orleans, Louisiana
TUESDAY, DECEMBER 13, 10:45 A.M.

Phin stared at his hands, clenched into fists on the tabletop in the NOPD interrogation room. *Interview,* the cop had insisted. *Not interrogation.*

But it had felt that way from the moment they'd taken him into custody, his bloody hands bagged—to preserve evidence, the cops had insisted.

His hands were clean now, at least. Clean and stinking of disinfectant.

He knew someone watched him on the other side of the mirror. He wasn't going to give them any more ammunition against him.

Once they'd put him in this room, they'd talked at him, asking him the same questions over and over.

Why did you come back today?

Who did you see running away from the building?

What's wrong *with you?*

That last question was because he hadn't answered a single question. He hadn't said a word, not when they'd cleaned the blood from his hands. Not when they'd done a test for gunpowder residue. He'd just stared at his hands.

Like he was still doing.

I'm okay.

But he wasn't okay, and none of the techniques his therapist had taught him were helping. His breaths were becoming shallow and sharp, his vision wavy. He could hear the explosions. The screams. The pleas for help.

The pleas for death.

No. You will not go back there.

A door opened, but Phin didn't look up. Not until a cold nose pressed against his arm, a rough tongue licking his skin.

The explosions faded. The screams and pleas subsided. He could hear himself think again. He shuddered out a breath, choking back a sob.

SodaPop.

Phin's hands were in the golden retriever's coat before he was even aware he'd moved, and he pressed his face against her neck. Phin hadn't wanted to be dependent on the dog.

Except that he was. In six short weeks, SodaPop had become his lifeline.

Phin found that he could draw air deep into his lungs.

I'm okay.

He would be, anyway.

Wiping his wet eyes, he looked up. The detective who'd first brought him in was watching him with sympathy. Not pity. Phin knew the difference.

Detective Clancy sat at the table. "Better?"

"Yes, thanks."

"I served. Iraq in the nineties." Clancy shrugged. "PTSD's a bitch. You should have asked for your dog when we first brought you in."

"I don't think I was capable of that then," Phin said honestly.

"Yeah. I get that, too." Then one corner of his mouth lifted in a smirk. "Your friend Stone's wife brought the dog in. The desk sergeant told her that she couldn't bring the dog into the station. I understand she read him the riot act."

"Yeah, Delores is a force of nature." Stone's wife was a tiny little thing. Looked like Tinker Bell, but she did not suffer fools. "She trained SodaPop to be a service dog."

For me. For free. Phin still couldn't believe it. It was the most amazing gift.

"They care about you, your friends," Clancy said. "Not just Stone and Delores. Burke and his crowd, too. I've gotten calls every ten minutes from one of them, demanding that I 'release you.'"

Sitting up straighter, Phin lifted his brows. "Will you?"

"You're not under arrest, Mr. Bishop. I told you that, but I don't think you heard me."

Phin remembered now. "Sorry."

"No need. Can you talk to me now?"

Phin's hands kept stroking SodaPop's fur as the dog sat at his side, leaning into him. Nuzzling him. "Yes."

"Okay. So, from the beginning. You and Stone O'Bannion were approaching Broussard's building. And then?"

"The door flew open. Made a loud cracking sound. Nearly sent me into a spiral, but then I saw the woman running out and I was distracted. She wore an old-fashioned cloak. Like Red Riding Hood, but gray. The hood covered her face, but her hair was black. Then we heard two shots, so we ran into the building and up the stairs. Joy was on the floor. Bleeding. So I helped her."

"Medics said you and your friend probably saved her life."

Phin's chest loosened. "She's alive?"

Clancy nodded. "She is. Still in surgery, though."

Still in surgery wasn't good. But Joy wasn't dead, so he'd hang on to that. "You don't think I did it?" Phin hated that he sounded so hopeful. Like a goddamn kid.

"No. Broussard's cameras, along with some street cams, corroborated your story."

Phin dropped his gaze to SodaPop, who licked his hand. "The cops got there really fast after Stone called them." That had confused him. "Too fast."

"Because someone had placed a call to 911 three minutes before you arrived. A woman. She was whispering that there was an intruder at Broussard's."

"So I didn't imagine her." He'd been so afraid that he had.

Clancy's smile was kind. "No, Mr. Bishop. You didn't. The cameras captured the woman running away and the man in black chasing her. I'm sorry it took so long to get all the security footage together, but you're clear. And you've given your statement, so you're free to go."

Phin got to his feet so fast that his chair fell to the floor with a clang. He righted it, then took SodaPop's leash. "No offense, but I'm out of here."

Clancy stood and handed Phin his card. "Call me if you remember anything more."

Phin followed Clancy to the lobby, where Stone and Delores were impatiently waiting for him. They both rose, Stone giving him a look of concern and enough space so that Phin could approach them.

Delores, not so much. She ran to him, stopping short of

hugging him. Phin could see that she wanted to, but she knew not to touch him when he wasn't expecting it. But he thought that she needed the hug more than he did, so he bent down to pull her close.

She was only five feet tall on the outside, but on the inside the woman was a warrior. She buried her face against his neck and let out a long breath.

"You're okay," she murmured, then pulled back, wiping her eyes. "SodaPop helped?"

"She did. I should have brought her with me today. As usual, you were right."

She pulled herself to her full tiny height. "And don't you forget it."

Phin felt his mouth tug up into a grin. "I won't."

She scowled. "That boss of yours is here. Him and the IT guy."

Phin scanned the room, and sure enough, Burke was standing with Antoine Holmes. Burke looked wrecked and Antoine didn't look any better.

Burke didn't trust you.

Stone ambled over, glancing behind his shoulder at Burke and Antoine before meeting Phin's gaze. "Your boss feels real bad."

"As he should." Delores scowled.

Phin rubbed her forehead with his index finger. "You're going to get frown lines. It's all right, Delores."

But it really wasn't. That Burke had, even for a moment, believed he could harm anyone—much less Joy—hurt. A lot.

"Burke *was* an asshole this morning," Stone said quietly. "But the way I see it, you can either walk away from them or you can work on patching things up. For what it's worth, I want you to come back to Cincinnati with us, so I might not give you the best advice here."

Phin found himself chuckling. "Honest as always."

"You got that right."

Phin met Burke's eyes across the lobby, his boss's contrition laid bare. Phin knew which option he needed to take. "He's been a good friend to me over the past two years," he murmured. "He's welcomed me back every time I've run, and he's given me support and opportunities. He even got me a therapist. And he's human, just like me."

"So no Cincinnati?" Stone asked.

"Not just yet. But soon." Because Cincinnati was Phin's hometown. His family was still there and he fully intended to return. When he was ready.

He still wasn't ready. He'd run from his family—his loving, caring family—just like he'd run from Burke and his New Orleans friends. Every time he felt an episode coming on, he took off.

Every time things got too heavy, he ran.

He'd make things right with Burke. And Joy. And then he'd go home and make things right with his family.

"What are you thinking?" Delores asked suspiciously.

"That I'm going to find out who hurt Joy. I'm going to prove that it wasn't me."

"Nobody believes it was you," Stone said.

But Burke had. For just a moment, he had.

"I still want to make this right. If I'd been there, I would have stopped that bastard from hurting Joy."

Stone sighed. "I'm not going to be able to talk sense into you, am I?"

"Nope."

Delores folded her arms across her chest, sending another glare in Burke's direction. "Then we'll help you. We'll stay with you until you've made this right."

Phin blinked. "You don't have to do that."

"Neither do you," Delores said, lifting her chin.

Stone's lips twitched. "You're not going to be able to talk sense into her, either. Come on. Let's make nice with Antoine and your boss. Delores, try to look like you don't want to rip them apart."

"I'm not that good an actress," Delores snarked, but schooled her features into a polite mask.

Together, the three of them—and SodaPop—approached Burke and Antoine.

Antoine was the first to smile. "Phin, my man. It's good to see you. We've missed you."

Phin gave Antoine a one-armed hug. Another army vet, Antoine had been the one to get Phin his job at Burke's two years before. Antoine and Stone went way back, and all it had taken was a single phone call from Stone, and Phin had a new start in New Orleans.

Phin owed his work family a lot. He was going to make this right. "Burke, it's okay."

Burke's eyes were filled with sorrow. "No, it's not. I'm sorry, Phin."

"Phin's going to try to find Joy's attacker on his own," Delores snapped. "Because he thinks you don't trust him."

Burke's and Antoine's eyes widened, and Phin sighed. "Thanks, Delores."

"You will not go after that bastard," Burke snapped back. "He's dangerous."

Phin got that. He could still feel Joy's blood dripping from his hands. "I know. But I owe it to Joy."

"Let's discuss this elsewhere," Antoine said reasonably. "Because I'm thinking the cops don't need to be hearing any of this."

It was true. Phin wasn't sure what he'd been thinking, speaking his thoughts aloud in a police station. "That's fine. Can I bring SodaPop?"

Burke nodded, his shoulders sagging a little in what seemed like relief. "Absolutely. She's your service dog. She goes where you go. Come on."

They'd turned for the exit when something caught Phin's eye. A woman was walking past them, her expression angry, her curly red hair bouncing with each step. The elderly man at her side wore a snazzy suit and a weary expression as he tried to keep pace with her.

The two strode to the glass door ahead of them and the

woman shoved it open, taking to the street at a fast walk, the man now jogging to keep up with her. She had a gray cloak draped over her arm. His gaze slid down her body to calves that were familiar. And then Phin noticed her feet—with their three-inch gray heels.

"That's her," Phin said, running for the door, SodaPop trotting along beside him.

"Who?" Delores demanded from behind him.

"The woman from this morning. The woman who ran away."

Phin wasn't letting her run away again.

2

ALAN LOOKED DIRECTLY into the camera, his lips curved into the smile he used with his parishioners. It was nonthreatening. Nonjudgmental. And the most likely to boost donations. They'd done research.

"Now, brothers and sisters, I'm not asking you to give if it's a financial hardship. But if God has laid it on your heart to give, we would very much appreciate it. Any little bit helps. A thousand dollars. A hundred. Even fifty, if you have it to spare." More than half of their gifts came in amounts less than fifty dollars, but those small sums sure added up. "If you have a special ministry you'd like to support, mark it on your check. Or if you're technologically savvy like my grandson, Sage, you can give through our website."

And, speak of the devil, there was Sage, slipping in through the door in the back of the sanctuary. Alan hoped he'd been successful. The alternative had been causing Alan sleepless nights for the past two weeks.

He wanted to stop the filming, to demand to know what Sage had discovered that morning, but they were making videos for the church's website, and every second cost money. You had to spend it to make it, though, and that was what these video spots were all about.

He leaned into the camera, making his smile self-deprecating. "Now, me, I'm not tech savvy at all. I still write checks." Actually, he didn't donate to his church. He hadn't needed to in years. Between his local congregation and his TV shows, he had fifteen thousand members all over the United States and abroad, many of whom gave faithfully every week. "You can choose to support one of our many missionaries, our mental health services, or our center for drug rehabilitation. And of course, if you want to support the church itself, we will use your donation to keep the lights on and to feed New Orleans' hungry." And to pay Alan's mortgage. God didn't want his servants living in hovels, after all. "Thank you all, and may God bless you and keep you. May his countenance shine bright upon you and bring you peace."

He held the smile until he heard the director say, "And . . . we're good. Nice job, Reverend Beauchamp. We got it in one take."

Which was Alan's norm. He'd been making that same speech for his entire adult life. He could do it in his sleep at this point.

"Thank you. I'll be in my office, planning this Sunday's service with Sage."

Gesturing for Sage to follow, Alan stepped away from the pulpit, fighting the need to rub at his temples. The lights hurt his eyes more every day. Macular degeneration was slowly robbing him of his eyesight, but he could still see his beautiful multimillion-dollar sanctuary with its gleaming wooden pews and shining stained-glass windows.

He didn't need to see to find his way to his office. Again, he'd been walking these halls for years. He sat behind his desk and shook out a few painkillers. His heart sank when Sage entered, a scowl marring his grandson's perfect features.

Unsuccessful, then.

"Well?" he asked the younger man. "Did you get the letters?"

"No." Sage drew a breath. "She got away."

Alan prayed for patience. "How?"

"She ran. I followed her, but she disappeared somewhere in the Quarter." He unzipped his backpack and pulled out a black bag. "I got two of Broussard's laptops. I figured these were more valuable than she is, so I came back."

Alan wasn't so sure about that, but it wasn't like *he* could go chasing Cora Winslow through the Quarter. Not anymore. His degrading eyesight forced him to depend on others for jobs such as this.

"Did anyone see you?"

Sage's gaze dropped for a moment before lifting to meet his. "Yeah. The receptionist was there. But I didn't think she posed a threat. She was in a wheelchair, for God's sake."

Alan abruptly leaned over the desk. "Do *not* take the Lord's name in vain," he hissed.

Sage rolled his eyes. "For *goodness'* sake."

Then Sage's words sank in. "You didn't *think* she posed a threat? What does that mean?"

Sage shrugged. "It was an electric chair. I yanked the battery pack so she couldn't go anywhere. I smashed the office phone so she couldn't call out for help and I took her cell phone. It's in the bag, too, by the way."

"But?"

Sage dropped his gaze. "But she had a gun. I was in Broussard's office, searching for a folder with Winslow's name on it, but I heard women's voices in the lobby— Winslow and the receptionist—and ran out of the boss's office with his laptop. The door to the stairwell was closing, and the bitch in the chair had a gun pointed at me."

"Did she shoot you?"

Sage took off his overcoat, revealing the black clothing he'd worn into the PI's office. He unbuttoned his shirt and held one side out.

Light shone through the round hole.

"I'm wearing Kevlar, but it hurts like a bitch, let me tell you. And don't tell me not to swear," Sage snapped before

Alan could do just that. "I got *shot* for you today, old man. I'll swear if I goddamn want to."

"Shh," Alan hissed. "If you're going to be crude, at least do it quietly."

Sage huffed a laugh. "I'm okay, thanks for asking."

"I'm glad you're all right," Alan said stiffly. Because he was. He didn't want Sage to be hurt. He didn't want anyone to be hurt.

Well, that wasn't true. He wanted whoever had gotten him into this mess to die a painful death. However, Sage was innocent. Of that crime, anyway.

But Sage was spinning out of his control, and Alan didn't like that.

Sage rolled his eyes again. "What's on these laptops that was so fucking important?"

Alan winced. At this point Sage was cursing to rile him up. "That's not for you to know. Did you leave any blood behind for the police to find?"

Sage hesitated again. "No. The vest stopped the bullet."

"What happened, Sage?"

"I grabbed the gun from her hand. Bitch was strong."

"*What happened, Sage?*" he repeated, using his most authoritative voice.

It worked. It always did.

Sage's shoulders sagged. "We fought over the gun and it went off. Shot her in the chest."

Horror had Alan sucking in a breath. "You *killed* her?"

Sage's gaze flicked up to meet his. "Maybe."

There was guilt in the young man's eyes. "What else, Sage?" Because there was more. There was always more these days.

"I was . . . mad. She'd *shot* me, for God's sake. So I took the gun and . . ." He looked away. "I might have hit her in the head with it."

Still more. "What else?"

Sage's chin lifted defiantly. "I pushed her chair over, okay? I stole her laptop, then chased after the Winslow woman. Cora was carrying a big purse and I just wanted to take it from her. That was all. If Winslow's letters aren't on the laptop in Broussard's email, then she was bringing them in to Broussard herself. But the old woman got in my way."

"You killed the receptionist," Alan said heavily.

Another shrug. "Maybe. Cops got there fast. They could have saved her."

Alan pressed his lips together, gathering his composure. "Did anyone see you?"

"Not my face. I was wearing a ski mask. Just like you told me to." He tossed the mask onto Alan's desk.

Good thing I told him to wear it. Sage's face and golden blond hair were highly recognizable.

Maybe more so than mine. The boy's face was on advertising billboards all over town. He brought in a lot of donations from their female viewers, young and old.

"Did Broussard's office have cameras?"

"Yes, but none of them caught my face. I was wearing my wig and glasses under the mask, so I was doubly protected. I'm in the clear."

That's what I thought, too, all those years ago. But the body Alan had left in that Baton Rouge parking lot hadn't stayed where he'd put it.

This was his worst nightmare.

He'd waited for a blackmail letter for years, but none had come. He'd waited for the police to show up on his doorstep, but that had never happened, either.

He'd grown complacent.

And then six weeks ago, *twenty-three years later*, a body had suddenly shown up. He hadn't known it was the body he'd left behind until two weeks ago when the authorities had ID'd the man and plastered the victim's face all over the TV news. That was when the Winslow woman had started asking questions.

Alan was tired of waiting for a visit from the police— or the blackmail letter that he thought more likely—so he'd sent Sage to follow the Winslow woman. Just in case she knew more than she was telling. Sage had searched her home several times and found nothing useful. But then she'd contacted a PI. Alan had thought *that* was bad.

Now his nightmare had suddenly become so much worse.

"Of all the people to kill, you picked the receptionist for a PI with a reputation for cracking difficult cases," Alan said mildly.

Sage flinched. "I didn't mean to." It was very nearly a whine, which made Sage sound like he was five years old again, not the twenty-five-year-old man that he was.

"That's not going to help you if you get caught," Alan snapped.

Sage's eyes narrowed. "If I get caught, I'm taking you down with me. I guarantee."

"You're not going to get caught." *And if you do, you are* not *taking me down with you. I* guarantee. "Leave the laptops with me. I'll have my network guy look at them."

Sage might be able to break into the machines, but the boy knew too much already.

He could crucify me, if he so chose.

Up until now it had been in Sage's best interest to keep Alan's secrets. But if that was no longer the case? *God help me, I do not know.*

He didn't know Sage anymore. Maybe he never had.

Sage huffed in irritation. "Fine. Have your toady tech guy check them out. But know one thing: I've cleaned up enough messes for you that I know this one is different. If you want my help again, you *will* tell me why the Winslow woman is so important to you."

No, I most surely will not *tell you why.* Because this *was* different. Normally Sage's off-the-books responsibilities included gathering intel on competitors. Most were upstarts, trying to steal Alan's audience. Some sought to blackmail him over nonexistent sexual scandals. So far, all had been easily dismissed by threatening them with their secrets.

Sage was good at finding dirt online, and what he couldn't get from a computer, he managed to learn by asking the right questions of the right people. His charm and good looks didn't hurt. Sage would make a good PI in his own right.

But never had Sage needed to physically touch someone, much less kill them.

A mocking smirk curved Sage's lips. "I'm right. The Winslow woman is fucking important."

"Sage," he barked, not so much offended by the word as he was by Sage's disdain for the rules. "Enough."

Sage took a step back, still smirking. "I'm so sorry, Grandfather. I'll leave you to your . . ." He waved his hand at the bag containing the laptops. ". . . whatever those are. If you won't tell me, I'll figure it out on my own. Digging up secrets is my forte, you know." His laugh was both bitter and full of scorn as he threw his arms wide. "May God bless you and keep you. May his countenance shine bright upon you and bring you peace."

With a sarcastic little wave, Sage took his leave, closing the office door carefully behind him.

The room was suddenly oppressively quiet, Alan's swallow audible. Sage had been digging up secrets for ten years and was the best assistant he'd ever had. He'd certainly been the most trustworthy. Until today.

There was now a body in a Terrebonne Parish morgue that had been missing for twenty-three years. Alan needed to find out what Cora Winslow knew.

And if Sage really started digging on his own?

Alan didn't know what he'd do.

Willing his hand not to tremble, he lifted the phone's handset to his ear. "Lana, please call Medford Hughes. I've forgotten the password to my computer again. Have him come to my office as soon as possible."

"Right away, sir. You have a meeting with Roy Grover in thirty minutes."

There was no way he'd be able to focus on a meeting

with that barrel of hot air. The chairman of the board of deacons never shut up. "Can you reschedule?"

His secretary's quiet exhale spoke volumes. Roy Grover would be very unhappy. "Of course, sir."

"Give him my apologies. Tell him I'll stop by his house some night this week." Or it might be never. He hated the man. There was always a problem he wanted to point out. More than half of Alan's job was soothing church politics. "You can take off early today, if you like."

Lana had worked for him far too long not to see that he was upset. He didn't want anyone to know he was upset.

Because Alan was very, very upset.

He hung up the phone carefully, staring at the bag containing the two laptops Sage had taken from Broussard's office. One of them might have information about Cora Winslow.

And if neither of them did, he'd have to . . .

Well, he wasn't sure what he'd do. But if the Winslow woman continued to push for the truth, she would have to meet the same fate as her father.

The stakes had been unbelievably high twenty-three years ago.

They were astronomical now.

The Quarter, New Orleans, Louisiana
TUESDAY, DECEMBER 13, 11:15 A.M.

Walking away from the police station as quickly as she could, Cora fished her cell phone from her purse. She'd given the burner phone to the detective in charge of investigating Joy's shooting.

"Cora," Harry said, sounding out of breath. "Stop."

She stopped abruptly, turning around to see her attorney huffing and puffing. Talking to the police had given her the headache from hell, but driving Harry to a heart attack would be a horrible end to an already shitty day.

She took Harry's hand. "I'm sorry. I didn't mean to make you run."

With his free hand, he took a handkerchief from his pocket and mopped his brow. "I'm not as young as I used to be," he said, still out of breath. "Where are you going, Cora?"

"To the hospital. I need to see Joy."

Harry frowned. "Not while her shooter is still at large. If the man was truly after you, it might be better to lie low for a little while."

If. Her own attorney doubted her.

"Maybe call in sick to the library," he went on. "Stay home where it's safe."

But her home wasn't safe. She'd told him that, too. He didn't seem to believe the break-in at her home had been connected, either.

Oh, he hadn't let the detective know that. Harry had been a tiger with Detective Clancy, demanding police protection for Cora, but the NOPD didn't have the resources for that. The detective had actually looked sorry when he'd told her that.

"I've already called in to the library. Took a sick day. I'll go home after I've checked on Joy. Thank you for coming, Harry. I wasn't sure who to call."

"I wish you'd have let me get you a criminal defense attorney. I do trusts and wills." He'd been her grandmother's attorney for years and the first name she'd thought to call when she'd decided to go to the police. "At least they don't suspect you."

"I don't know about that," Cora said dryly. "They took my fingerprints and did a GSR swab on my hands."

"You shouldn't have agreed to that," Harry scolded. "I *told* you that. Why did you even call me if you weren't going to listen to my advice?"

"Because I haven't fired a gun in months," Cora snapped, "so I knew they wouldn't find anything. If they're looking at me, they won't be looking for Joy's shooter."

Harry looked frazzled. "I can't go to the hospital with

you. I have appointments this afternoon that I can't miss. Please go straight home, Cora. I'll check on your friend as soon as I can."

"I'll go home," she promised. *After I see Joy.*

"Straight home?" Harry pressed.

"I have to make a few stops," she hedged. "I'm out of milk."

Which was true. It was also true that she never drank milk. That had been her brother. She felt the stab of sorrow deep in her heart.

She missed him. Every day.

Harry was shaking his head. "Will you at least call me when you get home from the hospital?"

The man had always been able to spot her bullshit. He'd attended her christening, after all. Had watched her grow up, had been an honorary uncle. He'd known her longer than anyone else. Anyone who was still alive, anyway. "I will. That I promise."

"Call, don't text. I want to hear your voice. And if you run into any trouble, we need a code word."

She huffed a surprised laugh. "A code word?"

Harry nodded, totally serious. "In case you're abducted."

She did smile then, a real one. "I didn't think you believed me."

"I'm not sure I do, but you've always had a level head. If you think he was after you, I have to at least assume it's a possibility." He grimaced. "And there is that business with your father. We can't ignore that there might be a link."

Well, that was something, at least. "How about 'help'? That's a good code word."

He narrowed his eyes. "You're as much of a smartass as your grandmother was. Your brother at least pretended to be respectful."

Another stab of sorrow made her chest ache. "Yeah. He was a suck-up."

But she said it fondly.

Harry smoothed his hand over her hair. "I'm sorry. I shouldn't have mentioned him. That was unkind of me."

"It's okay, Harry. It's been a year. I can talk about him now." She hadn't for the longest time, deep in her grief. "John Robert *was* more respectful than I am. How about 'gator' as a code word?"

Harry cupped her cheek. "That'll do, Cora. You be careful."

"I always am."

She really was. In whatever she did. Today it hadn't seemed to help.

He held out his hand to hail a cab, one miraculously stopping. Hailing cabs was Harry's superpower. That and managing her grandmother's trust. There was always money for the taxes with enough left to do the most critical upkeep on the house. Harry had been her rock this year.

"Call me, Cora," he ordered over his shoulder as he got into the cab.

"Yes, sir." She watched the cab drive away, then looked at her phone, wincing at all the text messages from Tandy. There were also fifteen missed calls and three voicemails from her best friend.

Glancing up and down the street, she relaxed a little. There was still no sign of the man who'd chased her that morning. He'd probably left town now that Joy's shooting was all over the news.

She hit Tandy's name in her contact list and held the phone away from her ear, bracing herself for the screeching. She was not disappointed.

"Cora Jane Winslow!" Tandy bellowed. "Where the ever-lovin' *fuck* have you been?" Then she whispered, "Sorry, Nala. Sorry, LouLou."

"Put her on speaker," Nala commanded in the background.

Cora winced as she pressed the phone back to her ear. Joy's daughters were the last people she wanted confronting her right now. If Cora hadn't gone to Broussard's, Joy would be okay. "Hi, Nala. Hi, Louisa."

Cora and Tandy had been best friends since the third grade. Nala had joined their group a few years later, when she'd transferred to their school. Louisa was a few years younger and had followed them around until they'd grown older, the age gap becoming less important. They were her rocks and Cora loved them dearly.

Except now, she was going to get some tough love. *Which I deserve.*

"'Hi,' she says," Nala drawled, her fury evident. "Scares the fucking shit out of us and all she has to say is 'hi.' Where have you been?"

Cora exhaled. "Can I tell you when I come to the hospital?"

"No, you may not," Tandy snapped. "You will tell us now. You said you were coming to the hospital and that was hours ago. We've been worried sick."

"Especially after what happened to Mama," Louisa said quietly. "You should have called us, Cora."

"I'm sorry. I got tied up. How's your mom?"

"In recovery," Nala said wearily, all fury gone. "Wayne is in the waiting room, along with Molly from Burke's office. Jerry's on his way from Tuscaloosa, so all of us kids will be here for her. Tandy made me and LouLou leave to get some food, so we're in the hospital cafeteria."

"Stay there until I get there. I'll explain everything."

The other side of the line went still. Very still.

"Cora?" Tandy said tightly. "What is going on?"

"Look, I'm standing here on the street. Plus, I'm hungry, too. I'll meet you in the cafeteria. I'm fine. I promise. See you soon."

She ended the call and turned off her ringer because Tandy would be calling back.

Of course there wasn't a single cab in sight now that she needed one. "Uber it is," she muttered, then looked down when a cold nose rubbed against the side of her leg.

It was a dog—a golden retriever with the sweetest face. The dog sat as pretty as you please, looking up at her hopefully. It wore a service dog vest, a collar, and a leash.

"Hello, precious," Cora murmured, looking around for an owner. "Where's your mommy or daddy?" She reached for the dog's collar, taking the leash in hand. "Are you lost?"

"No," a deep voice said in a tone that was not calm. The leash was yanked out of her hand as she looked up. A man was scowling down at her. He looked angry, his brown eyes dark and menacing. "She's not lost."

She took a step back from the dog, holding her cell phone tightly in one hand while she held the other out in surrender. "Sorry. I thought she needed help."

The man's scowl grew, and Cora took another step away, alarm skittering down her back. He was a big man. Cora was five-eleven in her heels, so this guy had to be six-three at least. Maybe six-four. And brawny. He'd be drop-dead gorgeous if he didn't look so intimidating.

He didn't seem to like her very much. Which was on par for the day.

The police station wasn't far. If she had to, she could scream and run back to the lobby. They likely wouldn't believe her again, but at least she'd be safe.

"Come with us," the man said. "We need to talk to you."

Cora's heart stuttered to a stop. *Oh no. No way.* The service-dog vest was a ruse. *Trying to get me to let my guard down.* She turned, then froze when she saw the people standing just a few feet behind her. Three more big men and one small woman, none of whom looked happy to see her.

Alarm became fear. The man with the dog could be the man from this morning. They were built similarly.

He's found me. I thought I was safe, but he's found me.

Stupid. She was so stupid. She should have gotten in that cab with Harry. She wouldn't be able to outrun all of them. Not now. She was exhausted and her feet ached from running in her heels that morning.

She lifted her chin and studied them. In case she had to report to the cops later.

All the men were dark-haired. The biggest one behind her was tanned and built like a tank. The shortest was at least six feet tall, but still broad-shouldered. Which was good for him, because he wore three computer bags slung over his shoulders like they weighed nothing. His silver smartphone stood out against his dark skin as he angled it toward her.

He was recording her, the sonofabitch. *How dare he?*

At least the fourth man seemed less angry than the others. He watched Cora like she was a puzzle to be solved.

But all four of the men seemed . . . grim. Determined.

And big. They could break her in two.

The woman was the outlier in the group. Only about five feet tall, she looked more like a pixie than a human killing machine.

She was probably their boss. She looked adorably cute but could likely order a murder with the snap of her little fingers.

And I read too many thrillers on my lunch breaks. Except that she wasn't imagining this. This was real, as was her heart smashing against her rib cage.

I will not pass out. That would make their job too easy.

"I don't want trouble," Cora said quietly, although every instinct was urging her to scream and run.

"Neither do we," the dog's owner said. "We just want to talk to you."

Cora took a step backward toward the street. "Leave me alone. Please," she added, unable to control the tremble in her voice.

"I'm afraid we can't do that," the woman said, her lips curving into a gentle smile. The smile was kind and Cora didn't trust it for a moment. Until the little woman gave the dog owner a shove. "Phin, honey, you're scaring her." The woman stepped forward, holding her hand out. "I'm Delores O'Bannion. And you're Cora Jane Winslow? We, um, couldn't help overhearing your phone call."

Cora swallowed, unwilling to believe the woman's overture was genuine. "Go away, please. I will scream."

"No need for that," the man named Phin said. He made a visible effort to soften his scowl, but it really didn't help. "I'm Phin Bishop. You have answers to our questions."

Cora took another step back. "No, I don't. I don't know any of you."

The biggest of the men stepped forward. "We work with Joy Thomas. My name is Burke Broussard. You came to my office this morning. I'd like to know why."

Broussard. "Oh my God," Cora whispered as her knees wobbled with relief. She stumbled backward, her shoe encountering nothing but air. A hand reached out, grabbing her arm and hauling her back onto the sidewalk as a car horn blared behind her.

She looked up at the dog's owner once again. Phin Bishop. His hand still clutched her arm and she found herself staring at his large fingers on her skin. His fingers were callused, like he worked with his hands. Numbly she looked up at him before finally regaining her composure. She yanked her arm back and looked over her shoulder.

Sure enough, she'd nearly fallen into the street.

"Thank you," she said stiffly, then lifted her phone to take photos of their faces, including the man who'd saved her from becoming roadkill. "I'm going to send these photos to my friends who are waiting for me. They'll let me know if you're really Joy's coworkers."

"Which friends?" Broussard—if that was really his name—asked.

"Nala and Louisa Thomas."

Broussard and Bishop both relaxed, as did the man with the laptops.

"That's fine," Broussard said. "Contact them."

"Hurry," Bishop said tersely. "We don't have time to dawdle."

She shot him an irritated glare. "Do not push me, Mr. Bishop. I've had a really shitty day."

"So have I," Bishop muttered. "Just . . . hurry. Please."

It was the "please" that got her brain in gear. She tried to write a text, but her hands were trembling. *Dammit.* Finally she typed in Nala's and Louisa's phone numbers and attached the photos.

Do you know these guys? she texted.

Nala's reply came first. *That's Mama's boss, Burke. Why is he there?*

Louisa's reply was next. *Burke, Antoine, and Phin. They're from Mama's office. Why are they there? Who are the other two?*

I'm not sure, Cora texted back. *But it has to do with your mother's shooting. Can I trust them?*

Her phone flashed with an incoming call from Tandy. Of course Nala and Louisa had shown the texts to Tandy.

Cora accepted the call, glaring when Phin Bishop tried to grab her phone. "Hands off, mister. Thank you for saving my life, but you're not entitled to invade my privacy."

She pressed it to her ear, not wanting them to overhear. "I'm here, Tandy."

"Who's there?" Tandy demanded, her phone on speaker. "You're scaring us."

"I'll tell you when I can. Nala, Louisa, can I trust Broussard and his people?"

"Yes," Nala said immediately. "But I don't know who the other two people are."

Cora lifted a brow at the woman, lowering her phone and putting it on speaker. "Delores? Who are you? And him?" She pointed to the man standing behind Delores like a bodyguard.

"My husband, Stone," Delores said calmly. "He and I are friends of Phin's. We need your help to catch whoever shot Joy Thomas."

"I heard that, Cora," Nala said. "Why are they asking you about Mama?"

"Because I was there this morning," Cora admitted. "I'll explain everything when I see you. Your mom told me to run, that she'd handle the man who broke in. I didn't know she'd been shot. I'm so sorry."

Nala sighed heavily. "That sounds like Mama. Are you in trouble, Cora?"

"I don't know. I'll talk to these people and let you know." She looked up at Bishop. "Where are we going to talk?"

Bishop looked at Broussard. "Where?" Bishop asked. "The office is a crime scene."

"My house," Broussard said. "Nala and Louisa have been there several times. They know the address."

"We know where he lives," Louisa confirmed.

"You'll be safe with Burke," Nala said. "Call us as soon as you can."

"Cora?" Tandy asked, sounding tentative and frightened. "What's happening?"

"I don't know."

"Is this about your dad?"

"I think so. The cops don't."

"I'm coming to this Broussard's house," Tandy said. "Just so you're not alone."

Cora's heart squeezed in gratitude. She briefly considered saying no, that Tandy didn't have to, that Cora would be okay. But she wasn't okay. And Joy's daughters said that Broussard was safe. She needed her best friend. "Okay."

"Okay?" Tandy asked, clearly surprised. "This has to be bad if you're allowing me to help you. Tell that man he'd better let me in or I'm calling the cops."

Good luck with that. The police hadn't been the biggest help so far.

"I'll tell him." She ended the call and faced Bishop and Broussard. "Let's go."

3

CORA JANE WINSLOW had been silent as Burke had driven them to his big house in the Quarter. She'd sat in the front passenger seat, staring out the window, tension pouring off her.

Antoine had followed in his own car, driving Stone and Delores.

SodaPop sat next to Phin in the back seat, nuzzling into his side. Keeping him grounded.

"I'm sorry," he whispered to SodaPop, because the dog had tried to follow him that morning when he and Stone had left his house for Burke's office. "I should have listened to you."

He looked up to find Burke studying him in the SUV's rearview mirror. They'd come to a stop in the courtyard behind Burke's house. "You okay?" Burke asked.

Phin nodded. "Mostly." He'd returned to New Orleans hoping for a fresh start, but that hope had been dashed the moment he'd registered Joy's blood on his hands.

Phin clutched SodaPop's coat gently. He wasn't going to fall into that hole again. Not with Cora Jane Winslow around.

She was . . . something. The black hair he'd seen that morning had been a wig. Her real hair was a vibrant red and curly, springing this way and that every time she turned her head. She was tall and elegant on the outside, but mouthy enough to call him on invading her privacy when he'd tried to grab her phone.

He'd barely been holding it together and she'd misinterpreted his intensity.

Best fix that right now.

"Miss Winslow," Phin said quietly, "I apologize. I didn't mean to scare you earlier."

She turned to meet his gaze. "Then why did you?"

Phin swallowed. Her eyes were the color of brandy, intelligent and piercing. "I have PTSD. I'd just been released from the police interrogation room and I wasn't doing very well at that moment."

Cora's gaze softened. "Accepted. I'm sorry I snapped at you. Thank you for keeping me from falling into the street. It seems like we both had shitty mornings. Why were you in an interrogation room?"

"Because he found Joy first," Burke answered. "And some of us jumped to a very wrong conclusion. I'm so sorry, Phin."

Cora flashed Burke a shocked glance. "You thought he did it?"

"No," Burke said quickly, then winced. "Maybe for a second. I wasn't sure what was happening."

"I'd never hurt Joy," Phin said. "Never."

"Me either." Cora's gaze focused behind them. "The others are here. Should we get this over with?"

"I like that idea." Burke got out and went to close the gate behind Antoine's car, leaving the two of them alone.

"What's her name?" Cora asked, looking at his dog.

"SodaPop. I tried to shorten it to Pop, because that's the truly correct word for a carbonated beverage, but she only answers to SodaPop."

She chuckled, a rich sound that he wanted to hear again. "You sound like you're from the Midwest."

"Cincinnati. So are my friends, Delores and Stone. Delores trained SodaPop for me. She's my service dog."

"I saw her vest. I'm sorry that I talked to her when she was working."

Phin's respect for her grew. "No worries. She got away from me to run to you. She hasn't done that before. I've only had her for six weeks, but usually she sticks to me like glue."

Cora smiled at his dog and Phin barely managed to keep from sucking in a breath. She was a very pretty woman, but her smile made her light up like the sun.

"She might have smelled my dog. Either way, I'm glad she ran to me," she said, then sobered. "I wanted to talk to Mr. Broussard, so this worked out. Should we go talk to him now?"

"We should." Phin got out of the car and opened Cora's door. "Burke's gone around to unlock the side door for us," he explained, offering his hand.

She took it, sliding out of the SUV, wincing when her feet hit the pavement.

"Are you all right?" Phin asked.

"Feet are sore, that's all. I ran quite a ways this morning."

"Which is part of the story that I hope you'll share," Antoine said, coming up behind them.

"Yes," Cora said simply.

Phin realized that he was still holding her hand. He dropped it, feeling his cheeks heat. He needed to get his head on straight. He needed to stop staring at Cora Winslow.

Burke met them inside the door and led them to his living room, a mishmash of styles from high Victorian to a 1990s duct-taped BarcaLounger to the modern, fully equipped kitchen. The kitchen was Phin's handiwork and he was proud of how it gleamed.

"I'll make some coffee," Burke said. "And then we can talk." He offered Cora a chair—without duct tape—and she sank into it, the lines of pain around her mouth easing as she rested her feet.

Phin sat on a prim settee from the 1880s that was surprisingly comfortable. SodaPop lay at his feet as Phin went back to staring at Cora Winslow.

She was younger than he was. Maybe thirty to his nearly thirty-seven. Her dark red hair reflected the overhead lights and surrounded her shoulders like a curly cloud. She wore a straight dark gray skirt and a light pink sweater set. A strand of pearls hugged her throat and a pair of glasses dangled from a chain around her neck.

She looked like a professor. Or a librarian.

A sharp knock at the front door startled him out of his study.

"Cora!" a woman shouted from outside. "If I don't see my friend in ten seconds, I'm calling 911."

Burke laughed quietly as he went to the front door. "She's a pistol, isn't she?"

Cora's smile was strained. "She's worried about me."

"Sounds like she has a right to be," Delores said, in her gentle way. "We've worried about both Phin and Joy all morning."

Cora's gaze flew to Phin. "Did the police book you?"

"No. The cameras confirmed my story. And the gunshot residue test on my clothes came back negative." There'd been too much blood to test his hands.

"So did mine," Cora said dryly, "but I think I'm still on Detective Clancy's suspect list."

"Me too."

"Cora!" Tandy rushed into the room, throwing her arms around Cora and hugging her tightly. "I was so worried. Don't do that to me again, okay?"

"Okay," Cora whispered. "Too tight, Tandy. Can't breathe."

Tandy loosened her hold immediately. Blond and curvy, Tandy was like a hurricane. Her energy almost crackled. "Sorry." She glanced at Burke when he brought over another chair. "Thank you. I'm Tandy Napier. Joy's daughters said we'll be safe here." She narrowed her eyes at Phin's boss. "I'm trusting you."

"You will be safe," Burke said, taking his chair—the duct-taped BarcaLounger, of course. "Now, let's get to the story. Joy's shooter is still out there and will be harder to track down with every minute that passes. Cora, can you start with why you came to my office this morning?"

Tandy frowned. "Yes, Cora. Do tell. This is about your father?"

"Yes. Mostly." Cora squared her shoulders and folded her hands on her lap. "My last name is Winslow, but my birth name is Elliot. My father was Jack Elliot."

Antoine frowned. "I've heard that name recently." His eyes closed briefly before flying open. "Elliot? The guy whose body was found in that building down in Houma when they demolished it?"

Cora nodded wearily. "Yes."

"Oh," Burke said, surprised. "That's not what I was expecting you to say." He looked at Stone, Delores, and Phin. "Do you know what she's talking about?" The three of them shook their heads. "It happened right after you left, Phin," he said. "The Damper Building down in Houma was damaged beyond repair by the last hurricane. Houma's an hour and a half southwest of here," he explained to Stone and Delores. "The last few storms hit the city hard. The Damper was demolished the first of November."

"And a body was found?" Stone asked.

"Yes." Cora cleared her throat. "The . . . um, victim was buried in the foundation. Not in the concrete, but in a crevice underneath. It was in the news for a week or so, and everyone forgot about it. The man had no ID." She looked down at her hands. "He was just a skeleton."

Phin made sure his voice was gentle, because she seemed to have become suddenly fragile. "But they ID'd him as your father?"

She nodded. "Two weeks ago. It took them a month to test the DNA in his hair follicles and match it with the genetic databases."

"How did they match him to you?" Antoine asked. "Did you submit DNA to one of the databases?"

"Yes. Two years ago. I was actually looking for him— or anyone else related to him." She looked up, her expression shattered. "Two detectives came to where I work. They were there to notify me. He had two bullet holes in his skull. He'd been murdered."

"Oh my," Delores murmured. "I'm so sorry, Cora."

Cora mustered a small smile. "Thank you."

Tandy leaned over to grasp Cora's hand. "But the police *are* investigating, right?"

"In Terrebonne Parish, yes, but they aren't offering a lot of hope. He'd been there for twenty-three years. Since the foundation was poured. That's not why I decided to contact a PI, though."

Tandy stiffened. "What happened, Cora?"

"I didn't tell you because I knew you'd worry. Someone broke into my house two days ago. I think they broke in more than once, but I'm certain they broke in two days ago."

"*Cora Jane!*" Tandy whispered.

Cora gave her friend a guilty look. "I went to the police, but they didn't take me very seriously. Nothing had been stolen, so they said there wasn't much they could do."

Phin could feel his face scowling and tried to smooth it, but it was no use. "Did they know that your father's body had just been found?"

"Yes. NOPD said it might be connected, and shared info with the Terrebonne Parish sheriff's department. But there wasn't anything that the NOPD could do about the break-in. They took prints, but whoever broke in wore gloves."

"What was disturbed?" Phin asked.

"Not much, really. If they did a search, they were neat. I kind of wish they'd ransacked the place, because then the cops would have taken me more seriously."

"How were you sure they broke in two days ago?" Burke asked.

Cora rolled her eyes. "I put Scotch tape over the doors. One of the pieces of tape was broken when I got home. I ordered a security system after the first break-in, but it didn't arrive until last night. I installed it right away."

"And you called us," Antoine said.

"I called Joy," Cora corrected. "I knew she worked for a PI. She said she'd get me in for a consult."

"I knew I had an appointment this morning," Burke said, "but I didn't know who with. What happened when you arrived?"

Cora visibly braced herself. "I didn't want anyone to know that I was going to see a PI, especially if whoever broke into my home was connected to whatever happened to my father. I mean, it could have simply been someone looking for information for a news story. That's what the cops said. Or a lookie-loo wanting a souvenir. People are weird that way. Joy was the only one who knew I was coming. I wore a wig and my cloak with the hood, hoping to hide my face. Stupid, huh?"

"No," Phin said forcefully. "Smart, actually. I thought we were looking for a brunette. But they must have been watching your house and followed you."

"Yes." Her eyes were suddenly wet. "I never meant for Joy to be hurt. She was my mother's friend. She's been in my life since I was a little girl. Please believe that."

"I believe you," Burke murmured. "What happened when you arrived at my office?"

Cora dashed at her tears with the back of her hand. "I was a few minutes early. Joy was just getting her coffee. She told me to go into the powder room and take off my ridiculous wig." She smiled weakly. "So I obeyed. I do everything Joy tells me to do."

"We all do," Antoine said soothingly. "So you went into the bathroom?"

She nodded. "I was getting ready to take off the wig when I heard voices outside the door. It was Joy and she was mad. She said that she was calling the cops. I peeked out and saw a man. He was wearing all black. Ski mask and gloves. Boots. All black. I called 911, told them that there was an intruder."

"So *you* called the cops," Antoine said. "We knew someone had called, but it was an untraceable number."

Cora winced. "I got a burner phone. It seemed prudent."

Burke's smile was gentle. "It probably was. Then what happened?"

"He went through the door behind Joy's desk. Your office door, I think," she told Burke. "I came out of the bathroom and started shoving Joy's chair to the elevator. The motor wasn't working. He'd broken it. She told me that she'd slow us down, that he'd hear the elevator."

"I need to have that old thing replaced. It's slow and loud. Dammit." Burke shook his head. "And then?"

"She told me to run, that he was after me, and that she could take care of herself." New tears filled her brandy-colored eyes and streaked down her cheeks. "I shouldn't have run, but . . . Joy told me to. I'm so sorry. This is my fault." Her voice broke on a sob. "Joy's hurt because I was a coward and I ran."

"No," Phin said. "If you hadn't run, he might have killed you. Or abducted you."

Tandy flashed him a grateful look. "He's right, honey. Joy would have tried to protect you. That's her way."

Cora just shook her head, covering her face with her hands as her shoulders shook.

Delores went to the kitchen and came back with a glass of water. She pressed it into Cora's hand. "Drink this and try to breathe. This isn't your fault. It's the fault of the man who shot Joy. You running didn't change the outcome."

"You can't know that," Cora sobbed.

"I can," Burke said firmly. "Joy's gun was missing from its holster. Our camera footage showed the intruder fighting her for her gun after she shot him. But either she missed or he was wearing a vest because it didn't slow him down. He took her gun and shot her with it. What happened when you ran?"

"I ducked into the kitchen of a diner and thought I'd lost him, but when I came out, he was across the street, so I kept running until I got to Tandy's art gallery. I didn't know Joy had been shot. I think the pots and pans covered the sound. If I'd heard the shots, I would have gone back, but he was following me, so I thought Joy was okay. Will Joy be all right?"

"Yes," Phin, Burke, and Antoine said together.

"She's tough," Burke added. "And she'd want us to use our time trying to piece together who shot her, not crying over her. She'd be real mad about that, Miss Winslow."

Cora's laugh was soft and watery. "She would. And you can call me Cora."

"Burke," Burke said. "Antoine, Phin, Stone, and Delores," he continued, pointing at each of them in turn. "You were a little scared when we introduced ourselves there on the street."

Cora's smile was tentative. "Thank you."

"Where did you go after we talked this morning?" Tandy asked, giving Cora a packet of tissues from her handbag.

"To the police station. I knew I had to tell them what had happened. I talked to Detective Clancy. He said he'd check into it. He swabbed my hands for gunshot residue and took my fingerprints."

Antoine's eyes widened. "You allowed him to do that?"

"I did. My lawyer told me not to, but I wanted them looking for Joy's shooter, not wasting time investigating me. My lawyer asked them to give me protection, and Detective Clancy straight-up said that wasn't happening."

At least she'd called her lawyer, Phin thought. Cooperating with the cops was usually a good thing, but Phin had seen it go the other way. Lawyers added a layer of safety.

"Who did you call?" Tandy asked.

"Harry."

"Harry Fulton?" Tandy squeaked, disbelieving. "Cora Jane, he deals with wills. Not arrests. What were you thinking?"

Cora sighed. "I was . . . rattled. Don't yell at me, Tandy Sue."

Tandy winced. "Don't call me that."

"Then don't call me Cora Jane," Cora snapped.

"Fine," Tandy grumbled. "You should have let me know you were all right. I was rattled, too."

"I know," Cora said, softening. "I'm sorry."

Phin was turning Cora's disclosures over in his head, and a number of things didn't fit. He tackled the biggest one first. "Cora, you said your father had been dead for twenty-three years. But detectives only just told you he was dead two weeks ago. Where did you think he was?"

Cora's gaze sharpened, a mixture of respect and appreciation. She threw her arms wide. "Thank you!" she said with heat. "The cops wouldn't pay attention to that fact." She drew a breath. "I didn't think he was dead. In fact, I was *positive* that he was alive."

"It would be hard to admit your father was dead," Delores said. "You must have only been a child when he disappeared."

"It was a month before my fifth birthday. He left one night to meet with a client and he never came home. But he sent letters nearly every single year on my birthday and other holidays. I received the last letter on my birthday a month ago, two weeks *after* his body was discovered but before he was ID'd."

The room went silent.

"Well, shit," Burke muttered. "Not what I was expecting at all."

The Warehouse District, New Orleans, Louisiana
TUESDAY, DECEMBER 13, 12:10 P.M.

Sage slammed his car door once he'd pulled into the parking garage of his condo. He was still seething and his ribs fucking hurt.

Sanctimonious old bastard.

Hadn't even offered to get him a doctor.

Not that Sage needed one. Luckily Joy Thomas's gun had been a small caliber.

He still couldn't believe the woman had shot him.

Then gotten herself shot, too. He hadn't wanted to shoot her. If she'd just let the damn gun go, he would have simply taken it and run.

Maybe she won't die.

He wanted to pray that Joy Thomas survived, but he didn't pray anymore. Prayer was for foolish old men who'd built televangelism empires they were terrified to lose.

Slinging his backpack over his shoulder, Sage made his way to the elevator. He needed a drink.

At least his grandfather was upset. That didn't happen often. Sage had never seen him quite like this.

Who was Cora Winslow? Why was she important?

Sage had done his research, of course. He'd been in the woman's house five times over the past two weeks. Three times he'd broken in when she was at work and twice when she was asleep. He'd gone through her personal papers and spied on her conversations. He knew that she was a librarian who spent all her time—and money—on that fancy house. He knew that she had a dog named Blue and that her best friend's name was Tandy.

He also knew that she was incredibly lonely. He'd heard it in her voice when she talked to her dog. He'd heard it when she cried in the night when she thought no one was listening.

Her father had died recently. Or at least his body had been found recently.

Her brother had died a year ago, her grandmother two years ago. Cora Winslow had seen some tragedy.

His grandfather interacted daily with people who'd seen tragedy. Some legitimately needed some help. Some were con artists whose only goal was to take from Sage's family. Sage's job was to deal with those people. He'd find out what their game was and how to thwart them.

Sage was very good at his job.

He believed that Cora Winslow's grief was legit, but his grandfather wasn't interested in comforting her.

Alan was *afraid* of her, and that, in and of itself, was unusual. The man was obsessed with getting his hands on the letters that Cora had been receiving from her supposedly dead father. Sage wanted to read the letters, too. He wanted to know what had Alan so damn scared.

Sage had even searched his grandfather's home study thoroughly for clues to Alan's obsession with Cora Winslow. He'd searched Alan's desk, the filing cabinets, and even Alan's computer. Sage had known the password since he'd been a teenager bent on trying his hand at hacking.

He'd even checked the big reference books for secret hiding places cut into their pages.

But he'd found nothing.

The elevator opened into Sage's penthouse apartment. He dropped his backpack on the sofa and walked to the wall of windows, gazing out at the unparalleled view of the river.

That he'd found nothing in his grandfather's study had bothered him, because not only had he not found anything on Cora Winslow, he hadn't found other files that he *knew* his grandfather had kept. Damning data that Sage had been sent to gather on anyone who had crossed his grandfather or who might become a hindrance in the future.

The old bastard wouldn't keep any of the truly important papers at work. There were too many prying eyes at the central offices, the risk of discovery way too high.

So the good stuff on Cora Winslow had to be hidden at

his grandfather's home. *Somewhere.* Otherwise the directive for Sage to break into Broussard's office didn't make sense.

There hadn't been any files on Cora Winslow on the PI's desk, and his filing cabinet drawer had held only a box of Ritz crackers and a jar of peanut butter. Broussard's group must have been keeping everything digitized.

Thus Sage stealing the laptops.

He hoped whatever was on those laptops was worth the receptionist's life.

He really hoped that he hadn't killed Joy Thomas, but if he had, he was not going down for it. He hadn't left any evidence behind. Of that he was certain. And his grandfather wouldn't implicate him, because he'd have to explain too many things that the old man clearly wanted kept secret.

Sage could keep his grandfather's secrets—for a price.

The old man paid him well, but his salary was a drop in the bucket compared to his grandfather's wealth. Once Sage figured out who Cora Winslow was to the old man, he could use it to get Alan's wealth for himself. His grandfather had the information *somewhere.* Sage just needed to find it.

Discovering the secret to Cora Winslow was now his full-time job.

The Quarter, New Orleans, Louisiana
TUESDAY, DECEMBER 13, 12:15 P.M.

Relief swamped Cora. Burke and his people believed her. *Finally someone does.*

"So let me get this straight," Burke said after a moment of silence. "Your father—who's been dead for twenty-three years—has been sending you letters every year?"

She took in each of their faces, seeing genuine concern. But on Phin's face she saw anger, and that helped her to relax because she knew that the anger wasn't directed at her, but *for* her. She kept her gaze fixed on his.

He might have had his own issues with PTSD, but right now he was the strength she needed and she'd take it. *Just a little. Just for now.*

"Well," she said, trying to sound logical, "clearly they weren't written by him. Not unless I believe in ghosts. Which I most likely don't."

Tandy huffed a laugh that sounded hysterical. "I thought he'd stopped writing the letters years ago."

"He did," Cora murmured, not taking her eyes off Phin Bishop. "But he started back up again a few years ago. I just didn't want to talk about them by then."

Phin's anger softened, mixing with compassion. "Why didn't you want to talk about them?"

Cora swallowed hard. "Because I was angry. He'd abandoned us, and my mother had to carry the load of everything on her shoulders. And there was a lot to carry. My brother was ill and needed care. Mama and my grandmother handled everything. *They* were my parents. He didn't deserve acknowledgment."

Except he'd been dead this whole time. She knew she shouldn't feel guilty for her anger, but she did.

"Understandable," Phin murmured. "But you kept the letters, didn't you?"

She nodded, her throat tight. "Every single one."

Tandy gripped her hand. "Oh, honey. Why didn't you tell me all this was going on?"

Cora glanced at her best friend. As she'd expected, Tandy's expression was as miserable as Cora figured her own to be. "Because someone killed my father, T. Someone else has sent me letters for twenty-three *years* pretending to be Jack Elliot. I was scared. I needed to know *who* wrote those letters and *why*. And I needed to know what they planned to do next."

Tandy looked devastated. "I always thought your mama wrote those letters. To make you feel better."

Cora shook her head. "I kept getting them, even after she died, all through college. That made me even madder at my father."

Burke shoved at the lever on his battered recliner, putting his feet up. His hands linked over his belly, and he closed his eyes. "So your father's been dead for twenty-three years. His body was discovered six weeks ago and ID'd two weeks ago, which was when you were notified by the Terrebonne Parish detectives. Did you tell them about the letters?"

Cora glanced around the room, wondering if anyone else thought that Burke's relaxed pose was strange. The two friends of Phin's were giving the PI odd looks, but Phin and Antoine didn't seem bothered at all. Antoine had taken out a computer from one of the three bags he carried and was typing something.

I guess that's Burke's thinking chair. She'd seen much stranger behavior in library patrons over the years.

"I did. I gave the originals to the detectives from the Terrebonne Parish sheriff's office." Her heart stuttered. "Should I not have given them to them?"

Burke waved his hand, not opening his eyes. "I'm sure that's fine. Did you keep copies?"

"Of course. I'm very organized. I told the detectives that I had the letters and would follow them back to Houma in my car. That they could make copies of the letters for me while I watched."

Burke's lips twitched. "You are thorough, ma'am."

"She's a librarian," Tandy said, as if that explained everything.

Phin's expression changed, looking . . . pleased?

She turned to him, irritation rising once more. "Why do you look so smug?"

Now Phin looked embarrassed. "Sorry. I was trying to figure out what you did for a living. I figured professor or librarian."

"She gets that a lot," Tandy put in, unconcerned when Cora turned her glare on her. "Well, you do."

"A librarian in the Garden District," Antoine said thoughtfully, staring at his laptop. "You work a few blocks from where you live. Nice house, Cora. Very nice."

Cora tamped down new irritation. Doing background checks on new clients had to be their standard operating procedure.

And her home was a very nice house. It was also an expensive house to maintain and the source of nearly every one of her headaches. Before her father's body had been found, of course. That new development was front and center. "It's been in my family for six generations."

Phin leaned over to look at Antoine's laptop. "Wow. I bet your handyman is rich."

He didn't know the half of it. "My handyman is mostly me." Still, the costs of maintenance were nearly unmanageable. "But we digress." She folded her hands in her lap and focused on the reclining Burke Broussard. "The detectives from Houma told me that they'd be investigating, but that after so much time, it would be a difficult case to solve."

"Who were the detectives?" Bishop asked.

"Dan Hardy and Liam Goddard."

Phin frowned. "Did you tell them about the break-ins?"

"I did. They said I should call the local police and file a report, which I already had done. They said they'd coordinate with NOPD. I told NOPD about my father's body being found and the letters. *They* said that if nothing was missing, there wasn't anything they could do."

"You've gotten a real runaround," Delores said sympathetically.

Cora sighed. "Yeah. I've wondered if I was losing my mind. Except then this morning happened."

Burke opened his eyes, focusing on her. "Did you walk or drive this morning?"

"I took a streetcar. I didn't want anyone to be able to follow my car, but they managed to follow me anyway."

"Where did you get on?" Burke asked. "Which stop?"

"St. Charles at Washington."

"Did anyone else get on at that stop?" He'd closed his eyes again, reminding her of a burly, Cajun Sherlock Holmes.

"Two elderly ladies and a middle-school-aged boy. The boy I know from the library. He comes in to read manga every Friday after school."

"The intruder *must* have followed you somehow. Or . . ." Burke's eyes flew open again. He abruptly slammed his recliner down and lurched to his feet, earning an alarmed squeak from Tandy.

Cora pressed her hand to her heart, which had taken off like a house on fire. "What?"

Burke shook his head, tapping his lips with his index finger. "Can I examine the contents of your purse, please?"

Cora clutched at her bag, a reflexive motion. "Why?" Then she understood. A tracker. Or a bug. "Fuck," she muttered and handed her purse to the large man.

Antoine got up as well and Broussard dumped the contents of her purse onto his dining room table. Both Phin and Delores's husband, Stone, rose and joined them at the table and the four men searched through the pile of stuff.

"There," Stone said.

"And there," Phin added.

Antoine made an annoyed sound. He went outside and returned a few moments later. "Stored in your garden shed, Burke. We can give them to Detective Clancy later."

Cora turned in her chair to stare at them. "Tracker or bug or both?"

"Both," Broussard said grimly. "They were in the lining. Do you always carry this purse?"

"No. I switched it two weeks ago. Maybe three. It was before the detectives came to the library to tell me my father's body had been found."

Phin's expression was equally grim. "Where do you leave your purse when you're home alone?"

"On my kitchen table." She sighed. "So at least one of the break-ins was to put the devices in my purse."

"Yeah," Burke said, perturbed. "I should have immediately checked."

Cora rubbed her forehead. "Dammit. I didn't even think about that."

"That's why you came to us," Antoine said kindly. "Do you have the copies of the letters with you?"

Cora shook her head. "They're in my safe-deposit box. Joy told me to bring them or email them to you, but I didn't do that. If I've been bugged all this time, whoever shot Joy knew about the letters. I had my purse with me when I took the box of letters to the Houma police, and again when I reported the break-ins to the NOPD. Maybe the letters are what whoever was looking for when they searched my house. And what he wanted from me this morning."

"Maybe," Burke allowed. "He stole two of our laptops, so he might have thought we knew about the letters, too."

Cora stared, horrified. "He stole your laptops? Did he get confidential information on your other clients?"

"No," Antoine said, his smile more than a little proud. "We don't keep confidential files on our hard drives. It's all stored on our network. The laptops are only the conduits to the data. Plus, I have a kill switch installed on all our hardware that I can detonate remotely. He'll get a nasty surprise when he tries to read anything on either laptop. Both have been completely wiped, except for a virus that will infect his system."

Cora knew a little about this. Information was her stock-in-trade, after all. "Leading you to him?"

Antoine nodded. "I hope so."

Phin was frowning. "Why didn't you have copies of the letters with you today if Joy told you to bring them?"

"I didn't plan to hire you all. I don't have that much

money. Joy said I could just do a consult with Burke to see what other steps I could take to protect myself and my home from intruders. I could afford one consultation. Now I honestly don't know what I'm going to do. But of course you can have the letters. Anything to help you find Joy's shooter."

Tandy squeezed Cora's hand. "You can't go home. It's not safe. Come home with me. Or stay with Dad. He'll be happy to have someone to take care of again."

Cora shook her head. "I bought a security system." That she hadn't truly been able to afford. It would keep her safe. "Plus, Blue will bark if anyone—" She sucked in a breath. "My dog. He's home alone. Could they—"

No, no, no. Nothing could happen to Blue. He was all she had left of John Robert. She brought out her cell phone, opening the camera app she'd installed the night before. Her pulse settled when she saw Blue curled up on his bed, sound asleep. "He's okay."

"Did the dog alert you when you had the break-ins?" Bishop asked.

"Friday night he was barking at my bedroom door. He doesn't bark often anymore. He's older and tends to sleep a lot. I went downstairs and a drawer was open in the desk in my kitchen. It's where I pay my bills. I thought maybe someone had stolen my checkbook or my wallet from my purse, but nothing was missing. But it felt off, you know? So I ordered the security system that night. The second time was two days later, on Sunday. I was at work."

Antoine frowned. "The library is closed on Sundays, isn't it?"

"Yes, but we had a staff holiday party and I went in to decorate. When I got home, that's when I saw that the tape I'd put over the doorway was broken. I don't know if Blue barked or not."

"Okay," Broussard said. "Next steps. One, we need to get those letters from your safe-deposit box. We'll do that this afternoon. Two, we'll beef up security at your house and install better locks. Unless you've installed new locks? Please say the locks aren't original."

"The house was built in 1878, and the locks are a whole lot newer than that. But they've been on the doors since I've been living there. Which is my whole life."

Burke turned to Phin. "Phin? Can you oversee the security upgrades to Cora's house?"

Phin blinked, looking surprised, but he rallied quickly. "Yes, of course."

Burke nodded his appreciation. "Thank you. Now, let's talk bodyguards."

Bodyguards? These people clearly thought she was much richer than she was. Which was, like, not at all.

Cora held up one hand. "Whoa. Stop. I don't need that. I can't afford your services. Joy said that I should talk to you once and you could recommend ways to keep myself safe."

Burke crouched next to her. He looked utterly serious, and she might have been intimidated had she not just seen him chilling in his duct-taped BarcaLounger. "Cora, I'm going to protect you. That is non-negotiable. You will not have to pay me. I only ask that you cooperate with our investigation, because we need to find out who hurt our Joy."

Cora exhaled. "Okay. I'll accept your protection, but only for Joy's sake. Just in case whoever shot her comes after me again, you can catch them. Who will be my bodyguard?"

"I'm not sure yet. Let me work on that while Phin is fixing your security. Do you feel all right with us going to your bank with you to get those letters?"

"Yes, but I need to eat first. I skipped breakfast and I really should eat."

"She gets hangricidal," Tandy said, patting Cora's arm. "Like hangry on steroids."

Cora glared at her best friend. "I do not."

"She gets real whiny, too," Tandy added. "Like she is right now."

That was fair. "Where can I find a deli or a restaurant nearby?"

"I'll make you a sandwich," Burke offered. "Will that do?"

She smiled at the big man. "Yes, thank you."

When Burke had gone into his kitchen, Cora met Phin's gaze. "Are you okay to work on my house today? You've had a really crummy morning, too."

Phin's nod was resolute. "Keeping my hands occupied is always good. Can SodaPop come with me?"

Cora smiled. "Of course she can. I'll put Blue in one of the upstairs rooms while she's visiting. I know service dogs shouldn't socialize with other dogs if possible."

"I don't think an afternoon of socialization will harm SodaPop's training," Delores said with a smile. "I trained her myself, and she's been around other dogs."

"Then I guess you're fixin' to visit the Garden District," Cora told Phin.

Phin smiled and Cora found herself staring. The man had a broody, dangerous bad-boy vibe, but when he smiled, he seemed young and carefree.

"I love those old houses in the Garden District," he said. "I repair things over there occasionally. Burke's had me doing repairs on this place for a few years now."

Cora returned his smile, feeling a sense of ease for the first time in a long time. She wondered why he'd seemed so surprised when Burke had asked him to do the upgrade, but then she remembered the exchange in the car. For a moment Burke had believed that this man had hurt Joy. A fleeting moment, but a moment nonetheless.

He was big and dark and a scowl seemed to be his resting face. *I should be afraid of him.*

Her smile must have faltered, because Phin abruptly sobered.

"I scared you earlier, outside the police station," he said quietly. "If you don't want me to come to your house, I understand."

Cora blinked, wondering if her feelings were that transparent.

But she wasn't afraid. There was pain in this man, deep down. PTSD, he'd said. Bad enough that he needed a service dog. But she sensed a gentleness there, too. And Joy's daughters had said he was safe. That would be good enough for the afternoon.

"I'm not afraid of you," she said honestly. "Not like this. But what will happen if you have another episode? Do you get . . . violent?"

"No," Delores said softly. "He always runs off before it gets bad."

Phin looked away. His feelings were also transparent. He was ashamed and that made Cora want to help him.

"Will you have any warning if you're about to have an episode?" she asked.

Phin reached for his dog. "That's what SodaPop's for. Early detection. And distraction."

"Will you look at me?" She waited until he did, then looked him square in the eye. "Have you ever hurt someone?"

He didn't blink. "Yes. Once. Five years ago."

"Phin was hurt worse," Stone said loyally. "The other guy started it, then shot Phin when he defended himself. Phin ended up in the hospital and the other guy just had a bruised jaw."

Phin was watching her intensely, waiting for her verdict.

She should ask for someone else. She really should. But the man's eyes were clear and honest. And more than a little vulnerable.

She couldn't hurt him. *Wouldn't* hurt him.

"I'd be grateful for your help, Phin. You're welcome in my home."

Phin's whole body relaxed, including the grip he'd had on his dog. SodaPop turned and licked his hand. He smiled down at his dog before lifting his gaze back to hers. "Thank you."

"You're welcome. We'll go to the bank first and get my father's letters. Hopefully that will give Burke somewhere to begin."

And, if she was lucky, Broussard Investigations would find out who'd killed Jack Elliot.

And why.

4

The Garden District, New Orleans, Louisiana
TUESDAY, DECEMBER 13, 2:30 P.M.

PHIN LOOKED BOTH ways along Cora's street,
making sure there were no men in black lurking in the
shadows. The coast seemed clear, so he stepped aside so
that Cora could unlock the front door.

SodaPop was stuck to Phin's side, keeping him calm.
He'd been worrying about Joy, but her children had assured them that she was stable. Still unconscious, but stable. She was currently in the ICU, but they hoped she'd be
moved into a normal room by the next morning.

He'd also worried about what they'd find inside Cora's
house, but neither concern had sent him into a spiral,
mostly because of SodaPop. *Good girl.* He'd felt confident
enough in his self-control to send Stone and Delores to
play tourist in the Quarter for a few hours. He'd see them
later that night, after Cora's house was safe. Phin was to
ensure that her home was physically secure, and Antoine
was to ensure that there were no more bugs and that the
alarm system she'd installed was working properly.

Step one, of course, was figuring out what was up with
the letters. After retrieving the copies from Cora's safe-
deposit box—there had been *three* sets of copies, because
Cora Winslow was *very* organized—Burke had taken one

set back to his own house, planning to go through the letters personally.

It made sense that Joy's attacker might have thought Cora had brought the letters with her to the office that morning, but why the attacker would want them, none of them knew. Hopefully Burke would figure it out.

Burke still wasn't sure who he would assign to be Cora's bodyguard.

Let it be me.

But Phin knew that was a truly stupid thing to wish. Not with his baggage. Plus, as confident as Cora had seemed in his ability to control himself, he had noted her relief when Antoine had tagged along.

Maybe it was because Antoine had come to check for bugs, but Phin was realistic, if nothing else. A man who needed a service dog was not qualified to be a bodyguard.

That he'd wanted the job since he'd come to work for Burke two years before was immaterial. He'd have to be satisfied going back to his old job—nighttime security and the firm's general fixer-upper.

And wasn't "fixer-upper" true in the metaphorical sense, as well? Phin was no catch. Especially not for a woman like Cora Winslow.

He flinched at the thought. He had no business even entertaining the notion that a woman like her could be attracted to a man like him. But he'd seen kindness in her eyes and an unwillingness to hurt him, and that would have to be enough.

"This place is amazing." Antoine had stopped two steps into the foyer, awe in his voice. "It's like a museum."

Phin hummed his agreement as he gazed up at the fifteen-foot ceiling and ornate archways leading to the rest of the house. "Greek Revival."

The house was a stunning example of the architecture that had been so popular in New Orleans during the mid-to-late nineteenth century. But it needed a lot of work. The light pink exterior was practically begging for a coat of paint. The interior walls were also faded, the baseboards and the tray ceilings chipped, and the area rugs frayed.

But the hardwood floors shone and the foyer, at least, was sparkling clean. The ornate chandelier over their heads was shining and spotless.

"You know your architecture," Cora said, dropping her keys in a bowl by the door.

"I've studied a little. Nothing official." Phin pointed to the keys. "One of the first things you'll need to do is find a safer place for your keys."

Wincing, she blushed and put the keys into her pocket. "You're right. I'm sorry." She started toward the living room. "I need to check on my dog."

Phin held up a hand. "Stay here. I need to clear the house." Just in case someone was hiding, waiting for her.

She frowned. "Blue's in the living room. He's old and missing a few teeth, but he won't like you coming into his territory. It's unlikely he'll attack, but I need to introduce you."

"Then I'll do that room last. Antoine, you ready to check for bugs?"

Antoine had already taken his scanner from one of his computer bags. "I am. I'll wait here with Cora until you're done."

"And you're carrying?" Phin said loudly, kind of hoping this morning's asshole was listening. The bastard would know that Cora was being kept safe.

Antoine grinned, understanding completely. "I am," he said, just as loudly.

Cora watched them with apprehension. "Am I allowed to make a few phone calls?"

Antoine sobered and fished a phone from his pocket. "Use my burner until I check your phone for listening devices, and don't say anything confidential."

"I just need to call Tandy at the gallery and let her know I'm home safe. Oh shit. My lawyer, too." She grimaced. "Everyone worries."

Phin understood. She had a delicate air, even though he knew she was tough. He had a lot of respect for Cora Winslow.

"I'll call down as I clear rooms," he said, then started up the grand staircase with a gleaming mahogany banister that looked original to the house.

Exceptional workmanship.

SodaPop at his side, he went all the way up to the third-floor attic, working his way down, clearing each room. When he opened a bedroom door on the second floor he stopped in his tracks, his mouth falling open.

Cora had an incredible computer station, comparable to the one Antoine kept at Burke's office. Multiple monitors, a sleek tower, and an ergonomic keyboard that looked like something out of science fiction.

He looked down at his dog. "What the hell does she do in this room?" The dog didn't answer, of course. Just gazed up at him calmly, making him feel calm, too.

He cleared the computer room and all the others save the living room before returning to the foyer, where she was still talking on the phone.

"I'm okay, Harry. I promise. I'm home and I'm about to set the alarm. Blue's here with me."

Phin had overheard her speaking to the older man after he'd followed her out of the police station and had quickly realized that Harry was the lawyer who'd accompanied her. *If I'd been Harry, I would have insisted Cora get in the cab with me and not left her standing on the curb after being chased by Joy's attacker.*

But maybe her lawyer knew her well enough to know she wouldn't have listened. Still, Phin had been annoyed that the old man had put his afternoon appointments ahead of Cora's safety.

"I'll call you in a few hours. Bye, Harry." She ended the call and rubbed her forehead. "Honestly," she muttered. "I'm not a child. But Harry's known me my whole life, so he still thinks I'm a little girl." She looked up at Phin. "All clear?"

"All but the living room. I'll do that while Antoine's doing his sweep."

Antoine saluted, then took the same route up the stairs that Phin had taken.

"This way." Cora led Phin to another amazing room with high ceilings and lush draperies that were only a little faded. He admired the details as he completed his search for any hidden intruders.

It, too, was clear.

This room had aged much better than some of the others had. It was furnished with modern, comfortable sofas and chairs, but the walls were covered in old portraits. Like, really old. "Who's this?" he asked, pointing to a severe-looking woman in a black dress with an elaborate pearl necklace around her throat.

"My great-great-grandmother, Blanche Winslow. She was married to him." She pointed to a man with an amazing beard in a naval uniform. "Seymour." She pointed to another portrait, newer than the others. The woman had Cora's red hair, piled atop her head. "My grandmother, Norma Winslow."

Phin studied Cora's profile. "You're wearing her pearls." They were a single strand, both simpler and classier than the ones that Blanche had worn in her portrait.

Cora smiled. "I am."

"What happened to the fancy pearls Blanche is wearing?" He wondered if someone might also be looking for valuables.

"Gone. They disappeared somewhere around 1900. Pirates," she said dramatically, making him chuckle. "Or maybe a thieving relative. Nobody knows."

Phin turned from the portraits to the old dog, who lay curled up on a braided rug in front of one of the room's two fireplaces. "Blue, I presume?"

Cora's smile held a tinge of sadness. "Yeah. He sleeps most of the time these days. He's twelve, which is getting old for his breed. We've had him since he was a puppy."

Phin studied the dog, who lifted his head to stare at him, growling menacingly.

"It's okay, Blue," Cora said. The growling immediately ceased, but the staring continued.

It was easy to see how Blue had come by his name. The dog was a blue merle color and his eyes were a strikingly light blue. He looked like a cross between a boxer and a pit bull.

"What breed is he?" Phin asked.

"Catahoula Leopard." Cora's speech changed, emphasizing her New Orleans accent, sounding more like Burke. "State dog of Loo-siana. Go ahead. Let him sniff you."

He went down on one knee next to Blue and let him sniff his fingers. He got a single lick for his trouble before Blue yawned and went back to sleep. Phin looked up at Cora. "He must have been really riled up to have barked that night. Doesn't seem like he's got a lot of energy for random barking."

"No. That's why I went down to check things out. He never barks at night. This neighborhood is usually quiet."

Phin gave Blue a soft scratch behind his ears before rising. "I noticed the garden in the back when I was checking out the kitchen." It was surrounded by a six-foot wall and he'd noticed the gate across the driveway when they'd pulled up. "Does the gate lock?"

The garden was large for the neighborhood. There was a small swimming pool as well as a koi pond. The pool had been covered for the winter, but the koi had been swimming happily, even though the temperature was brisk.

"It does, but I rarely lock it. Like I said, the neighborhood is usually quiet. I started locking it after the first break-in. I guess they didn't mean Blue any harm, even though he barked at them the first time. Someone was here while I was working at the library, but they left Blue alone."

"That's good, at least." He moved to the bookshelves that lined one long wall. The shelves were heavy with books. Most were decades old. Some looked centuries old. But there was a section of paperbacks with creased spines. There were fiction books of all genres, although the bulk seemed to be sci-fi and fantasy. There were also nonfiction books, mostly DIY fix-it books but also a ton of cookbooks.

"Yours?" he asked, looking over her shoulder.

Her smile was self-deprecating. "I *am* a librarian."

He tapped the spine of a book that had been a bestseller a few years before. "I like this one. I have it at home on my own keeper shelf."

Her smile bloomed. "You like to read?"

"Kept me sane when I was serving. People would donate books to the troops and I read every single one I could get my hands on." His mouth quirked up. "Even read some romances."

She grinned, delighted. "Me too. You can borrow any of mine that you'd like."

"Likewise," he offered, then realized he was still staring at her.

And that she was staring back at him.

Heat rising in his cheeks, he gestured to the portraits that covered the rest of the walls. "Your ancestors?"

She nodded. "I'm the sixth generation of Winslows to live here." She sighed. "I might just be the last. This house costs the earth to maintain."

"I know. Burke spends a small fortune on his house in the Quarter every year, apart from what he pays me to keep it up." Which was separate from his salary at Broussard Investigations, and honestly, more money than Phin thought he was worth. "Are you going to keep it?"

She looked around sadly. "I don't know. My grandmother passed away about two years ago. It's a lot of work to just keep it clean. I kind of let the house go that first year. No time or money. I had . . . other priorities." She glanced at a framed photograph on the mantel over the fireplace. The young man in the photo bore a strong resemblance to Cora, curly red hair and all. "My brother was ill."

Was.

Phin gentled his voice. "He passed?"

She swallowed. "Yeah. A year ago. He'd had Hodgkin's lymphoma and we thought he'd licked it with chemo. But it came back. He needed a bone marrow transplant, but we never found a match. Everyone we knew tried to donate, but . . ." She shrugged. "And then it was too late."

"I'm sorry," he murmured, saying a silent prayer of thanks that all his siblings were alive and healthy. He hadn't seen them in five years, but he followed their lives, largely with Stone and Delores's help.

"Thank you." She laughed bitterly. "I looked so hard for my father when John Robert's doctor told him he needed the transplant. My mother was dead by then, and my grandmother and I weren't matches. I thought, 'If only I can find my father. He'll donate. I know he will.' I searched and searched, but I could never track him down. Meanwhile I kept getting le—"

She cut herself off before she could say *letters*, then sighed. "I even donated DNA to one of those genetic tracing websites, hoping he'd done the same and I could track him—or his new family—that way. But he was dead all along."

Phin didn't know what to say, so he said nothing at all.

Cora sighed again. "I'm really tired. I guess this morning's caught up to me. Would you mind if I rested for a little while?"

"Of course not. Kick off those torture-shoes and rest your feet. I'll start checking doors and windows and make a list of the supplies I'll need to make the house intruder-proof."

"Torture-shoes is definitely true today. Thank you, Phin. I really appreciate it." She sank down into the sofa closest to Blue and kicked off her shoes.

Her toenails were painted neon pink with white smiley faces, which made him want to smile, too.

Instead, he clucked his tongue to call SodaPop and began checking entry points to her home. He'd nearly completed the first floor when Antoine came down the stairs, glowering.

He held out his hand, revealing five small listening devices the size of pebbles. He dumped them in a Faraday bag to keep them from broadcasting.

"And I'm not close to being done yet," Antoine said. "Sonofabitch bugged every bedroom and her bathroom, too."

Phin clenched his jaw. "Cameras?"

Antoine shook his head. "None that I can find yet. I'm going to my car to call Burke. I'll be back in a few. Stay here with her." He looked around with a frown. "Where is she?"

"On the sofa, hopefully asleep. I'll stand watch."

Uptown, New Orleans, Louisiana
TUESDAY, DECEMBER 13, 2:45 P.M.

Sage slipped into his grandfather's home study, confident that he hadn't been seen. He knew every nook and cranny in this monstrosity of a mansion, having grown up here.

He took a moment to look at the photographs on his grandfather's desk, a familiar sadness pressing at his chest. His father's photo was prominently displayed, one of the last formal photos they'd had taken.

The photo captured three generations: his grandfather; Sage's father, the firstborn son; and Sage himself, his father's only child.

Sage, his father, and his grandfather had posed for the camera, their suits dark, their ties perfectly tied. Their shoes had even been shined, which Sage hadn't understood as a five-year-old. Their shoes wouldn't even be in the picture, so why did they have to shine them?

His father had laughed, that booming sound one of the only things that Sage truly remembered about his dad. He'd murmured that his grandfather liked things a certain way, and it wasn't a lot of trouble to shine their shoes. Why not make him happy?

But Alan didn't look happy in this picture. He looked . . . sad.

And guilty. Sage had always thought his grandfather had looked guilty and didn't know why. He still didn't know why. The sadness he'd understood. His grandmother had recently died in a car accident, the car catching on fire. His father had been sad, too.

Sage didn't remember his grandmother. He and his father had lived in Mobile until he was two. That was when his parents had divorced and he and his father had moved back to New Orleans. He didn't remember the divorce, either, but he remembered the shouting every time his father dropped him at his mother's house in Mobile for the occasional weekend. He remembered his mother crying when his father returned to pick him up.

And he remembered that his grandfather had hated his mother. Still did.

Which was why Sage's mother still lived in Mobile.

And . . . *wow*. The realization that they'd gotten divorced twenty-three years ago was like a slap in the face.

Apparently, a lot of things had happened twenty-three years ago. He wondered if there was a connection between any of them.

But the clock was ticking and he had to start searching. His grandfather was waiting for his network guy to arrive at the central offices to try to get information off Broussard's laptops.

Good luck with that. Sage had already tried on his own. Whoever ran Broussard's IT department was good at their job. The machines had been wiped.

But it would take the IT guy a while to figure that out, so Sage had an hour or two.

From his backpack, he pulled three small cameras, wishing he'd done this years ago. That he hadn't was only because he hadn't been curious enough to bother. He'd already known all the information his grandfather kept, because Sage had gathered most of it for him.

That had changed when Cora Winslow had come onto the scene.

The cameras were the same kind that he'd planted in his grandfather's adversaries' homes and offices all the time, so he knew their capabilities well. He placed them so that he'd get a view of all areas of the study.

His grandfather would be hiding the Broussard laptops somewhere. Hopefully where the old man hid everything else.

Sage would finally find out where that was.

Metairie, New Orleans, Louisiana
TUESDAY, DECEMBER 13, 5:45 P.M.

A knock on his door had Alan glaring at the clock on his desk. It was about time.

"Enter."

Medford Hughes came in and closed the door behind him, looking like he'd rather be anywhere but there. Which was the same way he looked every time Alan called him in for a job. The man had his own business doing network stuff, but he always made time for Alan. He was too scared not to.

"Don't dawdle, Medford," Alan said, keeping his voice much calmer than he felt. "I need to get into my laptops."

Medford frowned. "Laptops, sir? More than one?"

"Two." Without touching the computers, Alan slid them from Sage's special mesh bag that kept them from connecting to Wi-Fi so they couldn't be tracked. But Alan had turned off his Wi-Fi in preparation for Medford's arrival, so they'd be safe.

Medford stared at the laptops on Alan's desk with open dismay tinged with fear.

"These laptops, sir?"

What was Medford's problem? The man had unlocked laptops in the past that did not belong to Alan and had never said a word. Alan always claimed he'd forgotten his password and Medford had always nodded as if that were the truth, even though he'd known that the laptops hadn't belonged to Alan.

But those previous computers had been taken from people Alan knew. He'd always had at least an idea of where to start with the password—pets' names and the like. This time, he had no clue. And this time, he had two laptops.

The laptops Sage normally collected weren't owned by tech-savvy companies like Broussard Investigations. They were owned by people who were trying to manipulate Alan, who might be trying to steal from him or even concoct blackmail scenarios. Ministers were always vulnerable to dishonest people who tried to paint them as less than holy.

Alan found that knowing the real intentions of those dishonest people was the best defense. Threatening to disclose their worst secrets always made them back down and walk away.

So he'd send Sage after their computers, and the boy had never failed to deliver.

"These laptops, Medford. Can you help me or not?"

Medford swallowed, clearly nervous. As he should be. Medford owed Alan too much to buck the system. Too much to question Alan's orders.

"Sir, without some idea of what you might have used as a password, I'd just be stabbing in the dark."

Medford always referred to the stolen laptops as Alan's, even though he knew they weren't. It was most likely how the man justified his actions to himself.

"You have programs to randomize passwords, don't you?" Alan asked impatiently. "Just let the program spin new passwords until it figures out the right one like you always do."

"Um . . . well, sir. These particular laptops will likely have . . . additional protections."

"What does that mean?"

Medford wouldn't meet his eyes. "Just that I might have put protections on these laptops to prevent unauthorized access."

Claiming that he'd been the one to set up the device security was another way that Medford justified the things he believed to be morally wrong. But it was also an attempt at self-protection because Medford suspected that Alan was recording all their conversations.

Which Alan was, of course.

Sometimes Medford was able to break a password and sometimes he wasn't. But he always tried. It looked like today might be a first. Medford was looking at these laptops like they were snakes, coiled to strike.

"What might these added protections do, Medford?" Alan asked.

Sweat was beading on Medford's forehead. "If I try to guess your password and get it wrong after even a few attempts, I could trigger the computer to wipe itself."

"I see," Alan murmured.

I won't know what's in Cora Winslow's letters.

It was possible, of course, that she hadn't given the letters to the PI—yet, anyway—but he wasn't betting on it. Sage's bugs had revealed that the PI's secretary, Joy Thomas, had told her to bring the letters with her to her meeting with Broussard this morning, or to email them. He had to assume Broussard had the letters.

If I can't get into Broussard's email, I won't know who sent them. Because it certainly hadn't been Winslow's father. He'd been dead for twenty-three years.

Alan should know. He'd killed the man himself.

He didn't know what was in those letters, but their very existence—and Cora Winslow's continued attempts to get the police to investigate them—had him nervous. He needed to make sure there was nothing in the letters that could lead police to what Jack Elliot had been doing twenty-three years ago.

Or my part in it.

Medford backed toward the door. "If there's nothing else, I'll just—"

"Stay where you are." He narrowed his eyes at Medford, hardening his voice. "You need to at least try. One of them might have passwords that include the names Nala, Louisa, Wayne, or Jerry." Because those were the receptionist's children.

Finding the woman's children's names had been simple enough. Joy Thomas didn't have a social media presence, but her kids did. He knew where they'd gone to school and the names of their significant others and their pets.

Medford shook his head. "I'll try, but I really think we set these passwords to be completely random, and I didn't write them down." His words sounded desperate. Panicked. "I'm not going to be able to guess them."

Alan wanted to snap viciously at the useless man, but he held it back, keeping his smile benign. "Please try."

"Yes, sir, as long as you know that there's a risk of wiping the entire drive." Hands trembling slightly, Medford pulled on a pair of disposable gloves and opened the first laptop.

And then Alan saw what had Medford so spooked. With his failing eyesight, Alan hadn't seen the holographic label on the laptop's lid. It was the same color as the computer itself, visible only when the light hit it a certain way.

But now he could see the label in sufficient detail.

It read *Broussard Investigations* in an elegant art deco script.

Sage was sure to have seen the label, but he hadn't said a word.

Alan seethed. He should have examined the laptops

more closely. Now Medford knew exactly where the machines had come from.

Which meant Medford knew that Alan was behind their theft, which had been all over the news that morning because of the shooting of Joy Thomas.

It also meant that Medford now knew that Alan was connected to the shooting of the Thomas woman, easily the worst thing that Sage had ever done.

Alan remained where he sat, trying to think as his heart raced faster and faster.

I'm not a violent man. The only time he'd killed was that one time twenty-three years ago. After that he'd been careful. He blackmailed. He manipulated. He did not kill.

But Sage might have. The Thomas woman was still alive for now, but that could change. Alan didn't have to ask to know that even attempted murder crossed Medford's moral line. He might tell the police everything.

That can't happen.

Medford was staring at the laptop's screen in what looked like disbelief. He was sliding his finger over the trackpad rapidly, his frown becoming more intense.

"What do you see?" Alan demanded.

"There's no password. It just . . . opened."

That was good, right? But it was also suspicious that Broussard hadn't taken precautions. Maybe the man was cocky, given his recent successes at catching some very bad criminals. Success did make a man cocky. Alan had fought against that himself.

"The drive isn't wiped?"

Medford finally met his eyes and the man's expression was one of reluctant knowing. "I don't think so. There doesn't appear to have been much on the hard drive. I think it's trying to connect to a server, but it can't because the Wi-Fi's turned off."

"And?"

"I think their content resides on a central server and

they use the laptops for access. Like old-time terminals that accessed a mainframe. There's nothing of use on the hard drive."

"But I can access the server with the computer if I connect to the internet? Just by plugging the router back in?"

"Possibly, but that will make the machine trackable." Medford hesitated, looking like he was dueling with the devil himself, but he finally spoke. "If you try to sign on, use someone else's Wi-Fi. And don't do it here."

"I see." He'd already come to the same conclusion. That Broussard would attempt to track down thieves was a given. It was good that Alan was smarter than those thieves. "And the other machine?"

Clenching his jaw, Medford opened the other machine, poked around the hard drive for a few minutes, then lifted his gaze. "It's the same." He pulled off his gloves and threw them in the trash can next to Alan's desk. "I'm done."

There was a tension in Medford's face that Alan did not like. *You're done when I say you're done.*

"Thank you, Medford. That's all I need for the time being." He rose and walked Medford out. "How's your wife?"

Medford flinched, just as Alan had intended him to. "About the same, sir."

A hopeless addict with a gambling problem, then.

"Give her my best."

Which translated to: *If you want her secrets kept, you'd best keep mine.*

Medford jerked a nod. "Yes, sir."

Alan expected him to leave, his head down, but Medford unexpectedly raised his gaze to meet Alan's. There was anger there. Despair as well. But there was a glint of determination that told Alan all he needed to know.

Medford had made his decision. The man was going to tell.

"You have something to say, Medford?" he asked sharply.

Medford shook his head. "No, sir. I'll see myself out."

Alan closed the door behind him, then returned to his desk to stare at the two laptops.

He needed to keep Medford quiet. He should make Sage take care of the man, but he couldn't ask that of his grandson. As much as he hated to admit it, that would give Sage one more thing to hold over Alan's head. For so long, Alan had been in control of his grandson. But that had changed sometime in the past year. Sage had become surly and mean, vicious and calculating. Bold and arrogant.

It's my fault. I never should have included him in any of this. But his old assistant had died suddenly. Had had a heart attack in his sleep, so Alan had needed someone new to research potential adversaries. Sage had been only fifteen but smart as a whip.

And loyal. At least he had been then.

Alan's ministry did so much good in the world. But staying on top required sacrifices. Alan had always been certain it had been worth it. He was still certain of his own role. He might have to rethink Sage's, though.

Pulling on a pair of leather gloves from his coat pocket, he closed the laptops and put them back in Sage's special bag. He'd follow Medford's advice and try to access Broussard's server from somewhere else.

Medford Hughes himself was a more pressing problem. He needed to take care of the man before he did anything else.

Alan rubbed his eyes, cursing his blurred sight. He'd have to drive tonight. He couldn't trust anyone to drive him to Medford's home.

From here on out, he'd have to handle things himself.

He picked Medford's gloves out of the trash can and slipped them into an envelope. He knew exactly what he needed to do.

5

PHIN WAS ON his knees in front of Cora's kitchen door installing the last of the new locks when the house alarm beeped to let him know a door had opened. He leapt to his feet, grabbing a baseball bat that he'd found in Cora's coat closet.

He didn't have a gun, but he'd be damned if someone would enter this house to hurt her. He stood in the kitchen archway, clenching the bat and squaring his shoulders to make himself look as big as possible.

"Whoa." Burke put both hands in the air as he closed the front door behind him, Antoine at his side. "Just us."

Which made sense, considering whoever had entered would have needed a new key and Antoine was the only one who had one. Cora would get a full set of keys, of course, but she was still asleep in the living room.

He'd checked.

Several times.

She slept deeply, the lines of worry that had creased her brow having disappeared for now. He'd dropped a hammer on his foot two hours before and she hadn't even reacted, even though he'd sworn very loudly.

If someone broke in, she'd likely sleep right through it. Luckily Blue had woken her when she'd had an intruder.

Phin glanced over his shoulder at the old dog, who lay on a thick dog bed in the corner of the kitchen. Blue was watching him, his eerie light blue eyes calm.

SodaPop, on the other hand, had jumped to her feet and was now leaning against his thigh. *Good girl.*

Phin pressed a finger to his lips before stepping back so that his coworkers could enter the kitchen. "I think she'd sleep through a hurricane," Phin murmured, "but I don't want to wake her. I don't think she slept last night at all. She put the contacts for her alarm system on every door and window in the house and there are a shit ton of windows. I don't think I've ever worked on a house with so many windows. There are over forty of them."

Antoine removed the ever-present laptops from his shoulders and placed them on the kitchen table. "She did a good job, too. I don't think I could have installed a security system any better."

"But the window locks are a joke," Phin grumbled. "I ordered some special locks for most of the windows, but I can't pick them up until tomorrow. Did you assign her a bodyguard?"

Burke nodded. "I did. Molly will be here soon for night duty and Val will guard her during the day."

"They're good choices." Molly was no-nonsense and the most logical person he'd ever met. Val was energy and light and friendship. He still wanted to guard Cora himself, but between the two women, she would be well protected.

Burke pointed to the kitchen table, where Antoine was already sitting, his three laptops open and arranged in a semicircle in front of him. "Can we talk?"

Phin wanted to say no, because he knew what Burke wanted to talk about. Burke had apologized for that morning and, as far as Phin was concerned, it was no longer an issue.

But Burke had that look in his eyes, the one that said that *no* wasn't an okay reply.

"I suppose." Phin took a seat and buried his fingers in SodaPop's coat. She leaned even more heavily against him, her presence welcome. Grounding. Necessary.

Antoine put his headphones on. "I'm not even here. Talk, talk, talk."

Phin knew that Antoine wouldn't pay them a bit of attention, although it wouldn't matter if he did. Antoine knew most of his story. It had been Antoine who'd gotten him the job with Burke's group to begin with.

Burke took the chair closest to Phin's. "I'm not going to tell you that I'm sorry again, even though I am." Then he sighed. "I'm glad you're back."

"Me too. This is . . . home."

"Good. So . . . Stone and Delores. Have you gone to them every time you've disappeared in the last few years?"

"Yes. Stone and Delores have given me safe harbor whenever I've needed it. I think it's cost them a lot to keep my visits from my family, but they gave me their word. It's why I've always felt safe going to them."

"I understand," Burke murmured. "So why did you come back today?"

"I didn't." Phin rolled his eyes. "I came back Sunday— or tried to. I got as far as the deli on the corner before I turned tail and ran. Yesterday, I got a half block closer. I felt like such a . . ." He sighed. "A coward. A failure. I wanted to be able to do the work you guys do, but I spiraled on my first real assignment. I ran. I wanted to be *normal*, Burke. I still want that. But . . . I'm just me."

Broken. But healing again. How many times would he have to heal?

Forever. This could happen again and again forever. The notion was depressing as fuck.

"We missed you," Burke said quietly. "*You*, Phin."

Phin's lips curved. "I know. I got all your texts. Joy said she was going to make me cut my own switch when I came back, because I was scaring her by staying gone."

Burke laughed. "She still might make you do that."

Phin closed his eyes, the memory of her bloody body on the floor coming back to assault his fragile peace. "But then I heard the gunshots, Burke. I had to come inside. To make sure she was okay."

"And you probably saved her life." Burke squeezed Phin's forearm briefly before pulling his hand away. "You ran *toward* the danger, Phin. You're no coward, and you're no failure. I talked to Joy on my way over here."

Phin's head shot up, adrenaline surging. "She's awake?"

"She is. Demanding to go home. But she also demanded to see you. She could hear you, begging her to hold on. Her kids say that if you don't come, they'll march over here and drag you to the ICU."

Phin's mouth stretched wide in a grin that felt odd. Like it belonged on someone else's face. He hadn't grinned like that in a long time. "I will."

Burke smiled back. "Are we okay?"

Phin nodded once. "Yeah. It hurt this morning, I'm not gonna lie. But you've been good to me, Burke. I owe you too much."

Burke frowned. "I don't want us to be okay because you feel like you owe me."

Phin exhaled. "I didn't mean it that way. I meant that you've proven your support time and again. One little slip doesn't wipe all that away. I still want to catch the bastard who hurt Joy, though. I may not owe you, but I do owe her. If I'd been there, he never would have hurt her."

"You don't know that. Antoine was asleep in his office and didn't hear the scuffle until it was too late." Burke held up a hand when Phin started to disagree. "Don't distract me. Why did you come back now?"

Trust Burke to realize that Phin hadn't adequately answered his question. "It's the holidays. I want to see my family. I'd set Christmas as my deadline for getting my shit together. But I couldn't face them until I'd faced you all. I'm sorry, Burke. I'm sorry I ran and I'm sorry I didn't come back till now."

"You came back, Phin. That's all that matters. The rest will take time. I'm glad you're here. I'm glad you're okay."

"I might run again if I spiral."

Burke met his gaze directly. "I know. As long as you come back. And let us know you're okay while you're gone." He nodded briskly, the conversation now over.

Thank God.

"Did you read Cora's letters?" Phin asked.

"I did. I can't figure out what's so important about them that someone would risk invading our office during the daytime. While Joy and Antoine were there. They're letters that a father would write to a daughter he hasn't seen in too long. Asking how she's liking school. Telling her that he'll always love her. But some of the items are things that shouldn't have been obvious unless he'd been here, watching her. Like . . ." Burke pulled out his phone and opened a file. "Here's one of the letters. I scanned them in so I wasn't carrying them around. I put the copies she gave me in my safe at home." He gave Phin his phone. "Read what I highlighted. This was in the very first Christmas letter she received."

"'You looked so pretty in your new green dress. Like a Christmas angel,'" Phin read. He frowned at Burke. "He— or she—knew what her dress looked like."

"Exactly. There are several small things like that over the years. There was also a four-year gap," Burke said. "There were no letters from about six years ago to two years ago, then they start back up again. I want to ask her why that is."

"Her grandmother died two years ago," Phin said. "And her brother was sick then. He died a year ago." He sucked in a breath as a thought occurred. "She said her brother needed a bone marrow transplant, but they couldn't find a matching donor. She said she looked for her father, hoping he'd be a match, but could never find him. That might have been two years ago. Whoever sent the letters didn't want her to think he was dead, because she was looking for him."

Burke nodded his approval. "You could be right. The letters that started back up had a different tone. More hands-off. He said he was happy where he was living and that he had a new family. He hoped she was okay. Said he'd love to come back and see her sometime, if she was willing. But there was no return address. No way for her to know how to answer him either way."

Fury started to boil in Phin's gut. "Someone's been manipulating her for *years*."

"And we're going to find out who," Burke promised. "I need to bring Antoine in on this. He's been waiting for us to finish." He waved at the man, who took off his headphones.

"Is the talk, talk, talk done?" Antoine asked hopefully.

"It is," Burke confirmed. "How many bugs total did you find?"

Antoine's expression became grim. "Twelve. Whoever was listening to her was not fucking around. No cameras at least."

"What about her phone and her computer upstairs?" Phin asked. "That is one nice setup she's got in her home office."

Antoine nodded. "I know, right? I was hoping she'd be awake to tell me the password. That's why I came back, to run a check of her system."

"I don't want to wake her up," Phin said quietly. "She was so tired." He realized too late how that sounded and wished the words back, but of course that was useless.

Burke gave him a sharp look, one that said he'd noticed that Phin was extra attentive to Cora Winslow and would be addressing it later.

Great.

Antoine didn't seem to notice. "Not having the password might be better. I really want to know how easy it would have been for the intruder to hack into her machine."

"Go see if you can break in, Antoine," Burke said. "I'll take the heat if she's mad about it. Also see if her phone's infected."

Antoine stood and closed his three laptops, leaving them on the table. "I'll be back. Are we eating soon?"

Burke snorted. "Yes, Antoine. We will feed you. Molly's bringing food."

Antoine did a smooth little dance. "Food from my favorite restaurant. Awesome."

Molly's fiancé owned Le Petit Choux, a restaurant in the Quarter. The food truly was awesome. Phin's stomach growled on cue.

Antoine smirked. "I'm not the only hungry one. Text me when the food's here. I'm going up to check her computer."

Burke turned back to Phin. "So, now that you're back, my furnace is making a racket."

Phin laughed, the request making him feel better than all of Burke's prettier words. "I'll take a look at it as soon as I can."

The Garden District, New Orleans, Louisiana
TUESDAY, DECEMBER 13, 7:20 P.M.

Cora blinked awake. It was dark outside and she'd fallen asleep on the sofa again. With a sigh she started to get up, then froze.

Voices. In her kitchen. Then one familiar voice cut through the fog in her brain.

"Then what were they looking for?" Phin asked.

Phin Bishop was still here and he apparently was not alone.

She stood and started for the kitchen, the cold floor feeling good against her swollen feet.

Blue was no longer asleep on the rug in front of the gas fireplace, which someone had thoughtfully turned on to chase away the December chill.

Probably Phin. Seemed like something he'd do.

Avoiding the mirror next to the front door—because she was sure that she looked a fright—she made her way into the kitchen, stopping in the doorway to study the group at her table. Burke Broussard sat at the head, where her grandmother had always sat. On his right was a medium-height blonde, her hair pulled into a sensible bun.

The blonde looked crisp and put-together, making Cora hyperaware of the fact that she'd slept in her clothes, which did not smell too fresh. She needed to shower and change.

On Burke's left was Antoine, the computer guy, and to Cora's surprise, he had the computer from her home office set up on the table in front of him, monitor and all. And it was on. He'd somehow bypassed her password protection. Annoyance welled up within her. How the hell had he done that? What had given him the right?

The words were on the tip of her tongue when she noticed the man half sticking out of the cabinet beneath her kitchen sink. Phin. He was wearing an honest-to-God tool belt, his jeans straining over his ass, and . . .

Well. That was a pleasant sight. And not what she should be distracted by right now.

Blinking, she refocused on the three people sitting at her table. Burke's gaze was fixed on his phone. The blonde, however, was regarding her with polite amusement and Cora knew she'd been busted staring at Phin Bishop's ass.

No problem. She could handle this. She was a Winslow, after all.

Channeling her grandmother, she smiled placidly. "Good evening."

Burke looked up and Antoine turned around in his chair, the two men studying her.

"Cora," Burke said. "I hope you slept well. We tried to be quiet."

"I did." First things first. "How is Joy? Have you heard anything?"

Burke smiled. "She's awake and irritable. Demanding they send her home."

Relief swamped her. "Thank God. I'd have checked my phone, but I'm not sure where I left it."

"You left it on the table next to the sofa," Phin called from underneath the sink. "It's on your charging pad now."

A glance at the countertop revealed her phone, exactly where Phin said it was. Blue was asleep on the rug in front of the kitchen door and SodaPop was sitting next to where Phin's very nice ass poked out of the cabinet. She wondered what he was doing under there, but there were other, more pressing matters.

"I see you've been busy." She aimed a pointed glance at her computer.

Antoine lifted his brows. "'John Robert twenty-five exclamation point' is *not* a secure password."

Phin backed out of the cabinet, a smudge of grease on his cheek. It made him look even better than he had before, which was ridiculous. "Sorry," he said, sounding like he meant it. "We considered waking you up to ask for your password, but you looked like you needed the sleep."

"Plus I wanted to see how easy it would be to break into your system," Antoine added. "It took me less than five minutes." The censure in his tone was clear.

Cora winced. His criticism was fair. "You're right."

Antoine's expression softened. "I'm sorry. I didn't mean that to sound harsh. But if I could break into your system, your mysterious intruder could as well."

The blonde rose. "Hi. My name is Molly Sutton. I apologize for what must seem like an ambush. These guys can get carried away when they're protecting your security. Your house is clean now, but Antoine found twelve listening devices planted throughout your house, and someone had broken into your computer and planted Trojan software to monitor your keystrokes."

Cora felt the blood drain from her face. "What? Seriously?"

What had she done on that computer in the past two weeks? In the past two years? What had the intruder found? What had he stolen?

Oh God. The accounts. All the bank accounts. Her grandmother's trust. Everything she was and owned was on that machine.

My research. The jobs she'd taken, the clients she'd supplied, all of it swirled through her mind in unrecognizable bits and pieces.

I'm going to be sick.

Phin was at her side just as she slumped against the doorframe. He gripped her elbow gently, his quiet voice grounding her. "Hey. Breathe. It's okay. You're okay."

She did as he instructed, breathing, allowing him to lead her to the kitchen table. She lowered herself into a chair next to Antoine as Phin crouched beside her.

"Some water, Molly?" he asked, and the blonde opened cabinets until she found the glasses.

The water appeared in front of her and Cora dutifully drank it all.

Feeling more like herself, she nodded at Phin. "I'm okay."

I am not okay.

He clearly didn't believe her any more than she believed herself, but he took the chair beside her, at the opposite end of the table from Burke.

She closed her eyes. "I've meant to change that password for months, but . . ." She felt tears sting her eyes and willed them back. "I couldn't make myself change it."

"He was your brother," Antoine said, his words full of compassion. "I understand. I have brothers myself. Phin told us that John Robert passed last year. His obituary was easy to find." His voice remained so gentle. Too gentle.

Cora wished he'd go back to sounding harsh, because her eyes continued to sting.

She exhaled. "Anyone would know that he was important to me. Anyone could guess my password. His name
and his age when he died."

Leaving her lost and so alone.

She shook herself. *Focus. You can cry later.* Setting her
jaw, she opened her eyes to look at her computer screen. It
was filled with the directory of her hard drive.

So many files. So many that were confidential.

She felt a degree of control return. At least she'd
password-protected the folder where she kept her clients'
records. She pointed to the folder on the screen. "Did you
guess the password to that one?"

Antoine shook his head. "No. Not yet, anyway. That's a
good one."

Burke was watching her carefully. "Why do you have
password protection on individual folders?" He held up a
hand. "The contents are not my business, but we assumed
someone was after the letters in your safe-deposit box. Is
it possible they were looking for something else?"

Again she closed her eyes, pressing her fingertips into
her temples. "Besides money?"

To her right, she heard Phin get up from the table. The
refrigerator door was opened and closed. Moments later,
she heard something sliding across the table in front of her.

She opened her eyes to see a platter of fruit, cheese, and
crackers, still in the plastic tray from the grocery store.
She'd bought it the day before, intending to snack on it
while she worked at her computer, which was now on her
kitchen table.

"You need to eat," Phin said gruffly. "Your friend said
you get . . ." He shrugged, his cheeks reddening slightly.

His hesitation to repeat Tandy's term nearly made her
chuckle. "Hangricidal? Yeah. Thank you, Phin." She nib-
bled on a cracker, willing her stomach to settle.

Whatever they wanted, they'd nearly killed Joy to get it.
"I need to check my bank accounts."

Antoine adjusted the monitor so that she could see it

and slid the keyboard so that she could reach it. "I've cleaned the malware and viruses from your system. You're safe to check. I didn't guess the password to your bank account, either, but they were monitoring your keystrokes. I'd change all the passwords immediately."

Bile burned her throat and she swallowed it back. "Right."

She input her username and password for her personal account, then held her breath while it connected. She let the breath out in a whoosh.

"It's all still there." Quickly she opened the account for her grandmother's trust, and it was all there, too. "All the investments are still there."

"So it wasn't money," Burke said.

Cora frowned. "You don't think this has to do with the discovery of my father's body?"

"I didn't say that," Burke replied. "But we need to pinpoint what they want so we can figure out who they are. That your home was broken into and a lot of listening devices planted after you got a visit from the Terrebonne Parish sheriff's department makes for a pretty strong case in favor of your father. None of those letters were on your computer, were they?"

"No. I hadn't scanned them in."

Molly tilted her head. "You seem to be a digital person. Why not scan them in?"

Cora ate an apple slice while she considered her answer. "I don't really remember my father. I was only five when he left us. Or we thought he'd left us."

"I read all the letters," Burke said. "Him begging forgiveness for leaving your mother for another woman was a common theme throughout, so I get why you thought that. I would have thought the same."

She shot him a grateful smile. "Thank you. So . . . the letters were all I had of him. I hated them and hoarded them all at once. Which sounds crazy, I know."

"No," Phin murmured. "Not crazy at all."

"I would have done that, too," Molly said, her smile reassuring. "But why not scan them? You've scanned every receipt for every material you've bought for this house. Your taxes are impeccably recorded. What made the letters different?"

"The receipts have to be reported for reimbursement from the trust. My grandmother left her money to care for the house," Cora explained. "She figured that John Robert and I would live here with our families. We both had degrees and jobs that could support us and any families we'd have, but the house is . . . well, a lot. So she left the money in a trust to care for the property, pay the taxes, et cetera. It's invested well." She sighed. "She was considering changing the provision of the trust, to leave half the money to John Robert and half to me and will the property to us jointly. But then, about two and a half years ago, John Robert got sick again and the doctor said he needed a bone marrow transplant. A few months later, my grandmother had a heart attack and died without changing her will." She shrugged. "I spent the year between her death and John Robert's trying to find a bone marrow donor, but I never did. After John Robert died, I was in a bad place for six months. I didn't do anything with the trust, or the house, or anything. I went to work and came home. Honestly, I didn't have the mental energy to worry about the letters."

"And the last six months?" Molly asked.

Cora laughed, but it was flat. "I've been cleaning the house. Harry Fulton, my attorney, has been keeping the taxes paid and the investments going. This morning was the first time we'd actually talked in person in two years. It was all emails and texts. But you asked about the letters. I hated my father, but, like I said, the letters were all I had. I kept them in a strongbox under my bed. I didn't want my mom to know I was keeping them. She'd get this hurt look on her face every time one would arrive in the mail. I don't think she ever got over the betrayal."

Her throat thickened and she had to clear it. "She died thinking he'd left her for another woman, when he was dead all along."

A warm hand covered hers. Phin Bishop. Trying to comfort her.

Cora tried for a grateful smile but couldn't muster one.

He just patted her hand. "Scanning in the letters would have made them seem more important than you wanted to admit they were," he said softly.

"Exactly." His hand was warm and solid and she missed it when he pulled it away. "So I just left them in the strong-box. I nearly burned them after John Robert died. I was so angry. I'd tried to find my father so many times, so that he could get tested for a marrow match, but the letters kept coming, talking about inane topics that I didn't care about." Her voice broke. "His son was *dying*, and he didn't *care*." She dashed at tears, hating that she'd hated him when he'd been dead all along.

Antoine hmmed thoughtfully. "Did he send letters to your brother?"

"Yes. But he sent more to me. John Robert burned his. I told him I'd done the same," she admitted. "I figured I got more letters because John Robert was so young when our father disappeared."

"That's a theory," Molly said. "Let's back up. The intruder targeted you either because of your father or for some other reason. Let's talk about what other reasons there can be. I assume that if they'd been going to steal your money, they would have done so already, so for now let's take money off the table." She leaned forward, resting her forearms on the table. "What's in the password-protected folder, Cora?"

It didn't make sense to keep it secret. She hadn't done anything illegal. "Client information from my side job." They all stared at her expectantly. "I double majored in computer science and information science. My MS is in library science. Most librarians have some computer know-how. We help clients who come in to use the library's computers. Sometimes it's a simple Google search, sometimes we help them set up a Facebook account so that they can see their grandchildren's photos. And sometimes they're looking for someone—an old classmate or an old flame. I'm good at finding things. One day a client asked if he could pay me to find information on a daughter he hadn't seen in years. I found the woman with no problem. He paid me fifty dollars. I didn't want to take it, but he insisted. I put it in the collection box at my church. But word got out, and pretty soon other people in the community were asking me to find people, and other information, too."

Antoine's eyes widened. "You hung out your PI's shingle?"

"No, nothing like that. I never charge more than fifty dollars and I always put the cash in the collection box. But it made me feel useful at a time that I . . . wasn't."

Phin frowned. "Wasn't what?"

"Useful," she murmured. "John Robert was dying and I couldn't stop it. I couldn't fix him. I couldn't do anything."

"You felt helpless," Molly said.

Cora nodded. "John Robert knew what I was up to. He gave me this computer. He did network security before he got too sick to work." Her lips curved even though her heart ached. "He would have been so mad at me for making my password his name and age."

Antoine just smiled. "At least you protected the folder."

"People trusted me with their secrets."

Burke leaned back in his chair, folding his hands over his belly like he'd done at his house that afternoon. "Is it possible the intruder was after one of those secrets?"

Cora hated the very thought. "I suppose. I mean, a few were . . . questionable requests. One woman thought her husband was cheating—he was. One man thought his business partner was stealing from him because the man had bought a new boat, but the partner had inherited the money. I suppose that someone might want something like that."

Molly shook her head. "They've gone to extraordinary means. Breaking in here, planting bugs. Breaking into our office and shooting Joy. Chasing you through the Quarter. I think it would have to be bigger than what you're talking about. Would you be willing to let us look at your client records? Just to rule that out?"

"You'll keep it confidential? Even if someone did something not exactly legal?"

Burke huffed. "We're not the cops, Cora. We're not going to turn anyone in. Unless they were involved in the attack on Joy."

Cora blew out a breath. "Fine, you can check."

Phin had crossed his arms over his chest. "Back to your father. You said you tried to contact him. How did you do that?"

Burke's brows lifted. "Very good question. And when did you start looking?"

"I started two and a half years ago, when John Robert's doctor said he needed a marrow transplant."

"Before your grandmother died," Phin said, and she nodded.

"She lived four months after that. She didn't think Jack would help, even if I did find him, but I was desperate. I called around to all the places Jack mentioned in his letters, asking if they'd seen him. Nobody had. I tried to find him through credit cards and variations on his name. Jack Elliot is a common name, but I called every one in every state. I had an old video of him from Christmas the year he disappeared and I was looking for someone who sounded the same. I called morgues and hospitals and I even flew to a few places where he'd mailed letters from years before. I picked places he'd mailed from more than once. He traveled around a lot. I had an old photo of him and did an age progression program on it. I passed it around at police stations and train stations and restaurants and hotels." She sighed. "But I got nothing. Then the letters started back up and I got hopeful, that maybe he knew I was looking for him, but those letters were all postmarked from other countries. He was seeing the world. Or so the letter writer claimed. I was so angry that he never gave me a way to write him back. John Robert was getting worse and worse and then . . . he died. After that, I put Jack's letters in the strongbox without even reading them. I was too heartbroken and numb over my brother to think about my father. Until the detectives showed up at the library to say he'd been dead all this time."

"You may have stirred something up," Burke allowed. "But I'd think they would have made their move back when you were searching. Not now."

"Her father was still missing then," Phin said. "She wasn't a threat."

"You're right," Molly said with a nod. "It wasn't until his body turned up that someone would have wanted to know if Cora had anything incriminating."

Phin's expression was grim. "Like letters written by a dead man?"

"Yeah," Molly said. "Just like that."

6

---~~~===∞===~~~---

"THANK YOU, DRAKE," Alan told his driver as he got out of the town car. "I'll see you in the morning."

"You sure, Reverend Beauchamp?" Drake had been Alan's driver since long before the macular degeneration had curtailed his driving, and Drake knew that he often had late-night appointments with parishioners in crisis. "I can stick around."

"No need. You can take the rest of the night off. I'm planning to stay in."

Lie. He was planning to silence Medford Hughes, but he couldn't have any of his staff tracking his movements. He needed to establish an alibi. He was also aware of the time quickly ticking away.

Medford could be talking to the cops right now. But Alan had to do this right. There could be no trail. He'd involve no one else. He'd do this himself.

Two men can keep a secret if one of them is dead.

That was just a fact.

He climbed the stairs to his bedroom, smelling the dinner Cook had left for him in the oven. But the thought of food made him sick. He was stressed and . . . scared.

Yes, he was scared.

He'd been prepared for this all those years ago. Prepared

for the cops to knock on his door. He'd had an escape plan, fake passports, foreign currency.

But the fake passports had long expired. And now people would recognize him, no matter where in the world he tried to hide. Like Sage, his face was on billboards and in ads on the television.

So he'd have to make sure the cops never knocked on his door.

Medford would be the fall guy. It was the best choice.

Quietly he entered the bedroom he'd shared with his wife Lexy for the past eighteen years. They'd been happy together, for the most part. Lexy didn't know his secrets.

Not like Anna had. His first wife hadn't even known the worst of the things he'd done. Still, she'd left him. Violently and permanently.

He pushed the memory aside. He didn't need the distraction. He needed to be focused.

He went into the massive closet that held his suits. So many suits. So many shoes. But they provided a necessary armor for the man he'd become.

He changed out of the suit he'd worn that day and into a pair of black jeans and a plain black sweater. They'd be burned later.

He packed a gym bag with a change of clothes, and then, checking to ensure that he was still alone, he went down the hall to his home office, where he locked the door behind him. He moved to the massive bookcase that held all his reference books and pulled at a hinged shelving unit. It had been custom made by the home's original owner, who must have also had his secrets.

Alan had discovered the little alcove quite by accident when he'd first bought the house. He'd never told a soul of its existence.

The shelf swung wide, revealing his personal safe. He knew exactly what it contained and it took him only moments to twist the dial. One-zero-fifteen. October 15. The date his life had changed forever.

He reached just inside the safe, taking the gloves that he kept there. He pulled them on, then reached deeper into the safe, bypassing the photographs and stacks of cash to grab the gun and the silencer that were stored at the very back. The gun had been hidden in this safe for twenty-three years. He cleaned it once a year, religiously, but he hadn't fired it since that awful night.

One-zero-fifteen.

He checked the chamber and made sure the magazine was filled with bullets before slipping the gun and the silencer into one of his pockets. He contemplated his other guns, then chose a second pistol, an unregistered Glock. He put it in his other pocket. Just in case he needed to shoot someone that he *didn't* want tied to the remains of Jack Elliot via a ballistics report.

He hoped that "someone" wouldn't include Jack's daughter, but if Cora continued to poke into things that needed to stay buried . . . the consequences of her actions would be on her own head.

He closed the safe and replaced the shelving unit.

His last stop was Sage's old bedroom, where a few of his grandson's clothes still hung in his closet. This included the black hoodie that Alan borrowed whenever he needed to meet with someone discreetly.

"Alan?"

Alan wheeled around, startled. Lexy stood in the doorway, her brows furrowed. "You scared me," he huffed, pressing a hand to his heart. The guns weighed heavy in his jacket, but the hoodie in his hands would hide any evidence of his overstuffed pockets.

"Are you all right?" Lexy asked. "You look pale, dear."

"I'm fine," he assured her. "I need to do an emergency visit tonight. You should have dinner without me."

Disappointment flickered across her features. She was a beautiful woman, still young. Eighteen years his junior. She'd been twenty-five when they'd met, the same age that Sage was now.

Alan knew she'd married him for his money, but she'd been faithful to him. She'd never cheated. Which he knew because he had a PI on retainer who made sure Lexy remained the sweet, beautiful, submissive wife that Alan needed her to be.

"Okay," she said quietly. "I'll make you a plate and leave it in the fridge. Do you want me to call Drake to bring the car around?"

"No. I'd planned to stay in tonight, so I told him to take the night off. This call just came in. I'll call an Uber."

"I understand. Be careful out there."

"I will. I promise."

When she was gone, he put the hoodie on and zipped it up, camouflaging the guns in his pockets. One more stop to make before he was ready to confront Medford.

He called an Uber, putting in the closest hotel as his pickup point, then walked down the street and past the gated entrance to his community, waving to the security guard on duty. He often walked around his neighborhood in the dark. The guard ensured it was completely safe to do so. But sometimes, when Alan needed to clear his head, he left the community behind, walking the streets of Uptown. That he was doing so tonight would raise no suspicions with the guard.

The night was brisk, cooling his overheated skin. Sweat beaded on his forehead, trickled down his spine. His mind was all tangled around what he was about to do. It had been the same that night twenty-three years ago. Like then, he had no choice. No good choice, anyway.

He made it to the hotel, a headache brewing behind his eyes. Light hurt more every day, especially the headlights from cars.

He was relieved when the Uber pulled up. The driver was young and more interested in the music he had softly playing than the older man in his back seat. Which was fine with Alan.

Within minutes, he'd been dropped off at the Xavier

University campus, where he could get lost in the foot traffic. He walked a few blocks to the storage unit he'd rented in the name of a relative he hadn't seen in years. She had no use for the cars he kept there.

Alan, on the other hand, sometimes needed to go places that he didn't want his driver—or anyone else—to know about. He kept a delivery-style van and a common black sedan in the storage unit. His compromised eyesight made it harder to drive now, but he had his special glasses to reduce the glare and he didn't have to go too far.

He had an appointment with Medford Hughes.

The Garden District, New Orleans, Louisiana
TUESDAY, DECEMBER 13, 7:40 P.M.

Holy fucking shit.

Sage ripped his gaze from Cora Winslow's house to stare at the camera feed on his phone. He hadn't expected to hit pay dirt this fast, but his phone had beeped, notifying him that the cameras in Alan's office had been triggered.

And now his grandfather was opening a secret safe. *A secret safe*, for God's sake. In the wall. Behind a hinged shelf.

Sage had never known it existed. That *any* of it had existed.

And from it, his grandfather was pulling a gun.

And a silencer. *What the hell?*

And a second gun.

The old man had *guns*? Really? Sage had never known that. He'd never seen a single gun in the entire house growing up.

"I just wasn't looking in the right place," he muttered.

Now he knew exactly where to look.

As his grandfather closed the safe and spun the dial, Sage wondered exactly what else was in the damn safe, and how he was going to break into it. It appeared to be an old-fashioned model. No electronic components whatsoever.

That was both good and bad.

Good, in that he could try an unlimited number of combinations without setting off any alarms. His grandfather hadn't pressed any buttons, hadn't disabled any security systems. He hadn't done anything more than lock his office door.

No electronics meant there were no wires to trip or sensors to set off.

But the bad news was that there were a *lot* of possible combinations. Hopefully, his grandfather had set his combination with numbers that had personal meaning, because the cameras Sage had planted weren't at the right angle to see the numbers to which the dial had been spun.

He could plant another camera, one that would catch the combination. That was the best plan, because he could be trying random combinations until the end of time and not hit the right one.

Or he could do both. Install another camera if he couldn't figure out the combination. He'd try numbers that represented meaningful events in his grandfather's life. The old man's birthday. The birthdays of his first and second wives. Of his three children.

Sage remembered his own father's birthday, of course, but he didn't know the birthdays of his father's siblings. Uncle Walton was in the army and had been since Sage had been a baby. Sage could count on one hand the number of times the man had come home for any reason.

They weren't close.

His aunt Jennifer was an even worse case. He had no recollection of ever meeting her. She was in a mental hospital somewhere and had been for years. He'd once overheard one of the kitchen staff saying that she'd had a psychotic break after a drug overdose and had to be committed. To his knowledge, no one in the family ever visited her. Not even his grandfather. Sage had no idea in which year she'd been born, much less the actual date.

Everyone had seemed to have forgotten her. There were no photographs of Aunt Jennifer in the house. Not a single one.

And, now that Sage was thinking about it, that was weird.

There were photos of his grandfather's first wife in the study, but nowhere else in the house because it bothered Lexy, the second wife. But photos of his actual grandmother did exist.

None of his aunt, though.

Frowning, he put his phone away. He needed to compile all of the dates that might be important, and that included the birth date of the daughter no one discussed.

He wondered if his mother knew but ditched that thought right away. They'd had words the last time they'd talked, which had been on his eighteenth birthday. Seven years ago now. Their words had been angry, filled with the kinds of things that were hard to take back. On both their sides. She didn't approve of Alan, and Sage knew she wouldn't approve of him were she to know what Sage did for a living. His mother would have to be a last resort.

He'd try to find out about Aunt Jennifer on his own first. And if none of the other combos worked, he'd plant another camera.

Sage checked the clock. He'd need to wait until tomorrow. There were four guards that staffed the little guardhouse at the entrance to the gated community where Alan lived, and three of them normally kept regular shifts. The fourth was a backup or covered vacations.

Luckily for Sage, they were paid by the community and not by Alan, so they had no particular loyalty to his grandfather—at least no more so than to the rest of the neighbors. The guard who'd been on duty when Sage had gone by that afternoon disliked Alan because he was a televangelist and "bamboozled widows out of their money," which was pretty much true. But the guy liked Sage and would turn the other way whenever Sage entered, allowing Sage to come and go as he pleased. It didn't hurt that Sage tipped him frequently and well and had since he'd been a rebellious teenager with too much money, time, and anger.

Unfortunately, the shift change had already occurred. The next guard hated Sage and thought he was a spoiled rich-kid punk.

Which was also pretty much true.

The nasty guard would always make sure that Alan knew Sage had entered the gate at the community's entrance. Sage couldn't just sneak in.

Sage could claim to be visiting Lexy, but that wouldn't be believed, either. He and his stepgrandmother tolerated each other at best.

So he'd bide his time and wait for a better moment to go back to his grandfather's study. He'd attempt to open the safe and would definitely plant more cameras.

In the meantime, he'd continue to watch Cora Winslow's house. She was in there, along with several members of Burke Broussard's staff.

He could no longer track her, which sucked. Broussard's people had found the bug and tracker he'd slipped into her purse on the first night he'd broken in, the day after her father's body had been identified, his picture on the TV news. Sage hadn't known that at the time, of course. Alan had simply instructed him to find out who she was and what she was doing. Sage had done the research and connected some dots.

And then he'd gotten curious, because there were a lot of dots he couldn't connect. Not yet. He'd stayed in her house that first time only long enough to bug her handbag because he knew she had a dog. But the bug allowed him to discover her habits, chart her movements. The next three times he'd broken in had been when she'd been at work. The dog had never even noticed him, sleeping the entire time. It had made Sage too comfortable, which had gotten him into trouble the next time he'd broken in at night. The dog had started barking, waking Cora, who'd come down to investigate.

So he'd gone back to daytime incursions. But only once more. He couldn't go back again. Now she knew someone had been there when she'd been at work.

Now she had PIs working for her, dammit. Sage had planted a dozen of the bugs and Broussard's people had found every single one. One of the guys had replaced the locks on the doors, too. Sage had seen him on one of the upstairs balconies, fooling with the new lock until he'd gotten it right.

For all Sage's searching, though, he'd found nothing to explain why his grandfather cared so much about this one woman.

So Sage was back to old-fashioned surveillance. He'd wait and watch.

The Garden District, New Orleans, Louisiana
TUESDAY, DECEMBER 13, 7:45 P.M.

Cora shook her head—not in denial, Phin thought, but in confusion. "But there's nothing important in any of those letters supposedly written by my father," she said. "They talked about his life and occasionally mentioned something I posted on social media. Said I looked pretty in my prom dress. Stuff like that. Once, not too long after he left, he mentioned my Christmas dress, which was green. I thought that meant he was close by, that maybe he was coming home. But of course he didn't." She frowned. "Why even send me letters at all? Why make me think he was alive for twenty-three years? Why would someone be so cruel?" Then it seemed to click, and her eyes went wide. "Oh my God. It was so we wouldn't go looking for him."

That Cora's father's killer hadn't wanted anyone to go looking for Jack Elliot was something that Phin had thought obvious from the beginning. That the notion had only just occurred to Cora had to be rooted in her grief, because she was a highly intelligent woman. Any other time and she would have figured this out long ago. But she'd just lost a parent, even one she'd thought had abandoned her. Coming on the heels of losing her brother and her grandmother . . .

Poor Cora.

Everyone wore expressions of sympathy, but no one besides Cora was surprised.

Cora sighed. "And you all thought of that already. Because why wouldn't you? It's crystal clear. Now I feel even more foolish than I did before."

"No feeling foolish," Molly said firmly. "You haven't been exactly able to think clearly about all this, and that's why we're here to help. The fact is, someone knew that if you thought your father was still alive, you wouldn't get the police involved. Your mother wouldn't have reported a disappearance back then. Nobody in law enforcement would care about a man who left his wife and children. There would be no suspicion of foul play. No murder investigation. So now we have to ask why. Someone didn't want you or your mother looking for your father. What did he do for a living?"

"He was an accountant." Cora squared her shoulders and folded her hands on the table, but not before Phin saw them tremble. "He had his own company. He did Grandmother's books and those of her circle of friends. I remember all the ladies grumbling when he left, that now they had to find new accountants." Her jaw tightened. "I remember wanting to scream at them because my mother was crying every night and all they could talk about was what a pain it would be to find new help."

Molly and Burke shared a meaningful glance that seemed to irritate Cora.

"Spit it out," she said tersely. "You think my father was doing something illegal? Working for someone shady? That his murder was his fault?"

Molly held up her hands. "Whoa. I didn't say any of that. Although that is certainly a possibility. It's also possible that your father stumbled onto something one of his clients was doing that was illegal, something that he'd planned to report, and that's what got him killed. We don't know, Cora, but we're going to try our hardest to find out. We're on your side here."

Cora's shoulders sagged. "I'm sorry. I know you're right. I'm not usually this . . . unstable. How can I help you get the information you need?"

"Where did he work?" Burke asked. "Did he have an office in town?"

"No," Cora said. "He worked here. The office upstairs was originally his. Mom kept it intact for a few years, but then she converted it to her craft room." Her smile turned wistful. "So much yarn. John Robert took the room over after she died. We donated all her yarn."

Burke perked up. "When you say she left it intact, does that mean she kept his client files?"

Cora frowned. "I remember watching her making copies of what was on his computer shortly after he left. She inserted disk after disk into his computer, crying all the while. She'd made two stacks of disks and I asked what they were for. She said that one of the stacks was for my father's clients. They needed their records because soon it would be time to do their taxes and my father wouldn't be there to do them." She dropped her gaze to her folded hands. "I told Mama to stop. That my daddy would be back. That he was coming back."

"What did she say?" Phin asked softly.

She glanced up at him, her eyes full of remembered pain. "She stopped what she was doing and told me that she was sure my father would never stop loving me, but that he was gone. That he had a new family. That I'd have to get used to us being alone, but that she'd never leave me." She swallowed. "She never did. Not until she died."

"How did she die?" Molly asked. "And when?"

Cora looked startled for a moment before understanding crossed her features. "It wasn't foul play. She had a heart attack ten years ago. Mama was a physical therapist. She went back for her degree after my father left. That's how she supported us. Grandmother helped, but Mama made sure we never went without." She cleared her throat. "That's also how she met Joy. She did Joy's PT after Joy was injured on the job. She'd sometimes take us to work with her, me and John Robert. Usually when my grandmother had a committee meeting. Grandmother was on the board of St. Charles School for Girls."

Even Phin had heard of the school. Politicians, celebrities, and the city's wealthy sent their daughters there.

Burke whistled. "That's prestigious."

Cora nodded. "It is. Grandmother went there, as did my mother. I went there and Tandy did, too. Later, Joy's daughters attended with us."

"You met Joy's daughters through her PT sessions?" Antoine asked.

"I did. John Robert and I would do our homework in the outer office while Mama worked with clients in private. Joy was also a single mother and asked if she could bring her kids to do their homework with us. Mom said yes, of course." A smile flitted over Cora's face. "Friendships were born. Nala was the same age as Tandy and me. Joy's son Wayne was John Robert's age. Once Joy was through her PT, she got her CPA license and Mama would funnel clients her way. Folks who'd hired my father and who hadn't yet found a new accountant they liked. Joy did CPA work until she started working with you guys."

"Small world," Molly murmured.

"Indeed," Cora agreed. "Back to your question, I don't know if Mama kept my father's records, but we still have that computer somewhere. It's super old, of course. I don't think there are any of my father's client files still on it, but you're welcome to look. It should still be in the attic."

Antoine lit up at the thought. "I'll take a look."

Burke shook his head. "Hold on, Antoine. Cora, was your mother as thorough and organized as you are?"

"Not really. Sometimes, when it was necessary. Like with the client files she copied for Grandmother and her friends. But not usually. She'd pack everything in boxes, all willy-nilly, and never labeled them. She'd always mean to but would get distracted. That drove me crazy when I got older, and I'd go behind her and write on the boxes. But not after my father left. I was too young then. One day I came home from school and everything in my father's office was gone. Mama said she'd put it all in the attic, and for me to leave it be. Grandmother told her that she should have thrown it all away, but Mama said she wasn't ready yet. Why?"

"Because she told you one of the stacks was for the clients," Burke answered. "Maybe she kept the other stack for herself. Just in case. We'd like to search for anything she might have kept."

Cora gestured in the general direction of the stairs. "Let's go."

"Hold on just a minute," Phin said. Cora hadn't eaten more than half a cracker. "Antoine, you know the way to the attic, right?"

Antoine nodded. "Scanned it for bugs."

"Then get started searching. Cora hasn't eaten since that sandwich at Burke's house."

Molly's lips twitched. "You taking over for Joy, Phin? Feeding everyone?" But the question was asked so sweetly that Phin didn't take offense.

"Someone's got to."

Molly held up her fingers, counting. "We have shrimp and grits, shrimp étouffée, gumbo, and some fried fish. What would you like?"

Cora grimaced. "Um, I'm allergic to shellfish. Like . . . super allergic. I'm not great with fish, either. I have an EpiPen. Sorry."

Molly exhaled. "Well, shoot. I didn't know that. Everything I brought tonight might kill you. How have you lived in New Orleans all these years and not keeled over dead?"

"I'm very, very careful and I don't eat out often. Last time I accidentally ate some shrimp, I ended up in the ER. Not fun."

Phin pointed to the cheese and fruit platter. "Eat some of that while I fry you an egg."

Anything more than that was beyond his skill set.

Molly rose. "Cora, I'm to be your bodyguard, if you're okay with that. For now, Phin's got you. I'm going up to help Antoine search."

Cora sighed. "Thank you. I want to say I don't need the help, but I do."

Something they had in common, Phin thought as he glanced down at his dog. He didn't want to need the help, but he did.

The difference was that when this was over, Cora could continue independently, but Phin would still be dependent on SodaPop.

Swallowing his own sigh, he got up to find a frying pan. If keeping Cora fed was to be his contribution, he'd do one hell of a job.

The Garden District, New Orleans, Louisiana
TUESDAY, DECEMBER 13, 8:15 P.M.

Alone in the kitchen with Phin and the two dogs, Cora watched the man standing at her stove, frying her an egg. Affection squeezed at her heart. He was sweet.

And he looked good standing at her stove.

You're perving on his ass.

Yes, she was. After a years-long dry spell, she felt relief that she was interested at all. She'd thought she'd lost that spark.

Turned out she hadn't had the right man standing at her stove, frying her an egg.

"What were you doing under my sink?" she asked after eating more cheese and fruit. She was hungry and Tandy was right. If she let herself get too hungry, Cora became downright unpleasant.

He glanced over his shoulder. "Leaky pipe."

She sighed. "I've been meaning to fix that."

"You do your own repair work?"

"Small things, yes. Something's always breaking in this old house. If I hired a handyman every time, I'd be broke. YouTube is my best friend."

He laughed. "I thought Tandy was your best friend."

She made a hem-hawing sound. "There are times that it's a toss-up. Seriously, she is my best friend and has been since the third grade. She is appalled at the thought of climbing under a sink, though. She lives in a brand-new apartment that comes with a maintenance crew, which makes her very happy."

Phin moved around her kitchen easily, his dog watching him. "I thought that the folks who lived in this neighborhood were swimming in cash. I've worked on a few of their houses. Usually friends of Burke's."

That confirmed her assumption that Burke Broussard had some funds. His house in the Quarter was huge, with an unusually large lot.

"Well, some folks here are swimming in cash. Especially the celebrities." Actors and musicians tended to flock to the Garden District. Cora had spied a few very familiar faces out and about as she'd walked to work. "But I'm not. Like I said, my grandmother left all her money in a trust to care for the house."

"What happens if you sell it?"

The very thought made her queasy. "I'd get the money from the house and what's in the trust. I've considered it, of course, but I can't make myself do it."

He slid a plate in front of her, along with a cup of coffee. The fried egg and toast smelled good and her stomach growled. The scent of the coffee was too good to be true.

"Sorry it's not fancier," he said. "I can cook—kind of—but I don't do it often." He took the seat beside her and motioned for her to eat. "I installed new locks on all your doors. I'll come back tomorrow and do the windows. For tonight, the alarm system and Molly will keep you safe."

She swallowed the bite she'd been chewing. "I wish I knew what the infamous 'they' were looking for. Part of me wishes they'd just found it so they'd leave me alone. Not proud of that, but if I'm honest . . ."

"I get it. You're not going to feel safe in your home now, and that sucks." He glanced upward. "I don't know if whoever broke in got up to the attic. I searched enough to make sure no one was hiding there, but I imagine a thorough search would take a long time. There's a lot of stuff up there." He met her gaze, his becoming amused. "I always thought attics packed with antiques were only in the movies until I moved to New Orleans."

"All six generations of us Winslows have apparently been hoarders. I need to get up there and clean it out. I'm betting there are some antiques I could sell that would pay for some of the upkeep."

"Undoubtedly." He glanced up again, wistfully this time.

It didn't take a genius to know that he wished he were up there searching through the antiques, too. She finished off the meal quickly, wiped her mouth, then stood. "Let's go up and see what they're doing."

Phin grimaced sheepishly. "Was I that obvious?"

"You really were." She walked alongside him, aware that without her shoes, he was a good bit taller than she was. She liked that a little too much. "Are you into old furniture?"

"I am. My sister and I used to collect old, banged-up tables and chairs and fix them."

She stopped, looking up to study his face. "Used to? Is your sister . . ."

"Oh, she's alive and well." Discomfort flitted across his face. "I haven't seen her in a long time."

"Why not?"

He hesitated. "Delores told you that I run when I have my episodes. After that bar fight, the one where I got shot . . . well, I ran."

There was pain in his eyes and once again she wanted to fix it. "Why?"

He shrugged. "It was best for all of us. Or so I thought at the time. Let's go up to the attic."

Message received. Phin Bishop didn't want to talk about his family.

Cora could respect that. She changed the subject to another potentially difficult topic. "Why aren't you a body-guard, too?"

He flinched. Then pointed to SodaPop, who was following him closer than a shadow. "I'm not predictable. I need help, even though I don't want to need it."

It appeared that the admission cost him.

She backed off that topic, too, choosing one that she thought he'd be open to. "Do you have extra time in your schedule? I have a number of repairs that I can't do on my own and I've put off way too long. I'd like to hire you, if you're interested."

A smile tilted his mouth as they reached the staircase. He rubbed one of his big hands over the banister with reverence. "Work on this old beauty? Hell, yeah. Tell me where and when you want me to start."

She started up the stairs, looking over her shoulder. He was still at the base of the stairs, admiring the hand-carved banister. She couldn't blame him. It was one of the nicer details of the house. "How about tomorrow?"

He thought about it, then nodded as he began to follow her up. "I'll talk to Burke. See what he has for me to do at the office. I do night security there, but I have a few waking hours in the daytime."

Excellent. This way he'd be here while she was at work,

in case the assholes came back. If he couldn't be her body-guard, at least he could guard the house.

He stopped abruptly. "Maybe not tomorrow. My friends are still here in town."

"Oh, right. Stone and Delores." She was disappointed that he wouldn't be here while she was gone, but the new alarm would have to be enough. "Well, figure out your schedule and let me know."

"I will."

They climbed the rest of the way up in silence, the voices of the others growing louder as they reached the attic door. Cora knocked, then stuck her head inside. "It's just us. Don't shoot or anything."

Someone snorted.

"You're safe," Antoine said. "Come on in. There's room for a marching band up here."

Cora entered the attic. It *was* a large room, with windows and window seats and everything. No ladder to a crawl space for this house.

"I loved this room as a kid," she said. "I'd come up here and read for hours."

Molly was standing in front of a wall of Tetris-packed boxes, fists on her hips. "Then you becoming a librarian makes sense. I don't even know where to start. There's so much stuff."

Cora gently nudged her out of the way, aware of Phin shadowing her, much like SodaPop shadowed him. "This row of boxes in the front are ones I packed. They're John Robert's things," she said, feeling the sting of sorrow. But a hand stroked her hair lightly. Phin, giving her comfort. It helped. "These boxes are all labeled. The ones in the next row are boxes John Robert packed. He always said he'd label the boxes 'later,' but he ran out of time. I wrote 'JR' on those boxes, so you can ignore those, too. My grandmother's things are in the next row, and I packed those, so they're labeled, too. Same with the row behind that. Those were my mother's things." And seeing the boxes, all lined up so tidily, made her grieve all over again. She cleared her throat. "Anything behind these boxes that isn't labeled was packed by my mother. Those will be my father's things, but they're probably mixed with other things." She sighed. "This is going to take a while."

Standing on her tiptoes, she began tugging at a box on the top row, unsurprised when Phin took the box from her hands and gently put it aside.

"I'll move them, you just tell me which pile they go in," he said.

She smiled up at him. "Thank you, Phin. That's a John Robert box. It can go in that corner over there for now."

Phin did as she directed, and as a group, they began sorting six generations of Winslow stuff.

7

ALAN BLINKED HARD as he parked his van on the curb two houses up from Medford Hughes's home. His head ached from the bright headlights. He took off his special macular glasses and massaged his temples, hating the glasses and hating the pain.

He'd survive a headache, though.

He wouldn't survive if Medford went to the police.

Medford hadn't done so yet, at least Alan didn't think so. Medford was a coward, as evidenced by the fact that, at this very moment, the man was putting a suitcase into the trunk of his car.

Medford was going to run.

Alan couldn't let him do that.

Dread sat heavy in his belly as he slid Sage's ski mask over his face and pulled up the hood on the jacket he'd borrowed from Sage's closet. He then pulled on a new pair of disposable gloves and carefully tugged the gloves Medford had discarded over top of them. It would be hard to bend his fingers, but he'd have to manage.

Grabbing Sage's special bag with the two laptops, he forced himself out of the van. Medford had gone back inside his house, leaving his trunk open and his car unlocked. He probably thought he was safe, parked in his own garage.

He's not.

Alan got into Medford's back seat and hunkered down, drawing his gun from his pocket. It was the same gun with the same silencer that he'd used that night twenty-three years ago. He'd been tempted to throw it away hundreds of times since that night, but he never had.

He'd kept the gun as penance. And as a reminder of what he was capable of doing.

Tonight, it would serve another purpose. Tonight, it was the best way he could think of to redirect the cops' search for Jack Elliot's killer. If Medford told the police about the Broussard laptops, the police would quickly connect Alan to the shooting of Broussard's secretary and to Cora Winslow and her dead father.

Tonight, Alan would give them an alternate, indisputable connection.

Medford would make a perfect fall guy.

Alan had remained hidden for about five minutes when Medford finally left his house, tears running down his face. That made some sense, as Medford appeared to be leaving his wife behind.

And she'll call me crying, Alan thought with disgust. She always called, crying about whatever trouble her drugs and gambling had caused, and Alan would have to counsel her. Cheryl Hughes was an unpleasant mess of a woman. Nothing like Alan's own wife had been.

May she rest in peace.

The thought of his Anna still had the power to shred his heart. The way he'd found her body in her favorite chair, her blood and brains staining the paisley fabric, still had the power to crush him in his dreams.

It had very nearly crushed his real life, too. The scandal of suicide would have been terrible. He'd thought quickly back then, staging the car accident and fire that would be the story the media shared.

Over and over again.

A bribe to a corrupt ME had ensured that his wife's

suicide would remain Alan's little secret. The ME had died in the hospital a few weeks later as Alan had held his hand.

Alan hadn't used this same gun that time.

He hadn't actually killed the man, either. Not technically. He had held a gun on the ME until the man had taken a handful of his own pills, sending him into a coma.

Alan had been called to the man's bedside by his wife since they'd been part of his congregation. He'd held the man's hand and prayed for him to survive. Out loud, anyway.

In his mind, he'd prayed for the man to stop breathing. And he had. Alan had been there for the man's wife and children in the months that followed. They'd been better off without a man willing to take bribes, anyway.

He'd done all of that while missing his Anna so very much, hating her at the same time for leaving him. But now he felt only sadness. And, in his dreams, guilt.

Cheryl would have to live that nightmare, too, after she discovered Medford dead in his car. Alan might have felt bad about that had Cheryl's excesses not caused Medford so much pain.

Sniffling noisily, Medford closed the trunk and got behind the wheel. He picked up a phone—not his normal cell, Alan noticed—and typed something into a browser screen.

Alan sat up and pressed the gun to Medford's temple. "Drop the phone, Medford."

The phone clattered to the center console as Medford's mouth opened in shock. "Reverend Beauchamp. What are you doing?"

"What I have to," Alan said sadly. "Where is Cheryl?"

"Inside," Medford whispered. "She's dead."

That was a shock. "*How?*" And then he understood Medford's tears. "You killed her."

"I couldn't leave her alone. Nobody would be here to make sure she didn't shoot up. She'd hurt herself."

"So you killed her?"

"She didn't feel any pain," Medford whispered. "I didn't have a choice."

Neither do I. "I'm sorry for this, Medford." And he really was.

Not wishing to draw it out any further for either of them, Alan pulled the trigger, the silencer muting the blast to a soft pop. He winced at the spray of blood that hit the driver's-side window.

After Anna, he'd wanted to forget how messy a head-shot could be.

But he had not forgotten and had come prepared. Carefully removing the outer glove he wore on his right hand, he set it aside and pulled a pack of wet wipes from his jacket pocket, reached around the front seat, and pulled Medford's hand closer. He cleaned the spattered blood from the man's right hand and gave it a minute to dry, looking over his shoulder all the while.

It was a quiet neighborhood. Most of the folks nearby were in their homes watching TV. Nobody was paying attention to Medford Hughes's garage.

Thank the good Lord for that.

When Medford's hand was dry, he tugged the glove onto the dead man's hand and carefully placed it on the center console. He put the gun in Medford's hand, leaving his palm slightly open. Just as Anna's hand had been after she'd taken her own life.

There would be gunshot residue on the glove and, if CSI got creative, they'd find Medford's skin cells on the inside of the glove because he'd worn them in Alan's office earlier that day. It would look like a suicide.

He had the presence of mind to grab Medford's phone off the front passenger seat and glared at the screen. Medford had googled the number for the NOPD's tip line.

Alan checked the call log and was relieved to see that Medford hadn't made a single call. He slipped the phone into his pocket and quickly pulled the first laptop from Sage's bag.

The laptop screen came to life in the darkness of the car, the home screen containing only one folder. The only other detail on the screen was the logo for Broussard Investigations.

He clicked on the Wi-Fi icon and typed in Medford's home Wi-Fi password. He'd been given the code the first time he'd visited after Cheryl had called him crying. Medford had discovered that Cheryl had embezzled a great deal of money from her boss, all of which had been either injected into her arm or lost at the gaming tables.

Medford had planned to leave her that night, so long ago. Alan had convinced him to stay. Had convinced him that a good husband—with a knowledge of computers—could make his wife's misdeeds disappear.

Alan had controlled Medford then. He knew about Cheryl's crimes and what Medford had done to cover them up. Such a good husband Medford had been.

Alan exhaled in relief when the Wi-Fi icon appeared in the task bar. *All I need to do is find Cora Winslow's information.* He clicked on the single folder on the screen and held his breath.

Then frowned. It was gibberish. He scrolled down, his pulse ratcheting up as he recognized the phrases thrown in among the random characters.

Oh. Oh no. This was worse than gibberish. The words were the ones used as place markers in document templates. *Lorem ipsum dolor . . .*

This was a trap. Medford had been right.

Someone was probably tracking him right now.

Which was what he'd expected, but he'd hoped to get a payoff for the risk. Instead, he had nothing and, if Broussard's people were as talented as their press made them out to be, they'd already be on their way.

Alan shook the second laptop out of the bag and left both machines on the back seat, taking the bag with him. He got out of Medford's car, opened the driver's door, hit the trunk release, then shut the door, hoping he hadn't disturbed any blood spatter.

Grabbing the suitcase from Medford's trunk, he hefted

it up and out of the car, staggering a little at the unexpected weight of it. He had to grip the lid of the trunk to remain upright.

What had Medford packed? A load of bricks? Luckily the suitcase had rollers.

He closed the trunk quietly and, dragging the suitcase behind him, headed for his van, grunting as he lifted the heavy bag into the back. He then took off his gloves and shoved them into the pocket of the jeans he intended to burn.

As he drove away, Alan whispered the same words he'd uttered twenty-three years ago. "Forgive me, Lord. I didn't have a choice."

Squinting against approaching headlights, he drove away.

The Garden District, New Orleans, Louisiana
TUESDAY, DECEMBER 13, 9:05 P.M.

They'd been sorting boxes for half an hour before Cora began seeing the unlabeled boxes her mother had packed. There were boxes of photos and art from her childhood and knickknacks her mother had once adored—gifts from her father throughout their marriage.

That her mother hadn't simply thrown them away said quite a lot. "It still kills me that she died thinking he'd left her for someone else," she said to Phin, who'd stuck as close to her as SodaPop did to him.

"Maybe they're back together now," Phin said softly.

Cora swallowed. "I like that thought." She refocused on the boxes, opening one to find office supplies. "We could be getting to the right ones. This could be what you're wanting to search."

Phin set the box on the window seat. "You sit and search this one. Rest your feet. We'll check the others."

She did as he said, and it was a relief to take some pressure off her feet. She'd been lucky she hadn't broken an ankle during her run that morning. So many sidewalks in the Quarter needed repair.

She wondered what the man would have done had he caught up to her.

She wondered if he would have killed her.

And that kind of thinking was unproductive. *Focus, Cora.* She opened the box and stared at the contents, her heart hurting once more. On top of a stack of folders were the photos her father had kept on his desk. They were framed in a set of 3D twenty-sided photo cubes . . . or whatever a twenty-sided thing was called. Pictures of her, John Robert, and her mother filled each of the twenty faces. Another held photos of her parents when they'd been much younger, back when they'd met in college.

She remembered sitting on her father's lap, playing with the photo displays when he was on the phone with clients. She'd roll them like dice, needing both hands to hold each one back then. She'd march her Barbie dolls across his desk, making them take whatever number of steps she'd rolled. The dice had no numbers, just photos, but she'd made numbers up.

All while her father cradled her in his arms, dropping kisses on her hair from time to time. And when he'd ended his call, he'd tell her what a good girl she'd been. How proud he was of her. What a good helper she was.

Her eyes burned once more and she let the tears fall.

She knew the others could see that she was crying, but they left her to her grief and she appreciated it. For so long she'd hated her father for leaving. Now she knew the truth and it would take some time to fully process.

Except she didn't have that kind of time. Not right now. She had to find out who was after . . . whatever they were after. She would cry later.

She wiped her eyes, put the photo cubes aside, then pulled out the folders that were stacked beneath them. She glanced up, again unsurprised to see Phin watching her.

"I'm okay," she mouthed, then tried to smile.

He gave her a nod, then went back to moving boxes so that the others could search them.

She focused on the folder in her hand, startled at the three words written in her mother's looping scrawl—*For Divorce Attorney*. Her heart hurting anew, she opened the folder to find it filled with old credit card receipts. Like really old. They'd been created on the old card imprinters, the carbon copies faded. She pulled a receipt aside. It was signed J. Elliot. She turned on her phone's flashlight, squinting to see the vendor and the date.

She pictured her mother looking through these receipts, believing her husband had left her for another woman. *Oh, Mama.*

Steadying her voice, she called out, "Um, everyone? These are old receipts. This one's from a few weeks before my father was killed. A gas station in Baton Rouge. I think my mother thought they were evidence of my father's cheating. They might be useful."

Molly was at her side in seconds, gently taking the receipt from her hand and using her own phone's light to study it. "Did your father do business there?"

"I don't know. Like I said, he worked from home, but he sometimes went to see clients. I have no idea if they were all local. The first letters he wrote were postmarked from Baton Rouge. Maybe . . ." She winced. "Maybe he really *was* seeing someone else and got shot by a jealous husband."

"Possibly," Molly allowed. "We'll go through all of these and see if there's a pattern to his travel. Don't touch any of the other receipts. I'll go through them wearing gloves."

"I should have thought of gloves," Cora said with a sigh. If they'd simply been old papers, wearing gloves might have caused more damage than the oils from her fingers, but these were no longer simply old papers. Now they might be evidence.

"You've also had a pretty crappy day," Molly said kindly. "Cut yourself some slack."

Phin brought her another box and the search continued until Antoine crowed, "Bingo! Found them!"

In his gloved hands, he held a half dozen three-and-a-half-inch floppy disks, fanned out like cards from a deck. "They're all labeled 'Client Files.' There have to be fifty disks in this box."

Cora rose and carefully made her way through the maze of boxes littering the floor. She stared at the old disks. "Do you have a computer that reads disks? Because I haven't seen the old computer my dad used anywhere. I hope someone didn't pitch it."

Antoine grinned. "Of course I have one, expressly for this purpose. Don't you worry."

"What's wrong, Burke?" Molly asked, because Burke was staring at his phone in horror.

"I just googled 'do people still use floppy disks.'"

"And you didn't like the answer," Cora said knowingly. "Some airplanes still use them for their navigation systems."

"I'm never flying again," Burke muttered.

"Or you'll just get super drunk at the bar before you do," Molly said soothingly.

Cora returned her attention to Antoine. "You'll check the disks quickly?"

"As soon as I get home. I have my old computers there." He dropped the disks into a plastic bag and sealed it. "You guys can keep searching, if you want, but I want to see what Cora's dad was doing before he died."

"Call me as soon as you find something," Burke instructed.

"Yes, boss." Giving a salute, Antoine left the attic.

Burke tilted his head, studying Cora. "How did you know about disks and airplanes?"

"I'm a librarian. I know a little bit about a lot of stuff. This terrifying trivia came from some middle school kids doing a project on my library's computer. Their mother is a housekeeper in one of the houses near the library and they don't have internet at home, so they do their homework on our computers. One of them read this tidbit and shouted, 'Hell to the no!' I reprimanded him, of course, both for yelling and swearing in the library, but he said, 'Miss Cora, you gotta see this. I'm never flyin' again.' And then I read what was on his screen and whispered, 'Holy shit.' They were delighted that I swore, too," she added wryly.

Molly laughed. "I bet you notched up a hair in the cool category. Miss Cora has a potty mouth. Here's another box for you to check."

Phin was slicing at the tape when they heard a shout from downstairs, followed by footsteps thundering up the stairs.

Burke and Molly reacted immediately, each pulling guns from holsters.

Phin was standing in front of Cora before she could blink.

"Just me!" Antoine called out. "Don't shoot."

Burke and Molly lowered their weapons but didn't put them away. Cora felt a little safer, seeing how quickly they all responded. Especially Phin. He'd been willing to use his own body to shield her.

That shouldn't have been as hot as it was.

Antoine came back into the attic, eyes alight. "I just got a notification that someone's playing with our laptops. I've got a location and I need backup."

Burke holstered his gun, as did Molly. "I'll go," Burke said. "Molly, you're with Cora. Phin, you're with me."

His back was still to her, but his shock was unmistakable. "Me?" he asked.

"You," Burke said. "Bring SodaPop. We need to roll before they realize we're tracking them and toss our laptops. Let's go."

Phin looked over his shoulder at Cora as he was leaving the attic. "You'll be okay." It was mostly a statement, but there was a hint of a question there.

She gave him a firm nod. "I will be. Go. I wanna know who's doing this."

The alarm beeped as the front door slammed and Cora reset it using her phone. "Are you upset you're stuck with me?"

Molly shook her head. "No way. I've had my share of excitement on past jobs and will have more in the future. But I don't want to be up here in the attic all by ourselves. Phin hasn't secured all your windows yet and with the lights on up here, we've lit a big neon sign saying where we are. Let's take those receipts downstairs. You can help me catalog them. We'll be faster working together."

Mid-City, New Orleans, Louisiana
TUESDAY, DECEMBER 13, 9:50 P.M.

"How much farther?" Burke asked tensely.

They'd been driving for about twenty minutes, as fast as Antoine dared. Burke was in the front passenger seat, Phin in the back with SodaPop, her muzzle resting on his thigh.

Phin checked his phone's map app. "If the laptops haven't been moved, we're about three minutes out."

Antoine glanced down at his own phone before returning his eyes to the road. "They haven't moved. Still the same GPS coordinates."

That was good at least. "When do you want to call 911?" Phin asked, still not sure why he'd been included. Maybe Burke was still trying to make up for suspecting him that morning.

If so, the boss's concern was misplaced. Phin knew where he belonged. He was nighttime security and the firm's handyman. He'd be okay with that, even if everything in him yearned for more, because he was still a liability.

A liability with a service dog in tow.

Burke exhaled heavily. "I don't know. I think I want to wait until we get there before we bring in NOPD. It might not add up to anything. The computers could have been ditched in an open lot."

Phin didn't agree. As much as he didn't like the NOPD, his gut was telling him to call this in. "The address at these coordinates is a house, Burke."

"Could be a garbage can outside a house," Burke countered.

Phin didn't know why Burke was so loath to call the cops, but he trusted the man and knew his reasoning would be sound. So he pointed to the next stop sign. "Left up there, Antoine, then the house is third on the right."

Antoine slowed as they approached the house, a small but tidy two-story.

"Owners?" Burke asked.

"Medford and Cheryl Hughes," Phin answered. He'd stayed busy during the drive, looking up the owners and their professions, and had run a quick background check on his phone. All things that Burke and Joy had taught him to do over the two years that he'd worked for Broussard Investigations.

They'd been training him to take a greater role in the business and Phin had been ready to step up. Until six weeks ago when he'd spiraled again.

He shuddered at the memory, his fingers sinking deeper into SodaPop's coat. She turned her head, licking his hand and grounding him enough to focus.

Phin suspected Burke had thrown him the easy tasks tonight to keep his hands and mind busy. A busy mind was less likely to spiral.

"Medford is fifty-eight years old, his wife Cheryl is fifty-five," Phin went on. "Medford was an IT consultant with a firm in California for twenty years but hung out his own shingle ten years ago. His wife used to work for an insurance business but quit a few years after they moved to New Orleans."

"So an IT guy stole our laptops?" Burke asked, staring up at the car in the garage.

"Or he was hired to break into them," Antoine offered. "Although that seems unlikely. A good IT guy would be wary of tripping booby traps like the tracking software on the machines."

"Maybe he's not a good IT guy," Burke said.

"Maybe," Phin allowed. "But he makes a good enough living to afford this neighborhood." It wasn't as posh as the Garden District, but it was definitely nicer than Phin's area. "I found photos of this guy on Facebook. His body type is different than the guy who shot Joy. Medford Hughes isn't as tall and he's about fifty pounds lighter."

Burke opened his car door. "Then let's go see what's what. Phin, you comfortable coming with us or do you want to stay here?"

"I'll come with you." He'd pull his weight in the search for whoever shot Joy.

Together, the three of them walked up to the open garage, SodaPop at Phin's side. The car was a white sedan and needed a washing. There was a mud stain on the trunk lid.

Antoine got there first and made a harsh sound in his throat. "Goddammit."

Burke took a few more steps forward, then sighed. "Hell. You were right, Phin. We should have called 911. Just . . . go back to the car. You don't need to see this."

Phin knew that Burke was trying to shield him from something horrible, but Phin was feeling okay. "I need to see," he said softly, and Burke moved aside with no argument.

One close glance at the car revealed a bloody mess. The driver's window and part of the windshield were covered with blood.

And other things. Brains. Bone.

Beside him, SodaPop whined softly and Phin realized he'd tensed up. Employing the breathing exercises he'd learned in therapy, he felt the anxiety fade enough that his chest no longer felt constricted.

He didn't have to go any closer to know what he'd find. "Shot in the head?"

Burke nodded grimly. "Suicide." He went around to the passenger side of the car and looked in the window. "He's still holding the gun." He pulled a small flashlight from his pocket and shined it into the car's interior. "And our laptops are in the back seat." He frowned. "That's weird. The guy's wearing a latex glove on his right hand. Why would he wear a glove to shoot himself in the head?"

"Good question," Antoine said. He turned and gripped Phin's shoulder. "You okay?"

Phin nodded. He knew his limits and he was pushing them. "Yeah. I'll make the call. Should I contact André, too?"

Burke sighed. "Couldn't hurt. Otherwise, we'll get hauled in for questioning again and I'm tired. I want to go home and get a meal and some sleep, in that order."

Captain André Holmes was Antoine's older brother and a close friend of Burke's. The cop had been an invaluable resource to the firm.

In return, Burke's group helped the cop solve cases that NOPD couldn't. Theirs was a symbiotic relationship. More importantly, Phin trusted the man.

Stepping behind the car, he placed the call to André first and brought him up to speed. André was on desk duty for a few more weeks, still recovering from a recent injury.

"You guys," André said with a sigh. "Never a dull moment. Antoine's with you?"

"Yes. He was the one who traced the stolen laptops."

"I figured. I'll call it in. You guys sit tight. Stay away from the victim."

"*I'm* not touching him," Phin declared.

André sighed again. "But you can't make promises for Burke."

It was the truth. "Sorry, André. Listen, I checked into the dead guy on our way over and he has a wife. There's another car in the garage, so she might be inside the house. Just so you know."

"Thanks, Phin. I'll be there in ten minutes. Uniforms should be there in less than five. I'll let Detective Clancy know, too."

Phin ended the call. "André's calling it in. He'll be here in ten, uniforms in five. You okay, Burke?"

Burke was still staring inside the car, his brow furrowed. "*Why* is he wearing a glove? And why just one? His other hand is bare."

Phin felt like he should look because the others were looking, and he didn't want to seem squeamish or . . . broken. But SodaPop whined again, and Phin listened to her, taking another step back.

Don't push it. Better to be a little squeamish and broken than totally nonfunctional.

"Why did he shoot himself?" Antoine asked, wearing an equally puzzled expression. "I made sure that everything was wiped from the laptops. Was he so afraid of whoever hired him that he killed himself rather than take whatever punishment his boss would dish out?"

Phin kept his gaze on the back of the car, knowing that if he stared at the blood too long, he'd slip. Blood and bone and gore were all serious triggers for him. But as he stared at the car, his mind cleared and his gaze zeroed in on what he'd thought was a mud stain.

It didn't look right. It was thinner than mud would be. But it was just thin enough to be a smear of blood.

He pulled the flashlight from the carabiner clip on his belt and shone the light at the car. *Yep.* That was blood. It wasn't enough blood to trigger him, and it wasn't on his hands. Those were the things he had to watch for.

"Burke? Come and look at this."

Burke immediately jogged around the victim's sedan. "Shit. Either he cut himself before he blew his brains out or . . ."

Antoine joined them. "Or that's no suicide."

"Still doesn't explain the one glove," Burke grumbled.

"Let's wait by the curb. We've contaminated the scene enough."

Phin backed away, turning to walk down the driveway, flashlight still in hand. He kept the beam at his feet, not wanting to step on evidence by mistake.

He saw no more blood, but his light did pick up on something else. Something dark, down on the curb behind Burke's SUV. It looked like a backpack.

Abandoned backpacks had the potential of being very dangerous. Something else Phin had learned the hard way. He opened the SUV's door and patted the seat. "SodaPop, in." Because there was no way he was endangering the life of his dog. She jumped in obediently. "Good girl. Hey, Burke, Antoine, look at this."

Both men followed him to the dark object, which was indeed a bag of some kind. Phin shone his light on the bag, stopping when he got to a logo that he recognized.

"Holy shit," Antoine breathed. "That's a Faraday bag. I have several from this same company. What do you want to bet that our laptops were in that bag?"

"Sucker bet," Burke said. "But why is the bag here? Did it get dropped by Medford Hughes? Or by whoever killed him?"

Antoine crouched beside it, using his phone to snap a photo. "And is there still something in it? I want to check it so bad."

Burke's chuckle was a welcome sound. "Sorry, Antoine. Hopefully André will pass us some information."

"For now, step away from it," Phin said quietly. "It could be harmful."

Antoine looked like he'd object, then he nodded. "You're right. Pays to be careful."

"Pays to stay alive," Phin muttered.

Burke clapped him on the back. "That too. I'm glad you came, Phin. I was so stuck on the glove that I wouldn't have noticed either of the other things."

Phin's insides warmed with the praise, even though he knew that what he'd done was nowhere close to enough. They needed to find out who'd shot Joy. Because that person had intended to harm Cora Winslow, too.

Maybe they still did.

Gert Town, New Orleans, Louisiana
TUESDAY, DECEMBER 13, 10:05 P.M.

Alan was shaking as he approached his storage unit.

"Pull it together," he snapped at himself.

He was almost finished. He could fall apart once he got home. In the privacy of his study, where no one would bother him. But first he had to park the van and change out of his bloody clothes.

Blood had spattered in all directions, staining his hoodie, which Alan had expected. He'd burn everything he was wearing.

Just in case. He couldn't be too careful at this stage.

Medford's suitcase had to be dealt with as well. He didn't want to take it home, just in case there was something in it that could be tracked. He wouldn't put anything past Medford Hughes.

He'd search the suitcase in his storage unit. If it was just clothing, he'd toss it into a dumpster. Any electronic equipment would have to be destroyed. Which was fine. He had a hammer and a lot of stress to work through. He'd smash Medford's electronics to bits.

Starting with the man's burner phone. Alan took it from his pocket with a shudder. If Medford had been allowed to make that anonymous call to NOPD's tip line, Alan would have been put into prison and a lot of people would have been impacted.

Alan's business was caring for people. If he went to prison, everything he'd built would crumble. People would suffer. Their faith would falter. Many would fall.

He couldn't allow that to happen.

He'd done what he had to do. Now he had to clean up. Wearily he took his macular glasses off, got out of the van, and stretched his back. He was tired, but there were still things to be done.

He surveyed the front bumper in disgust. That list of things now included having the crunched bumper of his van repaired. Alan had hit a parked car when he'd swerved out of the path of an oncoming vehicle, the headlights having blinded him. He'd heard a loud crash behind him, but he hadn't looked back. He'd gotten out of there.

At least the bumper could wait a little while. He might even be able to fix it himself. That way if the owner of the parked car reported the damage, no repair shops would be able to report him to the cops.

Opening the back of the van, he unzipped Medford's suitcase and rifled through it. It mostly held clothes, but he found Medford's personal laptop.

He retrieved his hammer and a bag of trash bags from the shelf where he kept his tools. It was a basic solution, but it would do. He put Medford's laptop and phone in the bag and hit them with the hammer, the bag keeping shards of plastic from flying everywhere.

When he checked inside the bag, the workings of the laptop were exposed. He pulled out the hard drives and went back to hammering them to pieces.

Exhausted, he took the bag filled with the remnants of Medford's laptop and set it aside. He'd throw it in a dumpster on his way back to the college campus, where he'd catch a cab home.

And then he'd get a good night's sleep in his own bed. He'd earned it.

8

⚜

"THIS MAGNIFYING GLASS is amazing." Molly Sutton slid another credit card receipt under the large magnifying glass that Cora had brought to the kitchen table. "Where can I get one?"

Cora's fingers trembled slightly on her computer keyboard as she waited for Molly to read the details of the receipt. They'd been at it for an hour, Molly keeping up a steady stream of pleasant chatter as they'd built a spreadsheet of her father's business expenses from the year he'd died.

Cora knew the woman was trying to take her mind off the fact that they'd learned the man who'd possessed Burke's and Joy's laptops had been found dead in his car, a bullet hole in his head. Which would have been bad enough, but Phin had discovered evidence that made it look like the man had been murdered.

Just like my father. Bullet to the head.

"Cora?"

Cora jerked her attention back to the blonde. "I'm sorry. My mind drifted. Can you repeat the question?"

"I asked where I can get a magnifying glass like this. It's sturdy and hands-free. It would make my life so much easier."

"It was my grandmother's. I don't know where she got

it, honestly. She'd use it for her needlepoint and quilting. I'm sure you can find something similar on Amazon."

"Not like this. I think this is at least a hundred years old. Your house is full of genuinely old stuff. I love it."

Cora's lips turned up. "When this is over, feel free to come back and help me sort all the genuinely old stuff so that I can sell it."

"I might buy some of it. My sister would love something with history for her birthday." She lifted her brows. "We could get Phin to help us move boxes. And then you could watch him while his muscles flex."

Cora coughed. "I . . . I don't even know how to respond to that."

Molly chuckled. "He's a fine-looking man, our Phin. And, as far as I know, unattached."

"Are you matchmaking, Molly?"

"I am *so* matchmaking. He's a nice guy and he doesn't warm up to people easily. But he warmed up to you right away."

"I hope he's okay. I don't imagine it would be easy for him to see something so grisly as that man's body."

"That's true, but Antoine said the dog is making a big difference. I'm going to have to talk to the woman who trained him and get some tips for my fiancé's dog. Shoe is generally well behaved, but he's earned his name. He chews shoes."

"Your shoes?"

"No, it's always Gabe's shoes. I think it's because Gabe's spilled something delicious on them at the Choux. That's his restaurant."

Cora perked up. "Le Petit Choux? I *love* that place. You're engaged to the owner?"

"I am. I'll ask him to send over some supper tomorrow that's shellfish free. You ready for the next receipt?"

Cora nodded. "Go for it."

"'Days Inn; Tucson, Arizona; May twelfth. Memo: four nights' lodging.'"

Cora typed it in, her heart sinking a little more. During the last year of his life, her father had stayed at ten hotels in places far outside the New Orleans metro area. They still had three years of receipts to review, so this was likely to only get worse. "This isn't looking good for my father's fidelity, is it? Tucson, Austin, Wichita. As far away as Casper, Wyoming."

"Doesn't mean he was cheating on your mom," Molly said. "That's usually the first conclusion people jump to, but there are other explanations."

"Like?" Cora asked, desperate to discover a legitimate reason for Jack Elliot's travel. The thought of her mother seeing the receipts and believing the worst broke Cora's heart.

"I don't know. The first thing we're going to do is input as many of the receipts as we can still read. The ones that are too faded to read, I'm putting aside. Antoine might be able to help me get better resolution on the ink that remains. Then we look for patterns."

"So far, there are no patterns."

"That's a pattern, too. If he visited the same place repeatedly, he might have a business associate there."

"Or a lover," Cora murmured. "I won't shatter, Molly. If that's what it is, I'll deal."

"I know you won't shatter. You're too strong for that."

Cora hoped she would be when she learned the truth. "And if we don't find repeated destinations?"

"Well, first we'll cross-check locations against the client list that Antoine will pull from those disks he found. And if there are no out-of-town clients, then we have to assume one of two things. First, that maybe he was involved in something—not accounting related—where he did a job for one person and moved on to the next."

Which might be something legal. *Please, let it have been legal.*

"The second assumption?"

Molly met her gaze. "That he was going to different places to throw off anyone tracking his movements."

"Like my mother?"

"Or the governing board that regulates and disciplines accountants." Molly put the hotel receipt in the finished pile and pulled another from the folder. "But the very fact that he kept all these receipts is a mark in the legal column. If I were doing something shady, I sure wouldn't keep receipts."

"I hope you're right."

"Me too," Molly said as she slid the next receipt under the glass. "Huh. Your father bought something from a gun store in Twin Falls, Idaho, just two weeks before he died. Specifically, .30-30 shells. Three boxes. That's a fair amount of ammo." She straightened and looked at Cora. "Did your father own a gun?"

Cora blinked. "Not that I know of. Mama hated guns. I think they would have argued over him having a gun in the house when we were little, but I don't remember that."

"You were only five when he disappeared," Molly said gently.

"True. Those shells, the .30-30. That's rifle ammo, isn't it?"

"It is. He could have been hunting, I suppose."

Cora bit her lip. "Maybe. But you don't think so."

"I don't know what I think. Enter this: Bullseye gun store, Twin Falls, Idaho, October first. Memo: three boxes of .30-30 shells." Molly put the receipt in the finished pile. "We'll keep a lookout for more gun or ammo purchases." She'd started to reach for another receipt when her phone began to buzz. "Excuse me. This is Burke."

Molly put the phone to her ear. "Well?" She listened for a moment. "She's here. I'll put you on speaker." She set the phone on the table. "We're here, Burke."

"Hey, Cora," Burke said, his tone easy and unruffled. That had to be good, right?

"Hey, Burke. What happened with the dead man?"

"Cops are processing the scene. The ME came and took him to the morgue."

Cora frowned. "And I bet they won't share information with us."

"Maybe," Burke drawled. "We have a source inside the morgue who sometimes tells us stuff."

"One of Antoine's brothers is doing his residency there," Molly told Cora. "We try not to ask for info unless it's important, but this qualifies."

"It certainly does," Burke agreed. "André came to the crime scene, Molly. They're going to investigate it as a homicide."

"Who's André?" Cora whispered.

"Another of Antoine's brothers," Molly said. "He's a captain in the NOPD. He and Burke used to work together before Burke quit the force to start the firm. That's good, Burke. Hopefully we'll get some answers."

"Well, it got a little more complicated when the cops knocked on the door of the dead man's house. They figured they'd find the wife asleep, but she's dead, too. Dead in her bed. André said she appeared to be an addict. Track marks on both arms."

"How did she die?" Molly asked. "Was it an overdose?"

"Maybe, but the ME suspects suffocation."

Cora's hand flew to cover her mouth. "Oh my God."

Molly patted her other hand. "You don't have to stay here and listen."

"Sorry, Cora," Burke said.

"It's okay. I was just startled. Why do they think suffocation?" Her brain was racing through what she knew about this cause of death. "Petechiae?"

The small red pinpricks due to capillary leakage.

"Very good," Burke said. "More of your librarian superpower?"

"Unfortunately, yes," Cora said. "A woman came into the library searching the term because her elderly mother had been suffocated by a greedy relative."

Molly lifted her brows. "You really do see all kinds of stuff. I never knew librarians had such a stressful job."

Cora put the memory of the devastated woman aside. "Was I right? The ME found petechiae?"

"The standard answer is that they'll know when they get the body on the table, but I overheard the ME telling André that he thought he'd seen it. We'll know more over the next few days."

Cora's mind was spinning. "So . . . if the man was murdered, it was staged to look like a murder-suicide?"

"That's the cops' theory," Burke said. "I'm heading to the hospital to take Joy's kids some dinner. Choux food. Thanks, Molly."

Molly just smiled. "I dare you to try to keep Gabe from feeding Joy's family. He sent over meals all day long."

Cora hesitated, then blurted out the question she wanted to ask. "Is Phin all right?"

"He's good," Burke said warmly. "I just dropped him off at his house. His friends are there and they'll take good care of him. Plan on him arriving early tomorrow morning to finish securing your windows."

"Thank you." Cora wished she could have checked with the man herself, but she didn't have his phone number. "Have him call me when he gets here. I don't always hear the doorbell if I'm upstairs."

Plus, that would give her Phin's number.

Molly's sly smile indicated that Cora hadn't been as smooth as she'd hoped.

"Try to sleep tonight, Cora," Burke was saying. "Molly's on the job, and she's my right hand."

Phin wants to be a bodyguard, too.

Not my business.

"I'll sleep well. I didn't last night. I was up putting sensors on all the windows. There are too many windows in this house."

Burke chuckled. "That's exactly what Phin said. Night, ladies. Molly, you call if you need anything."

"Night, Burke." Molly ended the call, her eyes sparkling. "You realize that our protocol is for Phin to call me to let him in, since I'm your bodyguard."

Cora fought the urge to hide her face. "I've never had a bodyguard before. I don't know the protocol."

Molly laughed. "Touché. Do you want Phin's number?"

Cora knew her cheeks were burning. It was the curse of being a redhead. "Yes."

Molly tapped her phone and Cora's buzzed with an incoming text. "There you go. Get some sleep, Cora. You're safe with me."

"Thank you. Blue should go out once more before I go up."

Molly sobered. "I'll do it. You're not to leave the house without me or Val, who'll be your day bodyguard."

Cora shuddered. "Okay. I'm not foolish, Molly. I won't try to ditch you."

"Thank you. Go on, now. Sleep."

Obediently, Cora climbed the stairs. Her bedroom had been a sanctuary for so long. Now she jumped at every brush of a branch against her window. There was a door to the balcony outside—a door that sported a brand-new lock, courtesy of Phin Bishop.

That made her feel safer than the knowledge that a trained bodyguard roamed downstairs. She slipped under her blanket, her phone clutched in one hand.

Burke's people would keep whoever was after her from getting in. She had to believe that. Molly seemed like a very capable bodyguard.

Cora rolled to her back, staring up at the ceiling. She'd told Burke that she'd sleep well, but that might have been a lie. Here, in the quiet of her bedroom, the truth of the day was loud in her head.

I have a bodyguard. Because someone is after me.
Way to make it all about you.

But it *was* all about her. Well, her and Joy.

And Phin. She'd gleaned enough to know that he'd have

a hard time with whatever he'd seen tonight, especially after his ordeal that morning.

Worrying about Phin was preferable to worrying about herself. She'd learned that at an early age. Worrying about other people was always easier. Or at least it didn't feel as selfish.

Burke had said Phin was okay, but was he really? After all, Burke was the one who'd thought Phin was capable of hurting Joy, so Cora wouldn't put too much stock in his opinion on this.

Without overthinking it, she opened a text window to the cell number that Molly had sent her.

This is Cora. I hope you're okay after everything that happened tonight. Give SodaPop a pet from me. Hope you sleep well. She added a snoozy emoji, then hit send.

There. At least the man knew someone cared.

She glanced at the time. She'd been in bed for all of five minutes and it felt like five hours.

Someone was after her. And her father had gone to all those cities—without her mother.

He'd bought ammo in Twin Falls, Idaho. Why? Did he have a rifle? Why did he have a rifle? If he had had one, where was it?

Had he hidden it in the house? Her mind started spinning through all the places he could have hidden something that big. The attic alone would take forever to search.

I'm not going to sleep tonight, am I?

No, she was not. Heaving out a sigh, she opened her phone's e-reader app, wincing when she saw the cover of the true crime she'd been reading. That wasn't likely to make her any less worried.

She scrolled through her to-be-read list, happy when she found a fantasy novel. There were no guns in this story. Only swords and dragons. She'd sourced it for the library herself. She could lose herself in this story for tonight.

And she could sleep when the danger was past.

Or if Phin was in the house. She'd slept so well when he'd been working on her doors.

Maybe tomorrow he'd come over and she could sleep then.

St. Claude, New Orleans, Louisiana
TUESDAY, DECEMBER 13, 11:45 P.M.

Delores O'Bannion put a cup of coffee on the TV tray table that she'd placed in front of the sofa. "It's decaf," she said.

Phin glared at the cup. "I know I didn't have any decaf in my house."

Delores grinned like the pixie she was. "I bought you some. You're wound too tight, Phin."

That was true.

"It's just easier to drink the decaf," Stone said from the recliner Phin had rescued from the curb over the summer. He'd cleaned it, refinished the wood, and reupholstered the cushions. It was a damn nice chair now.

And that he'd taken before-and-after photos had been his first clue that he was almost ready to face his family. He and Scarlett had rescued furniture and fixed it up for donations to the church where their uncle was a priest. He wanted to share the photos with his twin.

But there was a mental blockage. The same blockage that had kept him from sending even a text for five years.

Burke was wrong. I am a coward. I'm a coward and a fraud and I don't deserve to be—

A lick to his face had him wrenching to look down at SodaPop, who was sitting nearly in his lap.

Phin exhaled, aware that he'd been ready to spiral once again. *Good girl.* He glanced up at Delores, who was still standing in front of him. "You were right," he murmured.

She smirked. "I know. Don't ditch her again, okay?"

"I won't. I promise."

Delores took the other side of the sofa, and the three of them sipped their coffee in silence for several minutes until Stone cleared his throat. "Tell us about it, Phin."

Stalling for time to think, Phin took a large gulp of coffee, grateful it had cooled enough not to scald his mouth. "It was ugly. The man, anyway. I didn't see the woman."

He was grateful for that, too.

"It was supposed to look like murder-suicide?" Delores asked.

"Yes. At least that's what the police were thinking." That he'd helped discover that Medford Hughes had been murdered gave him a spark of pride.

That was good. That was progress. The two sitting in his living room deserved to know that, so he told them about finding the smeared blood on the trunk and the Faraday bag on the curb. When he finished, both of his friends were beaming at him.

"You were part of the team," Stone said, like he was cheering on a kid in Little League.

Phin nodded. "I was. It was . . . affirming."

"I'm proud of you," Delores said, her voice a little thick. A glance her way revealed that her eyes were filled with tears.

"Delores," Phin started, but she waved his words away with a choked laugh.

"I'm just happy. Let me be happy for you."

So he did. He let himself bask in their approval. "And I didn't spiral." He stroked SodaPop's coat. "I started to and she distracted me."

"Huge," Stone said, still grinning. "Good girl, Soda-Pop. That kind of scene is your biggest trigger."

It was. Seeing blood and brains and . . .

Phin drew a deep breath when the coffee soured in his stomach. *Nope, not going there.* He lowered his head to SodaPop's, nuzzling her with his cheek. She gave him a lick.

"Thank you," he whispered.

"She's a good dog," Delores said.

"She is," Phin agreed. "I'm so glad you started training service dogs." There were too few organizations training animals for an ever-increasing population who needed them. *Like me.*

I'm lucky. I have friends who care about me, here and at work.

He also had a family who cared. A family he hadn't done right by.

"I'm going home for Christmas," he said abruptly.

Stone's smile softened into something even prouder than it had been before. "Good."

Delores grimaced. "When they find out we've been hiding you all this time . . ."

"I won't tell them," Phin said. "I wouldn't do that to you."

Delores pointed to SodaPop. "Everyone knows I was training her. They'll know where you got her."

Not for the first time, Phin considered what a difficult position he'd put his friends in. Stone's brother Marcus was married to Phin's twin sister, Scarlett. "I'm sorry. I've caused strife."

Stone shook his head. "Marcus will understand. So will Scarlett, once she's over her mad. You worry about yourself. Delores, just give Scarlett her pick of Angel's next litter. She'll be happy again."

Angel was Delores's wolfhound, and Phin loved her. That his twin did, too, was no surprise. He knew that Scarlett had adopted a dog from Delores's animal shelter, a three-legged bulldog she'd named Zatoichi, after the blind swordsman adventure movies they'd loved as teens.

Delores nodded, her smile returning. "Good idea." Her expression turned a little sly. "So, Phin. Tell us about Cora Winslow."

Phin's face grew hot. "She's a nice woman who needs our help."

Stone's laugh was the tiniest bit dirty. "You dog, you. You like her."

Phin rolled his eyes. "I do. She's . . . well . . . kind and pretty damn brave. I hate that she's scared. I know what that feels like."

"To be getting letters all these years from someone who was clearly watching her," Delores murmured. "That poor woman. She's got to be feeling betrayed."

"That too. It sank in with her tonight that whoever was writing the letters did so because they didn't want her to report her father's disappearance to the police. It's someone who's close enough to her to know that she was looking for her father a few years ago." He explained her brother's cancer and the search for a marrow donor. "We're going to have to make a list of people who knew that she was searching for him. That'll make her feel even more betrayed."

First on his list was that attorney from this morning. The man who'd known that someone was after her but left her to fend for herself. Who'd known her since she'd been born.

"Better to feel betrayed than to feel dead," Stone said, then winced when Delores hissed at him. "That didn't come out right. Sorry."

Phin shook his head. "No, you're right. But it's still hard to watch her figuring all this out. I want to do something. But I don't know what."

"Be her friend," Delores said with a smile. "That's what my guy did. He did all kinds of sweet things for me. Made me feel safe."

Because Delores had been a victim of an attempted homicide years before. It was how she'd met Phin's sister, a homicide detective in Cincinnati. Delores knew how important feeling safe really was.

Phin smiled back at her. "How did he do that?"

"He'd sneak around my dog shelter and clean the cages when I was asleep. And then he'd sleep on my front porch to make sure no one bothered me. He didn't leave, even when the mosquitoes ate him up."

Stone was staring at the ceiling, clearly embarrassed. "Delores," he whined. "You make me sound like a sap."

"You were," she said with a twinkle in her eyes before turning back to Phin. "I knew he was out there, and one night I invited him in. Made him coffee."

"Decaf?" Phin asked.

"Hell no," Stone muttered. "Decaf is swill. Sorry, not sorry."

"You're not wrong," Phin agreed. "And then?"

"Then I told him that if he was determined to haunt my property, he could sleep on my sofa so he wouldn't be all bug-bitten. From there, we just grew together. If you want Cora to feel safe, show her that she *is* safe."

Phin nodded slowly. "I replaced the locks on her doors today. I'll do the windows tomorrow. And she asked me to do some handyman work around her place."

Delores nodded. "Very good start. If you're working around her house, she won't be alone."

"She has bodyguards," Phin said. "Molly and Val."

"That's good," Delores said. "Even better, actually. You'll have backup and that should decrease your anxiety. When will you begin?"

That she thought this was a done deal nearly made him smile. It was so very Delores. "I told her that I'd have to work around you guys. I don't want to just leave you to your own devices. You won't be here that long."

"We'll be here as long as you need us," Delores said firmly. "Start on her house, Phin. Stone and I have a long list of things we want to see in New Orleans. And places we want to eat."

"The food," Stone said with a groan. "Oh my God, the food. Seriously, Phin, don't babysit us. If you need us, call. Otherwise, we are on a well-earned vacation. Delores has volunteers working at the shelter, so we're good for a while. We have a free bed here and a kitchen. Just pretend we're boarders. Fix that woman's house."

Phin's smile was slow and felt deep. "Okay." His phone buzzed, and he blinked at the screen. "It's a text from Cora."

This is Cora. I hope you're okay after everything that happened tonight. Give SodaPop a pet from me. Hope you sleep well.

Delores leaned over Phin's arm, reading the text with unabashed interest. "Awww." She read it to Stone, who looked pleased. "Well, answer her."

Phin froze. "I don't even know what to say."

Delores returned to her corner of the sofa, her expression one of challenge. "*Are* you okay?"

Phin thought about it. He'd witnessed a man's brains coating the inside of his car tonight. Then watched as the man's wife was wheeled out in a body bag. Not to mention being interrogated by the cops for the second time that day.

"Not really. Better than I've been in the past, though, thanks to SodaPop."

"Then tell her that," Delores instructed. "Do it, Phineas."

"Just do it, Phineas," Stone echoed, resigned. "It's so much easier."

"You've given-named me," Phin said, trying for light and not coming close. "I guess I have to do it now." But his fingers felt thicker than usual as he tried to type. He finally got the words on the screen and hit send.

"Now thank her," Delores said. "And wish her nice dreams."

Phin laughed. "Okay, Mom." He did as she said and was surprised when Cora texted back. ***Hoping to dream of dragons.*** The text was accompanied by a screenshot of the cover of a fantasy novel. "I don't think she can sleep."

Stone pointed to the stairs. "Then go upstairs and text with her until she can."

Phin stared at him. "And say what?"

Both of his friends just stared at him pointedly.

"Fine," Phin grunted. He pushed off the sofa and clucked to SodaPop. "Come on, girl. We've been dismissed." He took the dog to his tiny backyard and leaned against his house while SodaPop sniffed the dirt.

Tell me about the dragons, he texted, then smiled when she began to do so.

9

The Garden District, New Orleans, Louisiana
WEDNESDAY, DECEMBER 14, 7:30 A.M.

PHIN PARKED HIS old truck at the curb in front of
Cora's big house and took a moment to stare up at the
gorgeous structure. He loved the homes in this part of the
city. The architecture, the detail, the grace.

He didn't love the price tag for the maintenance. He
wondered how long Cora would be able to keep it up. It
sounded like she poured every free moment—and every
free dollar—into cleaning and fixing.

Well, now she'll have help.

He grabbed his toolbox and held the door open so Soda-
Pop could jump out. Then, following protocol, he texted
Val that he was here. She and Molly had switched shifts
and Val's car was in the driveway, parked up against the
gate that secured the back garden. Although, if someone
wanted to get onto the property, the gate wouldn't stop
them.

I'll be doing that. Hopefully with better locks on the
doors and windows. And if that didn't work, then . . . *I'll
keep her safe.*

He'd made it to the front porch when he noticed a car
out of the corner of his eye. It was driving slowly past
Cora's house. The hairs rose on Phin's neck and he herded
SodaPop in front of him.

The car came to a full stop behind his truck and Phin exhaled.

Surely an intruder wouldn't simply park and knock on her door, would he?

Or maybe it was a reporter. The police hadn't officially released Cora's name in their report about Joy's shooting, but someone inside NOPD might have loose lips.

"Siri, call Val Sorensen mobile," he said, putting the phone to his ear without taking his eyes off the car.

"Phin!" Val sounded joyful to be talking to him again.

"In a minute," he said quietly. "There's a car parked in front of Cora's house, behind my truck. It's a black Lexus. Can't see the plate. And now the driver's getting out. Older man. Maybe fifty-five or sixty. Gray hair. Mustache. Dark glasses."

"Hold on." There were voices in the background and then Val was back. "Cora knows him. It's Patrick Napier, her friend Tandy's father."

Phin relaxed. "That's good. I'm not carrying like you, but the cordless drill in my toolbox could do some damage if it had to."

Val chuckled. "I'm so glad you're back. I've missed you. Come into the house, so I can see your face. It's been too long."

It had been too long. He'd missed all his work friends, but Val had become almost like the sister he'd left behind. Scarlett would love Val. She'd love Cora, too.

Scar would love all his friends. He needed to give her the chance. He only hoped she'd forgive him when he finally got his act together to go home.

Not turning his back on the older man cautiously approaching the front porch, he stepped into the foyer when the door creaked open. Loudly.

Need to WD-40 that.

"Phin."

He looked down to see Val smiling big. He didn't have to look down far. Val was six-one in her boots. Just a few inches taller than Cora had been in those ridiculous heels. He hoped she wore more sensible shoes today. He didn't like that her feet hurt her.

Val opened her arms, then waited, expectant. "Okay to hug you?"

He grinned down at her, not missing the way her eyes opened in surprise. He really needed to grin more often. "Yes. Please."

She threw her arms around his neck and clung. "Thank you."

He patted her back awkwardly, knowing what she was thanking him for and rejecting the notion. When Val and her boyfriend Kaj had been in trouble six weeks before, he'd stepped in, providing backup. In the end, he'd folded, spiraling right there in front of them. But that was over and done and he wasn't going back there.

He hoped. He prayed.

"I didn't do anything," he muttered gruffly. "You and Kaj did it all."

She drew back, holding his face between her palms. "Say 'You're welcome, Val.'"

He rested his forehead against hers. "You're welcome, Val."

She sighed, a happy sound. "You still going home for Christmas to see your family?"

She was the only one he'd told before yesterday. "That's the plan."

"I'm going to nag you."

"And I'll say thank you."

Her eyes went shiny. "I'm sorry that I pushed you. You weren't ready."

He'd stepped up to be a bodyguard six weeks before, but he really hadn't been ready. He wondered if he ever would be. "I'd do it again. For you."

That was the truth. Even if he got triggered and spiraled afterward. He'd done what he'd needed to do and had managed to hold off the episode until everyone was safe.

The shininess in Val's eyes became full-on tears that she wiped away with her sleeve. "You sweet-talker, you."

A creak on the grand staircase had them both looking up. Cora stood on the top step, watching them, her face a carefully blank mask. Val took a step back, watching them both.

Phin wondered what had happened. Cora's sweet smile was gone. She wasn't even angry like she'd been the day before when he'd frightened her on the street.

Val's brows lifted. "Come on down, Cora. Your friend's dad is on the front porch. I think Phin scared him out of knocking."

Cora descended, her long legs encased in sleek black pants. And she wore flats.

"You sleep okay?" he asked.

They'd texted for an hour before she'd grown sleepy enough. Phin had stayed up another twenty minutes afterward rereading their conversation. It had been a lot of little things. Mostly books they enjoyed. Some stories about her library patrons that had made him chuckle.

She was a good storyteller. *My mom would love her, too.* His mother was a retired high school English teacher and books had been a huge part of their growing up. Bringing home a legit librarian would make his mother so happy.

She'll be so happy when you just come home.

And he would. Soon. For now, his job was helping Cora stay safe.

Cora, who was so pretty in a green silk shirt that set off her red hair, making it look like a flame. But she didn't smile. She was . . . frosty.

What had happened?

Finally, the older man knocked on the door and Cora stepped forward to answer it, but Val held up her hand. "My job, remember?"

Cora nodded, saying nothing.

Frowning, Phin leaned closer to whisper in her ear, "What's wrong?"

She cut him a sharp look. "Nothing."

Well, shit. He'd learned from his mother and sister that "nothing" always meant "something." But he couldn't press because Tandy's father was in the foyer, his arms outstretched to Cora, much as Val's had been for him.

He felt an unexpected spear of jealousy at the familiar way the man embraced Cora, and then he got it. Oh. *Oh.* Nothing *was* something. Cora had jumped to the wrong conclusion seeing Val hug him.

He spared a glance at Val to see her shaking her head at him, her lips twitching. "I'll explain to her," she mouthed.

He wanted to roll his eyes but didn't dare. The man was watching him suspiciously over Cora's shoulder.

"I'm Phin Bishop," Phin said. "This is Val Sorensen. We work for Burke Broussard."

"Oh." The man released Cora, sliding his left arm around her shoulders. "My daughter told me all about him. I'm Patrick Napier."

"Patrick's been my surrogate father since I was in elementary school," Cora said. She leaned her head on the man's shoulder. "He and Tandy are the only family I have left."

"I was out of town yesterday," Patrick said to Cora. "I didn't hear about any of this until I got home last night. I nearly drove straight over here, but Tandy said you'd hired Broussard. Bodyguards are expensive. I can—"

"No, you can't," Cora interrupted. "We've had this conversation before. I'm not taking your money. Tandy told you about Joy?" She glanced at Val. "Patrick, his wife, and Joy were my mother's friends."

Patrick nodded. "Lots of carpooling when Tandy, Cora, and Nala were kids. I stopped by the hospital on my way in. Joy was asleep, but Nala said I can come back later today. I'll take you and Tandy, if you want me to."

"I'll be accompanying Cora," Val inserted smoothly. "You and Tandy can meet us at the hospital. Bodyguard, you know."

Patrick winced. "Sorry. Bodyguards are new to me. Cora, are you really all right?"

She smiled up at him, but the expression was strained. "I'm fine. Val and the others are taking care of me."

The others. Phin had been relegated to *the others*. Val better explain things quickly or Phin would have to make sure that Cora knew what was what.

Patrick sighed. "I didn't know someone had broken into your house. I would have mentioned the van I saw in your driveway on Friday morning if I'd known."

Phin was suddenly on full alert. Friday night was when Blue had woken Cora, barking at what had been the intruder's entry.

Val straightened. "Can you describe it?"

Patrick shrugged helplessly. "It was a van. You mentioned that you were having trouble with that commode upstairs that leaks. I figured you'd called in a professional to fix it. I meant to call you to make sure it was okay, but I forgot. I feel awful, Cora Jane."

Phin tensed. A white van had been parked a few doors down from Medford Hughes's house last night. One of his neighbors had seen it and told the cops while he, Burke, and Antoine waited to give their statements. "What color was it?"

"White or maybe cream. Or gray? It was light, that much I remember. Or it was dirty. Sorry."

Val frowned. "What about the driver?"

Another helpless shrug. "I didn't look. I should have. I'm so sorry. I was in a hurry to make a delivery to Mrs. Williams at the end of Cora's street. She'd ordered a sculpture for her husband's birthday and it was delayed. It had come in the day before but she was too busy to come in. I told her I'd deliver it."

"Oh, that's right," Cora murmured. "I forgot it was Mr. Williams's birthday. I'll have to drop off a card. She did tell me that she'd bought him a sculpture."

"Carved out of a chunk of jade bigger than my fist."

Cora's eyes widened. "Wow. That sounds expensive."

"It was," Patrick said. "Which was why I hand-delivered it." He dropped a kiss on Cora's head. "I've got to get to the gallery. You'll call me later so I know you're okay?"

"I promise. What time did you see the van in my driveway?"

"Eleven, maybe? It was before noon, I know that."

"Were you home on Friday morning, Cora?" Phin asked.

She shook her head. "I was at work."

"We'll ask your neighbors for camera footage," Val said. "We'll figure it out, Cora."

Cora nodded. "I know." But she didn't sound sure of that at all. "You go on now, Patrick. Tell Tandy that I'm okay. She's been texting me all morning."

"She worries." Patrick pressed another kiss to her temple. "So do I. Make sure these folks have my cell number in case you need me."

"I will." She started to show him to the door, then sighed when Val gave her a quelling look. "Sorry."

"You'll learn," Val said as she ushered Patrick to the door, leaving Phin and Cora alone in awkward silence.

"She's my friend," Phin blurted, unable to keep the words in his mouth.

Cora looked doubtful. "Okay."

Phin huffed. "Like a sister. She was with me the last time I . . ." He sighed. "The last time I spiraled. When I ran."

Cora's expression softened. "I see."

"I don't think you do," he muttered. "She's a twin. Like me."

She stared up at him. "You're a twin?"

"Yeah. I have a sister. Scarlett."

"That you haven't talked to in a while."

He nodded, but now his neck was stiff. His whole body was drawn too tight. "Right."

SodaPop sidled up to him, her whimper quiet.

"You can tell me, you know," Cora murmured. Her smile was genuine, and his heart eased. "Only if you want, of course," she added. "Are you gonna do the window locks today?"

"Yep," he said, relieved at the topic change. "And I thought I'd look at your water heater. Your water's only lukewarm."

She grimaced. "I know. I'm reminded every time I wash my hair, but I can't afford a new one. Not for a few months. I had to take money out of the trust last month to get the roof fixed."

"It might be a heating element. Not as expensive as you think."

She brightened. "Will you show me how to fix it?"

"Absolutely. Stay with Val today, okay? She's fierce."

"I promise." She hesitated, then briefly squeezed his forearm. "I'm glad she's your friend. You need support."

"*Only* my friend," he reiterated.

She grinned. "Got it. See you later. Can you check on Blue every so often? He's asleep at the back door."

"Of course. Wait. Where are you going?" His eyes narrowed. "Are you going to work?"

Cora sighed. "No. Well, yes, but only to get my library laptop. I already had this argument with Molly and Val. 'It's too dangerous to go to the library, Cora,'" she sing-songed. "'Think of the people who could be hurt if someone came after you, Cora.' So I'm going to get my laptop so that I can work from home."

"It was a compromise," Val said dryly, closing the front door after seeing Patrick out. "Molly and I weren't happy with it, either, but Cora does have to earn a paycheck."

He didn't like the idea of her leaving the house, but he kept his mouth shut, watching as she gathered her purse and followed Val out to her car. He knew Val would keep her safe. He also knew that Val would be calling Burke immediately to inform him about the van.

The driver of a white van had murdered Medford

Hughes and his wife last night. Assuming it was the same person—and they had to assume so as to best protect Cora—the intruder would not get their hands on Cora Winslow.

Phin walked into the kitchen and carefully set his tool-box on the marble countertop. He wasn't ready to body-guard again but he had to do something.

He sent a text to Burke. *You heard about the van at Cora's on Friday?*

Burke's reply was instant. *Val just called me. Not a good development.*

Phin hesitated, then pushed forward. *I can ask neighbors for camera footage.*

There was a slight pause, the ellipsis indicating that Burke was typing. Stopping. Typing. Stopping. Finally, the reply came through.

Let's do it together. I'll be there in thirty minutes.

Phin could live with that. At least Burke was letting him be involved. *I'll be waiting.*

Until then, he'd work on the windows.

He swallowed a groan. So many windows. Where should he even start?

But the answer was obvious.

In Cora's bedroom. So she could sleep tonight.

The Garden District, New Orleans, Louisiana
WEDNESDAY, DECEMBER 14, 7:45 A.M.

Having been using her Bluetooth so that she could drive, Val ended the call with Burke and glanced over at Cora. "You okay?"

"No," Cora said honestly. "I didn't know the white van was at the dead man's house last night until you told Burke just now."

These people—whoever they were—were killers. But hearing that the same vehicle had been at the scene of the brutal shooting of that man in his car made everything real, and she was terrified.

"It might not have been the same van," Val said.

"But you think it was," Cora said.

"Possibly. Either way, we will keep you safe."

Cora nodded, turning her attention to the window. She normally loved walking down this street, especially around the holidays. "Everyone's decorated for Christmas. I didn't this year. I just haven't had the heart to."

"Hearing that your father was dead when you'd thought him alive all this time was a shock. You're allowed to feel what you feel."

"I know."

"Did you decorate last year?"

Cora sighed. "No. John Robert had just died. And the year before that, my grandmother had just died. It's been three years since I decorated my house for Christmas."

"It'll get better," Val promised. "My brother died a few years ago, and it's hard. Different circumstances, but the loss is still the same."

"Your brother was your twin?"

Val glanced over, her brows lifted. "Phin told you?"

"He said you were a twin. Like he is."

Val's smile was sad. "Yeah, we have that in common. It's hard for people who don't have a twin to understand the bond. I heard Phin tell you that we were just friends when I was showing your friend out the door. I want to make sure you believed him."

"I do."

"Good. Phin's a good man."

"I can tell." And Cora could. There was a vulnerability in Phin Bishop that called to her. But there was also a strength of character. A resolve that she respected. She wanted to ask about his PTSD, but that was a conversation she needed to have with Phin himself. When he was ready. "We're here." She pointed to the library's driveway. "Turn in here."

"That was fast." Val pulled into the parking lot. "I bet you walk this every day instead of driving."

"I do. It's a nice walk, and I pass by my favorite little coffee shop on the way. The woman who runs it always has a cup waiting for me."

"Is she an old friend, too? You seem to know the people in your neighborhood."

"I've lived here my whole life. There isn't a lot of turnover on my street. Many of the homes have been in families for generations, like mine. Myrna, who runs the coffee shop, is a friend and a library patron. I helped her locate an old high school boyfriend after her husband passed." She smirked. "They're getting married in three months."

"Burke told me about your extracurricular sleuthing," Val said. "I'm impressed."

Cora rolled her eyes. "Don't be. I'm just good at internet searches."

"I'm still impressed. So, this is what's going to happen. We're going to walk from here to the library and you're going to stay in front of me. I'll have your back. If I tell you to duck, you duck. When we get into the library, you get your laptop and then we're gone. You ready?"

"I am." Cora looked around the parking lot. It was mostly empty. Only two cars, one of which she recognized as belonging to the night cleaning service, who'd just be finishing. The other belonged to her boss, Minnie Edwards. "How do I explain you? I really don't want my boss knowing that I have a bodyguard."

"Say that I'm your friend, come for a visit," Val said as she got out of the car. "Do not get out. I'll come get you." She came around to open Cora's door and waited until Cora was on her feet. "Hustle, Cora Jane."

Cora glared. "Who told you?"

Val grinned before moving into place behind her. "Your friend Tandy. Molly and I were having coffee, doing our morning handoff while you were in the shower. Tandy knocked on the front door. Burke had sent us a photo of

her, said she was your bestie and she was okay to let in.
Tandy said that if we let you get hurt, she would make our
lives a living hell."

Cora sighed. "She would, too."

"I never doubted it for a second."

They hurried up the stairs and into the library. Cora
drew in a deep breath. The smell of old books had always
calmed her. "I love this place," she said as she sat behind
her desk, unlocking her drawer.

Val looked around. "It's nice. Lots of light. And not too
many dark corners. Get the laptop so I can get you home."

Cora was sliding the laptop into her handbag when her
boss emerged from her office, regarding her with concern.

"Cora?"

"Hey, Minnie. How are you this morning?"

"I'm fine," Minnie said. "But I thought you were working from home."

"I needed my laptop."

"And the woman?" Minnie pointed to Val.

"She's an old friend, here for a visit." Cora hated to lie,
but Minnie already knew too much of her business. She'd
been in the library the day the detectives from Terrebonne
Parish had shown up with news about her father.

Minnie was not discreet. Now everyone in the library
knew that Cora's father's body was the John Doe dug up in
the Damper Building down in Houma. Some of them
might have realized it by seeing Jack Elliot's face on the
news, but most wouldn't have, as their last names were
different.

Minnie frowned. "I'm glad you're working from home.
You had another reporter here this morning. He was waiting in the parking lot. Said you'd made a breakfast date
with him. I told him that you'd taken a day off, and he left.
I wrote down his license plate, just in case." She pulled a
yellow Post-it note from her pocket. "He was driving a
black Camry. Brand-new."

Cora sighed. Reporters had been a problem over the

past two weeks. If it *was* a reporter. What if it was one of *them*? Whoever had been after her? That Patrick had seen a van in her driveway had rattled her soundly. "What did he look like?"

"Young. Handsome. Familiar, but I couldn't place him. I've been shooing reporters away since those detectives showed up here two weeks ago. Anyway, you be careful. I didn't like the look of him."

Val took the Post-it note. "I'll make sure Cora gets this after I've taken her home. Thank you, ma'am."

"You're welcome." Minnie frowned at Val. "And your name?"

"Ingrid," Val said.

Cora wasn't sure whether to be appalled or impressed with Val's ability to lie.

Val grabbed Cora's handbag and cell phone. "Let's roll, Cora Jane."

Val ushered them to the car, her steps quick, her gaze everywhere. Cora looked around, relieved that no black Camry lurked. Nor a white panel van. Or a van that might have been white or cream or gray or just dirty. The parking lot held the same two cars as when they'd arrived.

Val seemed tense, so maybe she was also worried that the Camry driver wasn't a reporter. "If I say duck, you get your head down," she said as she drove them onto the main road.

"I will." That it could even be necessary was surreal. "Why did you tell Minnie you were Ingrid?" she asked to take her mind off the potential threat.

Val chuckled. "That's my given name. Val's a nickname, more or less."

"I like Val better."

"So do I. Only my family calls me Ingrid."

Cora's mind was still spinning, still worrying about the Camry. She hated this. Hated being afraid. Hated not being in control.

Then do something productive. It was how she'd coped

when John Robert was so sick. Searching for a marrow donor had helped her stay sane.

But what could she do? She was a librarian, dammit. Not a bodyguard or a PI.

But you do find out things. Do your job, Cora.

This mess had started when her father's body had been discovered. Jack Elliot was the key. And he'd bought .30-30 ammo in Twin Falls, Idaho, just weeks before he'd disappeared. Rifle bullets.

Why? What had he been doing?

She opened a browser page on her phone and typed *Twin Falls Idaho Oct 1 .30-30* along with the year he'd died. She hit enter, paged through the results, then froze, staring at her screen.

"What the hell?" she whispered. She clicked on the link and gasped.

Val glanced over at her. "What?"

"I googled those bullets my father bought and got an article. '*Local Man Found Dead, Victim of Hunting Accident.*'"

"Read it," Val said tersely. "What does the article say?"

"It's from a newspaper in Twin Falls. The victim was Jarred Bergeron, a prominent businessman. The bullet was a .30-30. He was found by a hunting party, his body still warm. The shooter wasn't found and the ME ruled the death accidental. Bergeron died two weeks before my father was murdered." Cora's stomach roiled. "Did my father kill him?"

"I don't know, but we need to tell Burke." Using her Bluetooth earbud, Val called her boss and relayed the information, then ended the call. "Burke says we need to meet at your house."

Cora nodded numbly. *My father killed someone.* It was all she could think about until she heard Val curse. The curse was followed by a sharp turn onto a side street.

Cora's heart began to race. "What?"

"Hold on." The blonde turned down another street, moving away from her house. "We have a tail."

Cora pressed the heel of her hand to her chest. "Is it the white van?"

"No. It's the black Camry. Keep your head down. If I tell you to duck, get down on the floorboard."

Cora didn't need to ask why. Because if it got to that point, someone would be shooting at her.

What had her father done?

10

PHIN WAS SITTING with Burke and Antoine at Cora's kitchen table when she and Val returned from the library by way of the entire Garden District. They should have been back thirty minutes before.

Burke frowned. "What took you so long?"

"We've been worried," Phin added quietly.

Val's expression was grim. "We had a tail. Black Camry. A man driving this same make and model was waiting for Cora at the library this morning. Her boss noted the plate." She handed a piece of paper to Antoine. "I drove around some more after we lost him. Wanted to be sure."

"I'm on it." Antoine was already typing the license plate into his computer.

Val gently pushed Cora into the seat beside Phin. "I'll make you some tea."

"Thank you," Cora murmured, far too pale for Phin's liking.

Phin laid one of his hands over Cora's where she'd clenched them on the tabletop. "You're like ice."

"You're safe here," Burke told her.

Cora swallowed audibly. "Thank you. That guy might have just been a reporter, but I'm shaken up. Not gonna lie."

"You have a right to be." Phin started to move his hand, but Cora surprised him by grabbing it and holding it tight.

"You're warm," she whispered, "and I'm so cold."

Burke left the room and came back with an afghan that had been on Cora's sofa. He draped it over her shoulders. "We're figuring it out, but these things take time."

Phin hesitated, then put his arm around her. Between his body heat and the blanket, he'd get her warmed up. She was shaking like a leaf. "You got a hit on that Camry, Antoine?"

Antoine frowned at his screen. "It's a rental. Getting the renter will take some extra effort. Did they seem hostile?"

"Didn't stop to ask," Val said as she placed a steaming cup of tea in front of Cora. "He was driving aggressively. I finally did a somewhat illegal move and lost him."

"Antoine, find out who rented it," Burke instructed. "In the meantime, Phin, tell them what you found out about the van in Cora's driveway."

Phin wished he didn't have to, because it wasn't good. "I got camera footage from one of your neighbors. The van that parked here on Friday wasn't the same one that was parked in front of Medford Hughes's house. That one was a white panel van. The one in your driveway was a white minivan, also a rental. The driver was in your house for two hours. A ball cap hid his face."

"Bold," Val murmured.

Cora frowned. "He knew I wasn't home."

Because he'd bugged her purse.

Phin hesitated, hating to have to tell her this part. "We saw the same van in your driveway two other times, both during the day. Each time a man got out, a cap hiding his face, stayed in your house for between one and two hours, then left. Twice he came at night and he walked up to your house and went through your back gate. The first time was the day after your father's body was identified. He stayed less than five minutes that first time. That was probably when he bugged your purse."

Cora shuddered, her face growing pale. "He was here five times. Twice when I was asleep."

Phin's arm tightened and she leaned into him. "He won't get in again," he vowed. Even if he had to camp out in her house every night. She would be safe.

Her hands trembled as she wrapped them around the cup of hot tea. "I know," she whispered so faintly that he almost didn't hear it.

"We'll keep you safe, Cora," Burke assured.

"I know," she said again, then lifted her chin. "I can't do anything about those break-ins now. I can only move forward. Is there any good news? Please say yes."

Phin squeezed her hand, proud of her. She was tough. He hoped she'd find the next bit to be good news, but he didn't think she would. "Antoine found out about Twin Falls."

Antoine turned one of his three laptops around so that Cora could see the screen. "This is Alice VanPatten. She was Alice Bergeron when she lived near Twin Falls, Idaho."

"The wife of the man who was killed?" she asked. "Her husband's name was Jarred Bergeron. Did Alice remarry?"

"She did, ten years ago," Antoine said. "But she relocated to Baton Rouge only a few months after her husband was killed."

"Which was two weeks before my father died." Cora frowned. "She moved just an hour from New Orleans? That doesn't sound like a coincidence, even though he was dead by then."

Antoine shrugged. "I don't think it is a coincidence, but I can't explain it yet. For a while, she was a suspect in her husband's death."

Val took the seat across the table, cradling her own cup of tea. "I thought the ME ruled it an accidental death. A hunting accident."

"At first, they did," Antoine said. "Then Alice was under suspicion because she'd filed a police report claiming domestic abuse six months before he died. She claimed she'd left him, but he'd come to her parents' house to bring her home, threatening to kill them if she didn't comply."

"And then he's dead," Cora murmured. "Why didn't they suspect her parents?"

Antoine pulled his computer so that his screen faced him again. "They had an unshakable alibi—they were in church. Alice also had an unshakable alibi. She was seeing a man in a hotel room in Salt Lake City, two hundred miles away. The hotel confirmed that she'd been seen going up the elevator."

Cora straightened beneath Phin's arm, but she didn't move away. "Was the man's name Jack Elliot?"

Antoine shook his head. "John Winslow."

Cora covered her mouth with her hand, a tiny whimper escaping her. Phin thought this might be a bigger blow than an intruder invading her home.

"He used my mom's last name," she whispered. "Were he and Alice having an affair?"

"I don't know," Antoine said compassionately. "But soon after she was cleared, she sold the property in Idaho and moved to Baton Rouge. I found her address. She's an interior decorator. She married Richard VanPatten ten years ago. They have a four-year-old son."

Cora was silent for a long, long moment. Then she lifted her chin once again. "I want to meet her. I want to find out if my father killed her husband. And why."

"We figured you would," Burke said. "Val's going with you as your bodyguard. Antoine and I will stay here and keep searching the attic for anything your father or mother stored that's pertinent. Phin, you're on window security."

Cora turned to Antoine. "Have you reviewed all of the disks you found?"

Antoine nodded. "I did. There's nothing on them that looks out of place."

"And nothing that matches any of the receipts Molly

logged last night," Burke added. "She entered all of them into that spreadsheet of hers. None of the names, places, or dates lined up with his client files. Based on what your mother copied from your father's computer, all of his clients were in New Orleans."

Cora's jaw grew taut. "So he was either having affairs or doing something that got him killed. Or both, I suppose."

"Or both," Burke agreed. "I say we ask Alice."

Cora tilted her head back to look at Phin, her eyes filled with exhaustion and pain. "Can you come, too?"

Yes. But he shouldn't. "I need to fix your window locks."

Cora's lips quivered before she pressed them together. "Okay. I understand."

"But I can do that when we get back," Phin said, hating that he'd upset her. "It might mean me working into the evening, late. Is that okay with you, Burke?"

Burke frowned. "I suppose so, but . . . why, Cora, if you don't mind my asking?"

Cora grew still, her composure morphing from tired and stressed to something almost regal. She looked polished, like she was heiress to this house and all it contained.

She looked like the portrait of her grandmother hanging in her living room.

"Because I've slept only three hours in the past two days and that was when Phin was in my house. No offense to Molly, but I didn't sleep a wink last night. I'm hoping to get some rest in the car on the way to Baton Rouge. I'd be most obliged if you'd allow him to accompany me."

Phin sat up a little straighter. He might have pulled her a little closer. And she might have leaned into him a little more. If he did nothing else, he'd make sure Cora got some rest.

Val hid her smile behind a cup of tea. "Let him join us, Burke. It's good training. Phin's always got my back. Plus, Cora feels safe with him."

Burke shrugged. "Okay, I guess. I can work on the windows."

Cora gaped at him. "You're going to put locks on my windows?"

Burke looked amused. "I can do handyman stuff, too, Cora."

"But don't you have work at your office?"

Burke's amusement faded. "The cops were going to release the crime scene this morning, but then Medford Hughes was killed with my laptops in the back seat of his car. They're holding the office closed a little longer. I've got a few bodyguards out in the field and they'll stay on their current assignments. I can work from here if I need to. And don't worry—I can work on the windows as well as Phin can."

Phin knew that was true. Burke was good at fixing things but had hired Phin to do the maintenance on the office and his house. Phin wasn't sure if it was to give him work or because Burke simply wanted to relax on his time off.

Probably a bit of both.

"We need to stop and see Joy on the way," Phin said.

Val nodded. "You betcha. Antoine, send me the file on Alice VanPatten, along with her current address. We'll say hi to Joy and then we'll hit the road."

Tulane Medical Center, New Orleans, Louisiana
WEDNESDAY, DECEMBER 14, 10:00 A.M.

Phin paused in the sterile hallway, bracing himself to walk into Joy's hospital room.

He'd been in the hospital too many times himself, and he had the scars to prove it. Memories began to rise from where he'd stuffed them down deep.

A heavy weight against his leg had him reaching his fingers into SodaPop's coat. God, was he lucky. Delores had cared enough about him to train this amazing dog especially for him.

The realization calmed him enough that he was able to take a breath, then another. The tightness in his chest receded just enough for him to take the next step.

But pressure tightened on his other hand, halting him once again. He looked down to see Cora's hand clutching his. She wasn't moving. In fact, when he tugged her forward, she tugged back, resisting. Slowly he lifted his gaze to hers and was rocked.

She was afraid, but there was something else in her brandy-colored eyes.

Guilt.

It took him a second to process the reason behind it, but then he squeezed her hand back.

"She told you to run."

Cora stared at Joy's open door. "I should have stayed."

"You might be dead now." And he couldn't stand the thought of that.

"Joy almost was," she whispered. "You saved her."

"Nah, it was the EMTs," he said, and she looked up at him sharply.

"Stop that," she snapped. "You stop that right now. You saved her life, Phin. Don't minimize who you are and what you mean to Joy and all the rest of them."

Phin blinked. "I don't do that."

Val snorted from behind them, startling him. He'd forgotten she was there.

"Yeah, you do," Val drawled, "and it drives me nuts. Come on, children. We shouldn't be standing in the hallway. We're blocking the road."

He tugged Cora toward the door. "Val's right. Let's do this. For Joy."

Cora squared her shoulders, but the guilt was still there in her eyes. She fixed her lips in a smile that wouldn't fool anyone who truly knew her.

Like Joy, who'd known Cora since she was a child.

The hospital room was less intense than Phin had expected. Not as many beeping instruments. And the room was filled with flowers and balloons.

Louisa stood when they entered, a relieved smile breaking over her face. "Oh, thank goodness. Mama's been going on about how you needed to get your butts in here."

"I said asses, not butts," Joy said from the bed. Her voice was weak, but she was alive and Phin felt relief crash over him in a wave.

He was suddenly aware that he'd been expecting her to look much worse than she did. She was staring at him with one eyebrow raised, demanding he come closer.

A smile tilted his lips as he obeyed the command, stopping at the foot of her bed. "Hi, Joy."

Joy's stare remained sharp as a blade. "'*Hi, Joy,*' he says, like he hasn't been gone for six weeks. Get in here, Phin. Both of you." Her gaze dropped to their joined hands. "How long was I asleep, LouLou?"

Louisa was grinning. "Less than a day, Mama."

"That's what I thought. You move fast, boy." She patted the side of her bed. "Cora Jane Winslow, get over here. Stop hiding behind Phin."

Cora had indeed retreated behind his back. "She feels guilty for leaving you," he said.

Joy huffed. "I figured that out myself. Don't make me get out of this bed, Cora Jane."

Cora eased forward, glaring at Phin. "Asshole," she muttered.

He chuckled, not offended in the least. In fact, he felt calmer than he had in a very long time. "I've been called worse."

Cora moved to the chair next to Joy's bed. "I should have stayed with you," she said stubbornly.

Joy's eyes softened. "No, you did what I told you to do."

Cora shook her head, sending her red curls bouncing in every which direction. "If I'd stayed, you might not have been shot."

"I don't think he meant to shoot me. Plus, I did shoot him first." Joy said this so proudly that Phin laughed.

Cora snickered. "You're a badass, Joy."

"And don't you forget it," Joy said tartly, then reached for Cora's hand. "I was scared for you."

Cora's shoulders hunched. "I was scared for you, too."

"He wanted you. Wanted your records. He said he was 'looking for the Winslow woman.' I knew you had to run. He meant business. I'll remember his voice for a long, long time."

Cora tilted her head. "If we find him, will you be able to ID his voice?"

Joy nodded, her eyes narrowing. "You bet your ass I will. And don't say *if*. Say *when*, because Burke will figure this out. Where did you go when you *very wisely* obeyed me and ran for your life?"

"Through the Quarter. I went to Tandy's gallery first, but she wasn't there. She called me and told me you'd been shot. I went straight to the police station from there. They took my statement and sent me on my way."

"They gave you no protection," Joy said, tutting. "Shameful. But you seem to have found some protection on your own." She leaned to look around Cora. "Hey, Val."

Val waved from where she leaned against the wall. "Hey, Joy. I tried to bring you coffee and cupcakes, but Louisa told me no."

Louisa gasped. "I did not. You're trying to make trouble for me."

Val looked pleased with herself when Joy laughed, a dry raspy sound. "You girls," Joy said fondly. Then she sobered. "Tell me what's happening, Cora Jane."

Cora looked over her shoulder at Louisa, her expression clearly asking for permission.

Louisa shrugged. "You might as well tell her everything. Besides, I want to know, too. So will Nala. So dish, girl."

Cora did, telling Joy about the files and receipts they'd

found in the attic, the death of the man found with the laptops, and the woman they were going to see outside Baton Rouge. The woman who might have been having an affair with her father. Whose husband Cora's father might have killed.

Joy sank back into the bed. "Mercy. That escalated fast."

Cora's laugh sounded startled. "Actually, I think it started with a bang," she said wryly.

Joy grimaced. "Don't make me laugh, girl. It hurts."

Cora instantly sobered. "I'm sorry."

"Hush. We knew this had to do with your daddy. It's still hard to learn the truth, sometimes. The one truth that isn't hard to learn is that Phin Bishop is a good man. You'll be safe with him, no matter what he thinks of himself."

"I think I figured that out myself," Cora said softly.

"Because you've always been smart." Joy looked up, met Phin's eyes. "Your turn, Phineas Butler Bishop."

Phin winced at being full-named, even as he shifted foot to foot over her praise. "I can't be in trouble, Joy. I saved your life."

Joy's lips twitched. "Yes, you did, but you can still be in trouble. Come here. Let me look at you."

Phin obeyed, sitting on the other side of the bed and clutching the bed rail with both hands. He wanted to say something, but his voice had deserted him.

Joy filled in the silence, her voice going a little hoarse, emotion in her dark eyes. "Thank you, Phin. You came home at exactly the right time. My kids told me what you did for me. How you saved me."

"My friend Stone helped." Phin's mind replayed the memories of her blood on his hands, and his chest tightened again. As was becoming her habit, SodaPop pressed close, leaning against his leg. He sucked in a lungful of air, his nose burning at the disinfectant smell. "You stopped breathing."

SodaPop licked his hand just as Joy snapped, "Phin."

She's not dead. She's not bleeding.

She's alive. You saved her life.

When he felt stable, he met Joy's concerned brown eyes. "I'm okay."

"I can see that." She nodded toward SodaPop. "Who is this pretty one?"

"SodaPop. She's mine. A service dog. For PTSD," he added haltingly and wondered how long it would take before he admitted that freely, without feeling ashamed.

"I wish I'd thought of that," Joy said. "Who did?"

"My friend Stone's wife. Delores trains dogs. She started training SodaPop for me over a year ago."

Joy nodded. "That's where you go when you leave."

Shame crept up his throat. Then he startled when Joy flicked his hand with her fingernail. "Ow, Joy."

"You always come back, Phin. We know that you'll *always* come back. I'm just glad you've had a safe place to land all this time. Tell me about them."

So he did, talking about how Stone and Delores had opened their home. He talked about all of Delores's dogs. And about how he was going back home at Christmas.

All the while, he was aware that Cora hung on every word. He wasn't sure if this pleased him or not, because now she knew how fucked-up he really was.

He couldn't fix that. Not today, anyway.

So he told Joy about his family. His mother, the retired English teacher. His father, the captain in Cincinnati PD. His twin, Scarlett, who had a smart mouth and a tender heart, who'd adopted a three-legged bulldog and spoiled him rotten. He talked about his brothers and his uncle, the priest, softening his voice as Joy's eyes began to blink, her eyelids heavy.

"You're going to love them," he ended in a whisper, smiling when Joy let out a most unladylike snore. Not that he'd ever tell her that she'd done such a thing.

"You think they'll visit New Orleans?" Cora asked softly.

He met her gaze over Joy's bed. "I hope so. I hope they don't turn me away."

It was one of his deepest fears.

"I hope they don't, too. But it's hard to believe they could, based on how you've described them."

She had questions, Phin could tell. Like *Why have you avoided your family all this time when they're wonderful?* But he was grateful that she didn't ask him anything more.

Cora rose stiffly and he saw her exhaustion. The dark circles under her eyes had grown deeper and darker. She'd sleep in the car on the way to Baton Rouge if he had to sing her a lullaby himself.

Phin met her at the end of Joy's bed, slipping his arm around her shoulders, gratified when she leaned against him. Why she'd latched onto him was still a mystery. He wasn't an investigator. He wasn't a bodyguard. He wasn't much of a friend or someone who could be depended on in an emergency.

But he wanted to be. He wanted it so badly he could taste it.

"Come on," he murmured. "You need to rest."

Val gave him a nod as she followed them out to Burke's company SUV. It was as bulletproof as a vehicle could be, and Phin felt safer having Cora in it.

"You drive?" he asked Val. "And I'll sit in back with her."

SodaPop sat on the floor, curled around his feet, while Cora leaned against him. Before they got on I-10 toward Baton Rouge, Cora was asleep.

Baton Rouge, Louisiana
WEDNESDAY, DECEMBER 14, 12:30 P.M.

Alice VanPatten's house was tucked behind some trees at the end of a cul-de-sac. Cora stared at it numbly, not sure what she should be feeling.

"Cora?" Val prompted from the driver's seat. "You okay?"

"I don't know," Cora admitted. "Logically, I should be angry at this woman for having an affair with my father. But all I feel is . . . nothing."

Beside her in the back seat, Phin squeezed her hand. "Let's go ask her what happened. Or at least what she knows. Then you can decide what you feel."

Val turned in her seat to meet Cora's eyes directly. "And if you zone out and can't listen, Phin and I will be there. Sometimes hearing things that you never expected to hear—and that are diametrically opposed to what you want to believe—can send your brain into a kind of stasis. If that happens, you're far from alone. I'm even going to record the conversation on my phone."

"And if you don't want to go in, I'll go in and ask," Phin offered. "Val can stay out here and keep you safe."

Touched, Cora patted his hand. "Thank you, but I want to meet her. I want to know why she moved from Idaho to Baton Rouge. I want to know what my father actually did."

"Then let's get this done," Val said, getting out of the SUV and coming around to the back to let Cora out.

Phin got out of his side, then hesitated. "What about SodaPop?"

Val shrugged. "Bring her. If they don't allow a dog, she can wait in the SUV. It's cool enough that she'll be fine for a little while."

"Okay." Phin clucked to SodaPop, who jumped out and fell into line beside him.

"Thank you," Cora murmured as they walked to Alice's front door. "I got some sleep. You make a good pillow, Phin."

His smile warmed her, inside and out. "All part of the Broussard service."

Still, Cora was grateful. She wasn't sure what it was about this man that made her feel safe enough to sleep, and for now she wasn't going to question it. She'd accept it until her life calmed enough for her to think clearly.

For now, she was taking one step at a time. Literally.

Val climbed the stairs first, waiting until Cora and Phin were on the porch before knocking. For at least a minute, no one answered. There were no voices to be heard.

Then, finally, the door opened, revealing a man who appeared to be in his fifties. He looked tense and wore no smile. "Yes?"

Cora took a deep breath. "We're here to talk to Mrs. VanPatten, if she's available. My name is Cora Winslow. I think your wife knew my father. I learned recently that he died twenty-three years ago. I'm hoping to learn something about him."

The man's face remained impassive, except for his left eye, which twitched. "What was your father's name?"

Cora didn't take her eyes off the man's face. "Jack Elliot."

His shoulders sagged. "I thought so." He opened the door wider. "Please, come in."

Cora exchanged glances with Val and Phin. Both of them looked as puzzled as she felt. But then Phin's hand caught hers and held it.

"We can leave at any time," he whispered. "Just say the word."

Cora squeezed his hand. "Thank you."

"May we bring the dog?" Phin asked. "She's my service dog."

Nodding silently, the man led them into the living room, where a woman sat in the corner of a sofa, her hands folded in her lap.

Cora's breath hitched. Alice Bergeron VanPatten.

Slowly Alice rose to greet them, her expression one of weary resignation. "Are you police?"

Cora blinked. "No. I'm a librarian. My friends Val and Phin are private investigators. Do you need the police?"

Alice laughed, but it wasn't a happy sound. "Oh no. Certainly not. Please sit down. I imagine you have questions, but I have one of my own first." She waited until Cora and Phin were seated on a love seat, SodaPop at Phin's feet. Val chose to remain standing directly behind Cora. The man sat beside Alice on the sofa and they held hands, their grips white-knuckled.

What had Cora's father done? Did the man holding Alice's hand know that she'd had an affair with a married man? Did he know that Alice's first husband had been murdered?

Maybe so. He looked stricken. And terrified.

Join the club, sir.

"I'm Cora."

Alice nodded, her smile faint. "I know. You look like your mother."

Cora flinched. That was not what she'd expected Alice to say. "You knew my mother?"

"Not personally, no. Your father talked about her. Once he showed me a photo. It was your mother with you and your brother."

Cora was unsure of what to say. "My father showed you a photo of my mother?"

Alice nodded. "He loved her very much."

Cora blinked again. "Were you . . . involved with my father?"

Alice's weary resignation gave way to what looked like guilt. "Yes, but not in the way you're assuming. Before I tell you the story, I'd like to know how you found me."

"We were searching my father's records and found a receipt from a gun store in Twin Falls the year he died. He bought .30-30 ammo. I googled those things and came up with the news story of the death of your husband. My PIs checked you out and saw that you'd moved here to Baton Rouge and remarried."

"I'm Richard VanPatten," the man said. "Alice saw the news report two weeks ago of your father's body being identified. She recognized his picture right away. She's been a nervous wreck ever since."

"And grieving," Alice murmured. "I'm so sorry for your loss, Cora. I didn't know he'd been killed before two weeks ago."

"Me either," Cora said. "Someone's been sending me letters signed by my father for the last twenty-three years."

Alice gasped and Richard's face went slack with shock. "What?" they said together.

"That's why Cora hired us," Val said. "Someone's been trying to get to her. She's had several break-ins at her house and she was chased through New Orleans yesterday."

"We're not here to get you into trouble," Phin added. "Cora needs information. We need to protect her. How did you know Jack Elliot?"

"I didn't know that was his name," Alice said quietly. "He said he was John Robertson. My parents hired him to help me."

Cora's heart didn't know whether to settle or race. John Robertson. He'd used John Winslow when he'd stayed with this woman at a hotel. He'd used her brother's name as another alias. "Given your history of abuse, I'm guessing why your parents hired my father. But why *my* father? Why hire my father to kill your husband?"

Alice shook her head. "No. My parents hired an eraser, not an assassin."

Cora frowned. "An eraser? What's that?"

Phin stiffened beside her. "An eraser, like in the Schwarzenegger movie?"

Alice nodded once. "Yes."

Cora looked up at Phin. "What's an eraser? It sounds like an assassin."

He grimaced. "Sometimes it is. Depends on the case. I take it that Cora's father did not work for the government."

"No," Alice said. "He most certainly did not. He was an independent."

Cora was confused. "Stop. Tell me what an eraser does."

Phin gripped her hand a little tighter. "Think witness protection without all the government's procedures."

It took Cora's brain a few moments to process that. When it clicked, she stared at Alice. "Your parents hired my father to find you a new identity? A new life away from your abusive husband?"

"Yes. And he'd done that, but things went south at the last minute." Alice sighed. "Jarred Bergeron was a brute. He'd beat me until I couldn't move. He isolated me from my family. He made me believe that my parents didn't care about me, that I was stuck with him. We lived several miles from town on a ranch, and we were alone out there except for a few ranch hands. Most of them didn't want to get involved in the boss's business—or they thought his young wife needed to be taught her place. But one of the ranch hands felt sorry for me. He told my parents what was happening. One day when Jarred was in town buying supplies, my parents showed up and took me home, to their house where I'd grown up."

"But Jarred came after her," Richard said, anger in his voice. "Threatened to kill her whole family, including her brothers and sisters. The youngest was only ten. So she went home with him."

"And he punished you," Cora said quietly.

Alice nodded. "It was . . . really bad. And then my parents' house caught on fire. They got everyone out, but it was close. Jarred laughed. Said he hoped they got the message to stay out of our lives. I considered suicide, but I couldn't make myself do it."

"I'm glad you couldn't," Richard said gruffly.

Alice leaned against his shoulder. "Me too. Now. Then, I was desperate to get out."

"And law enforcement was no help?" Cora guessed.

Alice's mouth twisted bitterly. "Jarred was from a wealthy family. He could get away with anything. And then one day, when Jarred was in town, this man knocked on the door. It was your father. He claimed to be doing a political poll. I was instantly suspicious until he surreptitiously showed me the letter from my parents as he was going on about the candidate up for reelection. The letter said that I was to listen to this man. He'd get me out and I'd get a new ID. A new life. I'd move east. So I listened to him."

"No affair?" Cora asked, hopeful.

"No affair. Your dad's plan was simple. I was to pack up one backpack's worth of things I'd need and leave the pack in the woods behind our house. He gave me some powder to put into Jarred's coffee so that he'd go to sleep and I could sneak out. Then I was to wait for your father in the woods."

"But something went wrong?" Phin asked.

Alice sighed. "Yes. Somebody snitched. Probably one of the ranch hands. After my parents' attempt to take me home with them, Jarred had me watched. I don't think that Jarred knew your father was trying to help me escape. I think he honestly thought I was cheating on him. He beat me so badly that I was unconscious. I missed the pickup, and your father came knocking again the first time that Jarred left the property, a few days later. He took one look at my face and told me to come *now*. Not to worry about a backpack. He had me lie down in the back of his car and he drove. We stopped at the gun store on the way out of town and he bought the ammo. He already had a rifle. Then he stopped at a drugstore and bought bandages. Unfortunately, he didn't see Jarred lurking."

"Your husband was following you?" Cora guessed.

"He was. Your dad drove me to a hunting cabin he'd rented. He told me stories about Louisiana, about you and your brother, Cora. About your mother. He kept talking to keep me relaxed because I was still in bad shape. He hadn't even gotten the car stopped in front of the cabin when Jarred started shooting, but your dad was so calm. He stopped the car, took that rifle, told me to keep my head down, and fired one shot. Jarred was dead."

"Which put Alice in a bad place," Richard said. "If she disappeared then, she'd be suspected for his murder. Her face would be everywhere and cops would be looking for her. Starting over would have been even harder."

"So your father created an alibi for me. Jarred had already told everyone that I was cheating on him. So your father just used that. He took me to a tiny little roadside motel outside Salt Lake City and left for a few hours. When he came back, I had an alibi. I was supposedly with a man in a fancy hotel in downtown Salt Lake. I think our local sheriff doubted the story because I was so beaten up, but the alibi was so solid, he didn't have much of a choice. Jarred's family insisted I'd done it, but the hotel manager in Salt Lake City swore I was there. I don't know how your father got him to swear that I was there. I was cleared, which meant I could leave Idaho as a free woman—with an inheritance. I got the ranch and everything that went with it, much to the consternation of Jarred's family. Everyone thought I was a whore, but I didn't care. I just wanted out. I sold the ranch and moved east."

"You and your parents came to Baton Rouge," Phin said. "Why here?"

Alice smiled genuinely for the first time. "Cora's father made Louisiana sound so wonderful. We stayed in that roadside hotel overnight, so that I was recovered enough to walk unassisted the next day. He just kept talking to me. That's when he showed me the photo of his family. He called your mother once. I could hear how much he loved her. He told her he was in Baton Rouge with a client, and that sounded like a nice place. I didn't know he was from New Orleans, but I knew it was somewhere in the South because of his accent. I honestly just liked the sound of Baton Rouge. My parents had used all the money they got from the insurance on their house that burned down to pay for your father to hide me, but by then I had the money from the ranch, so we got a place together. I changed my name from Bergeron to my maiden name, which was Smith. I didn't change it again until I married Richard." She shrugged. "That's all."

That's all? Cora's mind was spinning. "I don't even know what to ask."

"I do," Phin said. "What about Jarred's parents? You said they were influential. Jack Elliot was killed only two weeks after he killed your husband. Could they have found out about what Jack did and killed him?"

Cora sucked in a breath. *Good question.*

Alice flinched. "I never considered that. I didn't know he was dead until two weeks ago. I suppose it's possible, but I don't know how you'd find out. They both died ten years ago. But they left me alone after I moved and they didn't fight my inheriting everything from Jarred. They tried to, because they said I was cheating on their son, but your father had given me something else—photos of my injuries. I hadn't had any of those before. Every time I went to the hospital, any records were somehow 'lost.' But your father gave me photos from when he'd rescued me. I showed them to his parents and said that I'd go public. That their reputation would be ruined. I'd already reported Jarred to the local police and nothing had happened, but I'd go to a big newspaper and tell them. Jarred's folks were furious, but their reputation was important to them, so they let me go. I told them that if anyone in my new town got wind of who I'd been in Idaho, I'd bring out those photos. Your father had told me to put them in a safe-deposit box, which I did. He was a good man, your father. I'm alive today because of him. I'm so sorry about what happened to him."

Phin nodded. "Mrs. VanPatten, how did your parents find out about Cora's father to begin with? It's not like he would have advertised in the newspaper."

Another good question, Cora thought, glad that she'd asked Phin to come along.

"I don't know," Alice said. "I asked once, and my father changed the subject."

"Does he still live nearby?" Cora asked.

Alice shook her head. "He died five years ago. Mom's gone, too. I only asked him that one time. I realized that if anyone found out what he'd done, he could be in a lot of trouble. He'd risked a lot for me. So I . . . let it go."

Cora understood but wished Alice had pushed a little harder for the truth. "Thank you for telling me. I wasn't prepared to learn that my father had this other life, but at least he was helping people who needed it." A sliver of doubt entered her mind. "He did just help people who needed it, didn't he?"

"I don't know," Alice said honestly. "He didn't seem like he was the kind of man to do illegal things for bad people, but I don't know."

"Did your father leave any papers behind?" Phin pressed. "Anything we can use to learn more about what Cora's father was doing? It's likely that if he offered this same service to other people, someone killed him for it. Ever since his body was discovered, Cora hasn't been safe."

Alice shook her head. "Richard and I wondered if my father left any explanations when he died. We've been through all the papers he left behind at least twice, and we've found nothing. My father was big on shredding and burning sensitive documents."

"What did your father do for a living?"

"He was a lawyer. He practiced family law until the day he died. He believed in the law until it didn't protect me. He was jaded after that. He did a lot of pro bono work for women who'd been in my shoes."

Cora managed a smile. "It was worth a try."

"Did Cora's father work alone?" Phin asked. "Did your parents maybe deal with someone other than Cora's father? It seems like a lot of details for one man to manage."

Another good question yet again. The government had

an entire division of people creating new identities for the witnesses they protected.

"I don't know," Alice said. "Like I said, I only asked my father about it once and he wouldn't talk to me about it. I only interacted with the man I knew as John Robertson." She studied Cora for a long moment. "Richard and I were finally blessed with a son. We named him John Robert VanPatten, after your father."

Cora's breath hitched. "What?" she tried to ask, but the word wouldn't come out.

Alice frowned. "I'm sorry. I know that John Robertson wasn't your father's real name, but it's the name I've known him by all these years."

"Cora's brother was John Robert," Phin explained when Cora could not. "He died from cancer a year ago."

"Oh," Alice breathed. "I'm so sorry, Cora. I didn't mean to hurt you."

"No, it's okay." She breathed slowly because she felt like she was about to hyperventilate. Phin let go of her hand and put his arm around her shoulders.

Grounding me. "I think," she finally said, "that my father would have been very happy to hear that. And I know that John Robert would have. He was involved in charities supporting victims of domestic violence. It's like his memory will go on."

Alice smiled. "That's lovely."

Phin cleared his throat. "I'm sorry to ask this, but one more question. When did you two meet? And when did Richard learn about your background?"

Cora's mind took a minute to parse the meaning behind Phin's question, but when it did, her eyes widened. Could Richard have been involved somehow? It didn't seem possible.

Richard VanPatten didn't seem offended. "Alice is an interior decorator. I bought this house twelve years ago and hired her to redecorate. She moved in a year later and we were married the year after that. She told me all about her past and the man she knew as John Robertson before we got married." He swallowed. "I saw the photos of what her husband did to her. I've thanked God for your father every day since. If it hadn't been for him, I wouldn't have Alice in my life. I wouldn't have a son."

"Thank you," Phin said, apology in his voice. "I'm sorry that I had to ask." He twisted around to look up at Val. "Any other questions?"

"No. You asked the ones I had. You ready to go, Cora?"

"I am. Thank you, Alice," she said sincerely. "Now we know what to look for."

Val got them out to the car and Cora slumped into the back seat, exhausted once again.

"That was not what I was expecting," she said once Val had them back on the road. Phin sat beside her, SodaPop at his feet. "Thank you both for coming with me. For asking the questions I wouldn't have thought to ask."

"Phin asked all of the good questions," Val said. "Nicely done, Phin."

Phin's cheeks became flushed. "Thank you," he mumbled.

Val laughed. "You just took a compliment without making noise about how it 'wasn't anything special.' Progress. I'm going to call Burke." She called her boss, talking through her earpiece as she drove.

Cora leaned her head back and closed her eyes, trying to ignore Val's rehash of what they'd just learned. "She's right. You were really good, Phin. Thank you."

He put his arm around her shoulders. "You're welcome. Get some more sleep. I'll wake you when we get back to New Orleans."

So she leaned into his shoulder and let herself drift off to sleep, knowing down deep that this man would keep her safe.

11

WEDNESDAY, DECEMBER 14, 1:10 P.M.

SAGE WAITED UNTIL the big black SUV carrying Cora Winslow had driven past before pulling onto the road, keeping a safe distance behind them. He wasn't taking any more risks, especially after he'd been confronted by that old-lady librarian that morning.

The old woman had rattled him, which was embarrassing. He should have said he was waiting to research something, but did he? Noooo. He'd mentioned Cora Winslow. Said he had a date with her.

She'd claimed that Cora wasn't coming into work that day, so he'd gone back to the Winslow house and followed Cora back to the library from there. But then the tall blond bodyguard had spied him tailing them once they'd departed, losing him in a move that had been pretty damn impressive.

And now things were starting to get interesting. Why had Cora Winslow come all the way to Baton Rouge?

And who the hell was Alice VanPatten? He'd searched online while Cora had been inside the VanPatten home, finding that Alice was an interior designer and wife to Richard. But there was no meaningful connection to Cora. Not yet, anyway.

He wondered if his grandfather knew.

He wondered what he'd be revealing if he asked, although it didn't really matter. Sage would have the upper hand in any conversation with his grandfather from here on out.

At least I didn't intend to shoot Joy Thomas. It really had been an accident.

His grandfather, however, had fully intended to kill Medford Hughes. He'd gone into his secret safe in the study, taken two guns, and had returned hours later with only one gun.

The news of Medford's death had already hit the news by then. Dead by a bullet to the head. It wasn't hard to add two and two and get four. But Sage had already figured it out by the time the news had broken.

He'd followed Burke Broussard and two of his men— and a dog—from Cora Winslow's house to Medford's. He'd parked a block away and used his long-range microphone to eavesdrop.

And had been stunned to learn that Medford was dead in his car. The guns his grandfather had removed from his safe had then made sense.

Mind. Blown. No pun intended.

That Alan had killed Medford Hughes had been a shock. His grandfather had not, to Sage's knowledge, ever killed someone. Like, ever.

Medford must have figured out that the laptops were stolen. Well, Medford had to have known that *all* the laptops that he was asked to break into were stolen. He just didn't know where all the prior laptops had come from.

Sage thought about the Broussard laptops with a smirk. More likely than not, Medford had been tipped off by the Broussard logo on the laptop's lid. His grandfather might not have been able to see that level of detail, but Medford would have.

Sage hadn't been one hundred percent sure that Alan

had pulled the trigger, until he'd learned that the stolen Broussard laptops had been found in the back seat of Medford's car.

That tidbit had come courtesy of the cops, who were talking about the crime scene loudly enough to wake the dead. Sage had barely needed the long-range microphone to hear every word they said.

Medford was supposed to look like he'd shot himself in the head, but the cops didn't think that was the case. Medford's wife was dead, too. Alan had killed them both.

That was harsh.

The wife was an addict—drugs and gambling—but she hadn't deserved to die. Unless Medford had told her what he'd found, which was possible.

Sage still didn't know what his grandfather was up to, but he was going to find out. He dialed Alan's cell phone, smirking when the man answered.

"What?" Alan's voice was flat and angry.

Or maybe guilty. Sage guessed it depended on how many people his grandfather had killed over the years. What if Medford hadn't been Alan's first kill?

He wondered if Cora's father had been. But he still didn't know why.

Why was important.

"Who is Alice VanPatten?"

"Who?" Alan asked impatiently. "Don't waste my time, Sage."

Such a pompous bastard. "If I thought I was wasting your time, I wouldn't have called, Grandfather. A simple answer would be nice. Do you know who Alice VanPatten is with relation to Cora Winslow?"

There was a moment of silence, a long, long moment. "What are you talking about?" Alan asked, his voice now quiet.

And maybe a little scared.

The scared part pleased Sage greatly.

"Alice VanPatten lives in Baton Rouge with her husband. Cora Winslow just left here with her bodyguards. Broussard's people. They stayed about a half hour, and Cora looked shaken when she came out."

Another beat of silence, then all hell broke loose. "You've been following Cora Winslow?" his grandfather thundered. "I never directed you to do that."

This was good. Alan was getting hot and bothered. Which meant Sage had struck a nerve.

He feigned confusion. And guilt. "I'm sorry, Grandfather, but you actually did. At least I thought you did, which was why I followed her to Broussard's yesterday morning. Was I wrong?"

Alan huffed. "No, you're right. But we're done following her. Don't do that anymore. If her bodyguards see you . . ."

Sage wouldn't mention that he'd already been caught tailing her once that day. "You don't know who Alice VanPatten is?"

"I do not. And I'm ordering you to leave the woman alone."

Hold on. Hold the fuck on. Was that fear in Alan's voice?

Sage had obviously hit the jackpot. He just needed to figure out what the payoff was. "Cora or Alice VanPatten?"

"Both of them," Alan snapped. "Stay away from both of them. You will only do what I instruct you to do. You will not follow either of those women. You are hereby forbidden to do so."

Forbidden? Really?

Did his grandfather not know him at all?

Sage made his voice meek. "Of course. I promise."

"All right."

It was clear that Alan didn't believe his act, so Sage abandoned the fake meekness. "I heard that Medford Hughes died. It was on the news this morning."

"He killed himself," Alan said, with just the right amount of sorrow.

His grandfather was too good at this.

"His wife's dead, too."

"I know. I saw the same report. A murder-suicide. It's tragic, but I'm surprised Medford didn't snap before now. His wife's condition has been weighing heavy on his heart for a long time. Either way, it's a tragedy. I'm devastated for them both."

"Yes, it is." The news hadn't mentioned the Broussard laptops and Sage was tempted to throw that detail into the conversation just to rile the old man, but he held himself back. He'd wait until he figured out what Alan was up to. "I guess I'll head on back to New Orleans. Do you need me for anything more?"

"Not at this time. I'll call you if I need you again."

Alan ended the call and Sage checked the time on the dash clock of his rented Camry. He had time to get back to New Orleans before his grandfather finished at work. Sage's friendly guard would still be on duty. No one would tattle back to Alan that Sage had slipped into the neighborhood.

It was time to try to open that safe.

The Garden District, New Orleans, Louisiana
WEDNESDAY, DECEMBER 14, 3:00 P.M.

Burke, Molly, and Antoine were waiting for them at Cora's kitchen table, and it looked to Phin like they'd been busy. There was an easel and a whiteboard with markers and sticky notes.

Food, too, which was a welcome sight. Phin was starving.

Molly held up a hand when the three of them entered the kitchen. "The three dishes on the stovetop have no fish or shellfish. Those are Cora's. All the stuff on the countertops is for the rest of us."

Cora's smile was grateful, but shaky. "That was kind of you, Molly, but I'm not hungry just yet."

Phin made her a plate anyway. "Eat," he commanded quietly when he put the food in front of her. "You need to eat something."

Val sat beside Cora, her own plate piled high. "He's right. We need you brainy and alert. You've had a shock, and I know what that feels like. But you can do this, Cora."

Cora squared her shoulders. "Brainy and alert, huh?"

Val grinned. "Yep. Too bad about the fish allergy. It's supposed to be good for braininess."

"That's not a word," Antoine complained.

Molly held out her phone. "It is. It's right here in *Merriam-Webster*." She put the phone away and picked up a marker. "We made some notes while you were gone. Just the case basics."

Organizing what they did and didn't know was Molly's strength. Phin took the chair on the other side of Cora and studied the whiteboard. What they already knew was organized by category.

There were the highlights of the receipts Molly had logged in, the information Antoine had gathered on Jack Elliot's CPA practice, and everything they knew about Alice Bergeron VanPatten.

Then something new caught Phin's eye. "What are those numbers in the lower right corner?"

Antoine looked pleased with himself. "I found your father's old computer in the attic while you guys were driving to Baton Rouge. Your mother had buried the computer in a box with sheets and blankets, probably so that the machine didn't get damaged. I plugged it in and voilà." He gestured to the numbers Phin had asked about.

Cora slowly lowered her fork onto the plate, frowning at the whiteboard. "Are those bank account numbers?"

Antoine held out his hand and Burke slapped a twenty onto his palm with a sigh. "You were right," Burke grumbled.

"I bet Burke you'd recognize the numbers as bank accounts," Antoine explained, tucking the twenty-dollar bill into his shirt pocket. "But they're not just any numbers. They're Swiss bank account numbers."

Cora sat back in her chair, expression dazed. "What?"

Antoine nodded. "There was a Word document on the computer with your mother's name as the title. I thought it was odd, because the rest of the files were named in a consistent format—a subject with the date in European style. Day, month, year. This document is a poem, though." He passed the document to a frowning Cora.

"A poem?" She scanned the piece, her frown growing. "It's from 'The Courtship of Miles Standish' by Longfellow. John Alden loves Priscilla Mullins, but she's being courted by Standish. Why would he leave my mother this poem?"

Burke held out his palm and Antoine pouted as he gave Burke the same twenty he'd taken earlier. "Burke bet you'd recognize the poem. We had to google it. It's not the poem itself that's important. It's the way the paragraphs are lined up. They're grouped oddly, not like the way the original poem was written."

"It was a cipher," Molly explained. "The first letters of each paragraph make up the password to a section of the hard drive your father had partitioned off."

Cora rubbed her forehead. "Partitioned off?"

"A hard disk partition is a way to split up a hard drive," Phin told her. "You can store different documents in different sections and password-protect each section individually."

"Like my password-protected folders," Cora said.

Phin lifted a shoulder. "Kind of. But it also allows the use of different operating systems on the same computer. It's more efficient and makes the machine more productive."

Antoine's brows shot up. "Where did you pick that up?"

"A product of my misspent youth," Phin confessed. "I

partitioned the computer I had to share with my brothers and sister. It was the only way to have privacy. I . . ." He grimaced, feeling his cheeks heat in embarrassment. "I journaled."

Antoine coughed. "That's your deep secret? You were a journaler?"

Phin shook his head. "It's what I wrote in the journal. I had issues with anxiety and anger even before I went into the army. Journaling was the best way I knew to keep my head level. But it wasn't anything that I wanted my family to read. They would have worried about me more than they already did."

Cora reached under the table and squeezed his hand. "I journaled, too. It helped. I needed a therapist to recommend it, though, so you were ahead of me."

He wasn't sure what to say, so he squeezed her hand in return, touched at the support.

Antoine had sobered. "I get it. Well, the partitions your father created, Cora, are password-protected remarkably well. I can't get into any of the others. Only the one with the password from the poem. It has a document with the Swiss bank account numbers."

Cora blew out a breath. "If my mother saw this, I never knew about it. Maybe she did, but she was so hurt by his leaving that she didn't notice that it was a code. We might never know. Do you know which bank the account is in?"

Antoine nodded. "It's a Swiss bank, but they have a branch downtown. I can't do more without you. Well, not quickly."

"And because it's a Swiss account, it hasn't been closed out," she said. "About ten years ago, the Swiss set a sixty-two-year deadline for account owners to claim their funds. At least we have a little time," she added dryly.

"Librarian trivia?" Phin asked, earning him a real smile.

"Yeah. Another project I was helping a student to research." She drew a breath. "I suppose we have to assume that whatever money is in that account came from this eraser side business."

"That makes sense," Burke said gently. "Are you okay, Cora?"

"No, but I will be. Meeting Alice turned my brain inside out. Everything I'd thought about my father has been a lie. I thought he was alive. I thought he'd left us to start another family. I thought he was cheating with Alice." She looked down at her hand, still holding Phin's. "I almost wish all those things were true. Now I know my father was a paid killer. Or at least he killed once." She looked up and her eyes were filled with tears that hurt Phin's heart. "Did he just erase people like Alice, giving them a new start, or did he kill for greed and gain?"

Burke passed a box of tissues across the table. "We don't know, but we're hoping there's more on that old computer."

Cora dabbed at her eyes. "So what next? And I don't mean about the money. I don't care if it's one dollar or a million. I don't think I could take it, knowing it was blood money. Even if most of it wasn't for killing, at least some of it was."

"Jarred Bergeron might have been an anomaly," Burke said. "He *was* shooting at them at the time, after all."

"According to Alice," Cora said.

Burke nodded. "Yes, but you believed her, didn't you?"

Cora sighed. "I did."

Burke looked at Phin. "Did you?"

"I did," Phin said. "She had much more to gain by lying and telling us that she didn't know Jack Elliot. She had much more to gain by not letting her husband open the door."

"I agree," Val said. "I believed her, too."

"Well," Burke said, "hopefully, Jack kept files on his eraser clients like he did with his accounting clients. I think that's what's next, Cora. It makes the most sense that someone from that side of your father's life killed him. It could have been someone like Bergeron, trying to stop him from rescuing a client. It could also have been a client, especially if your father didn't deliver."

Phin had been turning the facts over in his mind the entire way back from Baton Rouge. "Burke, when did Cora and her mother get the first letters? How long after Jack disappeared?"

"Her mother received a letter the day after the foundation was poured," Burke said. He gave Cora a look of sympathy. "Antoine and I found the letters your mother kept. They were in another one of those boxes in the attic."

Cora went still. "I thought she burned them. I *saw* her burn them."

Burke shrugged. "She might have burned them later, but she kept the first few. I set them aside in case you want to look at them."

Cora's lips trembled. "I don't think so. What did he say to her? Or whoever wrote the letters?"

Burke hesitated. "He said that he was leaving. That he had a girlfriend in another state and that she was pregnant with his child. It was a very cold letter, not at all like the letters written to you."

"So she not only wouldn't look for him, but she wouldn't read any other letters he might have left for her," Cora said. "Like the poem on the computer."

"That's what we think," Burke agreed. "The signature on the letters looks like your father's, though."

"Can we get a handwriting analysis?" Val asked.

"I'm setting that up," Antoine answered. "But we should also find out if the Terrebonne Parish sheriff has done one."

Cora rubbed at her temple. "Detective Goddard said it was on his list. I think we need to talk to him again. He's the one leading the investigation in Houma."

"Tomorrow," Val said. "You need to recharge after today."

Cora's smile was wry. "Because you already tried to call him, but the operator told you that he was out on another case and would return your call as soon as he could."

Val rolled her eyes. "I did. I thought you were asleep when I did that."

Cora waffled her free hand. She still held Phin's hand with the other. "I was in and out. Mostly out, but I did hear that part." She looked up at Phin. "Why did you ask about the date of the letter?"

"Because only his killer would know exactly when he was killed. Only his killer would have known that he needed to act fast to keep your mother from looking for your father. I wonder if his killer knew about his Swiss bank account."

Molly got up and wrote the question on the whiteboard. "I've wondered that, too. What else are you wondering about, Phin?"

Phin took a moment to organize his thoughts. The partitioned hard drive just raised more questions. "Why would he keep the receipts where Cora's mother could find them? They had to have been in plain view, because she boxed them up."

Antoine nodded. "You mean, if he had the hard drive all partitioned up and secret, why leave the receipts out where she might start asking questions?"

"Exactly," Phin said. "I think it was so she'd see it as a clue and start digging in his computer, but she didn't because she was so hurt at being left for another woman. But he was worried that one day he might not come back. He'd nearly been killed by Jarred Bergeron just a few weeks before. A lot of us had letters ready for next of kin when we were deployed."

Phin remembered the one he'd written in excruciating detail. He'd told his family that he was sorry for so many things. Things they'd never been aware of. Things they hadn't caused, like his anger and anxiety. And that he'd felt like a stranger in his own home more often than he'd felt like a legitimate part of them. He was glad they'd never read those letters. He'd burned them when he'd been discharged.

And then you left them without a single word.

He'd make up for that. He would.

"Jack had to have been aware of how dangerous his work was," Phin went on. "So he left his wife clues in case he didn't come home. I wonder if his killer knew that, too."

Cora blinked. "You think that's what someone is looking for in my house? The clues he left behind?"

He met her startled gaze. "I don't know, but it's a possibility."

Molly wrote that on the whiteboard. "A decent possibility, actually."

"But why look for these clues now?" Cora asked. "Why not back then?"

"You don't know that they didn't," Phin said gently.

She sucked in a breath. "Oh. I never thought of that."

"That's what we're here for," Val said, patting her shoulder. "Clearly, it's come up again because the body was found and identified. It wasn't just that the body was found, because that was six weeks ago. The break-ins didn't start until *after* he was identified. That means that whoever put him in that foundation wasn't paying attention to the news saying someone had been found during demolition. They didn't focus on Cora until his photo was publicized, after the police had ID'd him."

Molly scribbled. "You're right, Val. Keep going, people. What else has you scratching your heads?"

"Why the building in Houma?" Phin asked. "That was a very specific time frame—after the pilings and subfoundation were readied and the next day when the foundation was poured. How did his killer know about that building?"

Molly kept writing. "His killer was in Houma or somehow connected to the construction. Good thought, Phin. What else?"

"Did he have a partner—or partners?" Phin asked.

"You asked that of Alice," Val observed.

Phin shrugged. "That's a lot of work for one person, gathering clients, vetting them to make sure they weren't undercover cops or Feds, because this was an indie operation. Someone had to be arranging the new identities and the logistics of the client's erasure. WITSEC has a whole division of people to manage this."

"Here's a question, Molly," Antoine said. "Who knew where Jack was the night he died? His client, clearly, but who else? Whoever the client was running from, like the case with Jarred Bergeron? Or maybe a partner?"

Molly wrote it down. "Cora, did you have any break-ins here in your house in the days after your father disappeared? Did any of his things go missing, like he might have tried to come back for them? If I'd killed someone and tried to make it seem like they'd left of their own volition, I'd want some of their things to disappear with them. Photos or trophies from high school, or even a passport. Your father's passport was in one of the boxes in the attic."

"My mother never told me anything like that, but I was only five and I think she was trying to shield me from the worst of it. I was devastated that he wasn't coming home. I didn't understand that he'd found another woman, but I heard my mother crying to my grandmother that he'd found another family. That I understood." She sighed. "I hated him so much."

"You should have, given what you knew," Phin said. "Don't beat yourself up."

She shrugged halfheartedly. "It's hard."

"Who might your mother have confided in back then?" Molly pressed.

Cora frowned. "My grandmother, but they're both gone and neither of them left diaries or journals. Mama depended a lot on Harry Fulton over the years, and he knew her from before I was born. He's my attorney."

"The one you were talking to yesterday?" Antoine asked. "Before we approached you?"

"Yes. He was at my christening. Harry's always been around. He might know something. I can call him and ask." She reached for her phone with her free hand, but Phin stopped her by grabbing that one as well.

"Wait. We need to check him out."

Cora's brows arched. "What? Why?"

"I didn't like how he treated you yesterday. Getting in a cab and leaving you there when you'd been chased through the city because he had *appointments*."

Cora stared up at him, outrage flashing in her eyes. "You think Harry's involved? *Harry?*" Her voice rose on each word. "That's not possible. It's just not." Then her outrage crumpled into something sad and vulnerable. "Is it?"

Phin wanted to lie to her. He wanted to tell her that her old friend was perfectly trustworthy, but he couldn't do that. Not yet, anyway.

"Maybe not," Phin said, not wanting to hurt her, but the man's attitude had rubbed him wrong. "Let's just be careful, okay? He was in your life at the time that the letters started coming."

Cora's mouth opened, then closed. Her whole body seemed to sag. "Okay," she whispered. "Dammit."

"Did he know what color dress you wore for that first Christmas?" Phin asked, thinking of the letter to Cora that he'd read. "After your father disappeared?"

Cora was quiet for a moment before she nodded. "Yes. He accompanied my mother and us to church that Sunday. He always accompanied us to church. I've wondered about that green dress for twenty-three years. I thought that maybe my father was close by at the time, that he'd come visit me or even come back to us. But he never did. Knowing they were written by someone else changes everything. But I still can't believe that Harry is involved. I just can't."

"Did Harry have feelings for your mom?" Phin asked gently.

Cora hesitated, then nodded miserably. "Mama always laughed it off, but my grandmother used to ask him when he was getting married and he'd say that my mother had stolen his heart so he had none to give another."

Molly sighed. "Okay. He goes up on the board." She wrote Harry's name and added *Motive: Jealousy?* "He's a possibility we need to rule out. This might have been a simple case of Harry wanting Jack out of the way."

Cora swallowed, dabbing at her eyes with the tissue that was already wet. Phin grabbed another from the box and she offered him a watery smile of thanks. "I still think you're wrong about Harry," she said stubbornly, but Phin could see that she doubted her own words. "But I know you have to check."

Phin hated having put that wounded look in her eyes. "What about Medford Hughes? Was he around twenty-three years ago?"

"No," Burke said. "He didn't move to New Orleans until ten years ago. That doesn't mean he wasn't involved. He could have been a partner. If Jack did have a partner, they didn't necessarily work in the same city. It might have been preferable if they didn't."

"But Medford didn't kill himself," Antoine said. "He was murdered. And he wasn't the one to steal the laptops—wrong body type. He was a network guy. Possibly brought in to find out what we'd stored on our hard drives. I think Medford was set up, personal opinion."

"I agree." Burke studied the board. "My brain keeps coming back to Phin's point about a partner. Erasing people is hard work. Let's assume Jack did have a partner. How did they meet? How did they communicate? What happened to the partner after Jack died?"

"Some of that might be behind the partitioned drive," Antoine said. "I'll make breaking into it my highest priority."

"Do we know any more details about the crime scene at the office?" Phin asked. "Did they find any blood traces?"

"No blood at our office," Antoine answered, "except for Joy's, of course. There are the bullets from Medford's crime scene. Cops won't disclose anything, but the bullets are currently in the ballistics lab, waiting their turn."

"How do you know if the police aren't disclosing it?" Cora asked, then shook her head. "Never mind. I don't want to know."

Antoine grinned. "You learn fast. I'll keep peeking in on them. When they have ballistics results, I'll pass them on."

Cora frowned. "Doesn't your brother—the police captain—get mad when you hack into the NOPD's files?"

Antoine shrugged. "Ask me no questions, I'll tell you no lies."

Burke shook his head. "So we're going to keep searching the attic, Cora. And Antoine's going to work on getting into the partitioned hard drive. I'll take the lead on checking out Harry Fulton. If he looks clean, we can approach him with questions about break-ins immediately after your father disappeared. Someone could have been looking for your father's records, either a partner or a client. We need to know who."

"And we need to know who wrote those letters to Cora," Phin said. "Can we get a sample of Harry's handwriting?"

Cora sighed wearily. "I have letters Harry's written over the years. A few cards he gave my mother. I'll find them."

Burke looked over to Phin. "I got a few of those locks put on the windows, but I'm not as fast as you are."

Phin was relieved. He needed something concrete to do. "I'm on it. Cora, you can sleep in your room. It was the first room I did this morning. I'll work on the rest right now."

Her smile was sweet. "Thank you."

Sage slipped into his grandfather's study, unseen by anyone in the household. His stepgrandmother was at her
weekly standing appointment at the hair salon. She'd gotten her hair done every Wednesday at three o'clock for as
long as he could remember.

She had to look nice for the church services. Camera-
ready, even. One never knew when the camera would pan
over the faces of the people listening to his grandfather
with rapt attention. Lexy was *always* ready for her
close-up.

Sage glanced at his phone as he closed Alan's study
door. He'd slipped the guard at the gate a hundred dollars
to text him if his grandfather came through. Sage didn't
expect Alan to come home early, but he didn't want to be
surprised.

He walked to the bookshelf, finding the hinged area
only because he knew where to look. The workmanship
was remarkable. If he hadn't seen Alan open it, he'd never
have known it was there.

Carefully he tugged on the edge, just like he'd seen his
grandfather do in the camera feed. The bookshelf swung
open and there was the safe.

It was old. Maybe a hundred years old, like the house
itself. He pulled out his phone and opened the notes app
where he'd listed all the dates that were important to his
grandfather.

Alan's birthday? He twisted the dial and tugged at the
handle. Nope.

His first wife Anna's birthday? Nope.

He tried Lexy's birthday. Both of Alan's wedding an-
niversaries.

He tried all of Alan's children's birth dates, including
his aunt Jennifer's, whose birthday he'd found in the public
record after a lot of digging.

None of those worked.

He tried his own father's death date. That wasn't it, either.

Frustrated, he went back and tried all the dates again, just in case he'd made a mistake. But none of them worked.

Dammit.

He was going to have to go with plan B. From his pocket he took the smallest fiber-optic camera he owned and positioned it along the hinge of the secret bookshelf so that the lens pointed directly at the combination dial. It wasn't ideal and wouldn't give him a full view, but he'd be able to figure out the combination. Placement anywhere else would result in the view being blocked by his grandfather's hand as he spun the dial.

Sage stood in approximately the same place his grandfather had stood when he'd opened the safe. The camera was visible if you knew it was there, but he was hoping his grandfather didn't look too closely.

Besides, Alan's eyesight was pretty awful these days. He probably wouldn't be able to see it even if he tried.

Sage wondered how Alan had even gotten himself to Medford's house the night before. Although after seeing the guns he'd taken from the safe, Sage was suspicious of everything his grandfather had claimed.

The man he'd thought he'd known was a stranger.

Were Alan's eyes really going bad?

That probably was true. His grandfather hated weakness. He considered having to be driven around and having to use special glasses to be embarrassing. So the eyesight thing probably was true.

Reluctantly, Sage closed the bookshelf. He'd have to wait until Alan opened it again to see the safe's combination. Then he'd be back.

His phone buzzed with an incoming text.

Hellfire and brimstone heading your way.

Shit. Alan had come home early.

Sage quickly put his tools away and made sure he

hadn't left evidence that he'd been there. He slipped out of his grandfather's study, making his way to the back staircase used by the help.

Maybe he'd get lucky and his grandfather would go straight to the safe.

He really needed to see what it contained.

Until then, though, he'd go back to watching Cora Winslow. The librarian was turning out to be very interesting.

12

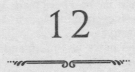

STONE'S EYES WERE wide as he lounged in Phin's recliner, Delores perched on his knee, as Phin gave them the highlights of the day. "Her father was an eraser? Seriously? I did not expect that."

"An eraser that killed someone on a job," Phin said. "I think that's the hardest part of that situation for her to deal with. She went to the woman's house today thinking she would be meeting her father's mistress. It was a shock."

"Poor Cora," Delores murmured. "To find out your father was a killer. She must be devastated."

"That seemed to make her numb more than devastated, I think." Phin stroked SodaPop's silky ear. "She'll have to process it and that takes time. She was far more devastated at the thought that her attorney could be involved. I wanted to ask her about the other man we met this morning, her friend's father, but I didn't want to hurt her any more than I already had by suggesting we investigate the lawyer. The friend's father is probably fine. He seems to care about her. But I'm checking out everyone that has any contact with her."

Antoine had done some checks, but Phin had needed to see for himself. So in between installing new locks on all those windows, he'd run some background checks of his own.

Delores's lips quirked up. "Are you talking about Tandy's father? Force-of-nature whirlwind Tandy?"

Phin chuckled because that was a good description of Tandy Napier. "One and the same. She came over tonight when we were all in the attic searching for more of Jack Elliot's records."

"Did Cora tell her everything?" Delores asked. "Because I got the impression that she wanted to keep Tandy out of this."

"Cora didn't have to tell Tandy anything. Tandy kept getting distracted by all the antiques, paintings, and sculptures gathering dust up there. Cora said they'd gone up there quite a few times, mainly searching for old dresses and jewelry, but Tandy always got sidetracked and they never found what they'd been searching for. Cora finally sent her downstairs to help me install window locks. She isn't handy and didn't help me a bit, but she did about talk my ear off."

Tandy had been good company, however, and he'd learned a lot more about Cora Winslow. Like how Cora had spent her teenage summers volunteering at the library where she now worked. How she'd set up a card catalog for all the books in her grandmother's home library when she was eight years old. How she'd always wanted to write books but had been frustrated because—and Tandy's voice had dropped to a conspiratorial whisper—she had no real talent for it.

How Cora had taken care of her mother after her father left, and then her grandmother as she got older, and then her brother as he was dying. And how she'd broken a little more with the passing of each one, withdrawing more into herself, which worried Tandy to no end.

Tandy had told him of every one of Cora's attempts to track down a marrow donor for her brother, about how

Cora had focused on finding her father or any of his "other children" with the "other woman." Who they now knew had never existed. He'd been impressed with Cora's ability to track down the leads she'd gleaned from the letters.

Phin's heart broke for her. She had to be cursing the time she'd spent away from her brother, now knowing that all those trips to seek her father had been for nothing.

For that alone, the letter writer needed to be punished.

"Phin?" The snapping of Stone's fingers had him looking up.

Stone was watching him carefully. "You okay?"

Phin nodded. "Not spiraling. Just thinking about all the time those damn letters cost Cora with her brother. She spent weeks trying to track her father down, weeks she could have spent with her brother while he was dying. Burke sent me a copy of all the letters. I read a few, but I'm going to read the rest tonight."

"How did she try to track her father?" Stone asked. "Did he drop any clues in the letters?"

"She used postmarks, mainly. She did an age progression on a photo of her father from twenty-three years ago, then took it to post offices and restaurants in the towns where the letters had been mailed. According to Tandy, she picked the smallest towns, figuring an out-of-towner would be noticed. But no one ever was able to positively ID Jack Elliot."

"Because he was dead," Stone said grimly. "I guess the question is, did the letter writer go to those locations to post the letters or was he—or she—able to get someone else to mail them?"

"I wondered that myself," Phin admitted. "So did Cora, apparently. She asked the postmasters at the various post offices if they'd been sent any letters or cards that had been requested to be postmarked locally. Tandy said that more than half the time, the letter had been hand postmarked by the postmaster after receiving it addressed to the post office."

"That happens a lot where we live," Delores said. "Especially around Valentine's Day. It's got to be annoying being a postal worker in Loveland, Ohio. I always feel sorry for them in February. People want their Valentine's Day cards postmarked with 'Loveland.' I never considered that people would do that for more nefarious reasons."

Stone kissed the top of her head. "Because you're an honest person."

She raised her brows. "Have you ever done that? Sent letters to another post office to be postmarked to fool someone into thinking it came from a different place?"

Stone's gaze slid to Phin. "*I* haven't."

Delores's eyes widened. "Phin? You did this? Why?"

Phin glared at Stone. "Asshole."

Stone shrugged. "I don't lie to my wife."

Phin sighed. "I've sent a few cards to my family over the years. I didn't want them to track me down, so I sent them to post offices out West."

"Phin." Delores's disapproval was evident.

"I didn't want them to think I was dead."

"He had reasons," Stone said quietly. "We've talked about this."

Delores shook her head. "I know, I know. And I'm glad you at least let them know that you're not dead. When was the last time you sent them a postcard?"

Phin winced. "When I first got to New Orleans. I had it postmarked in Denver. Sorry."

"That was two years ago!" Delores exclaimed. "They have to be thinking you're lying dead in a ditch somewhere."

Phin was about to apologize again when he noticed that Stone was shifting uncomfortably. "What?" Phin demanded.

"Well." Stone blew out a breath. "They don't think you're dead in a ditch."

Phin stiffened and SodaPop moved closer. His fingers dug into her coat. It was becoming habit now. "Why do you say that?"

Delores had turned to look her husband in the eye. "Yes, Stone. Explain."

Stone pinched the bridge of his nose. "Scarlett's known you were in New Orleans for a long time."

Phin's heart stuttered. "How?"

"You rented a house, man. Your landlord ran a credit check. Do you really think she didn't have searches set up for any mention of your name? She's a cop. And she's very smart."

Phin sank back into the sofa, poleaxed. "She never came looking for me here."

Stone gave him a look of incredulity. "Are you kidding me? Why would she after you ditched her in Miami? She knows you were there. She figured out that you avoided her when we visited. And before you ask, no, I never said a word to her. I promised you I wouldn't, and I haven't. She still has no idea that you stay with us when you need to get away. She doesn't know that you're only twenty-five miles away from her at those times." He sighed. "She knows that you don't want to be found, Phin. She makes do with knowing you're not lying dead in a ditch. Your whole family makes do with that."

Phin felt like he'd been slapped.

Which was fair. He *should* be slapped. "Shit." He rubbed his hands over his face. "I'm a selfish asshole." He heard no denials from his friends, which made him feel even worse. He dropped his hands, one finding its way back into SodaPop's coat. "I will make this right. And if they tell me to leave, I will."

"I really don't think they will," Delores said quietly. "And if they do, you can stay with us. Or come back here. You have support here, Phin. They care about you, too."

Phin thought of the support he'd received in the past forty-eight hours. "They do. Burke, Val, Molly, Antoine." Cora too. She'd been so strong, but she'd needed him. "They've been including me. Letting me do stuff that they

don't have to let me do. I've had so many second chances."
His throat thickened. "I don't want to be the one always
needing second chances."

"But you are," Stone said without an ounce of reproach.
"It's not your fault. Bad shit happened to you over in the
sandbox, and you were already depressed before you got
there."

Phin had been. He hadn't been lying to his work group
when he'd talked about journaling as a teenager. His journals and one kind guidance counselor had kept him from
doing something truly unfixable.

"Have you talked to your therapist lately?" Delores
asked tentatively.

"Not in a few weeks. But I'm okay right now and—" He
stopped himself, feeling himself falling into old habits,
where he'd mistake a slight improvement for not needing
any more help. Which wasn't true. At least not for him.
"And that's the best time to talk to her. When I'm level and
can think."

Delores brightened like he'd given her a new puppy.
"Yay! Progress."

Phin laughed. "I'll call her this week."

"Good." Stone nodded, pleased. "Since you are level
and can think, let's figure out how we can help you to help
Cora Winslow."

Phin was eternally grateful for the subject change. "Her
house is as secure as I can make it. I'm hoping she can
sleep tonight." He glanced at his buzzing phone, the notification on his screen making him frown. "What the hell?"

One of Cora's outdoor cameras had been triggered by
movement close to the gate.

Someone was lurking. Dressed all in black with a ski
mask.

Not the intruder who'd shot Joy, though. Wrong body
type. This person was several inches shorter and far more
slender. Gender was hard to tell from the camera angle.

He looked up to find Stone and Delores waiting for him to speak. "I need to get to Cora's house. Someone's trying to break in."

Stone patted Delores's back. "Let me up, babe. I'm going with him."

Phin opened a text screen. "I need to text Molly. She's on bodyguard duty tonight."

Stone shoved his feet into his shoes and grabbed his keys. "I'll start the car."

"I was afraid of this," Phin said as he sent his text. Molly replied right away that she'd seen the movement, too, and was on alert. "We've been searching her attic for two straight nights. Every fucking light on up there. We're like a damn lighthouse."

"Somebody knows you're looking for something," Delores said.

"Yes. And there are doors, windows, and a balcony on the attic level. At least they'll have a hard time getting in now. Lock up behind me, D. SodaPop, let's go."

The Garden District, New Orleans, Louisiana
WEDNESDAY, DECEMBER 14, 11:00 P.M.

Molly is a badass. Molly is a badass.

Cora kept reciting the words in her mind, hoping to quell her anxiety enough to sleep.

She had managed to get a decent nap after the debriefing meeting at her kitchen table. Phin had started replacing the window locks on the second floor and she'd been able to hear him moving around as she'd lain in her bed. The sound of him working had been better than a lullaby. Before she'd known it, it was dark outside and Burke's crew was up in the attic, looking for more clues her father might have left behind.

Most of Burke's crew, anyway. She'd stumbled out of her room and had nearly tripped over Phin Bishop's long legs. He'd been sitting against the opposite hall wall, his legs stretched straight out in front of him, the dragon book she'd been reading the night before in his hands.

He'd been "taking a break," or so he'd said. And maybe he had been. But he'd also been watching over her.

Which was so incredibly sweet. She wished he'd stayed. He would have if she'd asked, but she hadn't found the courage. She felt pathetic, needing him. But she did need him.

But he'd gone home, as had everyone else, after searching the attic until ten o'clock. Everyone was gone except for Molly, who was on night duty.

Molly, who is a badass.

Molly, who can take care of anyone who tries to hurt me.

Because people were trying to get to her. Because her father had killed someone. Or maybe because he'd pissed off the wrong person by making a client disappear.

Because her father was a goddamned eraser.

The words caused the fury to bubble up inside her. She'd been on a low-level simmer since she'd left Alice VanPatten's house.

Yes, Alice had needed help, but someone *else* should have been the eraser. Not an accountant with a wife and two little kids at home.

"What the hell, Dad?" she muttered. "What the actual hell?"

She rolled over and punched her pillow. And if her father were still alive, still here, she might be tempted to punch him, too.

How dare he do such a dangerous job? What if one of his clients' tormentors had followed him home? What if they'd hurt her mother? Or John Robert?

Had Jack even considered that? Did he have even the least bit of worry for his own family while he was off being a fucking cowboy, helping other people?

She had to draw a deep breath, because her heart was pounding and she'd clenched her teeth so hard that her jaw ached.

If he hadn't been in Idaho, Alice VanPatten might not be alive today.

But her father *wasn't* alive today, because someone had killed him.

And Joy Thomas might have died yesterday because some asshole had barged into Burke's offices in broad daylight.

Looking for me. For information about me.

The same asshole had broken into her home. Five times. She was no longer safe in her own home.

And I'm so angry.

She had to draw another deep breath because the first one hadn't worked. She was still tense. Still worked up. Still—

A loud thump from above had her sitting bolt upright in bed. She gasped and jumped out of bed, grabbing her bathrobe and her phone. The whole room had shaken.

Molly is a badass. Molly has a gun. Let Molly handle this.

But her feet weren't listening to her brain. Her home security system hadn't started blaring, so the doors and windows were still closed and locked. Right?

She charged up the stairs to the attic in her bare feet. And gasped again when she pushed through the door.

The moon was out and the attic glowed with a silver, ethereal light, illuminating four people in the room. It was . . . surreal.

Molly stood with her gun drawn, pointing it at the head of a . . . woman? Man? A figure lying on the floor.

The figure wasn't actually lying there, though. They were bucking and fighting the hands of the two men who held them down.

Phin and his friend Stone wore grim expressions as they struggled to contain the intruder, who was dressed all in black with a ski mask.

The window was wide open, letting in the cold night air. Cora shivered and considered closing the window, but that would mean walking around the four people in the surreal tableau.

The intruder was kicking now and Stone was cursing.

"Stop," Molly commanded, lowering the gun so that it was in the intruder's face. "I do not want to shoot you, but I will if you do not stop."

"Fuck you," the man muttered, and Cora had had enough.

She ran forward and dropped her full weight onto the man's legs, surprising him enough that he stopped fighting for a moment. Long enough for Phin to punch him in the jaw, subduing him.

The intruder yelped, then groaned. "Fuck all y'all."

Molly tossed Phin a pair of zip ties. "Cuff him."

"You can move now, Cora," Phin said, sounding amused. He wasn't even out of breath. Neither was Stone.

Cora, on the other hand, was panting like a dog. She rolled off the intruder's legs, coming to rest on her butt. Right next to SodaPop, who was *not* panting like a dog. On the contrary, she looked unruffled and calm.

Phin twisted the man so that he could get both hands behind his back and pulled the zip ties tight.

"Motherfucker," the man grunted.

"Fuck around and find out," Stone said, taking the other zip tie and restraining the man's feet.

Phin regarded Cora with a worried expression. "First, are you all right?"

Cora considered the question. "No, but I will be."

How many times would she say those words before this was finally over?

Phin nodded. "Good. Second, what were you *thinking*? He could have hurt you."

Cora sighed. "I didn't want you to get kicked."

Stone chuckled. "We appreciate the sentiment. Next time, don't engage with a bucking bronco, okay?"

Cora blinked. "Next time?"

Molly huffed her displeasure. "There better not be a

next time. And if there is, you stay put in your room. No running up to see what's happening."

Some of the anger that had been simmering all evening spilled over. "It's my goddamn house, Molly," she said coldly.

Molly's expression softened. "It is. I'm sorry. I shouldn't have talked to you that way. This is kind of a high-stress situation."

"Y'think?" Cora asked sarcastically. "What happened? Why didn't the alarm go off?"

"It did," Molly said. "But I'd set it to silent. Both Phin and I saw this guy lurking around your house. I went out to search and he ran away. Phin and Stone came over to give me coverage. They jumped the fence in the back of your property and we waited for him to come back."

"But that fence is six feet high."

"We're all trained for stuff like this," Molly said.

"And SodaPop? That's not part of a service dog's training, is it?"

"That was a little complicated," Stone admitted. "I went over first and Phin handed her over." He looked at the dog. "You're a good girl."

Molly smiled. "She is. I stayed on the bottom floor, Stone was on the middle floor, and Phin took the attic. We unlocked a few windows."

"You laid a trap," Cora said, her temper receding.

"We did," Stone said, then pointed at the intruder. "Einstein here picked the attic. Phin told us where he was entering and that gave us time to lock the windows we'd opened and get our asses up here to assist. The big bang was Einstein hitting the deck after Phin tackled him."

Cora glanced at Phin, hoping he was okay, that this hadn't sent him into one of his spirals. His eyes were sharp, his body tensed, but only in a hyperaware way. He looked okay.

She relaxed a little more. He looked better than okay. He looked *good* in the silver moonlight. *My knight in shining armor.* The thought nearly made her smile.

"So who is this little prick?" she asked.

Molly had lowered her gun to her side. "Phin, you want to do the honors? Hurry up, because I have to go downstairs. The cops are here."

Sure enough, Cora could see flashing lights reflected on the walls. "Wait a minute." She pulled her phone from her bathrobe pocket and started recording. "Go for it, Phin."

Phin pulled off the ski mask and the man glared up at them. He looked young. Eighteen or twenty at the most. His skin was pale in the moonlight, his hair a shade of red much lighter than Cora's.

Cora had never seen him before and she wasn't sure if she was relieved or disappointed. It would have been nice if this guy were the letter writer, but he probably hadn't even been alive when the first letter had been written.

"Cora?" Molly asked.

Cora shook her head regretfully. "Don't know him. Does he have ID?"

Stone patted him down. "No wallet. Who are you, asswipe?"

The man set his jaw sullenly and said nothing.

Molly holstered her gun. "I'm going to let the police in. Keep recording, Cora."

"Oh, I will." She glanced around her camera at Phin. "Thank you."

He nodded once. "I'm sorry we woke you up."

"I couldn't sleep." Because he hadn't been here. "It's all starting to hit me."

"I thought it might be," Phin said in his quiet way. "I'll make you some tea when we're all done here. Maybe that will help you sleep."

She smiled at him. "Maybe."

Stone was smirking. "I might want tea, too, Phineas. Aren't you going to offer me some?"

Phin flipped him the bird. "Shut up." But his lips were twitching.

Footsteps on the stairs had them all turning for the door. Two uniformed officers came in, followed by a rumpled Detective Clancy.

Clancy took one look at the scene and sighed. "Bishop and O'Bannion. You two again?"

"You're welcome," Stone deadpanned.

Clancy snorted a laugh. "Thank you." He crouched next to the intruder. "Not the same guy as last time."

"No," Phin said. "This guy is smaller. Tiny, even."

The man's eyes narrowed and he opened his mouth, then snapped it shut, pursing his lips.

Clancy turned to Cora. "Are you all right, Miss Winslow?"

"I am. It was mostly over by the time I ran up here. Phin and Stone had matters well in hand."

"She sat on his legs," Stone offered. "It was kind of a group effort."

Cora laughed and it sounded thin and hysterical to her own ears. "I think I really need that tea." She righted her phone so that the intruder was in the frame. Recording was the only thing she could do at the moment. She felt powerless and it sucked.

Clancy looked sympathetic. "You're sure you're okay?"

Cora shoved what probably would have been another manic sound back down. "No, actually. I'm not injured, though. Who is this man?"

Clancy shrugged. "I don't recognize him. Didn't you check him for ID?"

"No wallet," Phin said.

"Who are you?" Clancy demanded. The man deliberately looked away.

Clancy sighed again and rose. "It's gonna be like that, I guess. Get him on his feet," he said to the officers. "Cuff him and cut the zips, then pat him down." He pointed to the man, who now stood, his expression surly. "You will not give these officers any trouble."

Cora thought the detective wanted to deliver a more pointed threat, but Cora was still recording on her phone.

The man sneered but still said nothing.

The officers patted the intruder down as instructed and Cora's stomach dropped further. The man had a snub-nosed handgun and three different knives.

But perhaps equally terrifying were the matches they pulled from his pants pocket. There was a gas can on the balcony outside the still-open window.

"He was going to try to burn my house down?" Cora whispered.

"Well?" Clancy asked the man.

The man spat, his spittle landing a half inch from Clancy's shoe.

The detective shook his head. "You're just piling up the charges, aren't you?" He looked up and gave a satisfied grunt. "You've installed a sprinkler system."

Cora nodded. "Back in the nineties when my parents did some renovation." That was when they'd been newly-weds and had expected to live in this house forever. "My mother said it lowered the homeowner's insurance rate."

"Smart. I wish more of these old houses had that. Still could have caused some damage, though." He walked to the window. "Was it locked?"

"No," Phin said. "We unlocked it. We wanted to know who he was. But none of us know him, either."

Clancy shook his head at the now-handcuffed intruder. "Who sent you? Because they sure wasted their money. I hope they didn't pay you in advance. You walked right into a trap."

The man gave them all a look filled with hate.

"That's what I figured," Clancy said. "We'll run his prints through AFIS and if that doesn't get a hit, he'll tell us his name when it's time to call his lawyer. Why this room? What's so important in Miss Winslow's attic?"

"We don't know," Molly said, having returned at some

point. She leaned against the wall near the door. "I thought he might have figured it was the best way to get to Miss Winslow, but the matches and gasoline change things. We're hoping that he'll tell you."

Cora heard what Molly didn't say—that they'd been looking for her dead father's records and that was what someone wanted destroyed enough to risk sending this bozo. She wondered when they'd tell the police but decided to go with the flow for the moment.

The intruder shook his head at Molly's words, his sneer becoming a smirk that Cora wanted to knock right off his face. He didn't even look scared, despite possessing weapons, gasoline, and matches.

Cora thought that smirk might be the most frightening of all. Who'd sent him? And did that person have enough influence to get him out? Was that why he was so arrogant?

"We'll figure out what he was looking for," Clancy said, then looked down at Cora's bare feet. "It's cold up here. I'll be sending CSU up in a bit, but we can't close the window until they've dusted for prints. Why don't we all go downstairs? I can get your statements in the kitchen, where it's got to be warmer."

One of the uniforms dragged the intruder with them down the stairs, followed by Molly and the detective. Cora hit the stop-record button on her phone, then tugged Phin's jacket, keeping him from leaving, too.

"Why did you come back?" she asked. "I'm glad you did, but what made you?"

Phin met her gaze directly. "We've had the lights on up here for two straight nights."

"Oh. Come and rob me," she murmured.

"Something like that. Whoever's been watching you knows we're searching for something. I worried about that. And when I saw the asshole lurking near your gate on the camera feed, I just . . ."

"Rushed to rescue me?" Cora asked with a smile.

"Thank you." She turned to Stone, who was watching them with eagle eyes. "You too. Thank you both."

Stone nodded. "You're welcome. See you downstairs." He disappeared through the door, leaving her alone with Phin and the other uniform.

"Do you have to leave again?" she asked Phin.

Phin tilted her chin up, his finger gentle under her chin. "Still can't sleep?"

She shivered and it wasn't all from the cold. His finger was warm against her skin. She wished he'd cup her face in her palm. She craved the contact, but the simple touch on her chin was all he was offering at the moment. "No. I'm sorry. I hate to ask, but . . ."

"I'll stay. I'll sit outside your door like I did earlier. SodaPop and I."

"I don't want you to have to sit on the hard floor."

He shrugged. "I've sat in far more uncomfortable places and slept sitting against a wall more times than I want to count. I want you to get some rest and I can sleep out there. I'll wake up if anyone approaches. Army taught me that."

She wanted to argue, but fatigue was finally closing in. "Okay. Thank you."

"Now let's go get that tea. Your feet have to be like ice."

The Garden District, New Orleans, Louisiana
WEDNESDAY, DECEMBER 14, 11:45 P.M.

"Well," Sage murmured, watching through his binoculars as the cop pushed a man dressed in black into the back of the squad car. "That's interesting."

He'd been debating the wisdom of his own entry into the attic when he'd seen the man casing the Winslow house an hour before. It had been a golden opportunity, actually. If there was a security system, Sage could find out how long it took for alarms to screech. He also could judge the response time of Broussard's people.

The man in black had been Sage's canary in the mine. *Better that dude get caught than me.*

Sage had had his answer when one of the bodyguards opened the front door and shined a flashlight around. The man had run back into the shadows of the neighbors' homes and the bodyguard had gone back into the house. The whole episode had taken less than a minute, which meant that they had cameras and had seen the guy lurking outside.

Sage had decided that a search of the house was now too risky. Broussard's people had cameras and a quick response.

He'd been right to wait. Now there were a lot more people in Winslow's house. Three bodyguards plus the Winslow woman. He'd been able to see their silhouettes in the attic window as they'd taken the intruder down.

Throw in a detective and a couple of cops who'd responded to the scene, and the house was too damn crowded for him.

Broussard's people had been searching the attic for sure. The room had been bright as day for hours that evening, like a beacon lighting the night.

Which made Sage wonder what the hell they were looking for. But checking for himself wasn't worth the risk.

He'd been chafing at the bit, needing to do something, to learn something, but he wouldn't be doing that in Winslow's house.

Sage was frustrated that Alan hadn't gone back into his safe.

Not yet.

But maybe the old man could be nudged a little.

Sage dialed his grandfather's cell phone, gratified when a sleepy Alan answered.

"What?"

Sage grinned. He'd woken the old bastard up to boot. *Bonus.* "I know you told me to stay away from Cora Winslow, but I can't let it go. I failed in Broussard's office and I need to make it up to you."

"What have you done?" Alan asked coldly, the venom in his voice plain to hear.

Which meant that his grandfather had been sleeping alone. He'd never let Lexy hear him talking like that. The only people who ever heard that tone were Sage and one or two others who'd had the misfortune to be inducted into Alan's closest circle.

Sage made his tone properly respectful, even though it nearly made him gag. "Nothing, I swear. I haven't inter-acted with the Winslow woman or the woman she visited this morning. But I'm sitting on the curb a block from her house and the police are there."

"Why?" Alan asked, suddenly more alert.

"Those PIs she hired have been searching her attic and once they all left, some dude tried to break in. Climbed to the third-floor balcony with a gas can in his hand. I know we didn't hire him. Did we?"

"No," Alan snapped. "We did not."

Sage didn't know if he believed that or not.

Probably not. Considering the secret safe with secret guns, it seemed that Alan had a secret agenda going.

"How long was the 'dude' in the house?" Alan demanded.

"Not long at all. I think the PIs had set a trap for him. There were three people from Broussard's firm in the house, along with Cora Winslow. I don't think this guy expected that."

"I see. That's valuable information. When did they be-gin searching the attic?"

"They've been at it all evening tonight. Last night, too."

"See if you can find out what they were looking for, but do not take risks. One of the first things Broussard would have done is make sure she has a good security system. I don't want you to get caught."

How caring of the old man. But the care was only for himself. Alan used everyone. *Including me.*

"I don't want to get caught, either. The area's too hot right now."

Breaking into his grandfather's safe would be much less risky and a much more productive use of his time.

Ending the call, he pulled away from the curb and headed back to his condo. He wasn't going to call attention to himself by waiting around with so many cops on the scene. The bodyguards would be even more vigilant from now on. Everyone would be considered a threat, every parked car suspect.

He wished he knew exactly what Broussard's people had been looking for in the attic. He knew that Cora had been looking for clues into her father's death before she'd brought Broussard in. Sage had gleaned that much from the conversations she'd had with the Terrebonne Parish sheriff, with the NOPD, and with Broussard's people before they'd discovered his bugs.

That they'd been searching the attic for information relating to Jack Elliot made sense. But he might not ever find out exactly what that was.

He'd have to come at this from his grandfather's angle, whatever that was.

He'd just pulled into his parking place in his condo's garage when his phone beeped.

Yes. That was the camera he'd planted earlier that day.

He held his breath, watching as his grandfather twisted the dial forward, backward, and forward again before pulling the handle. He used the numbers he could see from his side view to extrapolate the exact numbers Alan had chosen.

One-zero-fifteen.

Huh. That date wasn't on the list of any that he'd considered.

He wondered at the significance of the date, then exhaled on a rush when it hit him.

He'd seen that date recently. Or a date close to it.

If the combination was a date, that would be October 15—one day before law enforcement believed Jack Elliot had been stuffed into the foundation of the Damper Building, because the concrete had been poured on October 16.

His grandfather's secret safe with secret guns had a combination one day earlier than the day that Jack Elliot had been murdered.

Hands visibly shaking on the camera feed, Alan put a single piece of paper into the safe. He started to close the safe, but after a moment's hesitation, he pulled out what appeared to be a photograph.

The angle was wrong, dammit. Sage couldn't see what—or who—the photo was of.

Alan stared at the photo for a long, long minute, expression weary and full of regret. Which was a big deal because Alan didn't seem to regret anything.

Alan put the photo back into the safe, closed the door, and twisted the handle. He leaned into the safe, resting his forehead on the metal for several seconds before straightening and closing the bookshelf.

Sage switched to one of the first cameras he'd planted.

His grandfather returned to his desk, immediately dropping his head into his hands.

Sage stared at the image of his grandfather. The old man had always been strength and self-control personified. Now? Alan was broken.

What have you done, old man?

13

~~~~~~~~•◦•~~~~~~~~

A LAN LAID HIS phone on his desk, trembling.
This was so much worse than he'd thought.

Sage had disobeyed a direct order. He'd continued to surveil Cora Winslow after Alan had told him to stay away from the woman.

His grandson tried to make it seem like he was being helpful, that he was trying to atone for his failure to get Cora's letters from Broussard. But Alan knew Sage. He'd raised him, after all. Sage had smelled Alan's blood in the water and was circling like a shark.

Alan had feared the day that his grandson would try to overthrow him. Would try to take everything that Alan had spent his lifetime building. Everything that Alan had sacrificed to achieve.

It was time to deal with Sage before Alan completely lost control of the situation.

Sage was ruthless under the charming facade, but Alan almost couldn't blame him for it. The boy had come by it honestly. Alan knew his own charisma was his greatest skill.

Sage thought he was in charge. He'd soon find out differently.

For now, though, Sage's information was as damaging as his blatant disobedience.

Hearing about the years of letters from her father on the recordings from the bugs Sage had planted in Cora's purse had been a shock, but they had explained one thing.

He'd always wondered why the police had never investigated the man's death. The man he'd known as John Robertson. The man who was really Jack Elliot.

Jack Elliot's body hadn't been discovered twenty-three years ago. Not by the police, anyway.

Someone had discovered it, though. *Someone* had moved it, burying the man in the foundation of new construction.

And someone had sent Cora Winslow letters all this time so that she wouldn't think her father was dead.

Who had found the body after Alan had killed him? Who had hidden it?

And why?

Someone had taken Jack Elliot's body from that parking lot in Baton Rouge where Alan had killed him and had driven nearly *two hours* to the building in Houma to hide the body somewhere else.

And then someone had continued to take great pains to make sure that no one searched for Jack Elliot, writing letters to his daughter for more than two decades.

Were they the same someone?

If so, that person had to be freaking out right now as much as Alan was, because they'd hidden Jack's body, thinking it would stay encased in the foundation of the Damper Building for decades to come.

But *why*?

Assuming it wasn't a random stranger, that meant that whoever had hidden the body had known it was there in that parking lot. Which suggested that someone had been following Jack.

And me.

Who was that someone?

Alan had thought of little else in the two weeks since seeing Jack Elliot's face on the news after the Terrebonne Parish sheriff's department had ID'd him. The cops had posted Jack's driver's license photo, taken only a year before his death.

Seeing that face on the news had brought back all the nightmares Alan had suffered for the past twenty-three years.

He wondered if the person who'd hidden the body felt the same way.

Alan had actually thought he'd gotten away with something all those years ago. The police hadn't come knocking on his door back then and, over the years, he'd just . . . let it go.

But now Cora Winslow was searching her house. Private investigators—good ones—were looking for clues. And it appeared that they'd found one.

He looked down at the document on his desk—the report from his own PI on Alice VanPatten. Usually, his PI's sole responsibility was to keep an eye on Lexy and Sage, to make sure they didn't fool around or do anything that might cause a scandal.

Scandals were very bad for churches. Donations tended to dry up in the face of scandal. Lexy had been a model wife. Sage's sins had been many, but no one had discovered them.

This scandal was Alan's. For the minister to stand accused was so much worse than if his family had created the problems. So he'd assigned his PI to investigate Alice VanPatten.

Dave Reavey had been ecstatic to do something other than following Lexy and Sage around. He'd thrown himself into a records search and had come up with facts that hadn't made sense to Dave but made perfect sense to Alan.

Until twenty-three years ago, Alice VanPatten had been married to Jarred Bergeron, an abusive man. Her husband had beaten her senseless, then had gotten himself killed in a hunting accident. Even though he hadn't been a hunter. The wife had been a suspect in her husband's murder, but a neatly crafted alibi had absolved her of guilt.

She'd been in a hotel room miles away with a man whose description fit the man Alan had known as John Robertson to a T. A man who'd called himself John Winslow.

She'd then sold her dead husband's holdings and moved to Baton Rouge.

That sent a chill down Alan's spine. The death of her husband had been only two weeks before his own trip to Baton Rouge twenty-three years ago. Jack Elliot *had* to have been involved.

The clincher, of course, had been the name of her child. John Robert VanPatten. She'd named her son after the man who'd rescued her from domestic violence. That John Robertson, a.k.a. John Winslow, a.k.a. Jack Elliot, had killed her husband was an undeniable fact in Alan's mind.

Cora Winslow and Broussard's people had found one of Jack's clients. According to Sage, Cora had been stunned as she'd left the VanPatten household.

So now she knew what her father had been.

And if she'd found one client, there was a chance she'd find more.

A chance she'll find me.

He hadn't given his legal name to John Robertson and he'd paid the man with cash a week before the job, so there was no linkage there. But there were plenty of other ways this could come back to cage him.

He couldn't allow that to happen.

Cora Winslow absolutely could not find the Caulfield family, who still lived in the same house in Merrydale with the green door and the tidy front yard. They weren't trying to hide from anyone. They'd simply been living their lives for twenty-three years.

Alan knew this because he'd driven by a time or two over those years. Just to be sure. Just to see for himself.

Another thought occurred, stealing Alan's breath. The Caulfields could have been of the same mind that he'd been twenty-three years ago. *Two can keep a secret if one of them is dead.*

Mr. Caulfield could have followed "John Robertson" away from the house with the green door and the tidy lawn that night. Caulfield might have been the one to witness Alan killing the man who'd been the go-between in their deal.

Their illegal deal.

Caulfield might have been the one to move the body to the foundation of the Damper Building. He might be the one responsible for the search of Cora's attic tonight.

Or it could be someone completely unrelated.

Alan didn't know and couldn't care. He just knew that Cora could not be permitted to locate that family. And if she did, she couldn't be permitted to speak with them.

There was no statute of limitations for murder.

Slowly he rose from his desk, his PI's report in hand. He opened the hinged bookcase and twisted the dial on his safe. One-zero-fifteen.

He put the report in the back of the safe with all the others his PI had generated over the years. He started to close the safe, then paused, his heart racing, his mind spinning. Carefully he pulled out the most recent photo he'd taken.

Of her. Ashley Caulfield.

One-zero-fifteen.

He stared at her face for a long, long moment, sorrow and regret weighing him down like bricks. But he couldn't change the past.

With a heavy heart, he put the photo back into the safe, closed the door, and spun the dial.

Ashley was innocent. She was just living her life.

But she and her family had to be silenced.

That this was all bubbling to the surface now was Cora

Winslow's fault. If she'd just left well enough alone, everything would have been fine.

Now he had secrets to bury so deep they'd never be found again.

But he couldn't do this himself. There was no way. He'd barely been able to drive to Medford Hughes's house in Mid-City. Driving to the Caulfields' home north of Baton Rouge was out of the question.

He'd ask Sage for this last thing.

If Sage agreed to his request, Alan would know that his grandson was irredeemable. If he didn't agree, Sage would have even more to hold over Alan's head.

Either way, he'd have to silence Sage, too. It was always going to end this way. He could see it now.

This will kill me.

But his life's work was important. He couldn't let it be tarnished. People would suffer.

He thought about his Anna, slumped in her chair, her blood and brains covering the paisley fabric. Anna had suffered.

So did I.

So had others. But if Alan was exposed, so many more would be hurt. His followers could lose their faith. He couldn't allow that to happen.

Sometimes the needs of the many really did outweigh the needs of the few.

Abraham had been prepared to sacrifice his only son, after all.

Sage would be Alan's sacrifice.

The Caulfields would have to be collateral damage.

Alan returned to his desk, placing his head in his hands. How did he present this to Sage in a way that would get the boy to agree?

He wished he'd eliminated the Caulfields years ago when he'd still had his independence, but he hadn't. Now he had to depend on someone else to finish the job.

He thought about the face in the photo. Ashley was innocent in all of this. In every single thing.

How was he supposed to package the murder of an innocent as a necessary evil? How could he frame it so that Sage would actually obey him?

I'll find a way.

He had to, because if Cora Winslow got to the Caulfields first, nothing would be salvageable.

The Garden District, New Orleans, Louisiana
THURSDAY, DECEMBER 15, 1:00 A.M.

Phin hadn't lied to Cora. He really had slept on more uncomfortable surfaces than the floor outside her bedroom door.

But this floor was cold. Luckily SodaPop was warm. She lay curled up against his thigh as he sat with his back against the wall and his legs stretched out toward Cora's door.

Cora had given him a blanket, and that helped.

It also smelled like her, which was a bonus.

He had no idea why she'd chosen him to guard her door tonight, but he'd gladly accept the responsibility. He thought that she'd be fragile, given all she'd lost. And a part of her was. A part of her had raised walls to keep from getting hurt again. She held herself aloof. As if allowing anyone too close would be more than she could tolerate without breaking down.

But she was not a fragile woman. Not by a long shot.

His heart had nearly stopped when she'd dropped her body onto that thug's legs. She could have been hurt in so many different ways, but he didn't think she'd even considered the risk to herself.

But he wasn't foolish enough to mention it again. Molly had scolded her and received the frostiest glare he'd seen in a long time.

No way did he want to be on the receiving end of that glare.

No, he wanted the warmth he saw in her brandy-colored eyes. The trust. He'd planned to camp out exactly where he was before she'd asked him to stay with her.

That she had asked was satisfying in ways that he couldn't explain.

Sure you can. You like her. You want to protect her.

You want her to find you useful.

You want her to find you . . . worthy. Worthy of keeping. Worthy of wanting.

Because you want her, too.

He wanted to tell that voice in his head to shut up, but it was right. On all of it. He wanted Cora Winslow. He wanted to feel her up against him, wanted to know what she tasted like. He wanted her to trust him with more than her safety. He wanted her to trust him with her pleasure, because he didn't think she'd had nearly enough of that in her life.

But he also wanted to be useful, and that was a more likely ending to their story. Being truly useful to someone he cared about was what got him through each day. It was what had kept him coming back to Broussard Investigations every time he'd spiraled and bolted, even though he'd never be an official member of the firm.

They cared about him, of course. They'd trained him to take on more responsibility, and he appreciated that so very much. But, at the end of the day, he was not a bodyguard. He was not a PI. He was their handyman and their night security.

Even when he hadn't been able to be what they were, they'd still needed him.

But not like Cora Winslow needed him. Hers was short-term need, but he didn't care. He felt more alive sitting on her cold floor than he had in a long time.

Maybe ever.

Her bedroom door creaked open, causing him to jolt to

full awareness. She stood in the doorway wearing her bathrobe and fuzzy socks.

At least her feet weren't bare this time.

In her arms, she carried more blankets and two pillows. "Still can't sleep," she said quietly.

He'd been afraid of that. She'd been completely wired when Detective Clancy had finally taken his leave after getting their statements about the break-in. Phin had hoped her adrenaline would crash and she'd sleep out of sheer exhaustion, but it didn't look like that was the case.

"The house is locked up like Fort Knox," he said. "The alarm's set and I checked all the doors and windows myself."

"I know, and I trust that." She crossed the hall and stood above him, looking down to meet his eyes. "I trust *you*. I'm just . . . my mind won't be quiet."

I trust you.

She probably shouldn't. He would let her down eventually. He wouldn't mean to, but it was pretty much a given.

"Did you finish the dragon book?" he asked.

She sighed. "I can't even read. I blink and realize that I've just been staring at the same page for fifteen minutes. I've never *not* been able to lose myself in a book. Even when John Robert was so sick." She bit at her lip. "Can I sit out here with you?"

Of course she could. It was her house. But he knew that wasn't what she meant.

He moved his gun to the other side of his body and patted the floor beside him. "We can make a pillow fort."

She laughed, her face lighting up for the briefest of moments. It made him feel . . . proud.

She settled next to him, offering him the extra blankets. "I don't have enough pillows for a fort, but we can stay warm. I think the furnace is on the fritz again."

"I think you're right. I'll take a look at it tomorrow."

Together they spread the blankets, SodaPop scooting up until only her head was visible. They stuffed the pillows behind their backs and Cora pulled the blankets to her chin.

Their arms were under the soft covers, but not touching. Not yet. His hand itched to reach for hers, but he'd let her make the first move. This was as vulnerable as he'd ever seen her.

Cora leaned against the wall with a weary sigh. Her shoulder was pressed against his, but her head rested on the wall. She turned just her head to look up at him. "Were you actually asleep?"

"No. I'm usually awake at night anyway. I'm the night security for Burke."

"Oh, right. You did tell me that."

They sat in silence for at least a minute, the only sound that of Blue snoring from inside her bedroom. "Your dog is an enthusiastic sleeper," Phin said.

She chuckled. "He's like a buzz saw. My own little white noise machine. John Robert couldn't sleep without him in the room." She sighed again. "How that dog grieved when he died. It broke my heart."

Phin flexed his fingers, telling them to keep to themselves. She'd reach for his hand if she wanted to. "When did you get Blue?"

"I was sixteen and John Robert was fourteen. Blue was his birthday present that year. He couldn't go to school because he was so immunosuppressed from the chemo. Mama got him Blue to keep him company. He was John Robert's dog from day one."

"Your brother had been sick a long time."

"He was. His first lymphoma diagnosis was when he was five years old. He'd been sick since he was younger, though. It started when he was two or three and got a virus. That may have triggered the lymphoma. He had a few healthy years off and on, but most of the time he was really sick. That was hard, seeing him so sick. He'd get through a series of treatments and we'd hope . . ." She sighed sadly. "And then it would come back again. Four times in all.

The last time . . . he was so tired. His body couldn't take the treatments anymore."

"I'm sorry. I shouldn't have asked. I've upset you."

"Oh no, it wasn't you. I don't mind you asking questions, Phin."

They were quiet for a minute or so, and then Phin couldn't hold his next question back any longer. "Why couldn't you sleep?"

"My father." She'd closed her eyes, her head back against the wall. "I'm so *angry* with him, Phin. Then I feel guilty for being angry with him because he's dead, which makes me even angrier. My mother had to bear the weight of John Robert's care. She worried all the time. She could have used my father's support, but he was gone. She thought he'd left her. Left us. Now I find out that he was dead all along, probably because of a job we never even knew about. I'm angry because he threw his life away, and I'm angry that we didn't know he was dead. That all this time we thought we were lacking somehow. That we weren't good enough. Or too much damn trouble. And that makes me *angry*."

She wasn't done. He could tell. So he remained quiet, waiting for her to continue in her own time.

Finally she exhaled, a tear escaping her closed eyes. "He knew John Robert was sick. He *knew* that. He had a wife and two little kids. Why did he need to do a job that was so dangerous? It got him killed, and for what? Helping strangers. And that makes me sound so selfish, and I hate myself for even thinking it."

More tears followed the first one and Phin gave up on letting her make the first move. She was hurting and he needed to help.

He put his arm around her shoulders and tugged her closer, gratified when her head came to rest on his shoulder. She was so soft. "You are *not* selfish. My dad is a retired cop. There were plenty of times we were afraid that he'd never come home. I get your anger. I felt it, too. Not every day, but sometimes. Often, actually. I understood why he did the job he did and my mother did, too. But it was something our family lived with, the knowledge that he might not come home after a shift. Because he was helping strangers."

It had been a source of his anxiety as a teenager and something he'd included in those journal entries he'd guarded so zealously.

He stroked her hair, breathing her in. She smelled like strawberries. "My brothers and sister . . . I don't know what they were feeling. On the outside, we were all supportive and proud of our dad. But it affected me. I always had anxiety and whenever he'd have a close call, I'd have to fight not to lose my temper with everyone else in the house."

She was quiet for a moment. "That's what you journaled, wasn't it?"

He wasn't surprised that she'd put that together. She was an intelligent woman. He liked that, too. "A lot of it, yes. My brothers and sister were always so . . . okay. So level. Not like me. I was up and down, all the time. I hated it. Hated me."

"No," she whispered.

"Yes," he whispered back. "It took a long time, but I've learned to cut that angry teenager some slack."

"Nobody helped you back then?"

"Nobody knew. I never let anyone know. I didn't want them to know. I was ashamed and mad and confused. And I wanted out. Out of the perfect family. I was the broken one. And that would hurt them to know I felt that way."

"That's why you haven't been home?"

"Part of it. Mostly I hate being the source of so much drama. I hate not being—" He cut himself off. This was about her, not him.

"Not being perfect like them," she finished. "But they love you."

"They do. I don't know why, but they do."

She pulled back enough to stare up at him. "You really don't know why?"

He shrugged uncomfortably. This was territory he rarely ventured into, even with his therapist. "I guess it's because I'm theirs."

"And you've got a good heart. Was . . ." She hesitated. "Was the anger a symptom of depression?"

"It was, which I know now. I've finally found some meds that help, but I didn't have them back then. I didn't think about depression being a thing then. I was just biding my time until I was eighteen and could join the army. Not my smartest decision."

"Out of the frying pan, into the fire."

"Exactly."

"But you're going back to see them?"

"On Christmas, yes. Even if I'm not perfect. I've got ten days. What are my chances of achieving perfection?"

She smiled up at him. "I'd bet on you."

Her smile . . . It warmed him like no blanket ever could. He couldn't tear his eyes away from her face. She was beautiful just like this, with her hair messy and her eyes a little red from crying. Because she was staring up at him, too.

As the seconds ticked by, the air between them grew charged, waiting for something to happen. Her eyes were no longer filled with anger and pain. There was heat there. Heat and want, and Phin's heart was pounding so hard it was all he could hear.

She wanted him, too.

Her smile faltered, becoming tentative, but the desire remained. "Phin?"

He couldn't manage a single word, so he brushed the wayward curls from her face, trailing his fingertips over her cheek.

She leaned into his hand, keeping her gaze on his. One of her hands emerged from the blankets to curve around his neck and he froze.

Her brows lifted. "Phin? You still with me?"

He could only nod.

Her lips curved. "I'm going to kiss you now. Blink once for yes, that's okay, and twice for no, don't do it."

Phin laughed, his brain and his mouth suddenly cooperating once again. "Yes. Please."

"So polite." She tugged him down and her lips were on his.

Sweet. So sweet. And soft and . . .

It was over too soon so he took charge, running his fingers into her hair and taking her mouth again. *Better, even better.*

It had been so long since he'd done this. Since he'd kissed someone.

So long since he'd let someone this close.

He wanted her closer.

He wanted so much more.

But not tonight. Not here, out in the hallway on the floor with Molly downstairs standing guard.

He pulled back and rested his forehead against hers. For a long time they said nothing. Just breathed.

And then the high of kissing her ebbed, and the doubts kicked in. This was insane. She didn't deserve a broken man. She deserved a perfect man.

At least one more perfect than me.

She pulled away to study him, her brow furrowing. "Whatever you're thinking, stop. I'm not sorry."

He sighed. "You should be."

Her jaw tightened, her expression the stubborn one he was quickly coming to know. "You don't get to tell me that. I like you. A lot. I think you're sweet. And you're a very good kisser."

His cheeks heated. "Out of practice," he muttered, looking away.

She gripped his chin gently, pulling him back to face her. "If that's out of practice, I'm volunteering as tribute to further hone your skills." She rubbed her thumb over his lip. "But I'll leave you alone for now. I didn't come out

here to kiss you. I came out here because I needed to sleep
and, for whatever reason, I can do that with you."

He rolled his eyes. "Because I'm boring."

She smiled up at him. "Because you're solid. And
smart. And loyal. And pretty damn hot."

He needed to say something. He opened his mouth, but
no words would come.

Her eyes crinkled at the corners as her smile grew.
"Blink once for thank you and twice for I'm not interested,
please go away."

He blinked once, hard.

"Good." She let go of his chin and snuggled into his
side. "I'll kiss you again tomorrow, fair warning. Now I'm
going to sleep."

Within minutes, she was breathing deeply and Phin
was still reeling.

But smiling. It was still insane, but he'd let himself have
this. This feeling of being enough. For a little while.

For as long as it lasted.

The Warehouse District, New Orleans, Louisiana
THURSDAY, DECEMBER 15, 2:10 A.M.

The ringing of Sage's cell phone didn't wake him, because
he hadn't been able to fall sleep. He'd been staring at the
ceiling for hours, wondering if he shouldn't be breaking
into his grandfather's study right now, so that he could find
out what in the safe had put that look on Alan's face.

That look of defeat and guilt.

What the hell had Alan done?

But the guard on night duty would surely inform Alan
that Sage had entered the gated community, so he was going
to have to wait. Even though the suspense was killing him.

Clumsily he reached for his phone, frowning when he
realized it was the burner phone. Only a few people had
that number. "Hello?"

"It's Sanjay."

His contact at the car rental facility. Sage had met Sanjay through Alan. Sanjay's parents had been some of Alan's most ardent supporters. They'd never missed a Sunday, always dropped cash in the offering plate, and generally hung on Alan's every word.

Sage and Sanjay, on the other hand, had been typical teenagers—stealing away to smoke pot. Sage provided the money and Sanjay had the connections. Years later, he and Sanjay rarely smoked anymore.

Sanjay had a job with a car rental company at the airport. Sanjay hooked Sage up with rentals whenever he needed to be discreet. His own Porsche was too recognizable.

Usually Sage borrowed the cars when he went clubbing in Gulfport, far away from Alan's watchful eyes, but sometimes it was for business. Like the Camry he'd picked up the morning before or the minivan he'd borrowed when he'd broken into Cora Winslow's house.

Sanjay rented the vehicles in his own name and Sage forked over the cash, usually twice the actual fee. He knew Sanjay was overcharging him, but discretion was sometimes expensive.

"What's up?" he asked with a yawn.

"We got a police inquiry about the Camry that I rented you off the books. Came in just before midnight. You need to ditch it, man. Leave it somewhere and I'll come and get it after my shift is up."

Shit, damn, and fuck it all. "Who made the inquiry?"

"Detective Clancy. Is that meaningful?"

Unfortunately, it was. He was the detective investigating the murder of Medford Hughes. Sage wondered if that old librarian had turned him in. Or someone might have spied him parked near Cora Winslow's house. Either way, this was not good. "No," he lied. "I'll move the car and text you. It'll come from my burner, so be watching for it."

"Will do. And . . . best not to call me again for a while. I think I can hide this, but not if it happens again."

Sage wanted to tell the man to go to hell, but he might need him later. "Of course," he said and ended the call.

Next time he'd buy his own damn car from a junkyard with cash. A car that still had a good frame and wouldn't look out of place on a street in the Garden District. That was why he'd rented a damn Camry. It blended in.

Clearly it hadn't, though. Someone had seen him or had at least seen the car.

Had they seen him personally, they would be knocking on his door.

They still might.

But they couldn't prove that it had been him parked on Cora's street. He'd worn a cap. His face hadn't been clearly visible. And he'd worn gloves the entire time. No prints.

The only person who'd actually seen him in the car was that damned librarian. Minnie Edwards. She could identify him.

He cursed himself for his own stupidity. She'd surprised him, knocking on his window and demanding to know why he was there. He'd been stupid, telling her he was there for Cora. *Dammit.*

If she had been the one to report the Camry to Detective Clancy, she'd likely given the police his description. But again, if the cops knew that he was the driver, they'd have arrested him already. Although they might still figure it out if her description was good enough. Sage thought that the old woman with the sharp stare would give a very detailed description.

She was a witness. The only person who could identify him in a lineup should he become a suspect.

She had to be silenced.

But . . .

He wanted to scream. He wasn't a killer. Not like his grandfather. But his other choices weren't good. The old lady had to go. He'd make it fast. She wouldn't feel any pain.

That was the best he could do.

He got out of bed and dressed all in black, hating that he'd left a loose end.

Two, actually. Because now that Detective Clancy had the Camry's license plate, the cops would press Sanjay hard. Sanjay was a good guy, but he'd fold like a cheap suit.

When Sage was only borrowing cars to go clubbing, it wouldn't have been a big deal if Sanjay blabbed.

This, though . . . This was a much bigger deal.

Dread settled on his chest, heavy as lead. Sanjay would have to go, too.

But that's all. After them, no more. I swear it.

He would not become like Alan. He swore that, too.

14

PHIN WOKE TO the smell of sausage. And coffee.
He stretched, his neck popping. He couldn't be
sleeping sitting up against a wall anymore. Thirty-seven
was too damn old for that.

He patted the floor to his right, unsurprised to find it
empty. Cora was gone. But her bedroom door was open
wide.

On his left, SodaPop blinked up at him and he scratched
her neck the way she liked. "Good morning, girl," he murmured, his voice craggy. "Thanks for sticking with me."

She nuzzled his hand and gave a small whine. She
needed to go outside. Phin got his body moving. He folded
the blankets and put them on the end of Cora's bed, already made. Blue was nowhere to be seen, so Phin guessed
the old dog was downstairs where the sausage was.

He found a crowd in the kitchen. Burke, Molly, Antoine, and Val were there, and Phin wondered when they
planned to return to the office. Or to Burke's house.

Cora was at the stove, a cast iron skillet sizzling. He
hadn't realized she could cook, but she looked completely
at home in her kitchen.

He stepped farther into the warm kitchen and did a double take. Stone and Delores were there, too, along with

Delores's Irish wolfhound, Angel. Stone looked up, a cup of coffee paused halfway to his mouth.

"You finally woke up."

"Sausage," Phin grunted.

From the stove, Cora laughed. "It's in the milk gravy," she said. "The biscuits are ready to come out of the oven. Can you get them, Delores?"

Delores hopped up from the table and grabbed oven mitts. "They smell amazing, Cora. I want the recipe."

"I don't know the recipe. I just make them like my mother did."

"Then you'll have to make them again." Delores gave Phin a quick glance as she passed by him. "You okay?" she whispered.

He nodded. "Fine."

Better than fine, actually. Cora had kissed him last night and said she'd do it again. But first he needed coffee.

Another whine cut into his thoughts and he remembered poor SodaPop. He opened the back door and went out with her into the garden, shivering as she sniffed every plant.

Why were Stone and Delores here?

He whistled and SodaPop came trotting over, her tail wagging. "Let's get warm, little girl."

He exhaled in relief when they were back in the kitchen. He rubbed his hands over his arms. "Cold," he said when Stone stared at him, one brow raised.

"You were raised in Ohio, Phin," Stone said, amused. "This isn't cold."

Phin would have flipped him the bird, but his hands were too cold. "Blood's thin now. Lived in the South too long."

Cora pressed a mug of coffee into his hands. "This is four spoonfuls of sugar, Phin. Delores swears this is how you like it, so if it's wrong, blame her."

Burke and his coworkers were watching him with interest, and Phin didn't like that. He liked to lurk on the sidelines.

Too many eyes were looking at him right now.

SodaPop detoured to her food and water bowls, leaving him all alone.

"Why aren't you all at the office?" he asked as he took an empty chair next to Stone. "Haven't they released the crime scene yet?"

Burke pressed a hand to his heart. "I'm wounded, Phin. Truly wounded. Yes, they finally released it late yesterday evening, but Antoine hasn't had a chance to do a sweep of the office yet, so we aren't talking business there until we know it's clean."

"You have a house," Phin muttered. He was not caffeinated enough to deal with his friends yet.

Burke laughed. "We love you, too, Phin. My fridge is empty. I was getting ready to do a grocery run when Molly texted all of us that Cora was making breakfast, so we descended. Mmmm." He inhaled deeply when Cora put the skillet of milk gravy on the table. "Smells so good. I haven't had good milk gravy in too long. Thank you, Cora."

It did smell good. So did Cora, as she put a plate and utensils in front of him. She was dressed in jeans and a Tulane sweatshirt. She was still wearing the fuzzy socks from the night before. That the socks made him happy didn't make sense.

Except that she'd been wearing them when she'd allowed him to see her vulnerable.

When she'd kissed him.

She smiled at him as she took her seat at the head of the table. "We're debriefing last night."

Phin's brain was finally waking up, thanks to the coffee. "Why are you and Delores here, Stone?"

"Because I wanted to see this house that you think is so grand," Delores said, going for seconds on the gravy. "So far, it is even nicer than you said."

Stone gave his wife a fond look before returning his

gaze to Burke. "And I have some information I thought you might want." He looked at Phin. "We were already here when they all arrived. I was holding my info until you wandered down."

Phin nodded, too busy eating to reply. Cora was an *exceptional* cook. He did a go-on motion with his hand.

Stone pulled a folded piece of paper from his pocket. "Your intruder's name is Vincent Ray." He unfolded the paper and, moving his plate to the side, flattened it on the table.

Phin focused on the photo, rage bubbling up inside him at the thought of the intruder breaking into Cora's home. "That's him. How'd you ID him?"

Antoine blinked in appreciation. "Yeah, how'd you do it so fast?"

"Facial recognition software," Stone said. "I use it sometimes when I'm investigating for a story. I work for my family's newspaper in Cincinnati."

That was true, but too modest, Phin knew. "Stone does investigative reporting for national news agencies and was embedded in the army."

"That's how I met him," Antoine confirmed. "He was embedded in my unit. I was going to do the facial recognition today, since I didn't have a photo of the guy yet. Thanks for saving me the effort. This is good work. How long did it take your software?"

"Seven hours," Delores said dryly. "He didn't sleep last night."

Which meant Delores hadn't slept, either. Phin shot her a look of apology and she just smiled at him.

Cora rose from her seat to lean on Phin's shoulder, staring down at the photo. "Vincent Ray. Why do I know that name?"

"He's the nephew of the leader of a drug gang," Burke said, reaching for the photo. "His family was in the newspaper a few years back. Vincent here is a junior. His daddy,

Vincent Ray Sr., is serving time for possession and distribution."

"Oh good," Cora said faintly, her fingers gripping Phin's shoulder. "Murderers, erasers, and now drug dealers who plan arson. This just keeps getting better."

Phin patted her hand. "He only got in because we allowed it."

Burke exhaled loudly. "And then our client sat on his feet. Don't do that again, please, Cora?"

"I make no promises," Cora said flatly, giving Phin's shoulder a pat before returning to her chair. "He invaded my home. With gasoline, a gun, knives, and matches." She lifted her chin, wearing what Phin called her regal heiress expression. "Surely you can't expect me to do nothing."

Burke pinched the bridge of his nose. "Just . . . Fine. Whatever."

Val chuckled. "You broke him, Cora." She held her fist out and Cora bumped it. "Now, the question is, *why* did this guy invade your home? Is he directly involved in this caper or was he paid?"

Everyone turned to look at her. "Caper?" Antoine asked. "Really?"

Val only grinned. "Elijah, Jace, and I are on a *Thin Man* movie binge. One of the reviews called it a caper film and it's a fun word." Elijah was the ten-year-old son of Val's boyfriend, and Jace was the fifteen-year-old she'd adopted.

Phin needed to stop by and see Jace. He'd promised the kid that he could help Phin build things. And then Phin had taken off.

To heal, he reminded himself. *I left to heal*.

And someday he'd be strong enough to heal in place. *No more running*.

He wanted that day to be today. He wanted it with every fiber of his being.

"So?" Val asked when everyone continued to stare at her. "Directly involved or paid? If directly involved, why?

What's Vincent's connection to Cora? If paid, by whom?" She looked over to Molly's whiteboard. "Is our best guess that someone wants Jack Elliot's records of the clients he erased? Or are we still pursuing the angle that Jack's killer was Harry Fulton, who wanted Cora's mother for himself?"

"My money's on the first one," Phin said. "Someone doesn't want those records found, so they sent this guy to burn the attic down. Vincent Jr. can't be the letter writer because he's way too young. But I haven't dismissed Harry Fulton. He could still be behind this. He's still the only one who was around when the letters started coming."

Cora's lips thinned. "It's not Harry. I refuse to believe that."

"That's fine," Molly said. "I get that you want to believe in him. Just promise us that you'll be safe about it. No meeting him alone, not until we straighten all this out."

"That's fair," Cora allowed, and Phin let out the breath he'd been holding.

She was sensible. That was one of the reasons he liked her so much.

"I ran some background checks on Harry last night, Cora," Antoine said. "He seems totally legit. It would be great if we could pin down where he was twenty-three years ago. Our lives would be easier if he was away on business, like in Europe or something."

"He doesn't travel," Cora murmured. "Always been a homebody. Stays in New Orleans or visits his sister in Shreveport. I don't think he's ever left the United States. Maybe not even Louisiana."

Molly squeezed Cora's forearm. "We will figure this out."

Cora nodded. "I know. I've been thinking about this, and there seem to be a few avenues to explore. First, uncovering the records on the partitioned part of my father's hard drive. Hopefully they'll list specific clients. Second, the Swiss bank account he opened. As his only heir, I should be able to get access to the account and we can find out where his deposits were coming from. And third, making this Vincent Ray person tell us who he was working for. Other than that, we're just sitting here, waiting for them to strike again, and that's not okay with me."

Burke's lips twitched. "I think we should be paying you, Cora. That's a good assessment. There is one more avenue we should add to your list, though—the Terrebonne Parish sheriff's department's investigation. Let's find out what they know. They might have evidence that they don't think is important, but given all we've learned, it might be exactly what we need."

"Specifically what?" Phin asked.

"Well, what you said yesterday," Burke said. "Who knew that the foundation was being poured in the Damper Building that day? Who had access to the property? Did anyone do a last-minute check on the pilings, or did they just start pouring? The thing about foundations for buildings the size of the Damper is that they can't dig that deep due to the water table."

Phin nodded. "Usually they pile rocks up to the top of the water table and compact them, then pour the concrete on top of that. The rocks anchor the foundation." He pictured the job and how Jack's killer would have hidden the body. "How was Jack's body found? Was it hidden in plastic of some kind?" He grimaced at Cora. "I'm sorry."

"It's okay. I didn't think to ask these questions. We can call Detective Goddard."

Phin glanced at Burke. "I'd like to see the building itself, if we can."

"And I'd like to see Goddard in person," Burke said. "We'll go this afternoon. This morning, I'd like to take Cora to the bank her father used. Like you said, as his heir, you can get access."

"I got a death certificate from the ME in Terrebonne Parish after they identified my father's body. That, along with my birth certificate, should be sufficient. I'd say that

we should take my attorney with us just in case they give
us guff, but . . ." Cora sighed. "But he's a suspect, too."

Burke folded his hands on his stomach, leaning back in
his chair. "Maybe we don't take Harry to the bank, but we
should call him. I want him to visit so that we can see him
when we question him. For today, I'll go with you to the
bank."

Cora met Phin's gaze. "You too?"

"Yes, of course." Phin wasn't even going to ask Burke
if it was okay. It would have to be.

Once again Burke's lips twitched. "Yes, of course," he
echoed. "Val, you're with us, too. You keep watch outside
the bank. I want to know if any cars drive by too slowly. I
want to know if anyone sneezes. Antoine, what needs to
happen to get into that hard drive?"

"I've had software running since yesterday, trying to
unravel the encryption. These things take time." Antoine
held up one hand like a traffic cop. "Don't ask me how
long. It takes as long as it takes."

Cora snapped her mouth closed, undoubtedly having
been about to ask that very thing.

"I might not ever be able to break it," he added reluctantly. "I figured he'd have a simple encryption, being so
long ago, but it's pretty advanced."

"And us?" Delores asked. "What do we do?"

"We can keep searching the attic," Stone offered. "Or I
can dig some more into Vincent Ray."

"I call dibs on the attic!" Delores said, clasping her
hands together in delight. "There might be a secret passageway. These old houses always had them."

Cora chuckled. "This one does. I'll show you before we
leave. It doesn't go anywhere, though. My great-grandfather
had it bricked over decades ago. One of my great-uncles
was using it to hide because he didn't want to do chores, or
so the story went. He tripped on a loose board on the stairs
and cracked his skull. Went undiscovered for more than a
day and nearly died. So they bricked it over."

"Wait," Phin said, he and everyone else staring at Cora. "There's a real, honest-to-God secret passageway? Could something be hidden on the unbricked end?"

"No. It's bricked over on both ends. But I'll show you and you can see for yourselves."

"That would have been so cool," Delores grumbled.

Cora patted her hand. "There are other nooks and crannies here, too. I've searched them all at one point. Found some old letters from World War I in one of them and a few old cookbooks in another. You can take a look at them. One of the cookbooks is from before the house was even built."

Delores brightened and made grabby hands. "Gimme."

"Now that Delores is sorted," Burke said with a smile, "we'll move on. Yes, Stone, please dig into Vincent Ray. Antoine, while your software is running, can you check the status of the NOPD investigation into Medford Hughes's death?"

"I did before I came over," Antoine said, "but that was before the NOPD shift change. I'll do it again."

A low growl got their attention. Delores's wolfhound had sat up straight, her teeth bared. A moment later, Soda-Pop was at Phin's side, pressed against his leg.

Even Blue lifted his head.

The doorbell rang.

Antoine checked his phone for the camera feed. "It's Detective Clancy. He looks unhappy."

Molly jumped from her chair and grabbed the white-board.

Cora's brows went up. "What's she doing?"

"Stashing our notes," Burke said. "As a rule, we keep our investigations to ourselves. If NOPD has a question, we answer it, but volunteering information is on an as-needed basis."

"Pantry," Cora said. "Hide it behind the mason jars, Molly. Val and I will let him in."

The Garden District, New Orleans, Louisiana
THURSDAY, DECEMBER 15, 8:45 A.M.

Val at her back, Cora opened her door to the detective, who wore a rumpled trench coat just like Columbo. "Detective Clancy? How can I help you?"

Clancy leaned to look around her and Cora leaned with him, blocking his view. He grinned. "Can't blame me for trying. I see all the vehicles on your curb. Broussard and his posse are here?"

"We just finished breakfast. Would you like to come in? We have some biscuits and gravy left."

"That sounds wonderful, thank you. I missed breakfast."

He followed her into the kitchen, where he took stock of the crowded table. His eyes flicked to the empty easel up against the wall and shook his head.

"You guys were brainstorming, huh? Maybe we can trade information."

Cora pulled out a chair for him. "How do you take your coffee, Detective?"

"Black, ma'am. Thank you." He waited until he had coffee and a plate of biscuits and gravy in front of him before saying another word. "I'm glad you're all here," he began, then took a bite of the food. "Whoever made this, I want you to marry me. My wife won't mind a third as long as you do all the cooking."

Cora laughed. "Thank you, but I'll pass." She sobered. "What's happened?"

Clancy squared his shoulders and met Cora's gaze. "We got the ballistics report back on the bullet that killed Medford Hughes. It was fired from the same gun that killed your father."

Cora stared as silence fell over the table. "What?" she whispered.

"I'm sorry, ma'am. There's no doubt. Whoever staged

Hughes's suicide was in possession of the gun that killed your dad. Whether it was the same person or not, we don't yet know."

Burke pinched the bridge of his nose. "I didn't expect that."

"Neither did we," Clancy said dryly. "I've been in communication with the Terrebonne Parish detective on Jack Elliot's case, so he knows our two homicides are connected. Given that ours is fresh and his is a cold case and that Miss Winslow has had several break-ins here, he's agreed to let us take over his investigation."

"The glove," Antoine murmured. "That damn glove."

"I knew it was weird," Burke said. "But why? How does that fit?"

Phin's hand dropped from the table to SodaPop. He was tense, Cora thought, wishing she could help him.

But he was doing okay. She wasn't going to interfere.

Phin drew a breath and let it out. "Detective, was there gunshot residue on the glove that Hughes was wearing?"

"Yes, there was. Why?"

"Because if there hadn't been, you wouldn't have assumed a suicide," Phin said. "His killer must have been wearing the glove, then put it on Hughes afterward."

Cora heard a low whine as SodaPop leaned in harder. *Good girl*, she thought, so glad that Phin had the support. He'd paled and sweat had broken out across his brow.

The scene of the murder. That's what he's thinking about.

He hadn't been okay that night, but he hadn't spiraled. She hoped he wouldn't now. He was visibly struggling.

"You're right, Phin," Burke said. "He shot Hughes with the gun from Jack Elliot's murder, put the glove on Hughes's hand, then put the gun in the dead man's hand. He was really careful."

Phin was breathing in deep measured breaths. "Not that careful. There was also the smudge of blood on the trunk lid. So, working backward, the killer touched the trunk as he was leaving. Couldn't have been when he got there or his hand wouldn't have been bloody yet. Hughes was only wearing one glove, so what about its mate?"

"Killer was wearing it," Molly said. "Were there any fingerprints on the trunk, Detective?"

"Only the victim's and his wife's. What are you thinking, Mr. Bishop?"

Phin was frowning, his lips moving, but no sound came out. He looked up and seemed taken aback that everyone was watching him. "Um . . . sometimes I work backward from the end when I'm planning to build something."

Stone smiled at him. "Or reading a book."

Cora faked a gasp. "You read the last page first?"

That seemed to break Phin's tension. "Sometimes," he said, his smile almost shy.

Cora wanted to kiss him again but contented herself with being his anchor should he need her. "So what happened at the end?"

"He touched the trunk," Phin said, "and left a smear of blood, but no prints. The smudge was at the base of the trunk lid, not the top. Like he'd touched it when the trunk was open, or he used that hand to open it."

"He got something out of the trunk," Val said quietly. "Detective, was the victim missing any clothes from his closet? Was any luggage gone?"

"It appears that some clothes were missing. Empty drawers, a lot of empty hangers in his closet. We found a suitcase in his wife's closet, but no luggage in the victim's closet or anywhere else in the house. But there was nothing in the trunk."

"The killer took it," Phin said, his breathing no longer labored. "He grabbed whatever it was. Maybe a suitcase, maybe something else. Then he touched the car with the other hand, leaving no prints, just blood. The hand that left the blood smear was also gloved."

"Was it heavy?" Delores asked. "The suitcase? If it was, he might have needed the support of the car. Otherwise, he would have grabbed the top of the trunk lid to slam it down."

"Or he might be small," Molly mused. "Or older. So . . . let's do this from front to back now. The killer arrives. I assume he had the laptops with him, since they were clearly meant to implicate Hughes in their theft. But we know it wasn't Hughes who stole them and shot Joy, because our intruder was much bigger than Hughes."

Val took up the story. "He gets in the car, probably in the back seat. Waits for Hughes to come out. Whatever the killer took from the trunk later was either already there or Hughes put it there while the killer waited. Hughes gets into the car, his killer—wearing gloves—shoots him. There's going to be blood and brain matter everywhere. Some of it had to get on the killer."

Phin's swallow was audible, but his voice didn't waver. "It got on both gloves for sure. The killer takes off one glove and puts it on Hughes. Puts the gun in his hand."

"He only needs the one glove for the gunshot residue test," Burke said. "If the killer wore the glove to shoot Hughes, you might find his DNA inside the glove."

"We got some skin cells," Clancy said. "Lab's testing them."

"Okay." Phin was nodding. "The killer gets out of the car, opens the trunk, then reaches for whatever he took. Was Hughes's wife's clothing also missing?"

Clancy shook his head. "According to her sister, no. Her clothes and shoes all seemed to be there."

"So Hughes didn't plan to take her," Burke said. "When was the wife killed, Detective?"

"It's not clear, exactly. ME says cause of death is suffocation. Lab found her saliva on the pillow on her husband's side of the bed."

Phin frowned. "The killer was so careful to make sure Hughes was wearing a glove with gunshot residue. Leaving the wife's murder weapon behind doesn't sound right."

"Didn't sound right to me, either," Clancy said. "I'm

wondering if the same person killed both Medford Hughes and his wife. She was an addict. There are track marks all over her arms and the inside of her thighs. Recent. She was also a gambling addict, according to her sister. The sister first thought that Medford snapped and killed her, then killed himself. When I told her that he might have been murdered, she was shocked. She had no idea who'd want him dead. Said he worked a lot. Volunteered at their church and took care of his wife after she'd shoot up. Tried to get her help, but it didn't take. The sister said she'd been ready for a visit from the cops for years, telling her that her sister was dead. She just figured it would be from a drug overdose."

"Why would Medford get scared enough to run?" Antoine asked. "Unless he'd been asked to process the stolen laptops. He did have his own network administration business. Breaking a password might have been in his skill set."

Cora frowned. "I want to know why the killer kept the gun that killed my father. For twenty-three years, he kept the gun."

"That," Burke said, "is a damn good question. Detective?"

"I have no idea." Clancy sighed. "People keep guns all the time, though. I can't tell you how many times I see it. You'd think they'd toss them in the river, but so many don't."

"Did Medford Hughes's neighbors hear the shot?" Cora asked.

"No, ma'am," Clancy said. "I think the killer used a silencer, but it was gone from the scene."

A cold shiver ran down Cora's spine. "Because he plans to use it again."

Phin's jaw tightened. "Not on you. We won't let him."

She believed him, offering him what felt like a shaky smile. "Thank you."

She wondered if Burke and the others would tell the

detective about the eraser business, but no one did, so she
followed their lead and kept her mouth shut.

"Did you find Hughes's computer?" Phin asked. "He
had our laptops in the back seat of his car. Where were his?
He was an IT guy. He had to have had at least one computer. Maybe you can figure out what his motive was in all
this."

Clancy looked impressed. "He didn't have one in his
car and we didn't find one in his house, either, which
strikes me as odd."

Phin nodded. "Maybe his killer took it. What about the
white van the neighbors saw parked outside Hughes's
house? Have you tracked it? We need to know where it is."

Clancy sighed. "We tracked it for a while, then lost it.
It shouldn't be hard to identify. It's missing half its front
bumper on the right side."

"The killer had an accident?" Cora asked.

Clancy nodded, looking even more tired. "We found
footage of the van on a Jackson Avenue street cam. It had
drifted into oncoming traffic then veered back into its
lane, hitting a parked car and driving away. The old Chevy
it had been approaching head-on wasn't so lucky. The
Chevy's driver must've panicked and wrenched the wheel,
because it lost control, went through an intersection on a
red light, and crashed into a bus. The driver of the bus
walked away, but the four college kids in the Chevy
didn't."

There was silence around the table. "Oh my Lord,"
Cora finally whispered, horrified. "He killed four more
people and didn't even look back?"

"He did not," Clancy said gravely. "We want to catch
him. Badly. So now it's your turn to help me."

15

DETECTIVE CLANCY CRADLED his cup of coffee in his hands. "Clearly this has something to do with Miss Winslow, given that someone's broken into her house several times now. Also, that someone broke into your offices, Burke, and stole two of your laptops, shooting Joy Thomas in the process and chasing Miss Winslow through the Quarter. *And* that the gun that killed Jack Elliot ended up in Medford Hughes's dead hand. *And* that some two-bit thug who still won't tell me his name broke into this house last night intending to burn it down. And, *finally*, that you *all* are here and brainstorming. I don't expect you're here for the biscuits and gravy, even though they're amazing." He pointed to the easel against the wall. "I'm betting that there's a whiteboard around here somewhere with your notes all over it. Captain Holmes has told me about how y'all work," he finished with a drawl. "So . . . what in the H-E-double-hockey-sticks is going on here?"

Cora froze, waiting for someone at the table to speak, but everyone was looking at her. Like this was her choice. She glanced at Phin, who was watching Clancy carefully.

"Do you trust him?" she asked Phin quietly.

Phin nodded slowly. "I think so."

"He's never given us a reason not to," Burke added. "Although lots of others hadn't given us reasons not to trust them until they did. It's up to you."

"At least I know it's going to be good," Clancy said. "Look, Miss Winslow, I know that you all have been searching your attic for the past two evenings, well into the night." He took a sip of coffee when Cora turned her surprised stare on him. "I put an unmarked car at the end of your street after you came to see me on Tuesday morning. After you fled for your life from whoever shot Joy Thomas. I apologize that whoever took your statement after the break-ins didn't treat the situation with the urgency it deserved. Had I known, I would have at least ordered drive-bys. Once I'd talked to you, I did put surveillance on your house. Last night it was me."

"I wondered how you'd gotten here so fast," Stone observed. "You walked in with the uniforms who responded to the 911."

Cora had to process that. "Wait. You were here, at the end of my street, for two days? You said that I couldn't have protection."

"It wasn't protection. It was surveillance. And I was only here last night. I had someone else here during the day and the night before. After my guys told me that you all had been searching the attic Tuesday night, I decided it was worth my time to check it out."

Cora turned to Antoine. "And we didn't know he was there? Our cameras didn't pick him up?"

Antoine looked embarrassed, as well he should, Cora thought, irritated. "There were no lurkers within our camera range," Antoine said. "How far down were you? I'll get wider-angled lenses on the property, stat."

Clancy chuckled good-naturedly. "I was sitting in my back seat, so you wouldn't have caught me on your cameras, even if they'd been wide-angled. The back seat's more comfortable and I could slouch down and watch without you seeing me."

Nasty shivers raced over Cora's skin. "Did anyone else do that?"

Clancy sobered. "Yes. There was a Toyota Camry parked not too far from where I was last night. Ran the plates. It was a rental. I was about to approach, but then all hell broke loose at your house. I saw the little asshole climbing into your window and then I heard Dispatch request a unit to your address." He gestured to Molly. "Miss Sutton had called 911, and I responded. I'd called in the license plate of the Camry right before Dispatch announced your 911 call, but the Camry was gone by the time we finished up here. I figured an intruder in your house outweighed a possible reporter." He looked around the table. "That was a mistake, I take it?"

"I don't know," Cora said honestly. "What was the license plate of the Camry?"

Clancy frowned. "He's followed you before?"

"Yesterday," Val said. "He tailed us when we were leaving the library. Cora had gone into work for her laptop, only to find out that the Camry had been there that morning, waiting for her in the parking lot."

Clancy straightened, putting his cup on the table. "Who saw the Camry at the library?"

"My boss, Minnie Edwards," Cora said. "She thought the guy was a reporter. She said that he was young, handsome, and somehow familiar."

"I'll go chat with your boss this morning," Clancy said. "I want to get her with a sketch artist. Now, don't think I've been distracted from my original question. What's going on? I need to know."

Cora sighed. "We aren't sure exactly. It has something to do with my father. He had some kind of . . . side business." She had to be careful with what she said. Her father's clients had escaped for reasons. Some of them might not have been legit, but some, like Alice VanPatten, were. "We only have hints. Like, he had a secret Swiss bank account. We were going to the bank today to find out more about it. He left receipts for items that had nothing to do with the accounting business he legitimately ran."

Clancy's brows shot up. "Legitimately? So the side business was not legitimate?"

Cora shrugged. "He had a secret Swiss bank account, Detective. You tell me. All I know is that he was involved in something that he kept very secret and that he was murdered. And that whoever killed him kept the gun and used it again on Medford Hughes. Or maybe it was stolen by whoever killed Medford Hughes. That person also wanted my private investigator's laptops, presumably for information about me. They got nothing from the laptops, by the way. They were wiped."

"We figured that ourselves, too," Clancy said dryly. "My IT people think you're a god, Mr. Holmes."

Antoine looked slightly mollified from his earlier humiliation. "It's true."

Clancy laughed. "God. You've surely got yourself a passel of characters, Broussard. So, Miss Winslow, you're looking for records of whatever your father was into, I take it."

"We are," Cora confirmed.

Clancy tilted his head, studying her. "And what have you found?"

"Receipts and a Swiss bank account." That was God's truth. She'd found Alice VanPatten through her own Google search. "We're still trying to learn who wrote me all those letters."

"Ah, the letters." Clancy picked up his cup again. "I got a hefty envelope from Detective Goddard in Houma late last night. He sent me copies of the letters. He said he'd be sending me the originals by courier today."

"What else did he send you?" Cora asked.

"Nothing yet. He's preparing to transfer everything he has in evidence. Mainly things found around the body." He hesitated. "Are you sure you want me to continue? The victim was your father."

"I'm sure," Cora said, and almost believed herself.

Phin tapped Delores, who was sitting next to Cora. "Switch with me."

Delores complied, giving Phin a sweet smile. "Of course."

Phin sat beside Cora, taking her hand. "If you want him to stop, you just say so. You and I can go out to the garden while he tells Burke."

What a sweet man. Cora squeezed his hand, grateful for his very visible support. "Thank you. I will say something if I can't handle it, but I've heard most of this before. I know he was found with one chipped rib, probably from a bullet, and two bullet holes in his skull. Those two bullets were found with the skull." Which was how they'd tested the ballistics of the weapon that had fired them.

"And so far, that's all I know," Clancy said. "He was wrapped in plastic, which didn't stop the decay but it did protect the bones."

Cora swallowed. "And his hair. That's how they got the DNA they used to ID him."

Clancy nodded. "You told me that when you came in on Tuesday morning. That you'd donated your own DNA to find out if you had any other relatives on your father's side because you'd been unable to locate your father to donate bone marrow for your brother. I'm sorry, Miss Winslow. That has to be hard, to discover that your search was in vain. But it did allow the Terrebonne Parish sheriff's office to ID your father's remains. So there was purpose."

"I know. I'm coming to grips with that. What else do you know, Detective Clancy?"

"Not much. I'll go see your boss as soon as I leave here. I want a description on whoever was following you. Does the library have cameras?"

"We do, but only around the book return slot." She grimaced. "People abuse that slot."

Everyone around the table grimaced along with her. "So gross," Val murmured.

"It really is," Cora agreed, pleased with how she'd

shifted the conversation away from her father's side business. She wasn't going to give Alice up. The woman had suffered enough.

She rose, ready to have the detective out of her house. He'd managed to clean his plate amid the conversation, but she could be charitable. "I can fix you a plate to take with you, Detective. But I need to be getting to the bank."

"I'm good, Miss Winslow, but thank you. You're a damn fine cook." He stuck out his hand for Burke to shake. "Call me when you're ready to tell me everything. Make it soon, please. Subpoenas are a pain in my ass."

Burke shook his hand. "When we get a clearer picture, we will."

Clancy frowned. "Translated, there *are* things you aren't telling me and probably never will. Miss Winslow, I can't help you if I'm flying blind. Can I at least get those receipts you mentioned?"

Cora turned to Molly. "We have copies, yes?"

"Of course we do," Molly said. She produced a folder from her large handbag. "They're right here."

"That was too easy," Clancy grumbled. "I'll be going now. Y'all have a good morning. Call me if the Camry tails you again. I'll get an unmarked car to your location and they can follow the Camry after you've lost it."

Val walked him to the door and Cora began clearing the breakfast plates, feeling grim. "That Camry better just be an overzealous reporter," Cora said, her jaw tight.

"We can hope," Burke said, equally grim.

"You were awesome, Cora," Val said when she returned. "Nice evasion. Burke really should be paying you."

"I'm not snitching on Alice VanPatten." Cora wished that she and Phin were back in their blanket fort. She'd felt safer there. But hiding wouldn't help. "My father's murderer is close by, isn't he?"

Burke shrugged. "We can't afford not to proceed that way, at the very least. You'll wear Kevlar when we go out today, Cora. Everyone will. To the bank, to see Detective Goddard in Houma, when you go out to walk your dog in the backyard. No complaints. Val, do you have an extra vest?"

"In my car," Val said. "I'll get it for you, Cora."

Phin had tensed, his fingers back in SodaPop's coat. It had been at the mention of Kevlar, which wasn't a huge surprise. Gunshots would likely be triggering.

"You don't have to go with me," she whispered, selfishly hoping he wouldn't take the way out she'd just offered. But she wouldn't ask him for more than he could give.

He gave her a grumpy look. "Don't even suggest it. I'm going. Besides, I've never been in a Swiss bank before."

Stone laughed. "Swiss banks look just like any other bank," he said. "When I was younger, I thought they'd wear those striped Swiss Guard uniforms, like the guys who guard the pope. I was very disappointed. Burke, how long before Clancy gets a warrant for Cora's attic? Because he's going to."

"We have at least this afternoon," Burke said. "We turned over the receipts we found readily. If Clancy figures out the tie to Alice VanPatten on his own, we'll deal with it, but I don't think he'll find it too easy to get a warrant on Cora considering she's been up front with the police so far."

"I'll call Alice," Cora said. "She has a life now. I don't want her blindsided by this. At least if she's warned, she can come up with a plausible reply if Clancy comes knocking."

Antoine dug into the pocket of one of his laptop cases, producing a burner phone. "Use this."

"Thank you. I had to give the police the one I used to call 911 from your office washroom. I'll get the papers I'll need for the bank. I'll take care of the dishes later."

Delores shook her head. "You cooked. I'll clean up. Don't forget about the secret passageway. And the antique cookbooks."

Cora smiled at the tiny woman. "I wouldn't dream of it."

Uptown, New Orleans, Louisiana
THURSDAY, DECEMBER 15, 10:15 A.M.

Sage slipped a hundred-dollar bill to the guard in front
of his grandfather's gated community. "Text me if he
comes in?"

"You got it. He just left an hour ago. He's unlikely to
return anytime soon."

"That's what we thought yesterday."

The guard grimaced. "His schedule has been less predictable lately."

Because Alan was distracted by whatever trouble Cora
Winslow had brought to his door.

Sage set out on foot, walking to his grandfather's mansion. He'd parked about a half mile away but hadn't driven
his own car. The Porsche was far too memorable. He'd
divested himself of Sanjay's Camry after driving it to the
old librarian's house and then to where Sanjay would have
picked it up.

Taking care of the librarian hadn't been that difficult.
Taking care of Sanjay had been much harder.

Sanjay had met him at the coordinates that Sage had
provided the night before. Sage had prepared himself to
shoot the man, but Sanjay's look of shock and betrayal still
haunted him.

Sage had made it quick, shooting Sanjay in the head
and leaving his body in the Camry. And then he'd taken
Sanjay's two-year-old Kia to a chop shop, trading it for a
clunker that the owner of the shop swore still ran like a
dream.

Sage cared more that the fifteen-year-old Toyota Corolla had clean license plates, like the guy promised.

Sage had worn the disguise he used when he went clubbing when he'd traded Sanjay's car. He didn't want anyone
recognizing him.

Like Minnie Edwards had.

He'd worn a ski mask when he'd broken the joke of a

lock on the old librarian's kitchen door, gaining entry in
seconds. He'd been armed with the small handgun he'd
taken from Joy Thomas, not that he expected to use it. It
would be too loud. He'd decided that a pillow would do.

But the old woman had woken as he'd stood over her,
one of her pillows in his hands. Surprisingly strong, she'd
fought him, yanking the mask from his head.

There had been a moment of terror in her eyes, and then
there'd been recognition—of him from the library, he'd
assumed. And then her expression had changed and he'd
seen true recognition.

He'd heard it in her whispered "Sage."

That had startled him. He'd hesitated for a heartbeat,
but knew that he'd have to follow through. She had to have
recognized him from his grandfather's TV ministry. Or
from one of the ads on billboards all over town. One pillow to the face later, and Minnie Edwards was no longer a
threat.

He should be feeling worse about what he'd done. It
kind of bothered him that he didn't. Yes, he felt guilty over
Sanjay because he'd known him. He hadn't known the librarian, but she was still a person. He should be feeling
worse about her death.

Regardless, it was done. His loose ends were snipped.
And now he'd find out exactly what his grandfather had
hidden in that safe. He took off at a jog, his workout attire
helping him blend in on the sidewalks of the high-priced
community.

He slipped into the house, avoiding the help. He knew
their routines. Knew that the cook would be watching television and the maid would be taking her hour-long smok-
ing break.

Alan was filming at the central offices today, so Lexy
would be there, too. The smiling couple with the perfect
life.

If their faithful parishioners ever found out . . .

Pulling on a pair of gloves, Sage locked the study door

behind him, making a beeline for the hinged bookshelf. A single tug had it moving fluidly aside, the shelf balanced perfectly. The builder must have known what he was doing.

He twisted the dial. One-zero-fifteen.

Holding his breath, he pulled at the handle and stuck his hand inside.

The photograph was near the back of the safe, lying on top of a stack of thick folders. Hands sweaty inside the gloves, he held the photo up to the light, just as Alan had done the night before.

It was a girl. She was wearing a graduation cap and gown, her smile bright. Her hair was golden and curly, her eyes wide and trusting.

Sage had never seen her before, but her face was familiar, as were her blond curls. Same with the dimple in her left cheek, deepened by her smile.

Sage's hair was the same color. He saw that same dimple in the mirror every time he shaved. Their eyes were the same.

She was family. He was certain. But who was she?

And what did she have to do with Cora Winslow?

The details around the young woman were slightly blurred, but he could still make out a few letters in the sign behind her. He hoped he could figure out who she was and where the photo had been taken.

He snapped a photo of the photograph with his phone. He'd work on deciphering the details later after he was back in his apartment.

He pulled the first folder off the stack and rifled through its contents. He recognized these papers. They were the reports he himself had made on the individuals Alan had him either follow or search their homes.

Those were people who sought to steal from them, to take advantage of Alan's generosity. Two had wanted to shake Alan down, demanding money for protection.

Nice auditorium you've got here. Pretty stained-glass windows. Be a shame if it all burned down.

Sage had found sufficient dirt on them to keep them all away. But most of the people Sage had investigated were just con artists trying to make a buck or two or a thousand. The details in Sage's reports had been used by Alan to get his enemies to back off.

Sage hadn't thought anything wrong with what they'd done. They'd simply used the subjects' own pasts against them. Everyone had at least one skeleton in their closet.

Sage had learned to exploit those secrets. Just like he'd do to Alan.

They'd never physically hurt anyone.

Until Alan had killed Medford Hughes and his wife.

And until I killed that old librarian.

And Sanjay.

Sage didn't believe in God. Didn't believe in hell, no matter how many times Alan had ranted about it. He wasn't afraid of eternal damnation.

But he'd never actually killed before. He thought about the way the old lady had struggled. How betrayed Sanjay had looked.

Stop. He couldn't dwell on them now. He'd have a crisis of conscience later.

He looked through the next folder and his eyes grew wide.

Holy shit. This is about me. Every detail of Sage's life, including the clubs he liked to frequent—far from New Orleans, of course, where someone might recognize him. He always went to Gulfport, Mississippi, and he wore the same wig and glasses that he'd worn to the chop shop that morning.

He hadn't thought that anyone had recognized him in the clubs. But clearly someone had known he was there.

There were pages and pages of information. Photographs of the men and women he'd taken to hotels after the clubs had closed. Each report was signed by his grandfather's private investigator. A guy by the name of Dave Reavey.

Sonofabitch. His grandfather had built a blackmail file on Sage, too.

He shouldn't have been surprised, but he was.

He shouldn't have been hurt, but he was that, too.

He set that folder aside. He'd be taking it with him.

The next folder was an eye-opener, too. Alan had been having Lexy followed for a long time by the same PI he'd set on Sage. Alan had been spying on Lexy since the very beginning of their marriage. *Seems like the PI's sole function is to keep tabs on Lexy and me.*

There was nothing here. Lexy had done nothing wrong. She met with charities and visited sick people in the hospital. She had standing appointments with her hairdresser and her personal trainer, but there was no dirt there, either.

Lexy was a model wife.

Sage wondered what she'd think about this. He grabbed one report at random and slid it into the folder with his own.

Leverage with Lexy, should he need it.

His phone buzzed with a text. *Dammit.* He wasn't finished yet.

He checked the message, expecting it to be from the guard at the gate, but it was from his grandfather.

I need you to meet me in my office at the church in 30 minutes. Do not be late.

Sage looked around the study. Had the old man installed cameras of his own? Was Sage being watched right now?

He was tempted to tell the old man to fuck himself, but he wanted to know where he stood. He was armed and now he had evidence on the old man. He wasn't sure what the photo meant, but he'd find out.

He'd begun to put the folders back when he found two manila envelopes in the back of the safe. One held cash—stacks of crisp one-hundred-dollar bills. There were five stacks of fifty. Twenty-five grand in all. The year on the bills . . . twenty-three years ago.

Lots of things happening twenty-three years ago.

If the money was connected to Jack Elliot's death, he wanted no part of it, so he put the envelope back.

The other envelope contained more photographs, all of the same girl. Most seemed to have been taken from far away, with a long-range lens, maybe.

They started when she was a toddler, playing on a jungle gym on a playground. Another was the same girl at about age eight. She wore a Girl Scout uniform and sat at a table outside, selling cookies. There was a photo of the girl in a formal dress with a corsage strapped to her wrist. Another of her walking down the street, an older woman at her side.

Sage captured all the photos with his phone.

This girl was the source of his grandfather's distraction.

This girl had something to do with Cora Winslow.

This girl could bring Alan down.

Now Sage just needed to find out who she was.

Closing the safe, he hurried out of Alan's study, out of the house, then caught a cab home. He'd come back for the chop shop's Corolla later, if it was still there.

He needed to change his clothes and do his grandfather's bidding.

He should be nervous, but he found himself only curious. What had the old man done now?

Houma, Louisiana
THURSDAY, DECEMBER 15, 12:05 P.M.

"I hope this goes better than the bank did," Cora grumbled as she freshened her lipstick. She was nervous about seeing the detective in Houma.

Today she'd be asking harder questions than she had on previous visits. Today she'd be asking for photos.

At least she had support. Three of their team had accompanied her—Phin, Val, and Burke. Val was driving the bullet-resistant SUV and Phin was in the back seat with Cora, SodaPop at their feet.

Burke followed them in his truck. If the black Camry or any other vehicle started to tail them, Burke would herd them away, so that the local cops could pick them up.

"The bank didn't go badly," Val said. "I'd have been shocked if they'd handed you the statements from your father's account. There's always paperwork."

There had been. Stacks of paperwork. And Cora had read every page before signing. Phin had stood watch over her while she'd pored over each document the bank handed her. Burke stood guard inside the bank, Val outside.

No one was getting to Cora on their watch.

Their investigation on Cora's behalf had started out as a way to get to whoever had shot Joy. Now it was personal for all of them.

Cora sighed. "I honestly thought that all I'd need to do is prove I was Jack Elliot's daughter and they'd at least give me a printout of the transactions."

The bank said they'd get back to them in a few days.

Plenty of time for Clancy to get a subpoena, dammit.

"Are we getting out?" Cora asked.

Val nodded. "Just waiting for Burke to park his truck. We're going to have you surrounded at all times."

Cora slumped. "And I appreciate it. It's just . . . confining."

"It won't be forever," Val said cheerfully.

Phin hoped it would be for a long time, though. He hadn't gotten his fill of Cora Winslow yet. Not by a long shot. He hoped she felt the same.

She took his hand and squeezed it. It was a good sign. He hadn't had a chance to kiss her again, but right now she was stressed. He made do with kissing her temple and she relaxed into his side.

Burke's truck rolled to a stop and he got out first. Phin tugged Cora to his side of the SUV, helping her out, his dog falling into step beside him. He, Val, and Burke surrounded her as they walked into the building that housed the Terrebonne Parish detectives.

Cora had called Detective Goddard when they'd been about twenty minutes out, letting him know they were coming. Burke had been against it, thinking that would give the man ample time to leave if he didn't want to talk to her. But Cora insisted that it was only polite and one caught more flies with honey.

She'd also already made the call before informing Burke, apologizing versus asking permission.

Phin liked her style.

Goddard ushered them into a meeting room. The man was a fourth-generation cop and had several awards. Phin had looked him up. He'd also served in the navy, and while that wasn't as good as the army, of course, it was still a mark in the man's favor.

Goddard gave Cora a smile as she sat at the meeting room table. "I figured you'd be calling me after I got the call from NOPD this morning. Hell of a twist, the gun that killed your father being found at the scene of a staged suicide."

"You could say that," Cora said quietly. "I need some information. I hope that you can help me."

He looked wary. "I'm sending everything I have to Detective Clancy."

Cora shook her head. "I'm not asking you to hold anything back from Clancy. But my life is now being targeted. Someone broke into my house again last night. He was armed and prepared to burn my house down. The intruder who broke into Mr. Broussard's firm on Tuesday shot one of Mr. Broussard's colleagues. She almost didn't make it."

"I heard about that," Goddard said. "You're okay, though? And Mr. Broussard's colleague, too?"

"Cora is fine, and our office manager will be," Burke said, taking control of the conversation. "We have some specific questions, especially given this morning's ballistics report. I think you might have held back information when you first talked with Miss Winslow, out of respect for her shock and grief. But she needs to know as many specifics about her father's death as is possible. We need to know so that we can help her. What can you tell us?"

Goddard studied the four of them for a moment, then glanced down at SodaPop. "Whose service dog?"

"Mine," Phin said, proud that he hadn't felt an iota of shame in the admission. "PTSD."

"I looked you all up when Clancy told me that Miss Winslow had hired your firm, Mr. Broussard. He said you'd be by sooner or later. I honestly wasn't expecting an entire entourage, but given that you've had an armed intruder and someone following you, I understand it."

Phin could see that Burke was irritated because Goddard was letting Burke know that he didn't hold all the control. "What can you tell us, Detective Goddard?" Burke repeated.

Goddard didn't even blink. "Clancy called again this morning with the ballistics report and asked me not to reveal anything we hadn't mutually agreed to."

Cora's shoulders sagged. "Then we've wasted our time."

"Maybe not. I can show you photos of your father's remains. And I can tell you about the summary of the handwriting expert's analysis on the many, many letters."

Cora nodded once. "All right, then. Let's see the photos."

Phin decided to step in. "Perhaps Burke, Val, and I can look at the photos. I'd prefer Cora not have those images in her mind."

Cora raised her brows at him, assuming her regal-heiress persona. "You'd *prefer*?"

Phin didn't back down. "You don't want the dreams, Cora. Trust me."

She deflated. "You're right. On this, anyway. What about the handwriting analysis, Detective Goddard?"

"First of all, I just got it myself a few days ago." He took a single sheet of paper from the folder in front of him. "I can't hand this over to you, but perhaps you can give us a lead. In the opinion of the expert, the same person signed all of the letters. Of course, the signature is just 'Your dad, Jack Elliot,' but there are nineteen years' worth of those same four words. There *was* a difference in the signatures before and after the four-year time gap."

"From when I was twenty-two until I was twenty-six," Cora said. "They started back up two years ago."

When she'd started looking for her father in earnest.

"Exactly. The signer's signature has grown a little more cramped, suggesting he's experiencing some mild arthritis. Since osteoarthritis is most commonly seen starting at about age fifty, we're estimating that the writer is now in his mid to late fifties or early sixties."

"He would have been in his early to midthirties when my father was killed, then," Cora said. "That's helpful. I guess."

"Your attorney's about the right age," Phin said.

Cora frowned at him. "Harry is not involved. I can't believe it."

"Harry Fulton?" Goddard asked. "Clancy told me that he accompanied you to the police station on Tuesday. Next time, hire a defense attorney," he added. "Clancy said the man was in way over his head."

"He's been my family's attorney since before I was born." She glared at Phin. "It's not him."

"Okay," Phin said.

"Do not patronize me, Phin," she said quietly.

"I'm not. Honestly. It doesn't matter what either of us thinks right now with respect to Harry Fulton. It matters what the evidence shows."

Goddard nodded. "He's right, Miss Winslow. For what it's worth, Clancy doesn't believe he's involved, either. He sent me a sample of the man's handwriting—from when he signed in at the station. His handwriting doesn't match the letters. But please, don't go anywhere with him alone until either Clancy—or your PIs, of course—have cleared him."

Cora gave a frustrated huff. "So the letter writer is a man in his mid to late fifties, early sixties right now. What else does the analysis tell you?"

"There's now a slight tremble in the *r* in 'your.'" Goddard put two more pieces of paper on the table and turned them toward Cora, handing her a magnifying glass. "Here's a pre-gap letter, and this one is the last letter you received. All of the post-gap letters have that tremble."

Cora squinted at the two pages, then nodded. "I see what you mean."

Burke leaned over to take a look, his admiration reluctant. "I didn't catch that when I read the letters. Your analyst has some expertise."

"Yes, he does," Goddard said. He pulled back the copies of the two letters and returned them to his folder. "He's very good. What else can I do for you?"

Burke frowned. "That's it? Seriously?"

Phin agreed with his boss, but it didn't look like Goddard was going to give them anything more unless they asked the right questions. "We'd also like to know about the burial site," Phin said. "Who knew they'd be pouring concrete that day?"

Goddard nodded. "Good question. I found the foreman who oversaw that building project. He's retired now. Very helpful fella. He said that when the body was recovered, he was stunned. He got two of the workers on that part of the project on a Zoom call the day the body was found. They figured the cops would be asking questions and they wanted to remember how that day went. But twenty-three years is a long time, so they didn't remember a whole lot. They did remember that it had been raining in the days before the day they poured, so their schedule was delayed. The foundation area was prepped and ready to go. One of the guys remembered covering the area with a tarp when the rain started, but it wasn't a tight fit, just enough to keep the rain out. Anyone could have lifted it and lowered the body into the hole they'd dug."

"Someone had to have known that," Phin said. "You don't just show up with a body if you don't know that you'll have a place to hide it."

"That's what I thought," Goddard agreed. "Unfortunately, the foreman said he'd been rescheduling the next steps, so all the contractors knew. He also said that all the business owners in the area would come by to check the progress. Nothing nefarious, just curious. They had to keep repairing the fences around the job site because kids would sneak in to look. It was their biggest construction project up until then—and since—so some of the details stood out."

"So a lot of people knew about the foundation," Phin said glumly. "Dammit."

Cora squared her shoulders. "What about the photos of my father's remains?"

Goddard handed an envelope to Burke. "Don't look at them, Miss Winslow. Please."

Burke took the folder. "Val and I will do that for you. Phin, are you okay to look at them?"

"Check them first. If there's no blood or body parts, I'll be okay." Bones he could deal with.

Burke opened the envelope and examined the photos, his expression neutral. He then handed them over to Val.

Val looked through them, then passed them to Phin. "Just bones."

Phin studied each one, stopping at the final photo. It was a picture of the clothing Jack had been wearing, specifically his pants, dark in color. But there was a darker patch on one of the pants legs. Phin held it closer, focusing in on that dark patch.

"What's this?" he asked Goddard, pointing to the area. There was a streak of blue and one of a yellowish brown. "It looks like a grease stain, but it's not the right color."

Goddard held out his hand for the photos and placed them back in the envelope. "That, Mr. Bishop, is the question of the day. I asked the lab to run tests to identify that spot."

"What are you talking about?" Cora asked.

"Stain on the thigh of the trousers your father was wearing that night," Phin told her. "What did the lab say?"

"First," Goddard said, "I want to remind you that Mr. Elliot's remains were found wrapped in a plastic sheeting that can be bought anywhere, and there's really no way to trace it after all this time. I tried. But the lab report yielded information that's more specific. I just got the report fifteen minutes before you got here and I haven't had time to research what the results mean. My lab guy had an appointment, so I can't dig deeper until he returns."

Burke scowled. "Detective, get on with it, please."

Goddard ignored him, his attention on Cora. "Your father's remains were clothed. Pants, shirt, undergarments, and a windbreaker. The lab found trace elements in the stain on his right pants leg."

"What kind of elements?" Burke asked.

"Lazurite, iron oxide, and manganese oxide." Goddard handed him the report.

Burke scanned it, then handed it to Cora. "What does that mean, Detective?"

Goddard shrugged. "I don't know. I was about to google those three things when you arrived."

Cora drew an excited breath. "Lazurite's in lapis lazuli." She looked up, her brandy-colored eyes wide. "That stain is paint. *Old* paint. Like paintings from the Renaissance. It went into the ultramarine pigments that are still so vibrant. Vermeer was famous for using them."

"I've heard of him," Val said. "Elijah and I watched a documentary about his ability to portray light. He was what . . . sixteenth century?"

"Seventeenth," Cora said.

Goddard was staring at her. "How do you know all that?"

"She's a librarian," Phin explained. Yes, he was proud of her. "Knows a lot of stuff."

"Remind me not to play Trivial Pursuit with her," Goddard said wryly. "What about the other two things? The oxide things?"

Cora was practically buzzing. "The iron and manganese oxides are in burnt sienna pigments, also used in old paintings. That's . . . wow. How would old paint have gotten on my father's pants? He wasn't a painter. He couldn't draw a stick figure with a ruler, according to my mother. And not just house paint or even oil paint, but paints used centuries ago." She frowned. "Not those exact paints, of course. Reformulations, would be my guess. But how did they get on his pants?"

"He could have brushed up against a wet painting," Phin said. "Or the paints might have been transferred from whoever was carrying him the night he ended up in the foundation. Picture your father's body being carried over a man's shoulder. Probably not a woman. Your father wasn't a small man. His thighs would have rubbed up against the clothing of whoever was carrying him. And the transfer had to have happened before his body was wrapped in plastic."

"What was someone doing with old Renaissance-period paints?" Val asked. "They aren't used anymore, are they?"

Cora bit at her lip. "Not widely. Mainly by art restorers. Or maybe by painters trying to re-create old masters. But not by any starving artists. Those old paints are super expensive."

"So," Burke drawled, "we're looking for a man in his late fifties, early sixties, with mild arthritis in his hands who restores artwork. I mean, that's very specific. I wasn't expecting that."

He was right, Phin thought. That was very specific.

And troubling.

Art restorers worked in museums, he knew.

But sometimes in galleries, too. He knew this because he'd repaired the sink of the owner of a gallery only a few blocks away from the gallery owned by Cora's best friend Tandy.

Tandy owned the gallery with her father. A father who was exactly the right age to be the letter writer. Phin wanted to blurt this out, but he stopped himself.

Cora was angry enough that they thought Harry Fulton should be investigated. And Tandy's father hadn't even known Cora until she was eight or so. The girls had met as third graders. The letters had started earlier than that.

He'd hold on to the thought and share it with Burke.

"I'm back to the plastic," Val was saying. "Was the plastic at the job site where Jack Elliot was buried? Did the killer have to go out and buy it? Did he have it on hand, planning the murder? It doesn't seem like it. If I were planning to kill someone, wrap them up, and shove them into a foundation—sorry, Cora—I'd be damn sure I had on clothes that wouldn't give me away. I wouldn't wear clothes that had Renaissance-period paint on them."

Cora turned to look up at Val, who stood behind her. "Are you suggesting my father's murder was unplanned? A heat-of-the-moment thing?"

"Either that or the killer didn't know he was sporting stains," Val said. "Would those pigments have come out in the wash?"

Cora frowned. "I don't know. I'd have to research that. If they didn't come out in the wash, the killer might not have known that he was wearing paint. If they do wash out, then the paint was fresh and the killer had just come from his easel."

Goddard was grinning. "I like you guys. This is amazing. I do have to share it with Detective Clancy, but you saved me a lot of time."

"Librarians to the rescue," Cora said wryly. "At least we have a place to start."

"Thank you," Burke said.

"Thank you," Cora echoed, then extended her hand to Goddard. "I appreciate the work you've put into this case."

"I really wanted to solve it for you," Goddard said with

regret. "But maybe Clancy can. Or your PIs. They have a good record."

"Yes, they do. We're going to drive by the site of the building demolition, just so you know."

"Figured y'all would. There's a diner down the street. Amazing shrimp, if you're hungry."

Cora made a strangled noise. "Shellfish allergies."

Phin settled his hand on her lower back. "We'll get a burger instead."

16

CORA WATCHED PHIN as Val drove them to the site of the demolished Damper Building. Something was bothering Phin, but she didn't know what.

"What is it?" she asked as Val parked the SUV in front of a pet store. It was as close as they could get to the building.

"Nothing," he said.

Cora scowled. "Nothing always means something."

Val cut the engine and turned around. "You okay, Phin?"

His hand had sought out SodaPop and Cora wasn't sure Phin had even known it had done so.

"I might not be after I tell you," he muttered, then sighed. "Tell Burke to park his truck and get in the front seat."

"Okay," Val said warily. "I just texted him. Are you okay?"

"Yeah."

But his fingers splayed and flexed in poor SodaPop's coat. His touch was always gentle with the dog, but Soda-Pop knew he was upset. Her little whine hurt Cora's heart, because when the dog made that sound, it meant that Phin was close to an edge.

"You don't need to tell me."

Phin sighed. "Yeah, I probably do."

Burke opened the front passenger door and climbed in. "What's going on?"

Phin closed his eyes. "So . . . I was thinking about who restores paintings."

Cora waited for him to continue, but he didn't. Unable to stand his silence, she said, "People who work for museums."

Phin opened his eyes and they were filled with misery. "Or galleries."

Cora flinched, her eyes going wide with shock. Shock quickly became fury. "*No*. It isn't Patrick Napier. I didn't even know him when those damn letters started. You're wrong."

Phin didn't look away. "I hope I am."

Dammit. Damn him. "You can't be serious."

But he was.

Cora looked to Burke, only to find him wincing. "Burke?"

"I have to admit that I hadn't considered that, but Phin makes a good point."

Cora's heart was racing, and she was so angry. How *dare* they? "You're forgetting that he didn't know me then. He didn't know my father. He didn't know what color dress I wore on Christmas the year my father disappeared. This is *insane*."

Burke looked at Phin. "She's got a point, too."

Phin sighed. "I'm sorry, Cora, and I hope I'm wrong. But how do you know that he didn't know your father?"

Cora's eyes burned and she shrank away from them, from their gazes full of pity and regret. Val too. *Damn them all.*

"He didn't even live in New Orleans back then," she shot back. "Tandy's parents moved to New Orleans when Tandy and I were in the third grade. I met Tandy first. She invited me to a slumber party at her house. Then I invited her to mine and we became best friends. Her father helped us—Mama and Grandmother. He fixed things. He made sure our roof didn't leak and that our faucets didn't drip. He was there when I needed a father. He took me and Tandy to all those father-daughter dinners. He is *not* the letter writer. He is *not*." She blinked, the tears in her eyes streaking down her cheeks.

Which just made her even angrier.

She turned her face away, staring out the window, needing a moment to compose herself.

They're trying to help.

Cora knew the little voice in her mind was right. She was behaving like a child. But Harry and Patrick? *No.* No to both of them. *Neither would hurt me.* She couldn't believe that either of them would have hurt her father, either.

Patrick had never even met her father.

How do you know?

She swallowed a sob. Because she didn't know. She didn't know anything anymore. Her life was out of control, a train tearing down a mountain slope, jumping the tracks.

Phin's touch on her arm was tentative. Gone within a second. "I'm sorry," he whispered. "I don't mean to upset you. But someone's after you, Cora, and I don't want anyone to hurt you. But especially not me. I don't want to hurt you."

Cora shuddered out the sob she'd been holding back. "I know," she whispered back. "Give me a second."

"Do you know where Tandy and her parents moved from?" Val asked, her tone . . . odd.

Like she already knew the answer and Cora wasn't going to like it. "Somewhere in Louisiana. I don't remember where." She wiped her eyes with the sleeves of her jacket and turned to face them. "Where, Val?"

"Thibodaux."

Cora shook her head. Thibodaux was only thirty minutes from Houma. "No."

Val nodded, sympathy in her blue eyes. "I just checked the property records for Lafourche Parish, just on a hunch. Just in case. Houma is in Terrebonne Parish, but Thibodaux is the parish seat of Lafourche. The property records show that Patrick Napier owned a home there until twenty-one years ago."

That made more sense. "Twenty-*one* years ago," Cora

said triumphantly. "He didn't arrive in New Orleans until *two and a half years* after my father was killed. *Two and a half years* after I started getting the letters."

Val, Burke, and Phin shared a sober glance that made Cora's stomach clench.

"It's a coincidence," she insisted.

Then heard herself. *Could it be?*

"It has to be," she whispered.

Phin brushed his fingertips over her hand, a fleeting touch. "I want him to be uninvolved. I also want you to stay alive."

So did Cora. "I shouldn't be fighting you all. I wanted you to find out who was breaking into my house. And then to find out who shot Joy." Sudden hope gave her heavy heart some buoyancy. "But Patrick wasn't in town on Tuesday. He couldn't have been the one to shoot Joy."

"That's true," Phin said steadily.

Cora sighed again. "But you need to be sure. *I* need to be sure. I'm not sure of anything anymore."

"I understand," Val said. "I think we all do. Patrick is close to your heart. He's important in your life. We can be objective when you can't. Let us look into him and we'll see what comes up."

Cora nodded. "Okay." She wiped at her eyes again because they kept leaking. "Are we going to see this hole in the ground?"

The hole where her father had been buried.

The father she'd hated for twenty-three years. Hated and loved at the same time. Twenty-three years later, she still did.

"We are," Burke said. "But you don't have to go, Cora."

"Yeah, I do." She pulled herself together. "As angry as I am with the man for doing a dangerous job that got him murdered, I do want to pay my respects."

Phin got out of the car and jogged around to her side, SodaPop keeping close. Phin held out his hand and tugged her to her feet.

"I'm sorry," he whispered.

"Don't be." She leaned up, gently patting his cheek. "You're right. We need to exclude him." She rested her head on his shoulder, able to breathe again when his arms came around her. His lips brushed the top of her head and she swallowed hard, tears threatening once again.

They *would* exclude Patrick. She was certain.

She pulled out of Phin's embrace and gripped his hand as they approached the area of the foundation where her father's body had been found. Val and Burke flanked them.

Burke, Val, and Phin were constantly looking around for threats.

Burke lifted the caution tape, gesturing for them to pass under. Cora held her breath as they edged up to the large hole in the ground. There were still pieces of broken concrete littering the ground.

And . . .

It was just a hole with some rocks at the bottom. Her father's resting place.

She should have been feeling something now. She knew she should have.

But until she found out who'd killed him and why, she didn't know what she should feel. Other than anger. That was still there, simmering in her gut.

"We had a good life," Cora said quietly. "At least I remember it being good. We lived with my grandmother, but that was just the way it was. We were family, sharing the big house. We didn't have a lot of money, but Mama said we were okay. Well, up until he disappeared. Then I remember Mama crying because she had bills to pay. Grandmother helped, but it wasn't like she was super rich. We held on to the house and Mama got her physical therapy certification. Things were better then."

"Tell me about the school you attended with Tandy," Phin said.

She clutched his hand gratefully. He was strength and goodness. She'd yelled at him and here he stood.

Supporting me.

They all supported her. Burke and Val, too.

"It was a private girls' school in the Garden District. Kindergarten through twelfth grade."

"Fancy," Val said. "Sounds expensive. How did your mom afford it?"

"Grandmother paid for it. I was a legacy student. Both Grandmother and Mama attended. It was assumed that I would attend, too." She stared down into the hole, casting her mind back to that time. "But there was financial assistance. I remember that pretty vividly. The other girls could be vicious. I was glad when Nala and Louisa started, because they were scholarship students, too."

"Not Tandy?" Phin asked.

Cora shook her head. "Her daddy had the money to pay the full tuition."

"How did Nala and Louisa get the scholarships?" Phin asked. "You got yours because you were a legacy student, I assume. But Joy didn't go to a fancy school like that."

"No," Cora agreed. "She didn't. Joy's parents ran a corner grocery store."

"In Tremé," Burke said gruffly. "I knew them. Good people."

"Had to be good people," Cora said, still staring down into the hole. "They produced Joy, after all. Mama and Joy became friends after Joy got shot on the job, back in the day. Joy's husband had passed a long time before that. Joy came to my mother for physical therapy. Her sister would bring her, along with Joy's kids. The sister was the kids' babysitter, as I remember. So she had to bring them with her when she drove Joy to PT. Mama didn't have a babysitter, either. Grandmother watched us when she worked, but sometimes Grandmother had plans, so John Robert and I went to work with Mama. When Nala and Louisa started coming with their mother, we all became friends. My mother got scholarships for Nala and Louisa the following year. Their mother was a hero—a cop wounded in the call of duty, in service to the city. The school was happy to have her daughters attend."

"And you had fellow scholarship students to hang with," Phin said.

"I did. Tandy was kind of the odd one out. She had a mother and a father, at least back then. She had a nice house that wasn't always falling apart and in need of fixing. She had new clothes and we didn't." Cora's lips tipped up. "Nala and I discovered thrift stores when we were high school freshmen." She chanced a look up and found the three watching her.

Burke looked contemplative, Val encouraging.

Phin looked like he wanted to hug her. All warm and safe.

She leaned against his side, gratified when he dropped her hand and slid his arm around her waist.

"Thrift stores in the nice parts of town have some super nice clothes," Val said. "I used to shop at them when I was a teacher. Now I just wear jeans and combat boots."

She made them look good, too, Cora thought.

"It's true. The thrift stores in the Garden District were special. We found things that were nicer than Tandy's." Cora smirked at the memory. "Pretty soon, Tandy was going with us. We all still shop at the thrift stores."

"When did Tandy's mother pass?" Burke asked.

"When we were in college. Aneurysm. Just . . . happened. So we were all there for Tandy. She, Nala, and I were in the same year, all at Tulane. We made it through." Cora frowned, a new memory troubling her. "It was Tandy's mother who introduced us to thrift stores. She was a champion shopper. I'd forgotten about that."

"So Tandy's mom didn't always have money?" Val asked carefully.

"Not always. She said that she'd learned to stretch a dollar after she and Patrick got married, before they came to New Orleans. Then his gallery business started growing and she didn't need to anymore, but she kept shopping at thrift stores. She saved for rainy days. She left everything in her savings to Tandy. I never asked how much it was."

Phin squeezed her waist lightly. "But you know."

She looked up at him, her smile wobbly. He listened, truly listened. Picked up nuances other people didn't. "Yeah. The next year there was a scholarship fund established at St. Charles School for Girls in her mom's name. Two girls a year get to attend for free. Harry manages the fund."

"You were surrounded by incredible women," Val commented. "I'm glad."

"Me too." She shook her head. "Patrick can't be involved. He just can't be." She squared her shoulders, something she'd done a lot lately. "How will you exclude him?"

"Background checks to start," Burke said. "We'll look for motive. Unexplained income. Gaps in employment. That kind of thing." He turned to face the buildings across the street. "But while we're here, I want to find out if any of those stores were in business twenty-three years ago. Someone had to have seen something. And maybe there's an art restorer who knew this area back then. Someone who wasn't Patrick Napier."

It had to be someone else. It just had to be.

She started to turn from her father's resting place. "Let's go, then."

"Just a minute." Phin pulled something from his pocket, his expression sheepish. In his hand was a rose, its stem cut short, its thorns stripped away. "For your father's grave, if you want to."

Her heart squeezed so hard that it hurt. "Phin. Where did you get it?" Her grandmother's rosebushes had gone dormant months before.

He glanced at Val. "Val's sister is a florist. When we talked about coming out here, I texted her, and she brought it to Val while we were in the bank."

"*That's* what was in the bag," Val said. "I wanted to peek, but I didn't."

Cora's eyes filled. "Thank you. Am I allowed to throw it down there? Is it still a crime scene?"

"Police released it weeks ago," Burke said. "Go ahead. We can step back and give you space. We can't leave you alone, though."

"You don't have to step back. Please stay." She took a moment to consider her words, then held the rose over the hole, her tears spilling over. "I loved you, even as I hated you. I don't know why you did what you did. But if every client was in trouble like Alice VanPatten, I'll try to understand. I'm sorry you're gone. I'm sorry Mama died thinking you'd left her. And if you're still lurking around somewhere, a little help would be appreciated. My PIs can only do so much."

She dropped the rose into the hole, then drew a deep breath and wiped her face once more. She had to stop crying. Her face was getting chapped from the brisk wind.

"I'm ready to go. Let's go talk to shop owners and get some food that won't send me to the ER."

Phin carefully turned her, keeping his arm around her. She slid her arm around his waist and let him guide her across the concrete-riddled property, the others walking ahead.

She looked over her shoulder, glancing one more time at the hole. Her father's resting place. *Rest, Dad. I hope you're happy, wherever you are*.

She looked up at Phin and found him staring down at her with pain in his eyes. *For me*. She didn't want him to hurt for her, though. He'd hurt enough.

She slid her hand around his neck and pulled his head closer. "Blink once for yes."

Slowly he blinked, one side of his mouth lifting. He closed the distance between them, taking her mouth in the sweetest kiss. It was no peck, but a full lush kiss that had her brain turning off the rest of the world.

For a long, delicious moment, the only thing she thought about was his mouth on hers, his shoulders under her hands, his hands running up and down her back. It made her want more. More with Phin.

He was the first to pull away, his mouth wet and his eyes slightly dazed.

She knew she looked the same. "Thank you," she whispered.

He pressed a finger to her lips. "Don't thank me. Not for coming with you today or for holding your hand, but especially not for kissing you. It was my pleasure." He hesitated. "I hope it was yours, too."

She swallowed. "It was."

He relaxed. "Val's waving for us to get a move on."

Cora looked over her shoulder and, sure enough, Val's expression was a combination of affection, exasperation, and impatience. Hand in hand, she and Phin crossed the street, nearly bumping into Burke when he stopped abruptly in the crosswalk. He was staring at his phone, his jaw tight.

Panic rose in Cora's chest. "Is it Joy?"

Burke shook his head. "Let's go. Back to the SUV." He, Val, and Phin shepherded Cora back to the secure vehicle, no one saying another word until they were all safely inside.

"What's happened?" Cora demanded.

"It's not Joy," Burke said grimly. "It's your boss."

Dread was like a bucket of ice water poured over her head. "Minnie?" she whispered. "Is she all right?"

But from the look on Burke's face, she already knew the answer was no.

"She's dead," Burke said gently. "Clancy went to her house to check on her when she didn't show up to the library today. She was lying dead in her bed."

"Natural causes?" Cora managed to ask, her voice choked and shaking. *Please?*

"No," Burke said. "I'm sorry, Cora. Clancy believes she was suffocated with a pillow."

Cora's mouth opened but no words would come. Her throat was tight and she couldn't breathe. Phin's arm tightened around her shoulders protectively.

"We need to get you back to the city," Phin said. "Where you'll be safe."

"I'll follow you," Burke said to Val. "You and I can come back tomorrow to talk to the shopkeepers. For now, Cora's safety is the most important thing." He turned back to face Cora. "I'm so sorry."

"It was the driver of that Camry," Cora murmured. "Wasn't it?"

"It makes sense," Phin said, pressing a kiss to her temple. "We'll make sure he pays. I promise."

Cora could only nod. She was numb.

Minnie had cared about Cora. And it had gotten her killed. Who would be next? Who should she warn?

Who can I trust?

For now, only Burke's people. And Joy and her brood. And Tandy, of course.

And Patrick? Was Tandy's father still trustworthy?

I don't know. I don't know anything anymore.

Cora had thought that seeing her father's grave would be the worst thing to happen to her today.

I'm sorry, Minnie. I'm so sorry.

Merrydale, Louisiana
THURSDAY, DECEMBER 15, 4:00 P.M.

MERRYDALE WELCOMES YOU.

Sage hoped so. Or at least he hoped that Merrydale would be generous with the answers to his questions.

The suburb north of Baton Rouge was full of nice, well-kept houses, but Sage was really interested in the high school. He hoped he'd gotten this right.

He was here in disguise. His personal cell phone was next to him in a Faraday bag, unreachable and untrackable. He was using his burner for all internet searches and GPS directions.

He checked the mirror on his car's visor to make sure

that the dark wig was on securely. The heavy, dark eye-glass frames obscured a fair portion of his face. He didn't look like himself, which was the goal.

He slowed as he passed the high school, studying the sign on the side proclaiming the school's name.

Yes. He'd gotten it right.

Putting on his blinker, he turned into the parking lot, just to make sure. He pulled out his phone and found the photo he'd taken of the graduating girl his grandfather had hidden in his safe. He zoomed in on the lettering over the girl's right shoulder. Only the lower half of the school's name was visible, but the girl's cap and gown were in the school colors, so that had helped his search.

The photo was several years old, based on the graduation-year charm dangling from her cap's tassel. He at least knew she'd graduated in a year that started with *201*. He couldn't see the final number.

It was a decent place to start.

The letters in the photo lined up perfectly with the letters on the school—Merrydale High School. He was in the right place, at least.

He didn't yet know the name of the girl, but hopefully he soon would.

He'd googled the public library's location on his burner phone. He had no idea what he was walking into in this little town, so he wasn't going to leave a tech trail. The library was less than two blocks from the high school.

It closed soon. He hoped he'd find what he was looking for easily. Otherwise, he'd have to come back later and he wasn't sure he had time for that.

It felt like time was running out.

His grandfather's behavior today had been weird. Alan had texted him to hurry to meet him, said that he needed him. But the old man hadn't said more than ten words the whole two hours Sage had sat in his office—mainly hello and goodbye. There hadn't been much more than that.

However, there had been several times when Alan had

looked like he'd wanted to say something. To command something.

It had put Sage on edge. He'd gotten out of there as quickly as he'd been able to and got the distinct impression that Alan had been all too happy to see him go.

Weird. That Alan's behavior was so upside-down was not a good sign.

It gave urgency to his mission. Sage wanted to find out who the girl was and what she had to do with Cora Winslow. He wanted to know why the combination to Alan's safe was one day earlier than the day Jack Elliot had been buried in concrete.

He hoped the library would have the answers he sought.

Ironic, him going to another library. At least this time he'd had the presence of mind to disguise his face.

He didn't want to have to kill another librarian.

That would suck.

He walked into the library and approached the librarian's desk with what he hoped was a shy smile.

"Excuse me, ma'am." He laid his drawl on thick. "I'm doing some research into my family tree. My granddad went to school around here and I was hoping you had some old yearbooks I could look through."

The woman smiled up at him. She had a pretty smile. If Sage had met her at a club, he'd have taken her back to his hotel in a heartbeat.

"We have some," she said. "What years were you looking at?"

This might work or it might not. He hoped that the library kept all the yearbooks in the same place, including the more recent ones.

"I'm not entirely certain. He died recently and we found conflicting information on his age. Home birth, y'know. Paperwork got messed up by the country doctor."

She rose and began walking toward one of the stacks. "I hear that sometimes. Let me show you where we keep them." She looked over her shoulder. "You can't check them out. They have to stay here in the library."

"I won't ask, ma'am. I promise."

"All right, then." They crossed the library, coming to a little room with glass walls. "Here they are."

Oh great. She'd be watching him.

He smiled nonetheless. "Thank you, ma'am. I'd best get busy." He let himself into the room and did a walk around the shelves, checking first to see if they had any cameras installed.

They did not appear to, which was lucky for him.

He took a second turn around to see what materials they kept on the shelves. They had a few yearbooks from the fifties and sixties and he chose those. Luckily, they had all the yearbooks from the 2010s. He grabbed them all and put them on the table with the old books.

He'd think of an excuse if she asked why he was looking at the recent ones.

He opened all the older books and made a show of examining the pages, all while checking to see what the librarian was doing. Every so often she looked up at him, but he thought she was checking him out rather than monitoring his activity.

Eventually she answered the phone and turned to her computer monitor. *Finally.* Sage grabbed the earliest of the recent yearbooks, then paused, thinking. He didn't have enough time to thoroughly check each yearbook.

This had to do with Cora Winslow. It had something to do with the date of Jack Elliot's death. If his hunch was right, if the girl in the photo was twenty-three now, she'd have graduated five years before. So he chose the book that was five years old and flipped to the senior class pictures.

He paged through the photos, looking for the girl.

Nothing in the *A*s or *B*s.

He found her in the *C*s. There she was, smiling for the camera. She looked fresh and innocent and his chest clenched as he was once again hit with a wave of déjà vu. He knew her, even though he'd never met her before.

And now he had a name. Ashley Caulfield.

The quote by her name made him smile. It was a line from the song "It's Not Easy Being Green," the quote assigned to "Kermit the Frog."

Then his smile faded as he let himself think of that photo in his grandfather's safe. Of all the photos capturing this girl's growing up.

Sage felt like he'd opened Pandora's box and this girl had popped out. He'd never be able to stuff her back in.

He knew she existed now.

He knew she was important. He just didn't know why.

He snapped a photo of Ashley's senior picture and quickly put the recent yearbooks away. He resettled in his chair, opening the old books. He'd planned to do this anyway, just to let the librarian believe his quest was a serious one.

Now he had another agenda. He wanted to find more Caulfields.

He checked the *C*s in every one of the old books, perusing not only the senior photos but those belonging to the underclassmen as well. The years represented were too spotty. If he only checked the senior sections, he might miss out on whoever it was he was looking for.

He finally found a single Caulfield. Timothy Caulfield had attended Merrydale High back in the midsixties. That would make him in his early seventies by now.

Was he related to Ashley? How? A grandfather, perhaps?

It could be. His own grandfather was in his late sixties, and Sage was only two years older than Ashley.

He snapped a photo of Timothy Caulfield and closed the yearbook. He made a show of standing and stretching, noting that the librarian was following his every movement again. He flexed a little, just to give her a show.

If her mind was on his body, she wouldn't be thinking about his face.

He put the yearbooks away and sauntered back out to the main room. "Thank you, ma'am. I put everything back the way I found it."

"Thank you. Did you find what you were looking for?"

"No, ma'am, but thank you anyway."

She tilted her head. "I noticed you taking a few photos. Why, if I might ask, if you didn't find what you were looking for?"

Fucking librarians. Always asking questions. Luckily, he'd prepared for this.

"I found a name I recognized from one of my granddad's stories. I figured I'd take the photo back to my grandmother and see if she recognized him."

"Oh, okay." This seemed to satisfy her.

He really hoped it did. He really didn't want to kill another librarian.

He got back to his car, buzzing with anticipation. He had one more thing he needed to check. On his burner phone, he pulled up the background check service he used.

Ashley Caulfield, he typed.

Nothing. She might have been too young to have any online presence, although that she had no social media seemed odd. Sage couldn't use himself as a comparison. He had dozens of pages on the internet dedicated solely to him.

He changed his search to *Timothy Caulfield*. He had a presence, thankfully.

And he owned a home not too far away. Had lived there for thirty years, which meant the man had been there twenty-three years ago.

Sage set a course for the Caulfield home, not certain of what he'd do once he got there. It wasn't a long drive. Nothing in Merrydale seemed far away from anything else.

The GPS on his burner phone took him to a neighborhood off the beaten path, each of the lots at least five acres. Timothy Caulfield's house sat a distance off the main road but was still visible.

Sage pulled over to the side of the road and opened his backpack. He had an old-fashioned paper map that he used to fool passersby into thinking he'd stopped to check his position.

No one had ever confronted him while he'd been parked, but there was always a first time for everything.

After unfolding the map—which would be useless if he was confronted, as it was a map of Gulfport, Mississippi— Sage took his binoculars from his backpack and used them to study the Caulfield home.

The house was a single-story ranch type with a green door. The lawn was well maintained and the flower beds had been freshly mulched.

His breath caught. There she was.

Ashley Caulfield ran around the corner of the house, from the backyard to the front. She was laughing, her face filled with joy. On her heels was a barking collie with a beautiful coat. Ashley held a ball high off the ground, and the dog was jumping for it.

She threw the ball hard and the dog gave chase. Ashley sat on an old tree stump, lifting her face to the sky.

Sage couldn't look away. On some level he *knew* her, even though he was certain they'd never met.

It was that damn dimple. *Just like mine.*

He became aware that he'd been sitting too long. He was lucky no one had come along, demanding to know what he was doing there.

He drove away, nearly reaching the interstate when his burner phone dinged with a text.

No one had this number, so it had to be a forwarded message. His personal cell phone was still in the Faraday bag, but it was synced to his laptop at home. All messages that came through to the laptop would be forwarded to his burner. He could return any messages using a spoofing service to make it appear that they'd come from his personal phone.

He'd been using this method to hide from his grandfather

for years. Of course, it had been for naught since Alan had hired a PI to follow him.

Irritated at the thought of his privacy being so invaded, he pulled over to look at the text. It was from his grandfather.

Because of course it was.

Where are you?

Sage considered his answer. If the man was still having him followed, the PI was really good, because Sage hadn't seen evidence of a tail.

Visiting friends in Gulfport, he replied. His grandfather knew he'd visited the Gulfport clubs, thanks to the PI. His grandfather was going to assume he was off getting defiled or something.

I need you here. In New Orleans. Now.

Sorry. I'm off the clock until tomorrow morning, Sage added, wondering what Alan would say to that.

There was no reply for so long that Sage had put his phone away and was about to pull back onto the little two-lane road that fed into the interstate, but his phone dinged again.

Report to my office at 9 am. Sharp.

Irritation rising, Sage typed back, *Sir, yes, sir!* He hit send before he could rein in his attitude.

Watch the attitude, boy. Tomorrow. 9 am. Do not be late.

"Asshole," Sage muttered, tossing the phone onto the center console.

He wondered if Alan would finally get to the point. He wondered if tomorrow would be another two-hour staring session where Alan said less than ten words.

He wondered what Ashley Caulfield had to do with Cora Winslow.

17

~~~

PHIN ROLLED HIS shoulders. "That was heavier than it looked."

Burke looked up from where he sat on Cora's attic floor, an open box at his side. "I told you that I'd help you with that shutter."

The third-story shutter, which had been hanging on by a single screw, had been bothering Phin since he'd first arrived at Cora's house two days ago. It was back in place now and would stay that way for another fifty years.

Phin crouched next to the box Burke searched. "What are you finding?"

Burke had come straight to the attic when they'd returned from Houma. Phin had followed him, helping him search for a few hours. Six boxes later, he'd become itchy and needed a break and some physical activity.

Fixing that shutter had settled him, and that was a good thing.

Stone and Delores had been searching boxes the whole time Phin and the others had been to Houma and back but had come up with nothing. They'd taken a break to go wander the Quarter for a while. That seemed like torture to Phin. He needed to keep his hands busy.

Cora was keeping hers busy. Amazing smells wafted up

the stairs from the kitchen. She'd retreated into the kitchen on their return, her eyes red-rimmed. She'd cried most of the way back from Baton Rouge. Phin couldn't imagine what she was going through. Still, she'd taken him into the darkened living room to kiss him before asking which cake was his favorite.

One of these days he was going to get to kiss her first. For now, he'd let her have the control. She'd lost so much control in every other part of her life.

"Not finding much," Burke admitted. "These boxes are mostly photo albums. Antoine's been checking online. There's hardly anything on Patrick Napier online, especially not from before he moved to New Orleans."

"Not too surprising." Phin reached for another box that had been labeled in Cora's mother's handwriting. He slit the tape with his box cutter. "The internet was still new then. Unless he'd done something amazing and gotten written up in the paper for it—or done something horrible and gotten written up in the paper for it—there shouldn't be much on him. Not much social media back then. MySpace hadn't even been created then, I don't think."

"I usually wish for the days before social media," Burke grumbled, "but sometimes I wish more people had used it."

A knock at the door had both of them looking up. Cora was poking her head in, her expression drawn but determined. "I brought you some sweet tea and red velvet cake."

She set the tray she carried on a stack of boxes. "Antoine found out that Patrick was a schoolteacher before he moved to New Orleans. Taught high school in Thibodaux."

Burke rose with a groan, his joints audibly popping. "Subject?" He took a glass of the tea. "Thank you, Cora."

"You're welcome." She closed her eyes and drew a deep breath. "Art. Patrick taught art." She opened her eyes and they were filled with confusion and doubt. "He had a painting included in an art exhibit in Houma, back in the midnineties. But that doesn't mean he was a restorer."

"It doesn't," Burke agreed.

But Phin thought that it was likely. He wasn't going to say a word, though. He'd what-iffed enough for one day. She was hurting and he hated to see it.

"I fixed the shutter outside this window and the faucet in the primary suite bathroom sink," he said, changing the subject, because Cora's eyes had grown shiny and even sadder.

She knew what they thought. She knew they suspected Patrick.

Of what, exactly, they weren't sure.

Patrick could have carried Jack Elliot to that hole in the ground that night twenty-three years ago.

He was the right age to be the letter writer.

Whether he'd killed Jack was unknown.

His involvement in Cora's life didn't make sense. Yet.

Cora sighed sadly, the sound cutting like a knife. "Patrick fixed that faucet for me a few months ago. It didn't stop dripping. A lot of the things you've fixed in the past two days are things he fixed first. I've spent years going back and refixing things he's tried to fix."

Phin had reached for a glass of the tea but halted. "He fixed things around your house?" She'd mentioned that once before, but it hadn't really sunk in. Patrick had been puttering around her house for years.

"He did. Tandy and I became friends on the first day of the third grade. My mother and Tandy's mom became friends, too. Patrick would come over and fix things because my grandmother and mother were really horrible at it. So was Patrick, but at least he tried."

Phin was conflicted. They had no hard evidence that Jack Elliot and Patrick Napier had ever crossed paths. Not even the night Jack died. At the moment, his killer was just some random guy with old-style paint on his clothes.

He hoped Patrick was simply a nice guy who was a bad handyman.

"Do you want to help us search?" he asked. "Plenty of boxes to go around."

"No, not really," Cora said quietly. "I asked Tandy to come over for dinner."

Burke's head jerked up, his hands stilling in the box he searched. "I don't think that's a good idea."

Cora shrugged and wandered over to the window seat. "She's my best friend, Burke." She sat, drawing her knees to her chest. She looked so very young in the afternoon light. And so very pretty, despite her swollen eyes. "I believe I trust Patrick, but I need to know for sure. You said you wanted to exclude him. So I'm going to ask Tandy some questions and hopefully we can glean the information we need."

Phin winced as he returned to his own box. "What kind of questions?"

"Like . . . what caused her parents to move to New Orleans? She would have been almost eight, so she should have at least a recollection."

Phin wanted to sigh. *This can only end in tears.* "You don't think she'll want to know why you're asking?"

"She will. I'll think of something to tell her. Maybe I'll tell her that I want some of those old portraits in the living room restored. She and I have talked about that before. She's offered to do them a few times, but something always comes up that distracts her."

Burke's brows went up. "Tandy does restoration?"

"She does. Usually for clients who buy work she sells in the gallery. They'll bring her the painting they found in the attic or in a closet. She gets jobs by word of mouth. She doesn't hang out her shingle."

Phin stared at her. "Why didn't you mention that earlier when we were talking about restorers?"

"Because I knew it couldn't be Tandy and you got me distracted worrying about Patrick. I'm still worrying about Patrick. Anyway, I thought I could tell her that I want the portraits restored, but she's so busy with the gallery, I was wondering if her father's ever done any restoration work." Cora looked satisfied with herself. "I don't recall hearing him talk about it, but he might have done some when he was younger. Tandy talks about it all the time. That Patrick hasn't makes me think that he doesn't know about it. Which would eliminate him as your suspect."

Burke heaved the sigh that Phin had been holding back. "I can't tell you who you can entertain in your own home but, for the record, this is a bad idea. She could tell her father that you're asking questions and force his hand."

"*If* he's involved," Cora said stubbornly. "But if he is involved and if she does tell him what I'm asking, maybe it'll force things to move along. I feel like we're in a holding pattern."

Phin wanted to shout *no*! That "moving things along" could get her killed. But Burke was slowly shaking his head at Phin, as if he knew exactly what Phin was thinking. So Phin held his tongue.

"I know it feels stagnant, Cora," Burke said calmly, "but we are making progress. However, like I said, I can't tell you who you can invite into your home. If you do get to talking about her past, ask her where her dad got the money for that gallery. Antoine found the deed in his name, but we want to identify the money trail."

Cora's satisfied smile faded. "What do you mean?"

"He bought a house in the Quarter and the gallery building at the same time," Burke said. "The proceeds from his house in Thibodaux wouldn't have been close to what he'd have needed for the purchase of those two properties. He sold the house in the Quarter after his wife died and bought a place in Uptown, but he's had that gallery since the day he moved to New Orleans. The value of the gallery property is astronomical now, but even twenty-one years ago, it wouldn't have been cheap."

Cora frowned. "Where do you think he got the money?"

Burke shrugged. "Don't know."

Swiss bank account, Phin thought. Hidden cash. He was starting to form connections in his mind and he didn't like them.

If Jack Elliot had had a partner in his eraser business, what skills would that person have needed? Which parts would Jack have done and which would have been left for his partner?

Someone had to have handled all the physical aspects—moving people, setting up a new house or apartment, shooting ex-husbands who tried to thwart their clients' escape. That someone seemed to have been Jack.

Someone would also have had to do a lot of computer work, identifying all the elements of a new life for their clients—social security numbers, passports, driver's licenses, work histories, medical histories. It made Phin's brain hurt to consider. He wasn't sure if Jack would have had the ability to do all those things.

Phin stopped thinking about skill sets when he looked in the box he'd just opened. *Oh. Oh wow.* "Cora?"

He looked up and found her watching him, her eyes filled with dread.

"What?" she asked in a croak.

Phin pulled an eight-and-a-half-by-eleven frame from the box. "I found your parents' college diplomas. They both went to LSU?"

"Yes. That's where they met, playing in a Dungeons & Dragons club, of all things. He was a grad student and she'd just started on her bachelor's. Dad was a few years older." She unfolded herself from the window seat and sat beside him. She picked up the diplomas and studied them. "Dad majored in accounting and Mom majored in biology. She'd started her master's after they got married, but got pregnant with me, so that slowed her down. And then John Robert came along. Mom had finished about two-thirds of her master's when Dad disappeared. She threw herself into it the year I started school, and she got her certification."

Phin smiled at her. "You were proud of your mother."

"I was. She picked herself up and did what she had to do." Sadness clouded the pride in her eyes. "She worked—and worried—herself into an early grave. One day she just collapsed. Her heart just . . . stopped. One day she was there and the next day she wasn't."

"You and Tandy had a lot in common," Phin murmured, ignoring the box for the moment. Cora was more important.

"We did. Her mom's aneurysm was also sudden. But my mother had warning and just didn't tell us. Turned out my grandfather had heart disease, but we didn't know. John Robert and I, I mean. My mother knew and she knew that something was wrong with her heart, but she was determined to work her job and take care of John Robert at the same time." She drew a breath. "What else is in that box, Phin?"

He peeked in the box. "Books that say '*Gumbo*.' Cookbooks, maybe?"

She laughed. "No, *Gumbo* is the LSU yearbook."

Pleased to hear her laugh, Phin reached in and pulled out a stack of yearbooks, each bearing the word *Gumbo* on the spine. He handed one to her. "Can you find your parents?"

"Hmm. This one is a few years newer than the ones you're holding. This is probably my mother's."

She opened the yearbook and thumbed through the pages until she came to the *W*s. "Here she is. Priscilla Winslow. She was so pretty." She held up the book so that Phin could see.

"She looks like you," Phin said with a smile.

Cora smiled back, muted but real. He wanted her smile to be unfettered, without worry. They'd make it happen.

"*Winslow* sounds very *Mayflower*," Burke commented. "This is pretty." He'd found a box filled with blown glass.

Phin wondered how much it was worth. Maybe Cora could sell some of it to pay for new wiring. He hadn't had the heart to tell her that she'd need to do a full electrical overhaul soon, and Phin wasn't a licensed electrician. He could do the job, but he'd need oversight by a licensed contractor.

"My grandmother used to talk about her grandparents and how they said our ancestors came over on the *Mayflower*." She huffed. "They really didn't, but it made for a good story. Huh. Maybe that's why my father picked that

poem for my mother—'The Courtship of Miles Standish.'
Miles Standish, John Alden, and Priscilla Mullens all
came over on the *Mayflower*."

Phin opened a different yearbook and started paging
toward the *E*s for Jack Elliot. But the voice in his head told
him to keep going.

To the Ns. For Napier. What if . . . ?

His heart sank when he found Patrick Napier's photo.
He'd been a handsome man then, his smile bold. He'd majored in both computer science and art history.

Computer science.

That didn't mean he'd been good at searching for and
procuring new passports and other identification papers.

It didn't mean he *hadn't* been good at it, either.

Patrick had also been part of a fraternity. So what about
Jack?

Hands unsteady, Phin worked his way back to the *E*s.

Jack Elliot was in the same undergraduate class as Patrick Napier. He'd also double majored—in accounting and
computer science. He and Patrick may have shared classes.

But they'd definitely shared a home.

Jack had pledged to the same fraternity.

Phin had found it. The connection between the two men.

Shit. How do I tell Cora?

This is going to suck.

Phin heard a little whine. SodaPop had wedged herself
against his side.

Because he was breathing too hard and too fast.

A soft hand covered his. "Phin?" Cora asked, her voice
thin. Concerned and scared, all at once. "What's wrong?"

He shook himself, clearing his mind. "Patrick Napier
graduated from LSU with his bachelor's degree the same
year your father did."

Cora's mouth fell open, her face gone slack with shock.
"What?" Then she shook her head in denial. "Lots of people went there, Phin. It doesn't mean anything. It was a big
school. They might never have met."

Phin exhaled. "They were both computer science majors. And they were fraternity brothers."

Cora's face crumpled. "No. *No.*"

Phin handed her the yearbook open to Jack's page, his finger marking Patrick's.

Cora looked at both pages, then closed her eyes. "Patrick wasn't *here* when the letters started. He didn't live here then."

Phin hated to burst her bubble of hope. "Let's find a way to ask Tandy if he made visits to New Orleans in those days. Do you have anything he's handwritten?"

She shook her head, her misery palpable. "I don't think so. I can try to get something. I'll . . ." Her voice broke. "It can't be true. Patrick could *not* have killed my father. I just can't believe that."

She turned away, choking back a sob.

Phin set the yearbooks aside and pulled her into his arms. "It's okay to let go."

That seemed to have been all the permission she needed. Her sobs racked her body. It was gut-wrenching to listen to, to see her fall apart like this. Phin looked helplessly over her head at Burke.

Burke looked grim. "I'll go down and see what else Antoine's found." He rose, grimacing, then gripped Phin's shoulder. "You okay, Phin?"

Phin nodded. Then shook his head. Because he wasn't. Cora's sobs were breaking his heart. "No, but I will be."

So would Cora. He'd make sure of it.

The Garden District, New Orleans, Louisiana
THURSDAY, DECEMBER 15, 4:45 P.M.

Cora's head hurt. Her eyes were sore. Her heart ached.

She'd known heartbreak before. She'd sat by her mother's coffin, saying goodbye. And by her grandmother's. And by John Robert's.

But this?

This was different. This was betrayal, and it cut so deep that she could barely breathe.

Patrick knew my father.

He had to have known him. Had they just attended the same university, even at the same time, Cora could have brushed that off. She might have been able to brush off both being in the same major. But they'd pledged to the same fraternity, and fraternity brothers knew each other.

"How is this possible?" she whispered.

Phin's arms tightened around her as they sat on her attic floor, surrounded by boxes filled with her past. "I'm sorry. I wish I hadn't had to tell you."

She sighed, patting his chest. "You're trying to keep me safe. I understand that. And what you found is . . . incriminating on its face."

But not set in stone. Not yet. There were explanations. There *had* to be explanations.

"We'll dig more," Phin murmured, dropping a kiss onto the top of her head. "I promise."

"It's not your job, Phin," she said quietly. "I'm not going to add to this bad situation by asking you to take on more stress."

He stiffened, his arms going rigid, letting her know that she'd misstepped. But he didn't let her go. And when he spoke, it was with a tenderness that made her eyes burn again.

"I would take on a lot more stress to keep you safe," he said. "And, while I'm not at a hundred percent, I'm much better than I would have been even a few months ago." He pressed another kiss to her temple. "Let's worry about you, okay?"

She breathed him in. This man was a little bit broken, but he was putting himself back together in real time. And he needed to help her. She knew that as well as she knew that she needed to help him, too.

"What are we doing here, Phin?"

His arms loosened only enough for him to flatten one hand over her back, rubbing in slow circles. "I'm not sure. But I haven't *felt* for a long time. I didn't want to feel a single thing. Because then I'd feel everything."

She was quiet for a moment, considering his words. "Everything is overwhelming."

"Yes." There was relief in that one word. "It really is."

"And now? Do you want to feel?"

He chuckled and it was just wicked enough to make her smile, too. "I definitely want to feel, but I'm trying to be a gentleman."

She smacked his chest lightly, her cheeks on fire. "You know what I meant."

He brought her closer, tugging until she was curled up on his lap. "I know. And my answer is the same, without the dirty double meaning. I definitely want to feel. I've missed out on a lot. I'm tired of missing out. I keep sticking my toe back into the water, y'know? Testing to see if I can handle it."

"Can you?"

"Better than I could two years ago."

"What happened two years ago, Phin?"

"I met Stone. And then Delores, of course. I'd been just existing. Moving from one town to the next. Crashing wherever I could find a semisafe place to sleep. I was homeless sometimes." He huffed a mirthless laugh. "I know where the soup kitchens and food pantries are in a lot of Florida towns."

Her heart hurt even more to hear this. But this hurt was tinged with hope, because Phin wasn't that man anymore. At least not now. Hopefully not ever again.

"Do you think that makes me think less of you?"

He rested his cheek on the top of her head, the movement weary. "It should."

"It doesn't. Phin, you entered the military as an eighteen-year-old boy with depression. Clearly you saw some things that have taken up residence in your head.

You worry that you're going to hurt someone, but, as far as I understand it, you only hit one guy in a bar after he started it and then shot you. You haven't hurt anyone. I'm not sure that you could."

"I wanted to kill that little bastard last night," he growled. "Trying to burn your house down."

That admission should not be hot. But it was. Swallowing that back, she patted his chest again. "But you didn't. You and Stone restrained him and held him for the cops."

She pulled back far enough to meet his gaze. She wanted to know why he was so worried that he'd hurt someone. She wanted to know what he'd seen that had so devastated his mind. There were so many questions she wanted to ask, but this wasn't the right time. He'd tell her those parts of his story in his own time, or he wouldn't. "How did you meet Stone two years ago?"

The relief flashing in his eyes was unmistakable, and she was glad she hadn't asked the more difficult questions.

"Stone's brother Marcus is married to my sister, Scarlett."

"The cop."

"The homicide detective," he corrected, his pride too cute. "Stone's good at figuring things out."

"Not hard to believe. He has facial recognition software on his laptop and knows how to use it. You and Antoine said that he'd been an investigative journalist. I need to look up some of his work. I haven't had a free minute to do that."

"I'll send you some links. Or I'm sure Delores has all his articles on her phone."

Cora smiled. "I'm sure she does. I like her a lot. She bubbles joy and contentment."

"She does now. She went through a lot of therapy after she was nearly killed. Which was how she met Stone. He watched over her during her recovery."

Cora had to set aside her horror at hearing that Delores had nearly been killed. She didn't want to distract Phin. "I guess that's why he's so protective of her. He's protective of you, too."

"He is. He's a good guy, with a lot of his own demons. He gets through each day by helping someone else. One day, two years ago, it was me."

"I'm glad," she whispered.

Phin smiled at her, a gentle thing that lightened her heavy heart. "Me too. When he met Scarlett, she'd been looking for me. Unsuccessfully."

"Stone found you."

"He did. Someone at one of the VA facilities in Miami remembered seeing me come in for my meds."

"Meds? For depression?"

"Yeah. I'd tried so many since I'd gotten out of the army, but none worked. Finally, a Miami doc tried one that clicked. It was such a relief to be able to *think*. To plan my life out past an hour at a time."

"Phin," she whispered, new tears falling down her face. She knew he wouldn't want her crying for him, but she couldn't help it. "Sorry. I'm all over the place today. I know you're here now and you're better, but I hate the thought of you not having a safe place to sleep. And now I've made it all about me. I'm shutting up now."

He kissed her, just a brushing of lips. "You're fine, Cora Jane."

She opened her mouth to protest the middle name but stopped herself. She didn't mind it coming from him. It was almost an endearment. "So the meds helped?"

"They did. I was able to get some handyman jobs, usually working for a licensed contractor for cash. All under the table, but I was doing well enough to get my own apartment. It was in a seedy part of town, but it was mine and I had a place to come home to after work and just . . . be."

"And then?"

"And then one day I was coming home from a job and saw three people on the street outside my place. Scarlett and two men I didn't know."

"Stone and his brother."

"Yes. I was . . . scared. Humiliated. I didn't want them to see me there. Suddenly the place that was safe and mine was dirty and run-down and made me ashamed." He shrugged, his muscles gone rigid once again. "So I did what I always do. I ran."

"You weren't ready."

"I wasn't. I walked around all night. Snoozed in an alley where some of my old friends hung out. Mostly other vets. We kept each other safe back in the day. Before I could think past the next hour. I thought maybe they'd throw me out because I hadn't come back after getting my own place, but they welcomed me. Said they were happy that I'd gotten out, that I was getting my life back. Said that it was a process and that some of them got out, only to come back, then they would escape again for a little while."

"That's sad."

"I know. I thought the same thing as I sat there in that alley, back against a wall, trying to get a little sleep."

"So that's what you meant when you said you'd slept sitting against a wall before?"

He chuckled. "Yeah, that. Plus all the years in the army. You slept when you could, in any position you could."

"So you left the alley?"

"At sunup. Figured Scarlett and the two men I'd seen her with would be gone. I came home, went up the stairs, and there was Stone hanging out at my front door. Scared the shit out of me at first. He introduced himself. Said we were family now. Said he'd been where I was and he understood." Phin sighed. "Said that he wouldn't tell Scarlett that he'd talked to me. Said that I didn't have to be perfect to go home, I just had to be ready."

"Did you leave with him?"

"Not that day. He gave me his cell number. Told me to call any time of the day or night and he'd be there. I kept thinking about what he said. What my buddies in the alley said. I didn't want to cycle back into that alley. I wanted to go home. To my mom and dad and my sister and my brothers. I just wanted to go home, but I was too scared to do that."

Those words were said with such desolation that Cora needed to comfort him. She wrapped her arms around his neck and held on.

His arms closed around her and they simply sat there. Together.

"I'm ready now," he finally murmured. "Ready for my family, ready to feel again. Because I've finally accepted that I'm not perfect and never will be. I'm just me."

"I like you."

She felt him smile against her cheek. "I like you, too. I'm not a good bet for you, Cora Jane. But I like you and I'd like to be a good bet for someone like you."

Her heart stuttered at the raw honesty in his voice. "Just someone like me?" she teased breathlessly. "Or me?"

He tipped her chin up and kissed her, long and hard and full of all the things they both seemed to be wanting. When he released her, his chest was rising and falling rapidly and his eyes were heated.

Yes, they were both wanting.

"You," he said gruffly, then cleared his throat. "You asked what we're doing and I gave you a long-assed answer. I want to be a good bet for you. I want you to feel safe. I want you to feel happy. I want you to just . . . *feel*. And I want you to feel all that with me."

"I'd like that. All of that." She rested her head on his shoulder, content in that moment. She wasn't thinking about intruders or erasers. Or Minnies or Alices or Patricks. She was taking a break and thinking about herself. And Phin. "Have you considered working with vets like yourself?"

"All the time. And then something happens, I get triggered, my anxiety ramps up, and I spiral. My therapist says I'm too hard on myself."

"She might have a point," Cora said dryly.

"She'd like you," Phin returned, equally dryly. He was quiet for a few heartbeats and she could almost hear him considering his words. "I sometimes think about going back to that alley. Asking some of the guys if they want to come live with me here in New Orleans. Work with me. They have skills, but they can't get a foothold in the real world. Getting a job's hard when you're homeless or when you're not sure if you can commit to an everyday responsibility. Knowing they'll get fired the first time they have to take time off to decompress keeps a lot of them from even looking. So they just stay where they are, and the days turn to years."

"Have you told this to Stone?"

"Not yet. He'd help me figure something out. He's good with jumping in to solve everyone's problems. He seems ornery and obnoxious, but he's got a soft heart under all the barbs and thorns."

"Delores loves him. She seems like she'd know what's what."

Cora wanted Phin to have someone like Delores. Someone who'd be there for him when he spiraled. Someone to help him surface and start again.

In time, Cora thought that someone could even be herself. In time.

"Thank you," she said quietly. "You shared a lot of personal stuff with me that you didn't have to share. I'm glad you did. It let me know you a little better and it took my mind off the elephant in the room."

"Patrick."

She closed her eyes, leaning into Phin. Taking a little of the strength he so unselfishly offered. "Yes. I need to talk to Tandy."

"Yes, you do."

"Burke thinks it's a bad idea. Do you?"

"I think it's going to hurt you and I don't want you hurt. But sometimes what needs doing isn't pleasant."

He was right once again. "I'm so tired, Phin."

"I know," he murmured. "One thing I have learned is that sleep is pretty miraculous. It will clear your head."

"Tandy will be here in a few hours. Maybe less."

"You have time for a nap."

Cora hesitated, feeling like a child. "Will you stay with me until I go to sleep?"

"Of course." He kissed her forehead. "I don't know how I can help you other than fixing your faucets and helping you sleep."

She laughed, surprised at the sound. "Are those euphemisms, Phin?"

He choked on a laugh of his own. "No." He stroked his hand over her hair, his tone going low and wicked. "Although they can be, when you're ready."

A shiver raced all over her skin and Cora thought she could be ready for *that* very soon. Her body, gone dormant for so long, was finally waking up. "It's been a while for me."

"Me too," he admitted. "Part of the whole not-feeling thing."

"Same. My last relationship was when I was just out of college. Then John Robert got sick and my life was wound around him. Treatment and care and looking for my father." Who'd been lying dead under a building all this time.

Time. *I wasted so much of it.* She couldn't waste any more. She *wouldn't* waste any more. It felt like a vow. It felt good.

She shrugged, remembering that last relationship. "The guy said buh-bye, that I wasn't fun any longer." It had hurt at the time but not enough for her to fight for the man. She thought she would've fought for Phin.

Phin made a growling sound in his throat. "Part of me wants to throat-punch him. The other part of me wants to send him a thank-you card."

"Is it wrong that the thought of you throat-punching him pleases me?"

"It's why I like you," he said, sounding satisfied. "Now, as much as I'd like to keep holding you, you need to take that nap."

Because Tandy was coming, and there would be a hard reckoning, one way or another. Tandy was no fool. The questions Cora would ask would infuriate her friend either way.

And if Phin was right? If Patrick was involved?

Cora hoped that she and Tandy could survive the fallout.

She rose and held a hand out to Phin. "Let's go. Can you bring the box of my father's college stuff with you? Just in case someone comes in and tries to torch my attic again."

Phin grabbed the box, lifting it easily. And if his muscles flexed a little more than they should because he was preening for her, she'd just be grateful.

Phin Bishop was a beautiful man, inside and out.

"You're a good person, Phin. Don't let your brain tell you otherwise."

He kissed her hard. "Same, Cora Jane. You are a good person and I'll remind you of that after you talk with Tandy, all right?"

"All right."

18

PHIN TRUDGED DOWN Cora's staircase, feeling fifty years older than he had only an hour before. Even SodaPop seemed subdued. Still, she stuck to his side like glue.

He reached down and gave her back a stroke. "Thank you."

He hadn't understood how much he'd needed the dog until he'd had her.

He hadn't understood how much he'd needed Cora until she'd patted his chest and listened to him tell her about hiding from his sister.

Burke, Val, and Antoine were at Cora's kitchen table. They gave Phin sad smiles as he pulled up a chair beside them.

"I know she's not okay," Val said, "but is she okay for now?"

Phin nodded, rubbing his hands over his face. "Yeah. She's asleep. Dammit, Burke. I hated finding that damn connection."

"I know," Burke said. "I hated it, too, but it was a necessary avenue to check. Too many coincidences for my liking."

"Mine too," Antoine said. "Burke told us about the diplomas and yearbooks."

Val patted Phin's arm. "Poor Cora."

Phin absently petted SodaPop, whose muzzle rested on his thigh. "Tandy might not know the answers Cora needs. We're probably going to have to go straight to Patrick himself, without giving away the game. We need to get a handwriting sample. A recent one."

"For the wobbly *r*," Val said. "Patrick's seen us. It's fair to say that he knows who Burke and Antoine and Molly are, too. If he visited Joy in the hospital the other day, then she may have told him about us."

"And, unfortunately," Burke added darkly, "we *do* have an internet presence. Too many cases have gone public the past year. One search on Broussard Investigations will yield photos of nearly all of us except maybe Antoine."

Even me, Phin thought. He'd been photographed on his last job. He'd been out of it by then, spiraled past bringing back. Too many triggers.

Too much blood.

He gave his head a hard shake. *Stop it.*

And then he realized that he hadn't needed SodaPop's intervention. He'd stopped his spiral on his own. *Progress.*

And then his mind careened away again, thinking of his sister and his mother and father seeing that photo of him from their last job, dazed and being led away by one of his friends.

He'd have to ask Stone if his family had seen it.

Stone.

He looked up. "Stone can get it," he said, interrupting whatever topic they'd transitioned to. Phin wasn't sure how long his mind had been spinning, but he'd missed the first part of the new conversation. He'd apologize later. "The handwriting sample. Tandy knows about Stone and Delores, but her father doesn't."

"It's a possibility," Burke allowed. "We'll have him go by the gallery tomorrow. The other option is Joy. I'll find out if Patrick has signed a get-well card or something. I haven't met the man yet, but is his body type consistent with the man who shot Joy? We can't even find a full-body photo of him online. Only his driver's license photo. You two saw him." He gestured to Val and Phin. "What do you think?"

Phin and Val looked at each other, considering.

"I don't think so," Phin said slowly. That he was relieved was an understatement. If Patrick hadn't shot Joy and stolen their laptops, maybe he wasn't involved.

Or maybe he'd had help.

Val nodded her agreement, then sucked in a breath. "Shit. I didn't think about this before, but his right hand trembled, too. Just a little. It was when he shook my hand goodbye when I was showing him to the door."

"Fuck," Phin muttered. "I keep hoping for Cora's sake, but it doesn't look good."

"No, it doesn't," Burke said. "We need to confirm where he was exactly on Tuesday morning when Joy was shot and the laptops stolen. He told Cora he was out of town, but let's follow up on that."

Phin rubbed his face again. "Dammit, I didn't want it to be him. That he could kill Cora's father and then insinuate himself into her life . . . That's scary-cold."

"*So* cold," Antoine agreed. "We may need to bring Clancy in on this, guys. If we ask Patrick these questions, he might bolt. If Clancy asks, he can have him confined to an interview room in NOPD headquarters. And if we don't trust Clancy, we can bring André in."

"Let's start with Tandy," Phin suggested. "If she leaves here angry that we're asking about her father, she might tell him and he'll still bolt."

"Clancy might come to the same conclusion we did." Val slid down in her chair, hands folded over her stomach. She resembled Burke in that moment and Phin might have laughed had the topic not been so serious. "Detective Goddard has to have told Clancy about the trace elements found on Jack Elliot's pants and what they mean in terms of art restoration."

"And Clancy isn't stupid," Phin said. "He might have already gone to the gallery to talk to Patrick himself." He winced. "Tandy might be mad before she even gets here. If we're going to get a handwriting sample, we should do it as soon as possible."

"Hold on." Burke took out his phone and dialed a number from his favorites list.

It rang twice before Joy's voice came through the speaker. "I thought you'd forgotten about me, boss."

Burke smiled. "Never gonna happen. How are you, Joy?"

"Fine," Joy grumbled. "Ready to go home, but this doctor says I have to stay. What does he know, anyway?"

"Lots of stuff he learned in medical school?" Val ventured.

"Lotta nothin'," Joy snapped, and then her voice softened. "Hey, Val. How's that adorable boy of yours?"

Val smiled. "Elijah is good. He and Kaj were going to stop by and see you."

"They did. Elijah brought me a stuffed coffee cup—a plush toy. He said that he knew how much I liked my coffee, but that the doctors wouldn't let me have any. So he got me a substitute. I don't even know where he'd get such a thing, but that boy sure is a cutie."

"He is," Burke said. "Have you had a lot of visitors?"

"Phin and that new lady friend of his stopped by," Joy said cagily. "They were holding hands."

"You're too late with that gossip," Phin said. "They already know."

"We saw him kissing her," Val said in a singsong voice. "We got the scoop on you, Joy."

"Well, shit," Joy muttered. "Taking away all my fun."

"Who else came by, Joy?" Burke pressed.

There was a momentary pause, and then Joy must have taken them off speaker, because she became suddenly clearer. "Why?" she demanded. "What's going on, Burke Broussard?"

"You really thought that line of questioning would work

without making her suspicious?" Antoine asked Burke. "She's way too smart for the likes of you, boss."

"That is the truth, right there," Joy said. "Who else is with you?"

"Just the four of us," Burke said. "Molly doesn't come on shift for a few hours. So . . . I will tell you, but can you first tell me who else has come by to visit?"

"André Holmes and his fiancée, Farrah. André's brother and his parents. Farrah's parents—her daddy says to tell you hello, Phin. He was worried about you."

Phin had met the man on their last job. He was grateful to Oscar for keeping him steady enough to be transported home. Where Phin had promptly gotten into his old truck and headed for Stone and Delores's house in Ohio.

"I'll stop by his house and tell him hello back," Phin promised. "Thank you."

"You're welcome, Phin. Let me see. My kids, of course. They haven't left. Those sweet girls from Marica's Bakery. They brought me chocolate cupcakes. They said they were for the nursing staff, but I knew the truth. I waited until the nurses were gone and ate one. Got busted by the nurse, who stole the rest of the box right out from under my nose." She sighed. "Tandy Napier's been here. Her daddy, too. We haven't really talked in years, not since his wife passed. We had a nice chat." She audibly brightened. "The ladies from Houston came. We had us a fine visit. That was so sweet of them to drive all that way."

Phin had met the ladies from Houston on an earlier case. They had become fast friends with Joy. It was no surprise they'd come to see her.

"How about get-well cards, Joy?" Phin said. "Any of those?"

"Why?" Joy asked, all levity gone from her voice.

"We think we have a lead on Cora's father's killer," Burke said quietly. "We need a handwriting sample. Did anyone leave you a card?"

"Only Jace. He was so proud of himself because he wrote the message himself."

Jace was Val's adopted son and struggled with dyslexia. That he'd written a note of any length was a major achievement.

I need to see him. The kid craved affection and male role models.

Not that Phin was the best role model, but he genuinely liked the boy. He'd make time for him as soon as he could.

"So nothing else?" Burke asked, disappointed. "Look, Joy. How well do you know Patrick Napier?"

There was a shocked gasp on the other end of the line. "He shot me?"

"No, we don't think so," Burke said hastily. "Wrong body type. But he might be somehow involved."

Joy was quiet a moment. "The letters."

"Goddamn, she's smart," Antoine said.

"Damn straight," Joy replied without missing a beat. "Don't you forget it. Did he write the letters, Burke?"

"That's what we're trying to find out."

"If he did, he could have been simply trying to make Cora feel better. Like her daddy still loved her, even though he was a lying, cheating sack of shit."

Val blinked. "He was dead, Joy."

"I *know* that," Joy said, disgruntled. "But Cora didn't. Nor did Patrick." Another pause, and then she seemed to understand it all. "Oh my God, Burke, you can't be serious. Patrick Napier can*not* have killed Cora's daddy. I've known Patrick since my girls were little. Nala went to school with Cora and Tandy. We did car pools and slumber parties." She sounded pained. "I don't know him as well as Priscilla did, but he's a good man. He fixed my garbage disposal once. I had to refix it, because he's a bad handyman, but his heart is in the right place. Tell me he's not on your suspect list. *Tell me.*"

Burke winced. "We don't want to be right. If we can exclude him quickly, more's the better."

Joy sighed. "What do you need from me? Want me to get him to write something?"

"Yes," Burke replied. "Something with a lowercase *r*."

"'Your dad, Jack Elliot,'" Joy said sadly. "For fuck's sake, this is a nightmare. Poor Cora. Does she know?"

"Yes," Phin said. "She's as upset as you'd expect. They knew each other, Joy—Cora's dad and Patrick. Pledged to the same frat at LSU."

"Motherfucker," Joy breathed. "I never knew about that. I don't think Priscilla knew, either. Motherfucker."

"Yeah," Burke said with a sigh. "That's what we thought, too."

"What other leads do we have?" Joy asked.

Burke brought her up to speed with what they knew, including the discovery of the weapon that had killed Jack Elliot in the dead hand of Medford Hughes, the presence of Renaissance-style paint on Jack's slacks, and the attempted arson of Cora's house the night before.

"Vincent Ray?" Joy murmured. "I knew his daddy. No-good sonofabitch. Apple didn't fall far from that tree."

"How did you know him?" Phin asked.

"Busted his daddy's ass a time or two when I was on the force." Joy had been a detective when she'd been shot on the job. "Petty stuff back then. Shoplifting, vandalism. Vincent Sr. didn't get into the drug trade until later. His older brother—your intruder's uncle—was always smarter. He always managed to slide free of any legal entanglements. That family has themselves some damn fine attorneys."

"Do you keep tabs on them?" Burke asked.

"Not specifically. I watch the news feeds and listen when I go to lunch with my old partner from NOPD and his cronies. I've met Vincent Jr. He's been in my house a time or two. My youngest son knew him from the basketball court in the park. Wayne thought he might save Vinnie from his family, but no dice. If Vinnie broke into your place, I'd look at his uncle's connections. Is Vinnie still in jail?"

"As of a few hours ago, yes," Antoine said. "But he's been there less than twenty-four hours. My sources tell me that he hasn't yet spoken to the cops. Hasn't even asked for an attorney."

"His uncle is probably letting him stew," Joy said. "For being dumb enough to get himself caught. He was going to burn Cora's house down? Because that wouldn't have worked. There are sprinklers throughout the house."

Phin frowned, because something didn't make sense. "Did Patrick also know there were sprinklers? Because Cora says he fixes a lot of things in the house."

Joy snorted. "Tries to. He tried to fix a loose electrical socket for Priscilla once and she had to call an electrician when the thing started to spark. He couldn't have sent Vincent to burn Cora's house down, if that's what you're insinuating. He knew about the sprinklers."

"Maybe he didn't want the whole house to burn down," Phin said quietly. "Just the contents of the attic."

"Shit," Joy muttered. "Did I make things muddier or clearer?"

"Neither and both," Burke said with a frustrated chuckle. "You get some rest, Joy. We'll be by tomorrow."

"With cupcakes," Joy demanded. "Val, you better bring me some or Antoine will be my favorite Burkette."

Burke blinked as Antoine sputtered.

"Burkette?" they said together.

Joy cackled. "I said what I said. Burke Broussard and the Burkettes. Cupcakes, people. Or don't bother showing your faces." She laughed. "Okay, that was wrong. Please bring cupcakes *and* your faces. I miss you guys."

"We miss you, too," Phin said.

"Love you, Joy," Val said.

"Not a freaking Burkette," Antoine said.

"I'll bring cupcakes," Burke said. "Sleep, Joy. Love

you." He ended the call and shook his head. "I do love that woman."

So did Phin. "I'm glad she's going to be all right."

Burke reached across the table and slapped Phin's shoulder. "Thanks to you and your friend Stone." He settled back in his chair. "What are our other leads? Where is Molly's whiteboard?"

"Still hidden in the pantry," Val said. "Want me to get it?"

Burke shook his head. "Antoine's been taking notes. It just feels . . . brainstormier if Molly's got her whiteboard."

Phin shook his head, laughing under his breath. His friends were ridiculous. "What about Medford Hughes? The gun that killed him was the same gun that killed Jack Elliot. Why was Hughes killed? What was his role with our laptops? He didn't steal them. Did he try to break into them before he died?"

"Somebody did," Antoine said. "That's what set off my alarm."

Phin rewound the conversation with Clancy in his mind. "What about the wife's sister? She might know who Hughes was connected with."

"She already told Clancy," Val said. "He works his job and volunteers with his church."

"He clearly did more than that, because somebody killed him," Antoine said logically. "The person who shot Joy and stole our stuff could have just thrown the laptops in a dumpster somewhere, but he didn't. Somehow they ended up with Medford Hughes. As did Jack's murder weapon."

Phin had a thought, because Clancy wasn't a stupid cop. "I wonder if Clancy wants us to talk to the sister. Maybe come at it from a non-cop perspective. He didn't have to tell us that the sister gave him that information, but he did."

Burke's smile was approving once again. "We need to talk to the sister. Dig more into Medford Hughes's life."

"I want to go with you," Cora said from behind them. They turned as one, Phin rising as Cora came into the kitchen. He cupped her cheek in his palm, happy when she leaned into his touch. "You're supposed to be asleep."

She shrugged. "My phone woke me up. Text from Tandy. She'll be here in a few minutes."

The Garden District, New Orleans, Louisiana
THURSDAY, DECEMBER 15, 6:30 P.M.

"Thank you, Phin." Sitting at her kitchen table, Cora cupped her hands around the mug of tea. She was so cold and her stomach hurt.

Tandy was coming and Cora was going to have to ask her some very difficult questions.

Phin put his arm around her shoulders and she leaned into him. "She's my best friend," she murmured.

"We can ask the questions," Phin offered.

Cora wanted to say yes.

"It might be better if we do," Val said with a sympathetic grimace. "We can be more objective."

Cora swallowed. "She's my best friend," she repeated, her voice flat and dull. Just like she felt inside. "She's been there for me every day of my life since we were in the third grade. She was with me when John Robert took his last breath. I can't hurt her this way."

"We can tell her that you've gone back to sleep," Burke said. "In my opinion, we shouldn't even be asking her any of this. Not until we can more deeply investigate her father. She's going to tell him, Cora."

Cora stared at the tea in her cup. "If it's not him, if you're wrong, it'll hurt him. If you're right and he did kill my father, he might up his efforts to get to me." She looked up, met Burke's gaze, fully aware that Phin was scowling beside her. "Then you can catch him."

"You will not be bait," Phin said harshly.

Turning her focus to him, Cora used her thumb to smooth away the deep, angry lines caused by his frown.

"I'm not going to hide in my house forever. I want this over. If being bait to draw Patrick out is necessary, that's what I'll do. You guys are good at protection, right? I'm in good hands."

Phin's eyes narrowed. "You're manipulating us. Me."

"I know. Makes it no less true." She drew a breath. "Let me start. It'll seem less intimidating if I start us out. I may blame you all for thinking Patrick could be guilty."

"That's okay," Burke said gently. "We can be the bad guys. It wouldn't be the first time."

A key turned in the front lock and Tandy called, "Cora? I'm here."

Val's brows were raised. "You gave her a key?"

Cora nodded. "When she was here last night, helping us search. Before we knew about the Renaissance paint." She turned in her chair. "In the kitchen, Tandy."

Tandy blew in like she usually did, wearing a chic pant-suit, her blond hair up in its usual ponytail. She dropped a kiss on Cora's cheek before grinning at the arm Phin had draped over her shoulder.

"You go, girl," she said happily, then looked at the faces around the table. Everyone was sober and suddenly Tandy was as well. "What's going on?"

Cora had to make herself breathe. "Can you sit down? I need to ask you some things that aren't going to be easy for either of us."

Frowning now, Tandy sat next to Antoine and across from Cora. "I heard about Minnie. I'm sorry."

Cora closed her eyes, the guilt and loss like a knife. "Me too." *Just do it.* She opened her eyes and met Tandy's gaze. "This is . . . well, I don't believe it, but there are loose ends and we need to . . ." She trailed off, unable to form the words.

She thought that Phin or one of the others would jump in, but they were respecting her wishes. They remained quiet as she searched for the right words.

There were no right words. Only thousands of wrong ones.

"I went to Houma today. Saw the detective who was investigating my father's murder."

"Okay," Tandy said warily, her glance flicking from face to face. "And?"

"My father's pants had a stain. Lazurite, iron oxide, and manganese oxide."

Tandy's eyes widened, the meaning of those compounds immediately clear. "Old paint formulas. Wow. I didn't know your father was an artist."

Cora wished there were booze in her mug instead of tea. "He wasn't. The detective—and all these guys—believe the paint was transferred from his killer's clothing to my father's."

Tandy sat back in her chair. "His killer was a painter? Or a restorer, maybe."

Cora nodded. "That was my first thought." She dropped her gaze to her tea. She couldn't look at Tandy for this part. *Coward. Look her in the eye if you're accusing her father of murder.*

So Cora looked back up and nearly broke her resolve because Tandy had the most loving, sympathetic, worried look in her eyes. That was not going to last.

"The letter writer has a tremor. Wobbles his *r*'s."

Tandy just looked confused. "Okay. What is it, Cora? Tell me. Have you found the letter writer?" She winced. "Is it Harry? I can't think of anyone else who's still alive who's known you that long."

"Harry is someone that they're looking at." Another deep breath. "Did you know that our fathers knew each other in college? That they belonged to the same fraternity? That they graduated the same year and shared a major?"

They would have lived in the same frat house. They would have shared meals, beers. They would have talked with each other.

They knew each other.

Cora couldn't bring herself to add any of those words and she didn't need to.

Tandy's expression changed. Wariness became cold defensiveness. "No. I didn't know that. How do *you* know that?"

Phin slid the yearbook across the table, two sticky notes marking the pages. "They're both in here."

"Are they." Tandy said it flatly, because she wasn't stupid. She knew what they were insinuating. She looked at the pages, one after the other, her lips firm and her eyes flinty. "And?"

Cora squeezed the mug so hard that she half expected it to shatter in her hands. "Tandy, I know you've done some art restoration for the gallery. Did your father ever do art restoration work? Or paint with the old paints?"

Face like a stone, Tandy lurched to her feet. "I don't believe this."

Val sighed. "Tandy, we're sorry. It's our job to put facts together and then rule things out or move forward with them. Cora says our theory isn't possible and wanted to get some information from you so that we could cross this theory off our list."

Still furious, Tandy sat back down. "What information?"

Cora had never heard her sound so cold. Tandy was vivacious and colorful, fun and loving. Unless you insinuated her father was a killer.

"You all moved to New Orleans when you were eight. Right?" Cora asked.

Tandy nodded, her jaw clenched tight. "We did."

"You lived in Thibodaux before," Cora whispered. "Near Houma."

Tandy was breathing hard and fast. "Yes. I have vague memories of the house."

"You told me about it when we first met. How you missed it. You had a tree house in the backyard and a room just for your plushies." Cora's voice cracked a little and Tandy's eyes softened, just a hair.

Please, don't hate me. Please.

"I did. Why, Cora?"

"You went from living in a small house in Thibodaux to owning a house and the gallery in the Quarter. Do you remember how your father paid for them?"

The softness disappeared, the coldness returning. "Do I need a lawyer, Mr. Broussard?"

"No," Burke said calmly. "We didn't make this up, Miss Napier. We're just following the leads. And the money. It's an adage for a reason."

Tandy squared her shoulders. "My father's aunt died. Left him an inheritance. He'd always wanted a gallery. So he and my mother started one."

"Did he do restorations?" Cora asked quietly.

"No." Tandy sounded sure.

Cora exhaled in relief. She'd known it wasn't possible. "Thank God," she whispered.

Tandy crossed her arms over her chest. "Go on, Cora. Ask your questions."

Cora's relief was momentary. Tandy wasn't going to forgive her for this.

"Did he do any travel to New Orleans before you guys moved here?"

Tandy laughed and it was a horrible sound. "You mean, did he come and spy on you? I remember the letters, Cora. Are you asking if he came to New Orleans to see what color your Christmas dress was?"

Cora's eyes filled with tears. "Yes."

Tandy was breathing hard, sounding more like a bull than the lady she was. "I don't remember."

Cora flinched, feeling like she'd been slapped. Because that was a lie. She'd known Tandy far too long not to know her tells.

Tandy had just lied to her.

She realized that she'd let go of the mug and had pressed her hand to her heart, which ached.

Lips pursed, Tandy arched a brow, daring Cora to say anything more.

Cora dabbed at her eyes with her sleeve. "My father had a secret Swiss bank account. He also had a dangerous side business. Like WITSEC, but private."

Tandy blinked. Her arms slowly released the death grip they'd had on each other, her hands falling to the table. "What?"

Cora nodded. "I met one of his clients, a woman who'd hired him to get her out of an abusive marriage."

"So anyone could have killed your father," Tandy said, cold once again. "A jealous husband or the mob, even. He probably deserved what he got."

Cora had considered both of those possibilities. Still, Tandy's words hurt. "Maybe. But his killer got Renaissance-era paint on my father's clothing."

Tandy drew a controlled breath and let it out. "I understand why your PIs are asking these questions, but you need to call your dogs off, Cora. My father has done nothing but love you and help you, and that you'd participate in this line of questioning is . . . I don't even know. Because I can *hear* your doubt. I can *hear* your suspicion. And it's ugly, Cora. So damn ugly. This isn't like you. I don't even know who you *are* anymore." She pushed her chair away from the table and rose, chin lifted. "I'm going to walk out of your house, and I don't want to hear from you again. I might be able to forgive someday, but right now, it's best if you don't contact me." She dropped something and it clanged as it hit the table. It was the key Cora had given her. "Do you understand?"

Cora felt numb, because she understood perfectly. Tandy had just cut her out of her life. "Are there any copies of my key?"

"No. And fuck you for asking. Stay away from my father, Cora Winslow." Tandy swept her gaze across the PIs' faces. "All of you. Stay the *fuck* away from my father. I'll get a restraining order. And I will sue you and everyone in your employ, Mr. Broussard, if you continue this defamation."

She swept out of the kitchen in a cloud of fury.

A moment later the front door slammed, shaking the house.

Cora bowed her head. *I'm sorry, Tandy.* She knew how it felt to have the rug pulled out from under you.

There was absolute silence around the table. Cora didn't want to look up. Didn't want to see the pity on their faces.

"Was there an aunt who left him an inheritance?" she asked, eyes on her tea.

"None that I've found so far," Antoine said quietly. "I'll keep looking."

She felt so damn tired. "Am I a fool for hoping there's an aunt?"

Phin hugged her to his side. "No. Go on hoping that, Cora. We'll keep you safe until we prove it either way."

There were a lot of *we*s in Phin's words tonight. He was finally feeling a part of Broussard Investigations.

At least some good had come of this day.

"She lied, didn't she?" Val asked.

Cora nodded, still not looking up. "Patrick must have done some traveling before they moved. Doesn't mean he came to New Orleans."

"No, it doesn't." Burke's tone was kind. "But it's another piece of the puzzle, and I think you know that."

She could only nod.

"Is it possible," Phin asked slowly, "that some of those trips could have been to search for any incriminating evidence in Cora's house?"

"He would have had to break in," Val said. "We can check to see if her mother filed a police report."

"We can ask Harry," Cora said, her voice barely a whisper. It was like she didn't have enough air to speak any louder. "If you trust him."

Phin stroked a hand over her hair. "I don't trust anyone in your past right now, but I'd like to see the man's face if and when we do ask him. Although he *is* an attorney. He might be able to hide his reaction. I'll go with you."

Thank you, Phin.

"We can talk to him tomorrow," Cora said. She gathered her courage and looked up, relieved not to see an iota of pity on their faces. It was more understanding and sympathy, but not pity.

Except for Phin. His eyes were filled with sadness.

For me. It was an unexpected balm on her sore heart.

It gave her enough of a respite to remember that this wasn't all about her. It was a fair bit about her, but not all.

Joy had been shot.

Minnie had been murdered.

And Medford Hughes and his wife were also dead.

Not all about you.

"So what's next?" she asked, gratified that her voice didn't shake.

Phin's expression shifted from sad to proud. "We keep searching in the attic for whatever your father left behind."

"We keep trying to break into his partitioned hard drive," Antoine said. "And I'm going to search Patrick's family ancestry. I'm hoping to find a rich aunt for you."

"We dig into that little punk who tried to set your attic on fire," Val said. She hesitated. "I'm going in with the assumption that Patrick hired him."

"I understand," Cora said, because she did. She didn't like it and couldn't believe it. But she understood it.

"I'm going back to Houma tomorrow," Burke said, "to check with all those stores across from the Damper Building. I want to know who was there twenty-three years ago. I want to find out what people remember about the days around the time your dad was buried there."

Cora needed to ask her next question, but it hurt thinking about. "What about Minnie? Do the police have any leads into her murder?"

"None yet," Antoine said. "None that have been up-
loaded to the online files. We can call my brother to ask."

"Captain Holmes," Cora said with a nod, then winced
at the sharp pain in her temple.

Her head hurt. Her heart hurt.

Everything hurt.

It didn't matter. She had to pick herself up and move on.
I've done it before.

"And the sister-in-law of Medford Hughes?" she asked.
"When do we see her?"

Burke made a face. "I was hoping you'd forgotten that
you heard that."

"Not a chance," Cora said. "I want to meet her. I think
Phin's right. Clancy mentioned her for a reason. Let's find
out what that reason was."

"Tomorrow," Burke insisted. "Molly will be here soon
to take over the night shift. She's bringing dinner. You will
eat, Cora," he snapped when she started to refuse. "Afterward, we keep looking through the attic. Antoine contin-
ues trying to break into that old computer of your father's
and looking for Patrick's aunt. I'm going to put one of my
guys on Patrick's condo. I'm counting on Tandy telling her
father straightaway what we told her. Including the fact
that your father had a private WITSEC business and a
Swiss bank account. Which, incidentally, I wish you hadn't
shared, but that's water under the bridge now. I don't want
Patrick running from us, and based on what we know, I
can see that happening."

Cora's nod was slight. It still hurt her head. "Okay."

Burke looked suspicious. "Which part is okay?"

"Most of it. If Patrick did this, he needs to be punished.
If he didn't, I've lost my remaining family. But Joy and
Minnie deserve the truth. *I* deserve the truth."

Phin's hand was warm on her back. "Yes, you do. And
we will find it for you."

Burke was frowning. "You said most of it was okay.
What part wasn't?"

Cora met the man's eyes. "The part where we wait until tomorrow to see Medford Hughes's sister-in-law."

"Goddammit," Burke spat. "I was afraid of that. It's a bad idea."

"*All* of this is a bad idea," Cora fired back, angry now. "Phin? You don't have to go with me, but I'd like it if you did."

"Then I will," he said. "You coming with us, Burke?"

Burke rolled his eyes. "Yes. Although I'm no longer sure who's running this investigation."

"Where does Hughes's sister-in-law live?" Cora asked.

Phin held out his phone. "I found her address. She lives in Mid-City. Let's eat first, then we'll go over."

She leaned her head against his biceps, so tired of all of this. "Okay."

19

VAL STOPPED THE SUV in front of Sara Morton's bungalow. Medford Hughes's sister-in-law lived in a nice neighborhood, only minutes from where both Molly and her fiancé lived.

This should be a low-key visit. No danger involved. Phin hoped.

He, Val, Burke, and Cora all wore Kevlar under their clothing, just in case.

"I think Miss Morton has company," Phin said, looking at the town car in the driveway. "She doesn't have a town car registered to her." He'd watched Antoine search the DMV database for the Camry earlier that day, and Antoine had given Phin his credentials to use as needed. Phin wasn't going to let Cora go into any situation that he hadn't personally vetted to be safe, so he quickly ran a check on the town car's plates. "Wow. That's unexpected."

"What?" Val asked.

Cora leaned over to see his phone. "Huh. I guess the church business pays well."

"It's registered to Reverend Beauchamp," Phin explained. "He has that big church in Metairie."

"Oh, I've heard of him," Burke said with obvious disdain.

"He does all that 'healing.' Takes advantage of desperate people. Calls it 'donations' but it's really a big scam."

Cora looked like she'd sucked a lemon. "My grandmother watched his show occasionally toward the end of her life, when she couldn't get to our own church on Sundays. She tried to get John Robert to go to one of their revival meetings in the hope of getting healed, but John Robert was not a fan of the reverend. Grandmother normally wasn't, either, but we were getting desperate."

"Detective Clancy mentioned that Medford Hughes volunteered with his church," Phin said. "Maybe it was Beauchamp's church."

"Maybe Beauchamp can tell us something about Medford," Val said. "Should we crash their party or be polite and wait?"

Burke got out of the SUV. "Let's try to crash. I'd like the reverend's take on Medford Hughes. Who knows, maybe Medford gave the reverend some last confession before he was killed."

Phin got out of the back and held his hand out for Cora to tug her across the seat. He liked holding her hand. He'd missed the simple intimacies.

"Protestant ministers observe sanctity of confession, too," Cora said as she slid out of the SUV.

"I know," Burke said. "But I can dream, can't I?"

Val patted his shoulder. "Dream away, boss. I've never seen this guy's show on TV, but I've seen the billboards all over town. I get the heebie-jeebies from televangelists, but if he can give us info on Hughes, I can say whatever I need to say to get on his good side."

"Are we supposed to know that both Hughes and his wife were murdered?" Cora asked. "It wasn't on the news. They covered it as a murder-suicide."

"Good point," Burke murmured. "We don't mention that we were the ones that found the body unless the sister asks. Clancy might have told her. We don't know. For now, Val, Phin, and I are here for information because Hughes had our laptops and the police aren't being helpful. You're here because the thief chased you and you haven't felt safe since."

"That last part's not a lie," Cora murmured, and Phin knew he'd give whatever he owned to make her feel safe again.

Strategy in place, they walked up the sidewalk to Sara Morton's front door, the three of them flanking Cora so she was covered from the back and sides.

Phin was at her side, of course, and SodaPop was at his. Cora was clutching his hand so tightly that he had to hold back a wince. "You okay, Cora Jane?"

Her smile was tremulous. "I will be. I mean, this was my idea."

"You'll be fine," Val said. "It's all good. This is just a chat."

"She's grieving," Cora said. "We're intruding on her grief."

"I'd hope that she'd want justice for her sister and Medford," Phin said. "I guess we'll see." They'd reached the door and Phin knocked.

A fortyish man in a suit answered the door, scowling at them. "We're not interested."

He started to slam the door and Phin slapped a hand against it. "We're not selling anything. We're here to speak to Miss Morton. Are you a family member?"

"No." The suited man stepped back. "I'll see if she'll receive you."

Cora blinked. "Receive us? He talks like my grandmother did."

"I think he's the driver," Phin murmured. "Probably a bit of a bodyguard for the reverend, too. Or at least he clears him a path."

The door opened again, revealing a middle-aged woman. "You're from Broussard Investigations, aren't you?"

"Yes, ma'am," Val said. "We don't mean to intrude, but we were hoping you'd have some time to talk to us."

"I've been expecting you. Detective Clancy said you'd be stopping by."

"Told you," Phin muttered, and Burke grunted his displeasure at having been wrong. "Is it okay if my service dog accompanies me?"

"Of course," Sara said. "Clancy said you'd probably bring her. Come in, please. I've been talking with my minister. Reverend Beauchamp, these folks are from a private investigating firm in the Quarter."

The minister rose, a smile on his face. It was a minister's smile, the kind that was supposed to be warm and welcoming.

It made Phin miss his Uncle Trace. Trace was also a holy man—a priest—but, unlike Beauchamp, his smiles were always so genuine.

"I'm Burke Broussard," Burke said. "My associates Val and Phin and our client, Cora."

"Pleased to meet you all. Sit down and rest." Beauchamp gestured to the sofa and chairs. He'd been sitting on a love seat and returned to it. They all took their seats, except for Val, who took her place standing behind Cora. "I'm sure you know that Miss Morton is grieving. I assume you have a good reason for the timing of your visit."

Ouch. The reverend had just politely chewed them out.

"Our apologies, Miss Morton," Burke said. "We're looking for information on Medford Hughes. The two laptops that were found in his car belonged to my company. The police haven't been terribly helpful in helping us find out why Hughes took them. The laptops themselves weren't worth much and they had no sensitive data on them, but our coworker was shot in the process."

"I heard about that," Sara said. "I also heard she's going to recover. I called the hospital and asked. I couldn't stand it if Medford had killed her. I was never so glad to hear that someone would be all right."

Sara Morton appeared to be under the impression that Medford had been the one to break into Burke's office and steal the laptops. Phin wondered if Clancy had told her that the man had been murdered. That detail still hadn't been shared with the media.

Of course, Sara Morton and Medford Hughes might have been working together. Seemed unlikely, but everything about this case seemed unlikely.

"Our coworker will make a full recovery," Burke confirmed. "Joy's important to us."

The reverend was watching Cora carefully and his attention made the hair rise on the back of Phin's neck. "Why are you here, Cora?" the man asked, his smile firmly in place.

Phin didn't like the way he was looking at Cora. Like she was a bug to study.

"The person who shot our friend chased me through the Quarter," she said. "I've had several break-ins at my house. I want to know why."

"Oh, that's terrible." Sara Morton looked genuinely upset. "I feel responsible."

The reverend reached over and patted Sara's hand. "We've had this conversation, Sara. You are not responsible for Medford's actions."

Sara didn't look convinced. "Will your friend have any issues paying her hospital bill, Mr. Broussard? Does she need help?"

That had not been what Phin had been expecting.

Burke actually blinked, so he'd been surprised, too. "We have good insurance. But you're kind to offer."

The reverend was shaking his head, an indulgent smile on his face. "She's one of my most generous parishioners. We're lucky to have her as part of our flock."

"I can see that," Burke said. "We were hoping we could get information on Medford Hughes."

"What do you want to know?" Sara asked. "I'll help you if I can."

"Was he involved in anything . . . sketchy?" Burke asked. "I hate to ask, but . . ."

"But he was found dead with your stolen laptops in the back seat of his car," Sara said sadly. "If he was, I never knew about it and my sister never mentioned it. I think she would have. She had kind of a love/hate relationship with Medford."

The reverend looked uncomfortable.

Phin wanted to ask why, but Sara Morton beat him to it. "What do you know, Reverend Beauchamp?" she asked.

The man hesitated. "I can't tell you everything. Some of it is confidential. But I can tell you what I saw and heard from others."

"From my sister?" Sara asked.

Beauchamp shook his head. "I can't tell you who, as that compromises another person's confidences, but Medford was involved with some bad people. Did the police find his personal laptop?"

"No," Sara said, her eyes wide and frightened. "Why? What do you know about it?"

The reverend hesitated once again. "Do you know what the dark web is, Sara?"

Dread took over the woman's expression. "Yes. Please, Reverend Beauchamp, just tell me."

Yeah, Phin thought, irritated. *Just spit it out, man.*

Sara pursed her lips when the reverend continued to say nothing. "He was *murdered*, Reverend. I've already told you that. How much worse can it get?"

Ah, so Clancy did tell her that much.

"He was into . . . children," Beauchamp said reluctantly.

Phin stared. He really had not been expecting that.

Cora looked horrified, and she wasn't alone. Val and Burke wore expressions of mixed horror and rage. Phin knew that Burke had dealt with those types when he was with the NOPD and still bore the emotional scars.

"Children?" Sara whispered.

"Yes," Beauchamp said. "Teenagers, actually. I thought Medford had committed suicide. That's what the news said. I thought maybe he'd become disgusted enough with himself to take his own life. But when you told me that he was murdered, well, that changes things. If he was killed by one of his associates . . ." He shook his head. "I don't want any harm to come to you, Sara."

Sara's hand was pressed tightly to her mouth, tears streaming down her cheeks. "Medford abused children? *Medford?* I can't believe that."

Phin couldn't blame her. It was a horrific crime, but it happened. He'd worked for Burke long enough to have seen a few investigations into child abuse situations.

Beauchamp's expression was full of sorrow. "I know it's hard to believe, but it's true."

Phin's temper boiled up when the reverend's words completely sank in. "Wait. You *knew*?" he asked, hearing the censure in his own voice and not giving a damn. "You *knew* Hughes was a pedophile and you didn't turn him in?"

Beauchamp closed his eyes, misery radiating off him in palpable waves. "He never admitted it to me. Someone else did. The victim is getting counseling and has chosen not to press charges."

"You're a mandatory reporter," Val said quietly, but her words were cold. "Your clergy-penitent privilege doesn't apply here."

"Don't you think I know that?" Beauchamp snapped. "When I first was brought in, the child's parents had already reported the abuse to the authorities. The child was in counseling but would not disclose who had abused him. All he would say was that there were pictures. Online. He's *thirteen*. It's—" His voice broke. "It's hideous."

Cora leaned in and rested her hand on the minister's. He jumped at the touch but then settled. "Reverend Beauchamp," she said softly. "That must have been a terrible thing to have to hear."

"It was." Beauchamp cleared his throat. "You want to help, you want to scream, you want to do things to the perpetrator that are *not* Christian. In the end, all you can do is provide comfort and counseling and pray for God's justice. I did get the child's parents into counseling, too. They had a lot of guilt."

"I imagine so," Cora murmured. "When did you know that Hughes was the perpetrator?"

Phin wasn't sure how she was being so calm. Phin was glad he'd brought SodaPop with him. He hadn't expected this interview to become so gut-wrenchingly awful.

"Today. The mother of the victim contacted me, asked me if she was sinning by being glad that Medford had killed himself. She never said why, but she didn't have to. I was . . . stunned. Simply stunned. I knew that Medford did some shady work on the side, but it was more like reconditioning stolen laptops—and that was only a guess. I never knew for sure."

"How did you guess that?" Cora asked.

"I'd forget my password sometimes and he'd fix it for me. I only used a few combinations of words and numbers, so he just . . . I don't know. He had this software he used. He'd get the right password more quickly than I could, leaving me time to do my actual work. Once he muttered that I was his only legit client. I asked him what he meant but he said he was only kidding. So I had nothing of real value to report to anyone. But if Medford was killed for what he had on his laptop, his killer could have been one of any number of people."

Cora digested this. "How would Medford have gotten his hands on Mr. Broussard's laptops?"

Beauchamp shook his head. "I have no idea. I wish I did know, but I don't. Maybe he stole them. Or, like I've said, he consorted with shady people."

Cora patted the man's hand and leaned back into her chair. "Thank you, sir."

"Can you assign someone to protect Sara?" Beauchamp asked, looking from Burke to Val to Phin. "I don't want anything to happen to her because someone after Medford thinks she knows something."

Burke nodded. "I'll find someone."

Sara shook her head. "No, thank you. I can't pay you for that."

"Now, Sara," Beauchamp gently scolded. "You have life insurance money from your sister. You can afford it."

"I'm giving that to the church. We've already had this conversation."

"But I don't want you in danger," Beauchamp protested.

Burke held up a hand. "If we put protection around your house, Miss Morton, anyone who comes after you will be someone we're looking for, too. They shot our friend. We want to catch them. Let's talk about compensation later. You'd actually be doing us a favor."

Sara nodded reluctantly. "All right. But you will bill me. I don't need charity, Mr. Broussard."

Burke gave her a business card. "My cell's on the back of this card. Send me a text with your email address and I'll have your number, too."

Sara clutched the card to her chest. "I'm afraid I haven't been much help to you. I don't know why anyone would have broken into your offices to steal your laptops or why someone broke into Cora's house and chased her through the Quarter."

Burke stood. "You might have helped us more than you know. We'll leave you alone now. Thank you for your time. And thank you, Reverend. We appreciate your candor."

Beauchamp nodded shakily. "You're welcome. I hope you find out who shot your coworker."

"We do, too," Burke said and led them back to the SUV.

They were silent until they were all buckled in and had driven to the end of Sara Morton's street, Burke behind the wheel this time.

Cora clutched Phin's hand again, even more tightly than the last time. She wasn't as all right as she seemed to be.

That Medford Hughes had been a pedophile was a shock.

"Well?" Burke asked.

"I didn't like him," Phin said. "But I think that was

because he goes on TV and gets old ladies to give him money."

"Same," Val said. "He was laying it on thick there at the end."

Phin nodded. "I agree."

Burke sighed. "I agree with both of you. Cora? You okay?"

"Not really," she said. "None of this makes any sense. None of this explains how it connects to me. Unless . . ." She rubbed her forehead with her free hand, still clutching Phin's with the other. "Unless my father was working a child abuse case and the perpetrator came after him, like Alice's first husband did."

"Then why kill Medford?" Val asked.

Cora shrugged. "Predators communicate on the dark web, right? If Medford got involved with a pedophile group and whoever killed my father was part of it and if Medford somehow betrayed them or threatened to expose them . . . Well, it would be a convenient way to silence Medford and set him up for the murder of Jack Elliot at the same time."

"I don't know," Val said doubtfully. "There's a lot of ifs in there, Cora."

There were, Phin thought, but he also thought that explained some of her calm back in Sara Morton's living room. She'd been feeling relieved that her father had been trying to rescue children abused by some very bad guys and had been killed for his effort.

It made Cora's loss more palatable, for sure. It was possible. And certainly better than the alternative—that Jack himself had been part of the crime. Phin was going to keep that thought to himself for now.

But there were a lot of ifs. The only way to get to the truth was to investigate Medford Hughes.

"We can check Medford's browsing history even without his computer, can't we, Burke?" Phin asked. "I remember Antoine talking about that, that he could access the browsing history on the router from the back end. That program he installed on our laptops was triggered when Medford logged in on his own Wi-Fi. We can find out who he was dealing with."

Burke met Phin's eyes in the rearview mirror. What had been approval in previous days was now admiration. "Yes, we can. I hadn't thought of that yet, but yes. Antoine should be able to do that. Can you text and ask him?"

Val reached her fist around the front seat and Phin bumped it. "Nice job, Phineas."

"Thank you, Ingrid," he said dryly. "Let's get Cora home. She needs to rest."

"I need to work," Cora corrected brokenly. "I need to know what my father actually did." And there was something in the tone of her voice that made him think that she was also wondering if Jack himself had been part of the crime. "I need to finish this."

Phin pulled out his phone and texted Antoine one-handed. He wasn't going to let go of Cora, no matter how hard she squeezed his hand.

When he'd sent the text, he turned to find Cora crying silently. "Hey," he murmured. "What's this?"

"*If* my father and Medford were killed by the same person and *if* my father was killed trying to stop child abusers and *if* Patrick killed him . . . does that mean that Patrick is a pedophile, too? Just like Medford Hughes?"

Phin sighed. "Let's see what Antoine finds out before you go there, okay?"

"No, you don't understand. I just remembered that Patrick was part of a mentoring program," she said hoarsely. "Teenagers from the community. For just a year, but what if he . . . ? What if he hurt those kids, too?" She shook her head. "I can't even think about it."

Val turned in her seat to stare at Cora. "Did you say a mentoring program? Was it called Invest in Kidz, with a *Z*?"

Cora nodded. "Yes. I wanted to participate, too, but I was in college and taking care of John Robert, so I didn't have time. It only lasted a year or so. Why?"

"Because Vincent Ray was one of the teenagers in that program," Val said grimly. "That could have been where he and Patrick met."

Phin hadn't thought Cora could look more devastated, but right now she did.

Phin, on the other hand, was furious. "Vincent Ray was going to set the house on fire. Sure, there were sprinklers, but what if they hadn't worked? Patrick could have killed Cora."

He hoped he didn't cross paths with Patrick Napier anytime soon. He might kill the man himself.

Cora wiped her cheeks with her sleeve, but the tears kept coming. "I hate this, Phin. All of it. It can't be true."

He unbuckled his seat belt so that he could slide closer to Cora, then wrapped his arms around her, his heart aching for her. "We'll figure this out." He kissed the top of her head. "And then it will be over."

He hoped he hadn't just told a lie.

Uptown, New Orleans, Louisiana
THURSDAY, DECEMBER 15, 11:15 P.M.

Alan's driver pulled his town car into his garage. "You okay back there, boss?" Drake asked, his voice gruff.

"I will be, Drake. Thank you."

"If that Hughes fella wasn't already dead, I'd kill him myself."

That was the reaction Alan had hoped for—the reaction he'd hoped Burke Broussard and his people would have as well. He'd been stunned to see them walk through Sara Morton's door. He'd only gone to visit her to ensure her life insurance proceeds would be donated to the church, which she'd already decided to do.

Then Broussard had walked in the door and Alan had panicked. Not that the visitors would have noticed. He was very good at covering up his true feelings. But he *had* panicked.

He'd come up with the idea of accusing Medford of pedophilia on the fly. He hoped it had worked, that Broussard would be so enraged that he'd focus his effort on trying to find a crime that did not exist.

Because Medford Hughes was no pedophile. Never had been. He'd been far too busy taking care of his wife and doing Alan's bidding to have any other nefarious hobbies.

If Broussard took the bait, he'd be spinning his wheels trying to find Medford's laptop, which Alan had crushed into bits and thrown into a dumpster near Xavier University.

And if Cora Winslow connected the dots, she might believe her father had been involved in a similar crime— murdered by someone targeting pedophiles. That would cause her to back off on her quest for the truth.

It had been the best he'd been able to do under the gun, as it were. It might just work. Either way, they couldn't prove he'd lied. Just that he was mistaken.

"I know how you feel, Drake. Some days the ministry is much more difficult than others. I'm going to bed. You can go on home."

"Sleep well, boss," Drake said.

Alan was certain he would not. "You too."

The Garden District, New Orleans, Louisiana
THURSDAY, DECEMBER 15, 11:15 P.M.

"That's pretty," Delores said, dropping onto the attic window seat next to Cora.

Cora held up the little shepherdess figurine. "It is. My father bought it for my mother for Christmas the year John Robert was born. I'm surprised I remember that. I was only three."

Cora hadn't been alone all evening. Phin's people and Burke's people had been taking turns sitting with her on the window seat, keeping her company after the fallout with Tandy and the new learnings about Patrick.

It had helped. A little.

Cora's chest still hurt, the lie Tandy had told echoing in her mind. Patrick *had* traveled that year that Cora's father had disappeared. *Had died.* Patrick might not have gone to New Orleans, but Tandy had been worried enough about the possibility to lie to Cora's face. It was difficult to accept. Both the lie and the fact that Patrick could have killed Jack Elliot.

And now? Knowing that Patrick had possibly abused a child? Children? And that he could have known Vincent Ray?

It was too much. She had to think about something else, or she'd go insane.

"Was it a happy day?" Delores asked. "That Christmas?"

Cora forced her mind away from Tandy and Patrick to remember that Christmas, so long ago. "It was. All the days were happy days. Until they weren't."

She put the figurine back in the box with the others. She'd been going through her mother's things all evening while the others searched the seemingly never-ending supply of boxes. Generations of Winslow boxes. "My mother collected little figures."

"She kept the gifts your father gave her," Delores noted.

"She did. I don't think she ever stopped loving him. She never got over losing him. Over what she thought was a betrayal."

"I'm sorry," Delores murmured. "The words don't mean much, but they're all I have."

"They mean a lot. That you train service dogs pretty much says that you've got a big heart."

"It started with Cap," Delores said. "One of my friends adopted a dog from my shelter, and he'd been a service dog but his owner had passed away. Somehow, he ended up with me. My friend's got anxiety like Phin, with a healthy dose of ADHD. I watched the dog and saw how good he was for her, so I got trained on how to train dogs myself. SodaPop is my fifth service dog. I've been searching for the right dog for Phin ever since we met him, and SodaPop was perfect."

Cora looked over to where Phin and Stone were wrestling to upend an antique buffet that had been behind rows of boxes for God only knew how long.

Phin's expression was focused but not frenzied.

"He threads his fingers through SodaPop's coat sometimes," Cora murmured, watching him. He was such a pleasure to watch, and admiring his flexing muscles was so much easier than thinking about everything else. "I don't think he realizes he's doing it."

"That's good." Delores smiled proudly. "I was so hoping they'd be good together."

"I've only known him a few days and I can see that they are."

"And they're not the only two that are good together," Delores said slyly.

Cora had been wondering when this was coming. "He's a good man."

"He really is. I wish he weren't so hard on himself, but after knowing his family, I think that's an inherited trait. They're all overachievers that take it personally when things go sideways. Even if it's not their fault."

"So you know his family well?"

Delores heaved a heavy sigh. "Oh yes. And they are going to be so mad at us when they find out that our house is where Phin comes when he needs a safe place to heal. But they'll get over it. Eventually."

"Sounds like they'll be more hurt than mad."

Delores nodded. "Yeah. I hate that. But Phin's recovery is what it is. The trips to our place had become less and less frequent. I think we all hoped he wouldn't feel the need to run anymore, but he showed up again six weeks ago. This one was really bad."

"Maybe it was because he'd thought success was at his fingertips since he'd gone a long time without a spiral. When he spiraled again, that success melted away."

Delores gave her a shrewd look. "You get him. I'm glad."

"Whew." Cora mimed wiping sweat from her forehead. "I thought this was going to be the 'don't hurt him or else' speech."

Delores snickered. "It was going to be. You just saved yourself by being so in tune with him."

Cora wanted to ask Delores what Phin had experienced that originally caused his PTSD. She wanted to know what had happened six weeks before to send him fleeing New Orleans for Ohio. But that was Phin's business. He'd tell her when he was ready.

"Are you going to ask?" Delores asked. "I can tell you want to."

"I can wait to hear it directly from him."

"Right answer. I wasn't going to tell you even if you'd asked." She looked over to where her husband and Phin were lifting the buffet onto its side, looking for a hidden compartment, most likely. They'd been checking for secret hidey-holes in the furniture for the last hour. Burke had stepped up to help them and it was quite a display of muscles. "That's a very nice view, isn't it?"

Cora thought about denying it, but what was the point? "It really is."

"Stone is the best of them, although I could be biased."

Cora chuckled. "I'm finding myself partial to Phin, so you're safe."

Delores laughed merrily. "Another right answer."

"You two are making me want to go home to my boyfriend," Val complained from behind them. "Stop it. And Burke and Phin are like my big brothers, so . . . eww."

Cora had almost forgotten that Val was back there looking through the shelves of books for hiding spots cut into the pages.

"Fine," Delores said, sounding put-upon. "I'm going to work on another box. Cora?"

"I'm going to go through these boxes of photo albums," Cora said, pointing to the box at her feet. "If my father tried to make it easy for my mother to find the Swiss bank account, I want to believe he left something for her to access the rest of that damn computer."

"Well, it's not in any of those old books," Val said, "and it's about time for my shift to end. Molly should be here soon. I'd love to stay, but I promised my son that I'd be home in time to watch a movie with him." She tilted her head. "That reminds me. When you were running from the guy who shot Joy on Tuesday, did you happen to run across a young man who asked if he could call someone for you? Behind a bakery?"

Cora stilled, a stack of photo albums in her hands. "Yes. Why?"

Val smiled. "That was my kid," she said proudly. "He was so worried about you. Described you to a T, right down to the pearls."

"He was sweet. Tell him thank you."

"When this is all over, you can come over to my place for a movie night and thank him yourself. You're welcome, too, Delores, if you're still in town." Val checked her phone. "Molly's downstairs." She turned to the men, all crouched next to the buffet. "I'm heading out, Burke. Y'all behave yourselves."

"See you tomorrow." Burke didn't look up, his gaze pinned to the buffet. He was nearly bouncing with excitement.

"What did you guys find?" Val asked.

"An honest-to-God secret compartment," Burke said.

Cora put the photo albums aside and hurried over. "Really? What's in it?"

Val huffed out a breath before picking her way around the boxes to join them.

"Phin's trying to figure out how to open it," Stone explained, his gaze fixed on Phin. "It's like one of those puzzle boxes."

"Phin's good at those," Delores said loyally.

"Phin's good at just about everything," Cora murmured, then winced. She hadn't meant to say that out loud or for it to sound so dirty.

Phin glanced up at her, his lips twitching and his cheeks pinking up. "Thank you," he said dryly.

Stone snorted. "Get back to work, lover boy."

Which wasn't fair. All they'd done was kiss, but Cora knew Phin would be equally good at what came after. She'd been letting herself think a lot about what came after as she'd watched him work around her house. It allowed her to feel something other than fear.

Anticipation. The stirrings of desire. It had been a long, long time. She felt like she'd been frozen for years and was only now thawing out.

She crouched down beside Phin, shining the flashlight from her phone at the area he was working on. It was set into the base of the piece of furniture. "I would have missed that, even if I'd been looking for it."

"Phin has magic hands," Stone said, waggling his brows.

Burke laughed. "Oh my God. Shut up."

Phin just shook his head. "I've seen these secret compartments before. Made a few myself."

Cora stared at him, fascinated. "You make furniture?"

"Sometimes."

"Lots of times," Stone said. "He's got a workshop in that house he's renting." He waggled his brows again. "You should ask him to show you his wares."

Phin barked out a laugh. "Stop. Just . . . stop."

Burke was laughing so hard that his eyes had teared up. Cora couldn't stop her own laugh that bubbled up. It felt so good to let go and laugh. "Tame your husband, De-lores."

"Nah. I like him that way."

"I'm perfect," Stone said with a cocky smile.

"You're so full of shit," Phin muttered then made a pleased sound. "Got it." He gestured to the edge of a drawer that had seemed to magically appear. "You want to do the honors, Cora Jane?"

"Not till we find gloves," Burke said. "If it's evidence, we need to treat it as such."

Val slapped a pair of latex gloves into Cora's hand. "I never leave home without them."

Cora had to steady her heart. She'd been laughing just moments before. Now she felt sick with dread. What would they find in there? What had her father left behind? Had he killed any other people?

Worse, had he been after Patrick? Because Patrick was hurting children? She didn't want to see. Didn't want to know.

She gave the gloves to Phin. "You found it, you get to open it."

Phin brushed the hair from her face, his expression un-derstanding. "I'll do it." He pulled on the gloves. "Hold the light on the drawer."

Cora had to wipe her now-sweaty palms on her jeans before holding the phone again. She couldn't keep her hands from shaking.

Stone took the phone from her hand. "I'll do it," he said gently.

Phin opened the drawer and Cora had to force herself not to look away.

"Letters," Phin said with surprise. "Old ones. I don't think your father wrote them." He peered at the writing on the envelope on top of the stack. "Who was Seymour Wins-low?"

"My grandfather's grandfather," Cora whispered. "Wow. He died in 1899."

"Can you get me a clean box or a bag, Val?" Phin asked.

Val pulled an evidence bag from her pocket. "Put them in here."

Phin did, then reached in again. And pulled out a shallow box.

An old jewelry box. The kind that came from a high-priced jewelry store. Cora recognized the name embossed on the box. It was one of the fanciest jewelers in New Orleans and had been in business for a very long time.

She held her breath as Phin lifted the box's lid. Then she gasped. "Oh my God."

It was a five-strand string of pearls, the quality so much better than the single strand that she wore every day. She'd seen these before. Many times, in fact.

She reached out and hovered one finger over them, wanting to touch, but not daring. "They were my great-great-grandmother's. She's wearing them in her portrait in the living room. Family lore says that they disappeared after her death. Her brother was suspected of stealing them. He was a pirate, according to the stories. If he did steal them, they never left the house."

"Is that all that's in there?" Val asked, as if Cora hadn't said a word.

"'Fraid so," Phin said, pulling the drawer out as far as it would go. "Empty."

"Dammit," Burke said with frustration.

Dammit?

Oh, right. They'd been hoping for clues left by her father.

Cora would be disappointed in a moment. For now, all she could think was that she could sell those pearls and replace the trust money she'd put into the house's new roof. And more. So much more.

An idea popped into her head, thrilling her. This was such a big house. It could shelter a lot of people. *More than just me.* People who needed help. A fresh start.

A safe place.

The idea needed time to percolate. There would be paperwork. So much paperwork. It would cost a lot of money. But now she'd have some more money.

She had options.

Phin put the lid back on the box and handed it to her with an indulgent smile. "Merry Christmas, Cora Jane. How many repairs will this necklace buy?"

She grinned at him, the worries of the day temporarily put aside. She got him, but he got her, too. This man was a keeper and she intended to try to do just that. "A lot. With a lot left over."

Burke sighed. "I'd say we should keep looking at boxes, but I think I'm done for the night. Let's lock up. Molly's downstairs. She'll stay with you tonight."

Phin caught her looking at him and nodded once. He'd stay, too.

She'd get to sleep again. Maybe not on the floor this time.

She held the box gingerly in one hand, her emotions on a roller-coaster high. She'd crash sooner or later, but for now, she felt downright giddy, like she'd had too much champagne.

She grabbed his neck with her free hand and pulled him in for a kiss that felt both celebratory and . . . more. He smiled against her lips before cupping her face in his big hands and kissing her back.

The kiss became hot immediately and Cora barely heard the groans around her. Barely felt Burke take the box of pearls from her hand, only vaguely hearing his promise to lock them in his home safe.

Barely heard the footsteps as the others stomped down the stairs.

Barely heard Val say, "Guys, take it downstairs. We're locking this door behind us, just in case we get more unwanted visitors tonight."

Phin pulled back, breathing hard, his cheeks flushed and his eyes dark with desire. "I'll lock up, Val," he said

without taking his gaze off Cora's. "See you tomorrow."
He took one more hard kiss that left Cora's lips tingling.
"Come on. Let's go somewhere that's softer than this hard-
wood floor."

Cora rose and tugged him to his feet. "I know just the
place."

20

PHIN HAD ENOUGH focus to lock the door to the attic—one of the new locks he'd installed himself—but every remaining brain cell was fixated on Cora Jane Winslow and the way she was kissing him.

He wasn't sure what had prompted this explosion of passion, but he wasn't going to question it now. His skin felt fizzy with sensation, his thoughts short-circuiting.

Every ounce of blood had fled his brain for his cock. He hadn't felt like this—so alive—in so damn long. Maybe ever.

Maybe it was the stress, maybe the momentary euphoria of discovered treasure.

Or maybe it was just Cora Jane Winslow.

"Careful," he muttered when he missed a step and they stumbled. He grabbed her close with one arm and gripped the handrail with his free hand, stopping them from plummeting to the landing below. "Don't want to break our necks before we can finish this."

Whatever this was. All he knew was that her body was pressed to his, her breasts soft against his chest and her arms linked tightly around his neck.

She laughed, a joyous sound. "Sorry. A little. But only a little." She slowed down, though, sliding her hands from around his neck down his chest, clutching his hand, tugging him down the remaining stairs to the landing, where SodaPop waited patiently.

The dog trotted over to the wall where they'd slept the night before, dropping to her belly and curling up in a golden ball of fur. Such a good girl.

Still holding Cora's hand, he threaded his hand through her curls and crashed their mouths together again, savoring her little moan. He wanted more of that sound. He wanted her looking up at him with dazed eyes, seeing nothing but him.

He pulled back, searching her face expectantly, and exhaled, releasing the tension he hadn't realized he'd been carrying. There was the look he'd hoped to see.

Like he was the only person in the world.

She tilted her head. "If you want to stop—"

He kissed her hard. "Not unless you do."

"No," she whispered, then grinned wickedly. "But we have to be quiet."

"Where?" he asked simply.

She tugged him again, this time down the hall and into her room. She clucked her tongue and SodaPop followed them in, curling up once again on the braided rug next to her bed.

"Is this okay?" Cora asked, hesitation clouding her eyes.

"Perfect." He kissed her again, his heart pounding even harder when she began to tug his T-shirt from his jeans.

He'd need to take SodaPop out, but his dog could wait a little while. He'd walked her only a few hours before. He also needed to check the locks.

That couldn't wait. "Stay here. Don't move."

He stepped back, headed for the windows. He tested the locks on the windows, then the door to the balcony just as the last of Burke's crew was pulling out of the driveway. Only Molly's big red truck remained.

Phin wished they could be completely alone, but Cora

was safe and that was all that mattered. His phone buzzed in his pocket, and he took it out to check, just in case it was something he needed to do.

It was from Stone. *Delores says to check your wallet. For the record, I didn't know anything about this.*

Frowning, Phin did as he was told, then blushed when he saw the condom tucked behind his cash. *Delores, you naughty girl.*

He returned to where Cora stood, just as he'd left her. A smile curved her lips. "Everything locked tight?"

"You're safe, Cora Jane."

"I know."

Then his mind cleared of everything when her hands slipped under his shirt, touching his bare skin. "Cora," he whispered.

She glanced up at him through her lashes. "Is this okay?"

"Still perfect." He stroked her curls from her face. "What do you want?"

She drew in a breath. "I want to keep feeling good. I want you to feel good. And I want to feel *you*. Against me." She exhaled. "In me." She nodded once, resolutely. "That's what I want."

"That's a very good answer, Cora Jane."

Leaning up on her toes, she kissed him again teasingly. "What did you put in your pocket, Phineas?"

He huffed an embarrassed laugh, because it was clear from the sparkle in her eyes that she knew exactly what he'd put in his pocket. "Delores wanted me prepared."

"God bless that woman," she muttered as she pulled his shirt over his head. Then spread her fingers over his chest, fanning them back and forth. Making him shudder. "Oh, Phin."

He had scars. Lots of scars. But that didn't seem to be what she saw. Her gaze had grown heated, not in the bubbly way that it had upstairs after finding that necklace, but in a slow, deliberate way that was so much better.

Her fingers found each scar as she explored his skin, but her touch didn't falter. Not until she got to the edge of his jeans. She glanced up. "Still okay?"

He could only nod, afraid that if he spoke, it would come out as a squeak or something equally embarrassing.

She tugged on the button of his jeans, then hesitated before exhaling and squaring her shoulders in the way he'd become accustomed to the past few days. She gripped the zipper of his jeans and pulled it down, the sound loud in the quiet of the room.

And then she was touching him through his briefs, her fingers light over his erection. He uttered her name on a gasp. "Cora."

His fingers were suddenly in her hair, his mouth on hers. Kissing her, his pulse racing when she opened for him, kissing him back. He grabbed the hem of her sweatshirt, stopping the kiss only long enough to drag it over her head. Then he was kissing her again, hard and desperate.

His fingers trembled on the clasp of her lacy bra and she took over, reaching back to release it. He stepped back, taking the bra with him, and stared.

She was as exquisite as he'd known she'd be. Soft skin, breasts that were the perfect size, just right for his hands. So he cupped them and she closed her eyes on a sigh that sounded relieved.

"You're beautiful," he whispered.

"So are you." She slid her hands up his body, twining around his neck, and he shuddered again at the feel of her nipples hard against his skin. He shucked off his own jeans, then unbuttoned hers, pushing them down her hips. She stepped out of them and he kicked his aside before covering her curvy ass with his hands and walking her toward the bed.

"Condom," she murmured, and he let her go with a mild curse.

He fished the condom from his pocket, then turned to

find her perched on the edge of her bed, watching him with an intensity that made him shiver in the best of ways.

"You have a really nice ass, Phin."

He blushed, hoping she couldn't see it in the darkness. He was a thirty-seven-year-old man, too old to be blushing like a teenager.

He dropped his gaze to the scrap of white that was all she was now wearing. They were far too tiny to be panties, and he loved them.

He couldn't wait to take them off her, so he did, his chest tightening when she lifted her hips to help him. And then she was completely naked except for the pearls she always wore around her neck.

She was the most beautiful sight he'd ever seen, and he wanted her.

He wanted everything, and he wasn't sure where to start.

An audible swallow had him yanking his gaze to hers, blinking when he saw insecurity there. That wouldn't do. Not at all.

He stepped between her legs and kissed her again, feeling her shudder. "So damn beautiful," he muttered when he came up for air, then gasped again when she pulled his briefs down and wrapped her fingers around him.

"Cora." It was all he could think to say, every nerve in his brain firing at the same time. He kicked his briefs somewhere near his jeans and scooped her up, placing her in the middle of the bed as gently as he could.

Then he crawled to meet her there, loving the way the moonlight filtered through her curtains, dancing across her skin.

He dipped his head to kiss her again and again until she was whimpering beneath him, undulating her hips against his.

"Phin, please. Please."

He slipped two fingers into her, groaning quietly when he

felt how wet she was. He'd forgotten how good it could be when he was with someone he actually cared for. "So wet."

She made a needy sound as she grabbed his ass and pulled him closer. "Stop teasing."

So he did, sheathing himself in the condom before sliding into all that wet heat. Her eyes were closed, her expression blissful.

He shouldn't feel as proud as he did. But he was proud. She wasn't afraid. Wasn't sad. Wasn't feeling anything but pleasure.

Because of me.

"Move," she whispered, eyes still closed.

"Look at me," he demanded. He needed to see her. Needed to know everything she was feeling.

Her eyelids fluttered open and, even in the moonlight, he could see her desire.

He began to move, setting a slow, steady pace, watching every flicker of her eyes, listening for every catch of her breath. Figuring out what she liked.

What they both liked.

And when she went over, she kept her eyes on his, her fingers digging into his shoulders as she shuddered and moaned his name. He'd have bruises in the morning, and he couldn't wait to see them.

He was so intent on her that his own orgasm took him by surprise. He arched his back, his body rigid as he came harder than he ever had before.

Shuddering, he braced his weight on his forearms, resting his forehead against hers. He couldn't move. Didn't want to ever move. He wanted to stay like this forever.

"Cora," he murmured.

"Mmm?" She sounded sleepy, but she was smiling.

"Are you okay?"

"I am *so* okay." She sighed, content. "You?"

"I can't feel my legs."

She snorted an indelicate laugh as she smoothed her hands over his shoulders. "Maybe we felt too much?"

He laughed. "No such thing." He kissed her softly. "Sleep now. I need to let SodaPop out and I'll be back to guard your room."

She frowned slightly. "You'll sleep with me, right?"

He hesitated. "I sometimes have dreams."

She met his gaze. "I can deal with dreams, Phin. Do you need SodaPop on the bed with us?"

That she'd think to ask was such a boon. He hadn't expected this. Hadn't expected *her*. Emotion flooded his chest and he had to kiss her again. "You are a good person, Cora Jane Winslow."

"So are you, Phineas Butler Bishop."

He didn't want to leave her, but he had to walk the dog before he passed out. Reluctantly he pulled out of her and dealt with the condom before pulling on his jeans and shirt.

She'd sat up in bed, watching him, her skin on glorious display. "You'll come back." It was a statement, not a question.

"I'll come back," he promised. He clucked his tongue at SodaPop, who obediently followed him down the stairs.

Where Molly sat with a cup of coffee. "She's asleep?"

Phin strode to the kitchen door, knowing his face was red. Blue was asleep on his bed near the radiator and he bent over to give the old boy a quick pat. "Almost. I'm going to sleep in that chair in her room."

It was only a white lie. Okay, it was a total lie.

Molly snickered. "Sure. You do that."

Busted. But he couldn't find it in himself to care. "Come on, SodaPop. Potty time." He stood outside, shivering while she sniffed the ground and did her business.

He ignored Molly's smirk as he passed her on his way back up the stairs. Cora had drawn back the covers and was snuggled beneath them.

Still naked, he discovered when he climbed into bed beside her. SodaPop lay on the floor next to the bed.

"Good night, Phin," Cora murmured as she cuddled up against him.

He hadn't slept with another person in longer than he could remember, but Cora wanted him to sleep with her and that was exactly what she was going to get.

He slid his arm around her shoulders, pulling her closer, her happy hum making everything right. Tomorrow they'd get back to work.

For now, he'd enjoy holding her as she slept.

It was good to feel again.

The Garden District, New Orleans, Louisiana
FRIDAY, DECEMBER 16, 4:30 A.M.

"No!"

Cora jerked awake at the shout. She'd fallen asleep in Phin's arms, but at some point, he'd pulled away and now lay curled into himself on the far edge of the bed. He was shaking and muttering "no" over and over again.

SodaPop was nuzzling Phin's neck, whimpering loudly.

He said he dreamed. Oh, Phin.

"Phin?" Cora gently reached for his shoulder, giving it a gentle nudge, before yanking her hand back. If he flailed, she didn't want him to feel guilty because he'd lashed out in his sleep and inadvertently hurt her.

He did flail, but it was immediately halted when someone knocked on Cora's bedroom door.

"Everything okay in there?" Molly called loudly.

Phin jackknifed into a sitting position, his eyes wild and disoriented. "What?" he demanded hoarsely.

"You were dreaming, Phin. It's okay." Cora slid out of bed and into her robe. Better to get Molly sorted first. She opened the door wide enough that Molly could see she was unharmed. "We're fine. Just a bad dream."

Molly's mouth bent down in sympathy. "I know those. Let me know if you need anything. Do you have any water?"

"I have bottles up here. I'll make sure he drinks something."

"Give him some aspirin, too." Molly gave her a nod before returning downstairs.

Cora shut the door firmly and sat on the edge of the bed closest to Phin. He still sat up, but his folded arms rested on his updrawn knees, his head in his hands. His body trembled and Cora's heart cracked.

She brushed a tentative hand over his head, working her fingers into his dark hair, massaging his scalp without saying another word.

Finally, he began to relax. "Sorry."

"Hush. Don't you tell me you're sorry, Phin Bishop. Not me."

He lifted his head, met her gaze. His eyes were devastated. "But I am."

"You are what?" she murmured, shifting so that she could work both hands into his hair, and he closed his eyes on a quiet groan.

"Sorry. Broken."

She didn't tell him that he wasn't broken. He was, a little bit. So was she, just not in the same way. "You're putting yourself back together, though. I'm proud of you, Phin. You've done so much for me this week." She injected humor into her tone. "You did so much for me a few hours ago."

He snorted a laugh. "I did do that, didn't I?"

She kept on massaging, working from his skull to his neck. "You really did. If you roll over, I'll rub your shoulders. You look tense."

He laughed again, this time bitterly. "Yeah, that's me."

"Roll over, Phin. Don't make me full-name you."

He opened his eyes, one side of his mouth lifting. "You're bossy, Cora Jane."

"I am." She stroked the side of his face. "I'm supposed to hydrate you, too. Hold on." She got him a bottle of water and dug in her nightstand drawer for some pain reliever. "I know there's some in here somewhere," she muttered, removing items and piling them on the nightstand as she searched.

Phin watched her, his eyes growing wide. "Why do you have a mousetrap in your drawer?"

"Because I don't have a cat."

"That makes no sense, Cora."

She sighed. "I set the traps out but then I trip them on purpose and put them away. I don't want to hurt any mice."

"*That* makes more sense." He reached over and grabbed a small mesh bag. "Why do you have twenty-sided dice in your drawer?"

"They were my mother's. I found them in one of the boxes in the attic and I remembered her fiddling with them when she was sad over my father leaving. She told me once that she and my father played with them in college."

"Dungeons & Dragons," he murmured, and she was surprised that he could remember details given how shaken he was.

"Yes. She taught John Robert and me how to play. We had game nights. Did puzzles. It was our fun time. Oh, here it is." She checked the expiration date on the bottle of pain relievers, satisfied that the pills were still good. "Take these and drink." She waited until he'd swallowed the pills and drunk half of the water in the bottle. "Now, roll over."

Shaking his head, Phin did as he was told. Cora scooted closer until her hip rested against his and began kneading the muscles of his back.

"You have very nice muscles," she said. "I like what I see."

He just hummed, groaning a little when she dug her thumb into a particularly tight muscle. SodaPop sat on the floor at Cora's feet, looking concerned.

She hadn't thought a dog could look concerned, but Phin's dog did.

"Good girl," she said softly. "You're such a good girl. He's okay."

Phin reached over the side of the bed and stroked Soda-Pop's silky ears. "Thank you, sweetie."

"Is she your sweetie or am I?" Cora asked playfully.

Phin winced. "Um . . . both?"

Cora chuckled. "That's okay. I know where I stand." She continued to work on his back and shoulders until he began to relax. "If you want to tell me about the dream, you can. If you don't want to, you don't have to."

He sighed. "You haven't asked why I have PTSD."

"I figured you'd tell me when you were ready."

He turned his head so that his cheek pressed into the pillow. "If you don't stop the massage, I'll tell you."

"You don't have to bribe me, Phin. You don't have to tell me at all."

"Not a bribe." He made a little noise. "There. That feels good."

She focused on that spot until the muscle beneath her hands became pliant. "What is it, if it's not a bribe?"

He sighed again. "Armor? I can't look at you when I tell it."

"Whatever you need. I assume it was something that happened when you were in the army."

"Yeah," he said roughly. "Not a very unique story. Our Humvee hit a mine. I was manning the turret and got thrown from the vehicle. The mine was in a backpack in the road. I saw it too late to warn the driver."

She thought about the scars on his chest and the one that slashed across his back. One of those scars was round and she thought that might have been where he was shot in the bar fight he'd mentioned. The others on his chest were scattered in an uneven pattern.

Shrapnel, she'd thought when she'd traced them with her fingers before they'd had sex. The scar across his back looked like a burn.

Oh, Phin.

"What happened to your friends?"

"Most weren't really friends. Colleagues. I didn't let many close enough to be a friend. Still . . ." He drew a breath and let it out slowly, his hand reaching for the dog again. SodaPop leaned into his touch, licking his hand.

Cora kept up the massage, both to make him feel better and to give herself something to do. She had a feeling this story, while not unique, would be hard to hear.

"They were . . ." His voice broke and he cleared his throat. "They were blown to bits. I was lucky. Getting thrown saved my life."

She traced the burn scar lightly before resuming the shoulder massage. "But?"

"But I was surrounded by . . . them."

Cora swallowed hard, imagining what he'd seen. "Did anyone else survive?"

"No." He choked out the word.

"Were any of the friends you did let close among the dead?"

He was quiet for a long moment. "Yes. He was hurt, but not dead. I crawled over to him and he was . . . bleeding. I tried to help him. Tried to stop the bleeding. Didn't work."

"What was his name?"

"Jamie. Jamie Darnell. He was twenty-six. Had a wife and a daughter. He was from Dayton, so we'd talk about Ohio. Sports and ice cream and Cincinnati chili."

"Cocoa and spaghetti noodles," Cora murmured.

"Library trivia?" he asked.

"Yep. Cocoa in the sauce, served over spaghetti. Always wanted to try it."

"Maybe someday . . ." He trailed off.

Maybe someday she could go to Ohio with him and try the chili. She hoped that was what he'd planned to say, but she wasn't going to push him.

"Maybe," she said, leaning down to brush a kiss over the scar on his back.

He shuddered. "I still see them. Blood and bone. Hands and feet. Arms and legs. All over the place."

Her hands faltered for a moment before resuming the massage. "I guess you would. Not something easily forgotten. Did you have to go to the hospital afterward?"

"Yeah. That was awful, too. I hate hospitals."

"Me too. Spent a lot of time in them with John Robert. Did you feel guilty that you survived?"

He nodded, his expression miserable.

She pressed a kiss to his temple, her hands still working his shoulders, but more lightly now. She was just keeping up the skin-to-skin contact at this point.

"So did I. Not the same, of course, but John Robert was my little brother. He wasn't supposed to get sick and if he did, I was supposed to be able to fix him. None of that worked out like it should have."

"Sucks," Phin muttered.

"It really does." She moved back up to his neck, then to his skull.

He shuddered again, this time in pleasure. "Feels good. Thank you."

"You're welcome. Can I ask another question?"

"What happened six weeks ago?"

"Yes. But if you don't want to tell me, you don't have to."

His mouth tightened. "I was helping Val and Kaj—he's her boyfriend."

"The prosecutor." Cora had read about their situation. Kaj's son had been targeted by kidnappers. Val had been the boy's bodyguard and had needed help taking the bad guys down. "You were there, at the end."

"I was. There was a . . ." He cleared his throat. "I saw some remains. Looked just like my squad. Arms and legs. Hands and feet. A lot of blood."

Cora kept her voice matter-of-fact when she wanted to cry for him. "Then your spiral six weeks ago makes logical sense."

Phin's fingers paused their stroking of SodaPop's coat. "Doesn't make it okay, though."

"Did you hurt anyone, Phin?"

"No."

"Did you help someone?"

"Yeah."

"You want to know what I think?"

He didn't answer for so long that she thought he wasn't going to. Then he sighed. "Sure. Hit me with it."

The weariness in his voice made her lay her cheek against his. She put her arms around his wide shoulders and hugged him. It was an awkward position, but he seemed to melt into her embrace.

"I think you're not God."

His eyes opened and he shifted to meet her gaze. "What?"

"That's what Tandy told me when John Robert died. I was so angry with myself. I'd failed him. Tandy finally lost her cool and told me that I wasn't God. I didn't get to rule the universe. It's not even close to what you went through, but you're not God, either, Phin. You didn't cause the explosion that killed your squad. You can't control the images that flood your mind. You saw them. It was awful. That would make anyone have nightmares and you already had anxiety and depression. That you spiral seems like a normal outcome. If I were God, I'd make it so that you'd never experienced any of that, but unfortunately, I'm not God, either. The fact is, it happened. You can't go back in time and make it un-happen."

"I hate that."

"I know. I hate that I can't go back and fix my brother. That I can't go back twenty-three years and beg my father not to go out on that last job. Then he might have been around to be a donor for John Robert. But we can't go back in time."

"Sucks," he muttered again.

"It does. But now that I know the details, I'm even prouder of you. You're putting your life back together. You have a job that you're good at with coworkers who care about you. You're planning to go home to your family and make that right. You're fixing the things you can control. You've even thought about helping the vets you shared that alley with."

He frowned. "How are you making me feel better? You

should think I'm too much trouble, but even *I* don't hate myself so much right now."

That pleased her. "Good."

He reached for her hand, bringing it to his lips. "Thank you, Cora Jane."

"You're welcome, Phineas Butler."

He made a face. "That doesn't make me feel better, you calling me that."

She shrugged. "Too bad," she said lightly. "Joy spilled your middle name and I can't let it go."

He rolled to his back and sat up, lifting her onto his lap like she weighed nothing. It was enough to make her swoon.

She kissed his jaw. "Do you think you can go back to sleep?"

"No, but you should." He settled her on the bed beside him, untying the belt of her robe so that he could lay his head on her chest.

She carded her fingers through his hair, gratified when he hummed his pleasure. "If you can't sleep, will you listen to an idea I have?"

"Uh-oh. Is it an idea I'll like or one that will make me want to lock you in this room and not let you out?"

"I think you'll like it. But you can lock me in here later if you want. As long as you're locked in with me."

He laughed. "I like you, Cora Jane."

"I like you, too."

"What's your idea?"

"Well, it came to me after you told me about the vets in that alley, how hard it is for them to get a new start."

He lifted his head to study her face. "Yeah? And?"

"And . . . I have this big house and it feels wrong to keep it for myself."

His brows went up, his eyes lighting up with interest. "And?"

"I wondered about opening the house up to vets who need a helping hand. Like a halfway house. A place they can stay while they learn a trade."

Phin's mouth opened and closed, his eyes growing shiny. "Wow. Not what I expected."

"Do you think it's a good idea?"

"Yeah. I think it is. More importantly, it makes you a good person. Which I already knew, but . . . God, Cora. The possibilities."

She smiled at him. "I know. I figured I'd sell that necklace and have enough money to get started. There are grants for this type of thing, too. I've helped library patrons find them."

"If they exist, you will find them. And if anyone can do this, it would be you. I'd like to help you."

"Of course. I figured you would, even before we did . . . you know. This."

His smile was slow and dirty. "Set the bed on fire?"

"Better you than some thug with a gas can," she said wryly.

He winced. "Sorry. That fell flat. I guess it's too soon."

Her lips twitched. "It's okay. You have time to think of something better. Lots of time." She lifted her head enough to kiss him. "Now I have to go back to sleep or I'll be mean to everyone come morning. Will you try to sleep some more?"

"I'll try." He shifted on the bed so that he could wrap her in his arms. "Sleep, Cora Jane. We'll figure all this mess out with your father and then we can fix this place up and help a lot of people."

21

SAGE'S MOTHER DIDN'T answer when he knocked on the front door, but her car was here, so he figured that she was home. He hadn't been here since he was eighteen. When they'd fought about him working for Alan. She'd wanted Sage to move away. To move in with her.

Sage didn't know why she'd tried to get him to leave his grandfather. He'd never asked. He'd just . . . avoided her. For years. He'd been happy with Alan then. Useful. Valued.

Or so he'd thought.

But she'd been right. Working for Alan had been the worst thing he'd ever done.

Sage had dreamed of Sanjay and the old librarian last night. He'd woken shaking, unable to go back to sleep. So he'd gotten dressed and made the drive to Mobile.

Maybe his mother had some of the answers he needed. That she and his father had divorced twenty-three years ago was not a coincidence. He was certain of it.

Sage only knew that Alan hated his mother, and that the feeling was quite mutual. Lisa Tupper had never divulged the source of their feud, but it went deep.

Hearing music playing faintly, he followed the sound, walking around her house to the screened patio. She was in the heated pool, cutting through the water in quick, even strokes. Letting himself in through the screen door, he took a seat at the patio table, waiting until she finally surfaced.

She startled, gasping. "Sage. What are you doing here?"

"Came to visit you, Mother. Is that a crime?"

She emerged from the water, grabbing a towel to dry herself off before dropping into the seat beside him and turning off the music coming from her phone. "Not a crime, but definitely unexpected. Are you sick?"

"No. Nothing like that. I have some questions, and I hope you'll have some answers."

"Ask whatever you like, son. If I can answer, I will."

He thought again of Ashley, of the dimple in her cheek that so matched his own. *Who is she and why is she living in Merrydale, Louisiana?*

But what came out of his mouth was "Why didn't you fight Grandfather for custody?"

She flinched, taken aback. "Oh. Well." She refilled her coffee cup, clearly stalling. Finally, she sighed. "It's a difficult story to tell. And when I tried to approach the subject, you cut me off. It's been seven years since we've talked. I figured you didn't want me in your life."

That had been true then. They'd argued about Alan. She'd said his grandfather was dangerous and he'd scoffed, calling her a liar. Then he'd ghosted her.

That had clearly been a mistake. "So Grandfather is the reason?"

"Yes. Your grandfather threatened me," she said baldly. "He said that if I fought for custody, he'd 'bury me.' I wasn't sure if that was hyperbole or not. He said he had photos of me with other men." Her gaze was sharp. "He did not, Sage. I was totally faithful to your father during our whole marriage. But the photos Alan had looked real. Even to me. He wanted me to go away and relinquish all my parental rights. I couldn't do that. So I bargained with him. Got a few weekends with you, a few Christmases. Until you were old enough to decide you didn't want to see me."

He frowned again. "Bargained with him? How?"

"I knew something he didn't want getting out. I threatened him with exposure. I wanted full custody, but I knew that wasn't going to happen. He was already too powerful and he had a lot more money than I did. His lawyers were sharks." She sighed. "So I was grateful to get what I got."

Sage knew his grandfather was capable of doing whatever he needed to do to get what he wanted, but that Alan had threatened to *bury* his mother? Knowing what he knew now, that Alan had killed Medford Hughes, maybe Lisa was being literal.

"Can you please just tell me what happened? I need to know."

"Why?" she asked, her fear obvious.

Sage pulled out his phone and found the graduation photo of Ashley that he'd snapped after finding it in his grandfather's safe. "Who is she?"

Lisa's eyes widened. "I don't know. How do you know her?"

"She looks like me."

Lisa nodded. "She does. Where did you get this picture?"

"I found it among Grandfather's things. He's done something. Something bad."

"Are you in danger, Sage?"

"Not at the moment." It was a prevarication and he knew it.

From the look on her face, so did she. "I have friends in Spain. Or Singapore or Australia. You can go any of those places to hide. Alan won't find you."

"I appreciate that." He put his phone away. If she didn't know who Ashley was, he'd have to come at this from a different angle. "What did you know twenty-three years ago when you bargained for visitation with me?"

Lisa sighed. "You know your father has a younger sister, right?"

Sage nodded slowly. "Right. Aunt Jenny. There's another brother, Uncle Walton."

"You don't really know either of them."

"Uncle Walton is never stationed near us, and Aunt Jenny is in a mental hospital."

"She got pregnant when she was fifteen," his mother said, as if merely saying the words was painful.

"Oh," Sage said quietly, a few pieces falling into place. "That wouldn't have been good for Grandfather."

"No, it wouldn't have been. It would have ruined his reputation. His career."

"His ability to fundraise," Sage added cynically.

"I hate that you know that. I hate that it's true."

"What happened to Aunt Jenny?"

"He sent her away."

"To the mental health hospital or to a home for unwed mothers?"

Lisa shook her head. "Neither. It was someone's actual home. Someone who owed him a favor, I guess."

"What happened?"

His mother suddenly looked twenty years older than she had when he'd arrived. "I found the address. Alan had it written on a scrap of paper in his wallet."

"You went through his wallet?"

"I sure as hell did. I loved Jenny. She was a sweet girl and needed her family. She'd told me that she was pregnant before she was sent away, and I asked if she knew who the father was. She . . . shut down. Said it didn't matter, that she didn't want the father of her baby in her life."

"How did Grandfather find out she was pregnant?"

"It wasn't difficult to figure out. I never said a word to your grandparents because I promised I wouldn't, and Jenny trusted me. But she was throwing up every morning. Her mother made her take a pregnancy test. The next day, Jenny was sent away."

"When was this?" he asked, already knowing the answer.

"Twenty-three years ago."

Sage thought he'd feel elated to have his suspicions about Ashley Caulfield confirmed, but all he felt was dread. "Did you visit her? At the address you found in the wallet?"

"I did. Jenny was still a child herself. She was miserable, lonely and sad and . . . traumatized. I asked her point-blank if she'd been raped and she nodded. I was . . . sick. Just sick."

"She never told you who'd done it?"

"No, never. I told her that I'd help her get an abortion. She just started to cry. She wanted the baby. Wanted someone who'd love her back, and that broke my damn heart. She was just a child herself and her parents had sent her away, like she was nothing. Just an embarrassment, an obstacle to their success."

"And then?"

"And then the owner of the house burst into her room and said she'd overheard our conversation. I should have known we wouldn't have privacy, but I was so taken aback by how distraught Jenny looked. The woman threw me out of her house and by the time I got home, both your father and grandfather were waiting for me. My marriage was over."

"*That's* why Dad divorced you?"

"Yes. He and your grandfather were so angry with me. For visiting Jenny, for offering her an abortion. I wasn't surprised by Alan's reaction, but your father's stunned me. I was just numb after that. That he'd throw me away for trying to help his sister? He didn't see it that way. Alan especially didn't see it that way."

"So you bargained with him. Told him you'd tell the world about Jenny's pregnancy."

"I did. He tried to buy me off with cash, but my divorce lawyer told me that I'd already get half of your father's money. I knew I'd be okay there. I bargained with him for you."

She said "you" so fiercely that Sage could actually see his mother as she'd been all those years ago. "Thank you."

Her eyes grew shiny. "I wish I could have done more, but

like I said, Alan came prepared. If he'd taken those doctored photos of me to court, I would have lost you entirely."

"He's a bastard," Sage murmured. Alan had been using him to further his own business needs for years. But he hadn't realized how truly ruthless his grandfather could be with family. "He told me that you didn't want me."

"Never true," she said with heat and finality. "Never."

He smiled at her sadly. "I believe you, Mother. I've seen his manipulations firsthand. I thought he'd just gotten worse recently, but it seems that he's been a bastard for a long time. I wish I'd listened to you when I turned eighteen."

"What did he do to you?" she asked, each word laced with fury.

"Nothing." Sage had done enough on his own and he felt . . . shame. It wasn't an emotion he was accustomed to feeling. "What happened to the baby?"

Lisa lifted her brows, her stubborn expression telling him that she wouldn't let him get away with keeping secrets from her. "She was stillborn. Or so Alan said. It appears that he lied." She pointed to Sage's phone. "Who is she?"

"Her name is Ashley Caulfield and she's twenty-three years old."

Lisa's expression darkened, her cheeks flushing with unhidden rage. "He told Jenny that she had a stillborn child. He told his wife that. What kind of man does that?"

A selfish, cruel bastard. "He didn't want his daughter to fight him over the baby," Sage murmured. "So he told her it was dead. But that in and of itself doesn't seem enough to have sent her to a mental health hospital. Not for all these years."

"I personally think it was more the rape than the supposed stillbirth, but I'm sure both were intertwined. Plus Jenny was never . . . stable. She had mood swings and depression. I didn't know it for what it was then. I just thought it was normal teenage stuff."

"How long has she been in a psychiatric facility?"

"Since shortly after the birth, so twenty-three years.

Your grandfather had her committed after she took some pills. Quite a few pills. She was in a coma for a while and wasn't quite right when she woke up. Duller, was how I thought of her then. She'd always been depressed, but at that point, there didn't seem to be anyone home, if you know what I mean. Her eyes were dead. The last time I saw her, she was so doped up, she didn't even know me."

"You went to see her in the psych hospital?"

"I did, a few times. Until the front desk told me I'd been put on a no-visit list, which made me so angry. It wasn't like I could do anything by then. She didn't even know me. Your grandfather actually filed papers to have my visitation with you revoked, too. I threatened to go to the press with Jenny's whereabouts. He very smugly told me that he'd already released a statement—that Jenny had experimented with drugs and was now basically a walking vegetable. His words, not mine. He'd used it as an impassioned plea for parents to keep their kids away from drugs. He was fundraising off his daughter's suicide attempt. I told him that I knew she'd been raped, and *that* got a reaction."

Sage went still. "What did he do?"

"He hit me so hard that I fell down. He had to leave the room because it looked like he wanted to hit me again. Your grandmother came in, helped me up. Told me that I shouldn't make him so angry, that he wasn't nice when he was angry."

Sage's mouth fell open. "He hit her, too?"

"I don't know. I'd never seen evidence of it, but it sure seemed like he had. Your grandmother said I should feel lucky that he'd only hit me. After all the cheating I'd done on your dad, I deserved worse. She said she'd seen the pictures and I was a harlot. I . . . broke. I told her everything, about my visit to see Jenny, about how she said she'd been raped. About how her husband had threatened me with those fake photos. Everything. I hoped she'd at least help her daughter, even if she didn't believe me about the cheating, but that's not what happened. At least I don't think so."

"She had a car accident and died."

Lisa's chuckle was mirthless. "That's what they told everyone. Again, had to keep up that reputation of his. Your grandmother killed herself. Your father blamed me for that, too. Alan had told him that I'd continued to harass Jenny to get back at the family. He said your grandmother was so broken up about Jenny's stillbirth, attempted suicide, and commitment to the psych hospital that she couldn't go on. So she shot herself in the head. Alan called your father and together they covered it up. They put her body in her car and wrecked it. Set it on fire. Bribed an ME to ignore the bullet hole in her head. Your father got drunk one night when he came to pick you up after one of my visitations and he told me everything. But I had no hard proof. If I had, I would have filed for full custody of you."

Sage flinched, thinking of Medford Hughes, of the gun found in his hand after he'd been murdered. He wondered if his grandmother really had killed herself or if Alan had killed her because she'd known about Jenny's rape.

And there was still the question of Cora Winslow's involvement. And the ominous-sounding meeting with his grandfather back in New Orleans. Sage needed to be getting back.

"I have to go, Mother. I have a meeting with Alan."

"My offer to send you to Spain still stands."

"Or Singapore or Australia." He'd meant his words to sound light, but they came out far too serious. "Thank you. I'll call you soon."

The Garden District, New Orleans, Louisiana
FRIDAY, DECEMBER 16, 9:00 A.M.

Cora stretched, sore in all the right places. She'd been right. Phin definitely knew what he was doing in bed.

But he hadn't stayed in her bed after his nightmare. She'd slept, but only fitfully. Every time she'd woken, he'd been sitting in the chair next to her bed, SodaPop at his feet.

He was gone now, the blanket he'd used neatly folded on the chair. She wished she could have woken with him, but she understood.

She checked her phone for any messages, hoping to see one from Tandy, but was unsurprised when there was nothing. She didn't expect Tandy to apologize for her anger. Cora knew what her friend was feeling.

Patrick had been like a father to Cora, too, and she still didn't believe he could have killed her father or hurt children. Not deep down.

But there were an awful lot of facts that pointed to the suspicions being true.

The pleasant buzz with which she'd woken was gone. *Dammit.*

She paged through her notifications. She'd missed a call from Harry late last night, right about the time they'd found the necklace, and she hadn't been interested in her phone after that. She'd call him back after breakfast.

She also had an email from the head of the regional libraries, expressing condolences for the loss of Minnie.

Cora didn't want think about her old boss right now. She hoped Minnie hadn't felt any pain.

She blinked tears away, determined to think about something else. Something productive. Something to keep herself busy.

Phin was right. Keeping oneself busy helped.

She thought about Phin and some of the tightness in her chest eased, making it possible to breathe again. He was one of the good things to have come of this whole fiasco. Phin and all the people he came with—Burke and Molly, Antoine and Val. Stone and Delores.

So get busy. She opened a browser window and typed *how to start a group home for homeless vets.* Her eyes gravitated to a link that explained how to provide transitional housing for military veterans.

This was exactly what she needed to know. Number one: choose a property. *Check*. Number two: permits and licenses.

This was the paperwork phase. Chasing down permits would certainly be one way to keep herself busy.

The aroma of coffee got her attention and she swung her legs over the side of the bed. She'd bookmark this website and work on it in between searching the attic and whatever else Burke had planned for the day.

She found Phin at her stove, frying eggs. SodaPop sat to one side, watching Phin work. Cora couldn't blame the pup. She liked to watch Phin work, too.

Molly sat at the kitchen table, looking at her phone. Blue lay on his bed by the kitchen door. Having people in the house again was nice.

"Good morning," Molly said, giving her a quick up-and-down appraisal. "You look rested."

Cora felt her cheeks heat even though Molly hadn't said the words with any hint of double meaning. *Of course she knows*. That she and Phin had kept their activities secret was too much to hope for when there were alert body-guards in the house.

Cora went straight to the coffeepot, bumping her shoulder into Phin's biceps. "Thank you for making breakfast."

His smile was easy. "It won't hold a candle to what you cooked yesterday, but it's food."

She was smiling up at him when her cell phone buzzed with an incoming call. She checked her screen and went still. "It's Harry."

Phin frowned. "What does he want?"

"I won't know if I don't answer it."

Molly patted the table. "Put it on speaker. We'll be quiet."

Cora obeyed, sitting next to Phin, who'd taken the eggs off the stove. "Good morning, Harry," she answered.

"Cora, I'm so glad to hear your voice. I've been worried."

Phin scowled. "Not enough to check on you sooner," he mouthed.

"I'm okay, Harry. I told you that on Tuesday. I have to say that I figured you'd be hovering over me, though." He hadn't called back and that was odd.

"I had to go to Shreveport. My sister took a fall and I just got home late last night."

"Is Henrietta okay?" Cora asked.

"She will be. She has a broken ankle. I brought her to my house and she's resting. I'm sorry I didn't call sooner. I drove by your house last night on my way home to check on you. I noticed a number of cars parked at your house and lights on in the attic. I called you but you didn't answer, so I called that detective we spoke with on Tuesday and he said that there was nothing to worry about. But I woke up with a bad feeling. What's happening, Cora? Are you all right? Say 'pralines' if you need me to call 911."

Molly smirked.

Phin rolled his eyes.

Cora just smiled. "I'm fine, Harry. I hired a PI firm to help me find out what happened with my father."

"That same PI firm you were visiting on Tuesday morning?"

"The same. They're good people, Harry."

"Why were you in the attic?" Harry persisted, sounding suspicious.

Molly turned her tablet around. She'd written *Ask him to come over. One hour.*

Cora nodded. "It's a long story. Can you come over this morning? Say in an hour? I'll tell you everything."

"Now I'm too curious to say no," Harry grumbled. "I'll be there in an hour."

"Do you have someone to stay with Henrietta?" Cora asked.

"My neighbor is here."

Cora grinned. "Miss Barbara?"

Harry cleared his throat. "Yes, Cora. Miss Barbara is here. She made breakfast for us."

"And dinner last night?" Cora teased.

"Cora Jane."

"Well, did she?"

Harry sighed. "Yes. She did. Are you happy now?"

Cora grinned. "You sly dog, Harry." This man was not guilty of anything. She was sure of it.

"Yes, well. I'll see you in one hour, Cora Jane."

She ended the call and looked at Molly. "Burke and Antoine are coming, I take it?"

"No. Burke's on his way to Houma to check out the shops around the Damper Building to see who was there back in the day. Antoine's back in the office. Said to record our conversation with Harry so he could hear it later."

Cora thought about Antoine, working with his headphones. Falling asleep wearing them, like he had on Tuesday when Joy had been shot.

"Will he be safe there?"

Molly nodded. "Lucien is back from a job. He's one of our other guys you haven't met yet, so Antoine won't be completely alone."

Phin put their breakfast plates in front of them. "Who is Miss Barbara?"

"Harry's neighbor. They've been doing a courting dance since I was in college at least."

"After your mother died," Phin said.

Getting his meaning, Cora nodded as she dug into her breakfast. "A few years after, yes. I guess he went on with his life. I'm glad. He shouldn't have been pining for Mama forever. Not like Mama did for my father."

"I brought down that box of your mother's things from the attic. The gifts from your father that she kept. I thought you might want to put them on one of the knickknack shelves in the living room, now that you know he didn't just leave you."

What a sweet man. "I'm still angry with him, but I suppose I won't be forever. When I'm not, I'll put them up where I can look at them and remember my parents."

Phin pointed to a box on one of the other kitchen chairs. "There's the box of photo albums you asked me to bring down."

Cora leaned over to kiss his cheek, smiling when he blushed. "Thank you."

"You two are making me ill," Molly groused, but she was smiling, too. "So tell me about these pearls you found."

"Burke took them with him last night," Cora said. "He put them in his home safe since I don't have one and people seem to keep breaking in."

"We *let* Vincent Ray break in," Phin said defensively.

Cora patted his hand. "I know. But I don't have a safe and if we all leave the house unattended, someone might get in that we don't want to let in."

"Fine, fine, whatever," Molly said. "What about the pearls?"

"They're pearls," Phin said with a shrug. "Pretty ones."

Cora laughed. "They're natural South Sea pearls set in a five-strand necklace with a diamond and emerald clasp and well over a hundred years old. I'm going to have them appraised and then I'll know more."

"Sounds like you know your pearls," Molly commented, pushing her empty plate aside. "But I figured you would since you wear those all the time."

Cora ran a finger over the pearls she wore. "They were my grandmother's. She wore them every day of her life, a wedding gift from my grandfather. They're probably worth a set of new kitchen appliances. I've tried to sell them a few times, but I've never been able to go through with it."

"I get that," Molly said. "Now I'm wondering what other treasure is just lying around this house."

"You can come help me hunt for fun when all of this is over," Cora offered.

Molly refilled their coffee cups. "I just might."

"You and Delores," Phin said. He gathered their plates and put them in the sink. "She was so excited about those pearls last night. Stone said she chattered about them all the way back to my house. He wants me to make a piece of furniture for their house and put a hidden compartment in it so he can hide things for her to find."

"They are a cute couple," Cora said. "I'm glad you've had them."

Phin lifted the box of photo albums onto the table. "Me too. We've got some time before Harry gets here. Let's take a crack at these albums."

Cora sighed. "Okay."

Phin tilted his head. "You don't want to?"

"It's just . . . seeing pictures of my parents together is hard. But I need to do it." She pulled a stack of the albums from the box. "Some of these are newer, after my father disappeared, so I'll look at them last." She frowned at the album with the photo of her parents inset on the cover. They smiled indulgently at something not in camera range.

"I wonder what they're looking at," Molly said.

"Me. That's what my father said, anyway. I remember sitting on his lap and looking at this album. It was his favorite, just photos of me and Mama and John Robert. 'Just us,' he'd say."

"Just us?" Phin asked.

Just us. She'd nearly forgotten the words her father had said so often. "This house is a Winslow house. It's filled with portraits and furniture and things that are Winslow things. My father loved this album because it was just us. Me and Mama and John Robert. No Winslows. He used to say that. 'Just us. No Winslows.'"

"He didn't like being part of the family?" Phin asked.

Cora ran a finger over the album. "I don't know. He loved us. I remember that. That's why him leaving was so hard to accept. I remember Grandmother telling Mama that she should throw these albums away. Mama promised she would when she was ready." Cora looked at the photo of her parents looking so happy together. "I guess she never was ready."

She opened the album to the first two pages, covered in pictures of her as a newborn with a lot of red hair. Her mother was in about half of the pictures, holding her with a big smile.

"You were a pretty baby," Phin said quietly, and she smiled at him.

"Thank you." She flipped to the next page and the next, a thought entering her mind as she noted that so many of the photos had been taken somewhere other than this house. "I don't think that he liked it here. In the house, I mean. Not New Orleans. He loved New Orleans."

"Why don't you think that he liked this house?" Molly asked.

"He loved to go other places, stay in hotels with us. I remember having Christmas morning at the Roosevelt Hotel in the Quarter when I was four. It was the last Christmas before he disappeared."

"Why?" Phin asked.

"They do such beautiful decorations there. That's what my mama said when I looked through the albums after he was gone, before she put them away. My grandmother . . . she didn't agree. She said that he was too proud for his own good and that she hoped his new wife would support him in the same fashion that my mama had." Cora winced at the memory, adulthood giving her a different perspective. "My father worked. But he hadn't come from money. Not that we had a lot by then, but we did have the house. And the Winslow name. That still meant something when I was younger. My grandmother was a good woman, but a little preoccupied with position. She'd always tell Mama that she dodged a bullet with 'that Jack Elliot.' That she'd known he'd be a bad fit. That was when Mama would get depressed and cry. I think that he didn't take any of these photos of us when he left really hurt her. It was like he left and never looked back."

Because he'd been dead. All this time.

"Your father didn't feel like he belonged here," Phin murmured. "Do you think he had plans to leave and take you all away from here?"

"Maybe. Maybe that was the purpose of the Swiss bank account. We might never know."

"Harry might know," Molly said.

"I'll ask him when he gets here."

Cora went back to the first page and flipped through the photos again. Her father had loved this album. If he'd left behind any message for her mother, it could be here.

The photos were held in place by corner mounts, not glued to the paper, thank goodness. Glue would seep through, destroying the pictures. These photos were still crisp.

I wonder . . .

Using her phone, she snapped a photo of the first page, aware that both Phin and Molly watched her curiously.

"I want to put them back in the right order," Cora explained before removing the first photo on the page and turning it over. "It's an archivist thing."

Sigh. There was nothing written on the back other than the date, written on a carefully cut piece of paper, the top attached to the photo with a small piece of tape. She wondered why he hadn't just written on the photo itself. "My father's handwriting."

"He made the album?" Phin asked.

"He did." Cora removed the other three photos on the page. They were the same—dates written on those carefully cut pieces of paper. Disappointed, she replaced the pictures, making sure they went back in the right places.

Molly and Phin continued to watch, saying nothing as Cora snapped a photo of the second page and removed those four photos.

She put them face down on the album page, looking at their backs. Again, all four had dates written on them in her father's scrawl. But one of the photos—the one of her mother holding her as a newborn—had something else written below it, the characters a brown color versus the black ink used to write the dates.

Cora leaned in to look more closely and gasped. "Oh my God. I think I found it." She turned the photo around so that they could see. "All those Nancy Drew books came in handy. Lemon juice. Look."

"Holy shit, Cora," Molly crowed. "You found it!"

"Mama used to write us notes in lemon juice. Looking back, she probably shouldn't have let us play with matches to read the secret messages. Luckily, we had the sprinklers. For John Robert and me, it was like a secret adventure. She once told me that my father had written her secret notes in lemon juice. I wonder if she kept them."

Phin was grinning. "Over time, and in the attic during the summer, it was warm enough to activate the lemon juice. What does it say?"

"It's numbers. A string of eight numbers. No letters." She read them aloud, and Molly wrote them down. "What does it mean, though?"

Phin shrugged. "Your dad used a code so that your mother could open the Word document on his computer to find the Swiss bank account number. Maybe this is a code, too."

Molly was frowning. "Seems a little subtle to me. Even if she thought he hadn't left her, would she have thought to look for clues or codes?"

"I don't know. Maybe he left her a letter telling her to look. Maybe we just haven't found it yet."

"Let's come back to that once we know if we have anything," Phin said wisely. "Do any of the other photos have secret messages on the back?"

Cora's heart raced at the very thought. "Let's find out."

"I'm texting the others," Molly said. "Burke can't get back, but Antoine and Val need to get over here."

"I'm texting Stone and Delores, too," Phin said. "If this is a real thing, it's going to make their day."

Cora wanted to rip all the photos from the album, but she forced herself to be methodical, taking pictures of each page before removing the photos and examining their backs.

Not every page had a photo with a string of numbers. And not every photo had only numbers. Two had combinations of letters and numbers.

"Twenty," she said finally, when they'd looked through the entire album. "Eighteen with single letters or numbers and two with letter/number combos."

She looked at the people sitting around her table. Time had flown by as she'd worked, the others joining them one by one. By then Antoine, Val, Stone, and Delores had joined them. Burke had been halfway to Houma by the time Molly had texted him, but he listened in by cell phone.

"What do we do with this?" Cora asked.

Antoine was frowning at the list. "The two with letter and number combos are some kind of password."

Hope surged and Cora barely kept her voice level. "To get into the hard drive?"

"Maybe." Antoine still frowned. "I can use it to get into the drive, but I probably won't be able to decrypt whatever's stored there without the encryption password. That could be what the eighteen single characters are—an encryption password. The problem is, we don't know what order the characters go in. They're all mixed together. There are too many combinations."

Delores waved to Antoine's three laptops. "You can't just set them up and make your computers . . . y'know, figure it out?"

Antoine made a face. "I can, but it will take a while. I don't know how long. Could be hours or even days. I won't know until I get there."

Cora understood the dilemma and it was daunting. "I

helped a kid with a problem like this once. It's a statistical thing. Combinations of eighteen individual characters? It would be a lot. Trillions."

"Six quadrillion," Val corrected, looking up from her phone. She turned it around and there were so many numbers that Cora's eyes crossed.

"Shit," Burke drawled through the speakerphone. "There has to be a way to know the correct order."

Phin made a humming noise as he studied the photos on the table. "Twenty pictures."

Cora turned to him. "What are you thinking?"

His eyes were dark and intense, sending a shiver down her spine. "I'm thinking about that bag of twenty-sided dice you keep in your nightstand drawer," he said.

"Nightstand drawer?" Stone asked, brows high. "Why were you in her nightstand drawer?"

Cora blushed as Delores elbowed her husband. "Hush, Stone. Cora, why do you keep a bag of twenty-sided dice in your drawer?"

"They were my mother's. She and my father played D&D in college and she taught John Robert and me how to play. It was our Friday-night family thing. We played games and did puzzles."

Phin was nodding. "And each side of a D&D die is numbered one through twenty."

Cora assessed the photos on the table. Each one was familiar. Each one she'd loved to look at, once upon a time when she'd sat on her father's knee at his desk. But not in this album.

She looked up at Phin, her heart beginning to race. "The custom-made twenty-sided photo cube up in the attic."

"It's not a cube if it's twenty sides," Antoine said.

"Antoine," Molly hissed at him.

"What do you mean?" Phin asked, ignoring Antoine and Molly.

"All of these photos are on that cube. If my father

marked even one of the photos on the cube with a number, we can figure the rest of the order from the dice."

Phin grinned. "I think you found the key, Cora."

"Where is the photo cube, Cora?" Stone asked, not even bothering to hide his impatience.

"In the attic. Hold on." Cora ran up the stairs, Val and Phin close behind her.

"Dammit, Cora," Val gritted out. "I'm on duty. Let me go in first."

"Sorry," Cora said as she made it to the top floor and burst into the attic. She exhaled with relief, half expecting the room to have been ransacked or burned. But it was just as they'd left it.

She went to the box by the window seat that had the special photo . . . thing. "Found it. It's an icosahedron," she muttered, the word suddenly coming to mind. "I know it's not a cube, Antoine."

Phin laughed. "I'm not sure if I want to know how you knew that, but good for you. Come on. Let's see what Antoine can do with this."

Then the doorbell rang.

Phin looked down from the window to the front porch and muttered a curse. "Harry's here."

"Dammit." Cora had forgotten all about him. "Val, can Molly and Antoine clean off the table? You and Phin and I can keep him busy in the foyer until it's safe to bring him into the kitchen. See, I know that I need to have you with me to do your bodyguard stuff."

Patting her shoulder, Val took possession of the photo icosahedron before heading down the stairs. "I'll give this to Antoine."

Phin made an unhappy sound. "Looks like we'll need to wait a little longer to explore what your father hid on that hard drive."

She was impatient, too, but Harry might have more answers. "Be nice to Harry, okay?"

"I reserve the right to continue disliking him for leaving you alone on the street on Tuesday."

She pulled his face down for a light peck on his lips. "I wasn't alone. You were there."

He smiled down at her. "Yes, I was."

22

Metairie, New Orleans, Louisiana
FRIDAY, DECEMBER 16, 9:15 A.M.

"YOU'RE LATE," ALAN snapped when Sage waltzed in.
"I stayed with some friends last night."

"Staying with friends" meant that Sage was at the clubs again. Fornicating and doing God only knew what else. At least Sage disguised his face, but all it would take would be one floozy he'd taken back to his hotel room to rip off his wig and he'd be recognized.

Sage's golden hair was his most recognizable feature.

Alan stopped himself before he said something that would make Sage too angry to follow his commands. "I have something for you to do."

This is it. The moment he'd been bracing himself for since Cora Winslow had tracked down that VanPatten woman. Because Cora knew. Or at least she thought she did.

If she learned the whole truth, all would be lost.

Sage studied him. "What is the job?"

"There's a family that's causing trouble for our ministry."

Sage slowly straightened in the chair. "What kind of trouble?"

"I don't think you need to know that."

"What do you want me to do?"

"I want you to . . ." Alan closed his eyes. Made himself say the words. "I want you to search their house for any files, take their laptops, tie them up, then . . . block the exits and set the house on fire."

He opened his eyes to see Sage staring at him, in obvious shock.

"You want me to *kill* them?" Sage hissed. "You're talking about burning them alive?"

"They'll likely die of smoke inhalation first." He hoped.

Sage shook his head. "No. I won't kill someone. Not even for you, Grandfather."

Alan gave him a bland look, hoping the boy couldn't hear his heart beating in his chest. "You killed for yourself. Little-old-lady librarian. Rental car clerk."

Sage's eyes flashed fury. "You had me followed."

"Of course I did. You've been a loose cannon for the past year, Sage. You need to straighten up and fly right. Which starts with proving you can follow orders, unlike the past few days when you practically stalked Cora Winslow."

"And if I don't agree?"

"Then the police will get an anonymous tip with footage of you entering the old librarian's house. You wore a ski mask, but you drove that rental Camry, which you later drove to meet the rental car clerk, where you did not wear a mask. They'll get photos of you shooting Sanjay, and the location where they'll find his car—with his body in the trunk. That will be enough to get them a warrant for your penthouse condo, where they will find sufficient proof that you killed two people."

His grandson had gone pale. "I left no evidence in my condo."

"Doesn't matter. The police will find that you did." Alan would make sure of it.

Sage's mouth twisted. "You sonofabitch."

"You watch your mouth."

His grandson laughed bitterly. "You are asking me to

murder someone, and you're more concerned that I *swear*? You are a piece of work." He shook his head, suddenly sober. "And if I do it? What then?"

"You get to keep your job, your fancy apartment, and that sports car you love so much."

Sage's eyes narrowed, contempt mixing with his horror. "What if I tell the police that you killed Medford Hughes?"

Alan couldn't help it. He flinched.

Sage smiled coldly.

Alan shrugged, his nonchalance back in place. "They'll think you're making things up because you were arrested for killing that sweet old librarian and an innocent rental car clerk."

"So we're killers now," Sage said quietly. "Is that accurate?"

"*You* are. *I've* never done anything like that."

Sage's laugh was mirthless. "You really are a sonofabitch. A lying sonofabitch."

Alan gritted his teeth. "Will you do as I ask?"

"How long do I have to decide?"

"Thirty seconds."

"Right." The muscle in Sage's jaw bulged. "Give me the address."

Alan had known the boy would fold. Still, he had to control his shaking hands. "Memorize it. I'm going to keep it and burn it afterward."

He handed the paper to Sage and watched as the boy dropped his gaze to the address, staring at it for a long, long moment. Finally, he looked up, his expression completely blank as he tossed the paper to Alan's desk.

"I hate you," Sage said quietly. "So damn much."

I know. Alan wanted to tell him that the job wasn't real, that it was just a test, that he didn't expect Sage to actually kill for him.

But it wasn't a test. It was reality. He needed the Caulfield family gone. He needed the truth buried so deep that no one would ever find it.

And then he'd deal with Cora Winslow. She was surrounded by bodyguards all the time, but that couldn't last forever. He'd kill her outside the library once she went back to work, and then he'd burn her whole house down.

No one would find anything in the rubble. No records, nothing incriminating.

Then it would be over. Finally, over.

Maybe then I'll be able to sleep.

The Garden District, New Orleans, Louisiana
FRIDAY, DECEMBER 16, 10:40 A.M.

Harry Fulton was in his early sixties, dressed in a suit and tie. He was about five-six and balding, a pair of skinny glasses perched on the tip of his nose.

Phin still didn't like him.

Cora opened her arms to Harry as soon as he walked into the foyer. She had to bend down to hug him. "Thank you for coming."

"Sorry I'm late," Harry said. "I texted you that I was delayed, but I don't suppose you saw my message."

"I've been a little busy this morning," Cora said after letting the man go. "Harry, these are my bodyguards, Val and Phin. Val and Phin, my attorney, Harry Fulton."

Harry nodded to Val, then narrowed his eyes at Phin. "He's looking at you like he's more than your bodyguard," the smaller man said suspiciously.

Cora laughed. "Because he is. And, no, I'm not interested in your opinion on the matter." She tucked her arm into Harry's. "Come, let's have some tea."

The table was neat and tidy, all the photos gone. As was Antoine.

Cora looked to Molly for an explanation. "He took all of our things and went up to your office," Molly said. "He's going to figure stuff out while we chat with Harry."

"Harry, this is Molly. She also works for the PI firm.

The others are Stone and Delores. They're friends of Phin's from out of state."

"Nice to meet you all." Harry gave Molly a once-over. "I've seen you before. I'm trying to remember where."

"Le Petit Choux," Molly said with a nod. "You eat there three times a week."

"That's it," Harry confirmed. "I've seen you there often as well." He pulled out a chair for Cora, in which she sat with a grateful smile.

"Thank you, Harry," Cora said.

Phin glared, taking the chair next to her before Harry could.

Val rolled her eyes.

Molly patted the chair next to her for Harry. "My fiancé owns the restaurant. I eat there a lot."

Harry smiled at Molly. "You, my dear, are a very lucky woman. That man is a culinary artist." He waited until everyone was seated before turning to Cora. "So what's this about? And why are all these people here? I wasn't expecting a kind of Spanish Inquisition."

Both Stone and Val snorted a laugh.

Phin had to admit that he might like the man a little bit. Anyone who quoted Monty Python couldn't be all bad. Still, he had his eye on the attorney.

Cora sighed. "I've had an eventful few days, Harry. Also, their boss is on the speaker. Hi, Burke."

"Hi, Cora," Burke said dryly. "And hello, Harry."

"I've heard of your firm," Harry said. "I'm glad you're helping Cora. But, Cora, this has got to be expensive. I'll move money from the trust into your bank account."

"No, you won't," Burke said. "We're doing this for free because whoever's after Cora shot one of ours. Joy will be okay, but it was close."

Harry looked relieved. "I'm so glad that she'll recover."

"We are, too," Cora agreed. "Harry, we need to ask some questions about my father."

"I figured you would. He's kind of been front and center

in all this, ever since they identified his body. Where would you like to start?"

Cora blew out a breath that sent her curls bouncing. "I guess I'll jump into it. Did you manage any of my father's financial affairs?"

Harry didn't answer right away, sending Phin's suspicion spiking. "I didn't," he finally said. "But he did ask me some questions that made me wonder what he was up to."

"Questions about a Swiss bank account?" Cora asked.

Harry nodded. "You found it, then. I never knew for sure if he'd set one up."

"Did my mother know?"

"She knew that he'd asked me," Harry said. "After he disappeared, I told Priscilla about our conversation. She figured it was money he'd used for the other family he'd left her for." The older man swallowed. "And all this time he was dead."

Cora's shoulders slumped, so Phin took her hand and squeezed it lightly. She leaned into him before returning her attention to Harry. "She didn't try to find the account?"

"No. She was so devastated when he left, she said he was welcome to it. She didn't want anything of his. Did you find the account?"

Cora shrugged. "I found the number. Went to the bank yesterday and filled out a metric ton of paperwork to get access to it."

Harry hesitated. "Do you know how he got that money?"

"Yeah, we do. I don't know how much to tell you, only because the less you know at this point, the safer you might be."

Harry paled a fraction. "It was illegal, then."

Cora tilted her head. "You suspected?"

"I hoped, actually. He'd tell your mother he was going to Mobile or Tupelo for business. She worried that he wasn't where he was supposed to be, that he was cheating on her. She asked if I'd follow him and see where he was really going. She couldn't, not with you and John Robert being so small. And John Robert always being so sick. I followed Jack once. He said he was going to meet a client in Mobile, but he went to Baton Rouge instead."

"You knew he wasn't where he was supposed to be, then," Cora said sadly. "And so did Mama."

"Yes, dear. I *hated* telling her that. I really did."

"Did you?" Phin asked. "You didn't want her for yourself?"

"Phin," Cora snapped.

Phin wasn't sorry. This was Cora's safety, her *life* on the line. He held Harry's gaze. Watched the man's face turn a deep red.

"It's all right, Cora," Harry finally said. "His point is fair. I loved your mother. I think my feelings started when she was in college, before she met Jack Elliot, but she was too young and I was too old. And then she was married and so happy. And I was still too old for her, anyway. I was content just to be her friend."

Letting go of Phin, Cora leaned across the table to cover Harry's hand with hers. "And after my father disappeared?"

"I loved her still, but she never got over Jack. She knew how I felt. Or she thought she did. I think she thought I had a crush, but it wasn't just a crush. She was everything to me. It killed me to watch her suffer when your father disappeared. And then, when she died . . . God. I wanted to die, too, but there was you and John Robert to take care of. I knew she'd want me to make sure you all were provided for."

Cora squeezed Harry's hand. "You did that. Thank you."

Harry swallowed. "I did it for her, but also for you two. You and John Robert were like the kids I'd never have." One side of his mouth lifted in an attempt at a smile. "Miss Barbara is well past child-bearing age."

Cora's laugh was watery, her eyes shiny as she released

Harry's hand and leaned back in her chair. "You really are a sly dog, Harry."

The man had tried to make her feel better when it was clear that he was hurting as well. Phin felt a little more grudging acceptance.

"Thank you for being honest," Phin said. "We had to ask."

Harry gave him a single nod. "I know. Cora is my heart."

"Then why did you leave her alone on the street on Tuesday when a shooter had chased her through the Quarter?" Phin demanded.

Harry rubbed his temples. "I was so angry with myself for doing that. I was flustered by that detective. I don't like police stations. They give me anxiety. I'm an estate attorney. I do wills and trusts. I don't deal with criminals. I just wanted to get away from the police station, and Cora was insisting she was going to the hospital to see her friend. I was flustered," he said again. "I'm sorry."

That made sense. Kind of. Phin hated to admit it, but he could understand. Kind of.

"I got halfway to my office, then had the cab turn around and go back, but Cora was already gone. Then I got the call from my sister and everything kind of crumbled."

"They're twins, too, Phin," Cora murmured. "Best friends."

Shit. Now he really had to be nice to the guy. "I hope your sister is better soon."

Cora laughed. "See, was that so hard?"

Phin scowled. "Yes. Yes, it was."

She kissed Phin's cheek. "Thank you." She turned back to Harry, her expression sober once more. "Was my father happy here? In this house?"

Harry hesitated once again. "He loved your mother and you kids. At least I thought he did before I thought he was cheating. But he and your grandmother were never going to be best friends. I think he wanted to move you all out of this house. I know he'd been looking for one. Why?"

"I was wondering if that might have led to him doing whatever it was he was doing to get the money he socked away in that Swiss bank account."

"Could have been," Harry allowed. "Your mother would have gone with him anywhere, I do know that. She was hurt that Jack and your grandmother didn't get along. Told me once that it might be better if no more Winslows lived in Winslow House."

Cora sighed. "My grandmother was a stubborn woman."

Harry's smile was slight. "And your father was a stubborn man. Your mother was always playing peacemaker. Anything else?"

Cora nodded. "Yes. Did anyone break into the house after my father disappeared?"

Harry started to shake his head, then he blinked, his mouth forming an O. "Oh my gracious goodness. Yes, there were a few odd occurrences, but we didn't consider them 'break-ins' at the time. Your father's clothing disappeared. His toiletries. Normal stuff. Priscilla thought he'd come back for them while you all were out."

"When was that?" Cora asked. "I don't remember going anywhere special and Mama didn't work outside the home back then."

"It was on Sunday while we were all at church. The first time was the Sunday right after he disappeared. That was also the day after the first letter arrived, the one to your mother saying he had another family. The rest of the 'break-ins' also happened on Sundays. Your mother assumed it was because Jack knew we'd all be in church."

Cora exhaled a quiet breath. "Harry, did you know Patrick Napier before he moved to New Orleans?"

Harry's eyes widened in shock. "*Patrick?* You think *Patrick* was involved?"

"I don't want to," Cora said. "Did you know him then?"

Harry stared a moment longer before nodding once.

The single movement seemed to shatter Cora, the color draining from her face. "You did?" she asked brokenly.

Oh, Cora. She'd still been hoping that Patrick had not been involved in her father's murder.

"I did. He'd inherited some money and wanted advice. I told him I wasn't taking any new clients and referred him to a few other attorneys in the city. I didn't hear from him again until he'd opened his gallery in the Quarter. I didn't even realize he'd done that until I met him again at a Christmas party your mother threw. You and Tandy were best friends from school and you dragged me over to meet her and her daddy."

"I don't remember that," Cora whispered.

"You were there and gone again with Tandy, off to do some mischief. I remember saying to Patrick that he must have gotten his inheritance settled and he said that he had."

Cora clenched her eyes closed for a few seconds. They were full of confusion when she opened them again. Confusion and hope. The hope was back again.

"Then the inheritance is real," she said to the table at large. "Burke, did you hear that?"

"I did, Cora," Burke confirmed. "But Antoine wasn't able to find any legal relatives of Patrick. He tried all night. Patrick's father was an only child and his mother had one brother. There's no mention of an aunt anywhere. Antoine went back a generation and there was no great-aunt, either."

"It could have been a family friend he called aunt," Cora said, her desperation clear. "Why would he mention it to Harry if there was no inheritance?"

"Maybe," Phin murmured, hating to hurt her even more, "to give his story credence should anyone ever ask."

"But if Harry had taken him on," Cora argued, "Patrick would have had to show him the will and he would have known he was a liar."

Harry shook his head sadly, as if he didn't want to hurt Cora, either. "It was a well-known fact around town that I wasn't taking new clients. My partner had just retired abruptly due to a health issue, and I was drowning in work.

My receptionist told Patrick that I wasn't taking new clients. He insisted on speaking to me anyway. I gave him referrals to other attorneys."

"Maybe he went to one of them," Cora insisted. Then her eyes filled. "I'm grasping at straws, aren't I?"

"I think so," Phin said as gently as he could. "But maybe Harry can ask around. Find out if Patrick did end up talking to any of those other attorneys. Harry?"

"I will," Harry promised. "I promise."

"When did he contact you, Harry?" Stone asked.

"It was sometime after Mardi Gras, I remember that. I had to work the whole week and missed all the parades. I'd promised Priscilla that I'd take her and I was irritated that I'd broken that promise. I told my assistant to turn away all new clients. Patrick called a few months after that."

"So maybe five months after Jack disappeared," Burke clarified.

"Yes. But it took another two years for Patrick to move here," Harry said. "Why?"

Cora covered her mouth with her hand, a little whimper escaping her. Phin wrapped his arm around her. "What?" he asked urgently.

"Jillian, Tandy's mom. She told me once that Patrick had had his heart set on St. Charles School for Girls for Tandy and that they'd been on a waiting list for two and a half years before they moved to New Orleans. *Two and a half years.* I don't want this to be true, dammit."

Hurting for her, Phin rested his cheek against her head, holding her closer. "I'm sorry."

She turned into his embrace, burying her face against his chest. That she'd had a moment of hope made the truth so much harder to accept.

He understood that, too.

Phin wrapped both arms around her and let her grieve that loss of hope. Delores had tears in her eyes. Stone, Val, and Molly wore matching looks of pity.

Phin felt helpless.

Harry sighed. "I . . . I don't know what to say. I don't know how to help."

"You've helped us a lot," Phin said. "Thank you."

Harry stood and rounded the table, going down on one knee next to Cora. "Do you need me to stay? I will if you need me."

Cora pulled out of Phin's embrace, shaking her head. "It's okay. You can go. I'll call you in a little bit. Thank you, Harry."

Harry rubbed her back, meeting Phin's eyes. "Call me if she needs me, okay?"

Phin nodded. "I will. I promise."

Molly rose. "I'll walk you out." She did so, then went to the bottom of the stairs. "You can come down now, Antoine," she called up. "He's been texting me," she explained when they all stared at her. "I wanted him to wait until Harry was gone."

"You need to go home and sleep, Molly," Burke ordered her from the phone.

"I will," Molly promised. "I want to hear what Antoine has to say first."

Antoine flew down the stairs, his eyes bright. "I have it. Jack left records on his hard drive." He stopped short and stared at Cora. "Dammit. I'm sorry."

"Let's take a little break," Val said. "I think we need some chocolate. I happened to bring some cupcakes with me, and Delores brought beignets from Café du Monde."

Cora squared her shoulders. "Maybe later. I need some aspirin, and then I want to know what Antoine's found. It's time to end this."

The Garden District, New Orleans, Louisiana
FRIDAY, DECEMBER 16, 11:30 A.M.

Antoine set a single laptop on the table. It seemed strange for there to be only one, Cora thought. Usually he had three.

She gulped down some aspirin with the glass of water Delores offered her. Her head was killing her. "Thank you."

Delores ran a hand over Cora's hair, only possible because Cora was sitting down. If she'd been standing up, Delores wouldn't have been able to reach.

"They'll figure it out," Delores promised. "And you won't be alone."

"Thank you." She put the glass on the table and folded her hands, bracing herself. "What did the photos give you, Antoine?"

Antoine looked a bit manic. "Everything. Well, everything on that old computer of your father's. The photo of you as a newborn was number one. Once I had that, I could figure out the order of the other photos and got two separate passwords. The password to the hard drive was the two letter and number combos, like we thought. And the other eighteen characters were the encryption password, which allowed me to read all the files."

Phin took Cora's hand. "Fine, Antoine. Now tell us what you found. You're giving Cora an even worse headache."

"I'm sorry, Cora. I got excited. So, there were three files on the partitioned drive." Antoine held out a sheet of paper. "The first was a letter addressed to your mother."

Cora took it, her hand trembling. The paper was shaking too hard for her to see the words. Her heart swelled when Phin took it from her hand, holding it so that she could read it. She truly wasn't alone in this. Drawing a breath, she began to read.

"'My dearest Priscilla. I knew you'd figure it out! You must have found the letter in my desk drawer and then the rest of the puzzle pieces. You've always been the smarter of the two of us. So . . . if you're reading this, I must not have come home.'"

Cora pressed her hand to her chest. It hurt to even think of her father writing this. "'You'll be angry with me, and

I guess you have that right. I hope someday you can forgive me. I've tried to help people, to make the world a better place. Hindsight being twenty-twenty, I probably should have left the work to someone else. In a nutshell, I've been helping people escape abusive situations, helping them start over. It started innocently enough. One of my frat brothers—PN—told me that a woman we were friends with back in college was being beaten by her husband. I dated her for a while, long before I met you. I couldn't let her be beaten up if I could help, so PN and I helped her. She became our first job.'"

What little hope Cora had retained simply fizzled. "PN. Patrick Napier."

"So Patrick was his *partner*?" Phin asked. "Not his killer?"

Antoine wobbled his hand. "Hard to say. Let her finish."

Cora drew another breath. "'PN and I started helping other people, mainly women like our friend who needed to escape abusive husbands. PN does the background research and he makes their new IDs. He has an eye for photography and can forge a signature.'"

Cora swallowed. "Your dad, Jack Elliot," she whispered, thinking of the signature on each of the letters she'd received. Squaring her shoulders, she forced herself to read on. "'I manage the money, setting up new accounts for the people we relocate. I set up an account for myself, too. If you've gotten this far, you probably found the poem I left you. The first letters of each paragraph are the password to another document which has the account number. If you haven't discovered it, here it is again.'" She read off the Swiss account number. "'At first everything was going well, but recently it's been falling apart. I've told PN that I want out. If you're reading this, either an abusive spouse has killed me, or PN has. I started suspecting him a few months ago. Two weeks ago, that came to a head when the husband of one of my clients shot at me.'"

She looked up. "Jarred Bergeron."

"Keep going," Phin murmured, hugging her to him with his free arm.

Not alone, she thought again. "'We had a third partner, TR. He was a cop and the source of most of our clients. He found the people who needed help and passed their names to PN and me. TR did the heavy work, getting people out and transporting them. On a few cases, he needed another pair of hands and I helped him. I say "was" because TR is dead.'"

"TR was a cop?" Burke asked through the speaker. "Do we know his name?"

"I haven't had a chance to search for him," Antoine said, "but I will. There's more. Cora?"

"'We worked together for three years, each of us living in a different city in Louisiana. We took care to never be seen together and were careful in how we communicated. Things started to go out of control when we took a job placing a young man who was supposedly running from his family because he'd inherited his grandfather's millions and the family was trying to kill him to get the money. This job didn't come from TR. It came from PN. He said he'd met the guy through a chat room. This guy on the run paid us a lot of money to get him out of the country.'"

"I don't like where this is going," Val said grimly.

Cora didn't, either. "'It turned out he'd killed his grandfather himself and the family was trying to find him to turn him in. They'd reported his disappearance to the local police and there was a manhunt underway. TR found out and had a fit. He was angry that PN hadn't done due diligence. PN was very sorry, or so he said.'"

"Until it happened again," Stone said quietly.

Antoine nodded. "Exactly."

"How could they have just accepted what this PN said?" Delores asked.

"It was the nineties," Phin said. "It was easier to fake a

story back then. Identities got harder to fake after 9/11 and the growth of the internet."

"He's right," Antoine said. "Things are very different now. Finish it up, Cora."

She didn't want to, but she would. "'TR and I felt that PN should have been more careful. But then it happened again. PN was devastated once again, but TR didn't believe him. Neither did I. TR and I had planned to confront PN, but then TR was shot in his own home. He was working undercover vice in Houma, and that's a dangerous job. But he wasn't killed in his cover house, it was in his own house and there had been no evidence of breaking and entering. PN and I both knew his address, and I know that I did not kill him. So I straight-up told PN that I wanted out. We had two more jobs scheduled and I told PN that I'd finish those, because I'd personally vetted both clients. PN wasn't happy with me leaving, but even he agreed the job was becoming too dangerous. I did one of the jobs and, like I said earlier, an abusive husband shot at me. I would have quit right then, but this last job is delicate and everyone involved is trying to do the right thing.

"'I don't believe it's dangerous, but I'm scared, Priss. Scared I'll die like TR did. If that happens, I don't want you trying to find PN. If I'm dead and he's responsible, he will kill you if you make trouble for him. I've included information on this drive that you can use to leverage your safety if PN ever threatens you. Please know that I love you and always have. I love our babies and always will. Your husband, Jack Elliot.'"

Cora thought she'd be sick. Patrick and her father had been partners with one other man. Her father had been killed doing that final "delicate" job, and now Patrick was the only one left standing. *How could you, Patrick?*

That he'd done such an awful thing and then cozied up to her family? Rage battled with betrayal, making her swallow back bile.

"Wait." Delores held up one hand. "Cora's mom was a physical therapist, not a computer guru. How was she supposed to put all these pieces together? I knew that encryptions existed, but I'd have no idea how to actually use one. How did Jack expect her to get this letter?"

Antoine grinned at her. "That is an excellent question, Delores."

"It really is," Val said with a frown. "I wish I'd thought of it. Working with Antoine makes all this stuff seem like it's easy-peasy, but it's really not."

Delores looked pleased with herself.

"There's another letter somewhere that we haven't found," Antoine said. "At the beginning of this one, Jack tells her that he's glad she found the first letter and 'the rest of the puzzle pieces.'"

"Mama loved games and puzzles. We used to have races to see who could do the Sunday crossword fastest. Mama would come up with these amazing games, like a scavenger hunt crossed with a trivia game." The memory had once been a sweet one. Now all Cora would remember was this intricate puzzle that Jack had left for his wife. "But there was no such letter in his desk drawer. Mama would have said something. She would have *done* something."

Cora's mama wouldn't have cried for the husband who'd left her. She would have cried for the husband who'd been murdered. And then she'd have tried to get justice.

"Maybe it'll turn up," Antoine said but didn't sound like he meant it.

"Or maybe PN found it when he was searching our house while we were at church," Cora said bitterly.

"Maybe," Antoine acknowledged. "We might never know that. So there were three files on the partitioned drive, like I said. The first was this letter. The second was a ledger of the money he'd taken from the clients and how it was spent. He was very meticulous. Every penny was accounted for, with the initials of the client. Some of the cases they did for free. Some, like the killer who paid them to get him out of the country, paid a lot."

"Did Jack or the cop report this killer to the authorities and tell them where they'd stashed him?" Molly interrupted.

"Jack made a note in the third file that they did—anonymously—but the police never found him. He wasn't where TR had left him." Antoine shrugged. "The same thing happened with the second bad guy they helped, which was what triggered TR to blame PN. Jack just wanted to get out after TR was killed."

At least her father's goal had been to truly help people. Strangers, yes, but his heart had been in the right place.

Cora figured that would have to be enough.

"What is this third file?" she asked.

Antoine's eyes gleamed. "The client list. It's only initials, no names. But there are addresses. For example, Alice's says AB for Alice Bergeron and gives her address in Twin Falls, Idaho. Most of the homes at the addresses on this list have been sold over the years, but we can get some information from the property records in each of their locations. The few I looked at had one or both owners simply disappear, and the house went into foreclosure. But." He rubbed his hands together in excitement. "Jack's last job was in Merrydale, Louisiana. That's a suburb of Baton Rouge. The client was TC. Timothy Caulfield has owned that home for more than thirty years. He still lives there with his wife and daughter Ashley. She's twenty-three years old. Her birthday is the fifteenth of October."

Cora felt the room spin and clutched Phin's arm for support, grateful when he wrapped his arms around her. The girl had been born the day before her father died—or at least the day before the concrete had been poured. "Did Caulfield kill my father?"

Because Patrick had been his *partner.* Not necessarily his killer.

But Patrick had been the partner who'd had a personal agenda. The partner who might have killed the cop. TR.

She cursed the hope that rose every time she learned something that could exonerate Patrick. But she loved the man.

Like a father.

"We can find out," Molly said, steel in her voice. "But, Cora, Patrick is somehow involved. We can't gloss over that fact."

"The paint," Cora whispered.

"The paint," Molly repeated. "That this Timothy Caulfield was a painter who used Renaissance-era paint formulas is . . . Well, I suppose it's possible. At this point, anything is possible."

"But not likely," Antoine said gently.

Cora swallowed hard. "It's bad enough to think that Patrick may have written the letters. I don't want to believe Patrick killed him, too."

"I know," Phin murmured. "And you can keep hoping. But let us watch your back until we know for sure."

"Okay." She turned to face the table, still in Phin's arms. "So when do we leave for Merrydale?"

23

❧────◦◦────❧

SAGE'S CHOP-SHOP COROLLA rolled to a stop on the street near the house with the green door and the neatly kept lawn. He had no idea what he was going to do.

This had been the address on the piece of paper Alan had shoved at him. He'd recognized it immediately, of course, dropping his gaze so that his grandfather wouldn't see his surprise.

This was where the girl lived. Ashley Caulfield.

The girl whose photos Alan kept in his secret safe.

Alan's own granddaughter.

His grandfather had lied. Had told his own daughter that her baby had died. And then . . . what? Had her placed here?

Who were the Caulfields? How had Alan found them?

And what part had Cora Winslow's father played in the entire fiasco? That Jack Elliot had been involved was only common sense.

The police had listed his probable date of death as the day the foundation had been poured in the Damper Building. The day after Ashley's birth.

And the moment his body had been identified, Alan had been fixated on Cora Winslow. Sage might have been a fool, but he wasn't stupid. He could add two and two and get four. Jack Elliot was definitely a part of this.

Had Jack brought her here? Had he been a go-between, getting rid of the baby that Alan had sworn was stillborn?

Why had Alan killed him?

Because Sage couldn't think of another explanation that made sense.

This is insane.

And now Alan had ordered his own grandson to kill his own granddaughter.

Sage felt sick.

I killed that old lady and Sanjay. I'm just as bad as he is.

And if he killed the Caulfields? What then? Alan would have an even greater hold over him.

Or he'll turn me in. Sage hadn't noticed a tail as he'd driven out of New Orleans, but that didn't mean that Alan's PI wasn't lurking. Sage hadn't realized the PI had been watching him for years.

Sage hadn't realized the PI had followed him to the librarian's house two nights before, or to where he'd met—and ended—Sanjay.

It would be just like Alan to have Sage set fire to the Caulfields' home, only to have law enforcement waiting to arrest him.

Sonofabitch.

Sage stared at the house with the green door, his mind swirling with too many thoughts. If he didn't kill this family, Alan would turn him in for killing the old librarian and Sanjay.

His grandfather had a sterling reputation in New Orleans. And any truths Sage could tell on his grandfather would only boomerang back at him. He'd be charged for the deeds Alan had directed him to do.

I'm screwed.

And angry. So very angry.

He couldn't just sit here, though. Either he left and let Alan do his worst or . . .

Or I get out of this car and do the devil's bidding.

He tugged on his wig and pushed the fake glasses up on his nose, then got out of the car and closed the door quietly. He'd scout out the area and then decide. No reason to announce his presence. There were trees on either side of the house and he walked through them, keeping out of sight.

"Hello!"

Sage wheeled around at the chipper voice and found himself face-to-face with Ashley Caulfield. His mouth opened and closed, words refusing to materialize.

She was his cousin.

She looked like she could be his sister.

He was supposed to kill her.

Grandfather, I truly hate you.

"Hi," he managed. "Who are you?"

"I'm Ashley." She smiled winningly and patted the collie at her side. The dog was old, his face white with age. Sage remembered the dog jumping after a ball, so the old boy still had some kick left in him. He'd have to remember that. Old dogs could bite, too. "This is Toto," she added.

Sage found himself smiling. "I thought Toto was supposed to be a little dog."

"Well, my Toto was little once." She made a face. "He grew."

Sage's smile faded. There was something . . . different about Ashley Caulfield. She was almost childlike. "Dogs do that sometimes. I've never had a dog."

Alan hadn't allowed it.

I should have gotten myself a dog when I moved out. But he hadn't. He'd still been under his grandfather's thumb, even though he no longer lived in the same house.

He still wasn't free.

"Where are your parents, Ashley?" he asked gently.

"Oh, they're in the house." She waved at the house with the green door. "Probably taking a nap. But they have to wake up soon and take me to work."

"Where do you work?"

"At the drugstore in town." She smiled again. "I stock shelves and see if people need carts."

"Do you like your job?"

"I do. My boss is nice, and I like the people who come in to shop."

"I'm glad."

She tilted her head. "Who are you?"

"That's a very good question," another woman's voice said. "Who are you?"

Sage wheeled around again to find an older woman watching him warily. She looked to be in her early sixties. Late fifties at the youngest.

Once again, Sage's mouth opened and closed with no words forthcoming.

These people were like stealth ninjas. He hadn't heard either woman sneak up behind him. The older woman would be Timothy Caulfield's wife, Beatrice. Sage had found her name associated with Timothy's.

Beatrice studied him for a long moment and Sage could see the moment she recognized him. Which was not possible. He did not look like himself. He wore a wig and glasses.

"Who are you?" she repeated, this time in a whisper. Fear was now in her eyes.

"What's wrong, Mama?" Ashley asked.

Mama? He'd thought Beatrice was Ashley's grandmother.

"Go in the house, Ash," Beatrice said. She was firm but not snappish.

"But—" Ashley said.

"Ashley," Beatrice said again, still patient. "Please. Go wake up your father. Tell him we have company."

Sage made himself smile. "Please, Ashley. Go inside."

I'm supposed to kill her. To kill them all.

"O-kaay," Ashley said on a long-suffering huff of air. "Come on, Toto."

Sage and Beatrice stood staring at each other until the front door slammed.

"You have her eyes," Beatrice said stiffly. "And her dimple. So explain, please. Start with your name."

Sage exhaled, his hand going to his pocket where he kept the gun he'd taken from Joy Thomas. "Alan," he said. "My name is Alan."

Merrydale, Louisiana
FRIDAY, DECEMBER 16, 1:10 P.M.

Sage's mother answered on the first ring. "Sage? Are you all right?"

No, he was not. "Is the offer to send me to your friends in Spain still open?"

"What have you done, Sage?"

Sage looked down at Alan's unconscious PI in disgust. Dave Reavey was a middle-aged man with a beer gut who couldn't take a punch. Sage had spied the man following him from the Caulfields' house and his anger had taken control.

His grandfather hadn't trusted him to do the job. Or maybe the PI had been there to send proof of Sage's deeds back to Alan so that Alan would have even more to hold over Sage's head.

Not today. Sage had pulled into the parking lot of a restaurant and walked inside, watching where the PI had parked. The restaurant had two entrances, so he left through the other one. It hadn't been hard to sneak up on the guy.

Now Sage felt stupid for missing the man following him all these years. Alan's PI was really bad at his job. *Probably gone soft watching me and Lexy all this time.*

Sage had knocked the man out and tied him up with the PI's own ropes—what kind of PI carried ropes in his trunk, for God's sake? He'd checked the man's phone to

ensure he hadn't sent anything incriminating to his grandfather.

The PI hadn't. Not yet. But he'd been planning to. There
was video on his phone. Sage deleted it from the phone
and from where the PI had backed it up to the cloud.

He shut the PI's car door with a slam, trapping the unconscious, tied-up man in the back seat. He got in his old
junker, ready to head back to New Orleans. He had a ton
of things to do before he made his escape to Spain or Australia or wherever he ended up.

He shook his head, even though his mother couldn't see
him. "Best you don't know what I've done, Mother."

He wasn't telling her anything, for her own good. *And
for mine.* "Can you send me your friends' contact information? I need to lie low for a while." A long while. Maybe
forever.

"I'll do you one better. I'll get us both tickets on the first
flight to Madrid."

He blinked. "You're going with me?"

"I am. Pack a bag, darlin'. We're going to Spain."

His throat closed and he had to blink again, this time
because his eyes were burning. "Thanks, Mother."

"Just get here safely, Sage. I'll take care of the rest."

She ended the call, leaving Sage reeling. She was going
with him. He hadn't even considered asking her to do so.
He needed to tell her what he'd done. She might choose not
to help him.

He couldn't make himself do that, though.

He gave himself a shake, focusing on traffic as he
merged onto the interstate. "Fall apart later."

He had another call to make.

"Siri, call Lexy Beauchamp, mobile." He waited several rings this time before his stepgrandmother answered.

"Yes?" she said warily. "Sage? Is that you?"

"Yes, ma'am. I have some information that you might
find interesting."

Merrydale, Louisiana
FRIDAY, DECEMBER 16, 1:45 P.M.

MERRYDALE WELCOMES YOU.

Phin watched the sign go by, hoping they'd find what they were looking for at the Caulfields' house. They needed answers.

Burke and Molly had tried to convince Cora to stay behind, but Cora Jane Winslow was having none of that. Phin and Val had supported her. She had a right to know.

Val was driving their SUV with Stone and Delores tailing them closely, giving Phin some semblance of safety. Burke was on his way, coming up from Houma, probably twenty minutes behind them. Molly had gone home to sleep and Antoine had stayed behind in New Orleans to work the other cases on Burke's docket.

They'd seen no trouble on the road, but Phin was anxious. SodaPop wasn't whining, though, so it couldn't be too bad.

It was progress and he'd take it.

"There isn't anything on the Caulfields online," Cora complained. She'd been on her phone the entire drive from New Orleans. "No social media, no articles, no nothing. Just a single mention of them in the white pages and in the property records. But nothing else. How can someone have no social media presence in this day and age?"

"You don't," Val said smugly from the driver's seat of the SUV.

"I do," Cora said. "Through the library's website."

"One photo." Val held up her forefinger. "One measly photo in the 'About Us' section. You don't have Facebook or Insta or Twitter. So you're not one to talk."

"Tandy does all the—" Cora halted abruptly, pain tightening her expression. "She's the social media butterfly. I just floated in her wake. Besides, there are plenty of mentions of me now. 'Jack Elliot's daughter.' 'Jack Elliot survived by daughter Cora Winslow.' You can find me online."

"But nothing about *you*," Phin said. "Nobody would know that you wear pearls to bed or that you smell like strawberries."

Cora turned to him, a smile on her lips and a blush on her cheeks. "You sweet-talker, you."

"I'm going to gag," Val said. "And I did not need to know about the wearing pearls to bed. Call Antoine and see what he's dug up. I tried and he didn't take my call."

Phin did, putting his cell phone on speaker. "It's Phin," he said when Antoine answered.

"I know," Antoine said dryly. "Caller ID. I wouldn't have answered for Val, so this is your lucky day."

"Mean!" Val called.

"You know you love me," Antoine said. "So you want to know what I've found, right?"

"Yes, please," Cora said.

"Tell Val she should say please, too, and I'll take her calls."

"No, he wouldn't," Val said.

"Actually, I would, but I was working on something else when she called. I didn't get a text telling me to answer the damn phone, so I didn't. I still don't have a lot on the Caulfields. Husband is Timothy, he's seventy-five years old. Wife is Beatrice, she's sixty-eight. Daughter is Ashley, she's twenty-three. No parking tickets, no felonies. No record of any kind. They've been married for thirty years, the same length of time they've owned their home. He's a retired electrician, and she's a seamstress. Ashley graduated from Merrydale High five years ago. Timothy graduated from the same high school fifty-seven years ago. That's all that I know."

"That's not much," Val said. "What were you working on when I called before?"

Antoine sighed. "I asked my brother André about any thirteen-year-old boys who were reported as victims of molestation, trying to get at who Reverend Beauchamp was talking about. André went through all the reports of sexual assault on children in the New Orleans area. He even went back five years, in case the parents reported it a while back. None mentioned pictures. Not one. And none were members of Beauchamp's church in Metairie."

Phin frowned. "I don't understand. Are you saying the reverend made a mistake?"

"Or lied," Antoine said. "Either way, there isn't a case that matches what the reverend told you all last night. I was trying to locate the family so that we could find out if Medford Hughes really was the perpetrator."

"Why did you check that out?" Cora asked.

"Well," Antoine said kindly, "partly for you, Cora. I wanted to let you know for sure either way if Medford was guilty, because I knew you were wondering if Patrick was, too. I can't definitively say that either man is innocent, but I can tell you that Medford wasn't using his home Wi-Fi system to either browse or download child porn on the dark web. That was a good idea, by the way, Phin. I was able to get into Medford's Wi-Fi records. He might have been searching elsewhere or using a VPN to hide his movements, but it wasn't happening from his home router. When I found that out, I called André. I figured he could tell me that there really was evidence of abuse, but he said there wasn't."

Phin thought about the reverend and his dramatic delivery. "Let's assume for a minute that Beauchamp lied. Why would he?"

"Good question," Antoine said. "I'll be pissed if he did lie, because I've just spent hours of my time chasing facts that don't exist."

Which could have been the reason for the lie. To distract them and make them waste their time on a wild-goose chase.

"Let's pay him another visit when we're done here," Val said. "Maybe he'll be willing to say more in front of people who aren't part of his church. He'd worry about his reputation as a secret-keeper if he told one of his church

members. We're almost to the Caulfields' house, Antoine.
We'll call you back once we've talked to them."

They turned onto the Caulfields' road and reached their
driveway just in time.

"Phin," Cora hissed. "What are they doing?"

"Leaving," Phin said, because the Caulfields had loaded
up both of their cars, boxes filling the back seats and luggage piled on the roofs.

It appeared that they were leaving for a very long time.

Val pulled into their driveway, slanting the SUV so that
it blocked the Caulfields' exit. Stone pulled his minivan in
behind them, further blocking the driveway.

Two older people ran from the house, a man and a
woman. Timothy and Beatrice Caulfield. A young woman
sat on a front-porch swing, a collie at her feet. She was
frowning in confusion, clutching a large stuffed bear that
had seen far better days.

Timothy had a shotgun in his hands, and both husband
and wife looked like they were about to pass out from
fright.

"Okay," Val said quietly. "This is not what I expected."

"They knew we were coming," Phin said. "Why else
would they run?"

"I think I'll ask them," Cora said and then, to Phin's
horror, she got out of the SUV before he could stop her.

"Fuck," Val whispered. "Phin, go stand behind her.
Don't look threatening. I'm calling Burke. He can't be far
behind us."

The trip from Houma to Merrydale was only twenty
minutes longer than the trip from New Orleans, and Burke
was a speed demon. He'd be there in ten minutes, easily.

Telling SodaPop to stay, Phin got out of the SUV
slowly, his hands extended to show he held no weapons.
He wished he did have a gun, but weapons were Val's bai-
liwick. He turned once to meet Stone's gaze. His friend
had rolled down the window of his minivan and had his
head stuck out.

"Hold," Phin mouthed and Stone nodded, so Phin turned back to where Cora stood in front of the couple, her hands in the air like she was being held up.

"We're not here to hurt you," Cora was saying. "I promise."

"You have to leave," Timothy said. "We have to go."

Something had terrified this couple, yet the daughter—Ashley—looked more confused than afraid.

"Sir," Cora said quietly. "Have you been threatened?"

Beatrice's face crumpled. "We have to go. Please, let us go."

"We will," Cora promised. "But can you spare me a few minutes? My father knew you. Helped you, I think. His name was Jack Elliot. You might have known him as John Robertson."

Timothy slowly lowered his shotgun, his face slack with shock. "You're his little girl. CJ."

Danger from the gun diminished for the moment, Phin stepped to Cora's side, taking her hand. "My name is Cora Jane," she said. "That's what he called me."

Beatrice blinked hard. "You said his name 'was' Jack Elliot. Has he passed?"

Cora looked surprised. "He was killed twenty-three years ago. It's been on the news. His body was found in a demolished building down in Houma. They ID'd him a little more than two weeks ago. He was shot in the head and hidden in the building's foundation."

Beatrice staggered. "What was the date of his death?"

"October sixteenth," Cora said. She glanced over to the young woman on the porch swing. "The day after your daughter was born."

"Oh my God," Timothy breathed. "Oh my God."

Beatrice's hand was covering her mouth. "We didn't know."

"I know," Cora said with a kindness that made Phin marvel. She was hurting, but still so kind. "Can we ask you a few questions?"

The SUV's door opened and closed. "I can make sure you're safe," Val promised. "My boss is on his way. He'll be here in five minutes. Together we will keep you safe. And we can help you find a place to hide if you need to."

"Why should we trust you?" Timothy asked, but it was a question born of fright, not belligerence.

Cora shrugged helplessly. "You don't have to, but I've been trying to solve this mystery for two and a half weeks. Someone killed my father and sent me letters, signed by him, for the last twenty-three years. Someone has repeatedly broken into my house and they also shot my friend. My boss was murdered in her own bed. Two other people were killed. We know that you're afraid and that you have a right to be. These people are private investigators I hired to protect me. If you'll help us, they'll protect you, too. I can only give you my word."

Timothy and Beatrice looked at each other, communicating as long-married couples did. Finally, Timothy nodded. "We'll talk to you, but not here. There's a motel in town. We can stop there. I don't want to be here when he comes for us."

"Who?" Cora pressed. "Who threatened you?"

"Not here," Beatrice said stubbornly. "I won't risk my family."

"All right," Cora said reluctantly. "We'll drive with you to the motel."

"Ash!" the woman called. "Time to go."

Ashley came down the porch steps, the collie trotting at her side. "Who are they, Mama?"

"She's the daughter of an old friend," Beatrice said, cupping her daughter's cheek in her hand. "Get in the car with Dad. We've got one stop to make and then we'll go on our vacation!"

The perky way the woman spoke made no sense initially. Ashley was twenty-three years old. But then she turned her smile on them and began to speak and Phin understood. She had a cognitive disability.

Her parents' need to protect her made even more sense now.

"Hello! I've met a lot of new people today. I'm Ash. Who are you?"

Cora's smile was gentle. "I'm Cora, and this is my friend, Phin. The lady behind us is Val, and Phin's friends are in the minivan. They're Stone and Delores. I like your dog."

"His name is Toto."

"That," Cora said, "is an excellent name for a dog. My friend Phin has a service dog named SodaPop."

Ashley giggled, a childish sound. "I like that name."

"You know about service dogs?" Cora said.

Ashley nodded soberly. "You don't pet them or talk to them while they're working."

"Yes," Cora said. "That's exactly right. My dog is Blue. That's his name because he's blue. I'll show you pictures when we stop. We need to get moving, though. Your folks are anxious to leave."

Ashley turned to her house, her expression sad. "We have to go."

"Maybe you can come back soon." Cora extended her hand, and Ashley took it. Cora led her to the family's car, accompanied by Timothy Caulfield. "I'll see you soon, okay?"

Ashley smiled. "Okay!"

Merrydale, Louisiana
FRIDAY, DECEMBER 16, 2:45 P.M.

Phin had thought the couple might try to lose them, but they were true to their word. Their little convoy of vehicles had left the Caulfields' house and headed for a motel in the middle of town.

Burke had been waiting at the motel, Val having called him once they'd gotten started. Between them, they had three vehicles and six people—including Cora—to guard the Caulfields.

Cora had taken Ashley under her wing once they were in one of the motel rooms, chatting about hair and makeup and how sweet Toto the dog was. The motel had an adjoining room, and Beatrice had put Ashley in there with Toto. Ashley had a tablet loaded with movies, so she'd be okay.

Delores offered to stay with Ashley, but Beatrice politely declined, locking Ashley's outer motel room door and putting a chair against the door.

Stone stood guard outside the doors to the two rooms, which Phin knew was far safer than a chair against the door.

"Okay," Cora said once everyone had found a place to either sit or stand. The Caulfields were sitting against the bed's headboard and Cora sat at the foot. Phin stood directly behind her, his hands on her shoulders, SodaPop sitting at his side.

Cora reached up and held his hand, linking their fingers. "I found records that my father left. Client records. It's taken us a long time to break into them, so he did guard your privacy zealously. We've told no one else what we've found, so don't worry about that. I assume my father was involved somehow in Ashley's . . . birth?"

Beatrice's smile was grim. "He was. We adopted her in a private transaction. Your father was the go-between. He found the baby, found us, made it happen. We paid him fifty thousand dollars for the mother's expenses and medical care."

"That was every penny we'd saved," Timothy added. "Plus, we refinanced our house and dipped into our retirement, but he gave us Ashley and the necessary documents to make the adoption legal."

"And his partner? Did you talk to him as well?" Cora asked.

The couple shared a puzzled glance before turning to Cora. "He didn't have a partner," Timothy said. "We only dealt with John Robertson. That's the name he gave us."

"Okay," Cora said. "That's odd, because he said he had a partner in the documents we found."

Beatrice shrugged. "We only dealt with your father. He emailed us, made the ID documents, and brought us the baby just before dawn. She was just a few hours old."

Patrick had been the one to email the clients and forge the documents, Phin thought, wondering if Patrick had used Jack's alias to divert risk from himself. After the death of TR, Jack Elliot had become the face of their business—and the sole focus of anyone who wanted to stop them, like Alice's husband.

Patrick was becoming more contemptible with every new thing they learned.

"How did you pay him?" Phin asked.

"Wire transfer for the deposit," Timothy said. "We paid him half up front and the other half in cash when he brought us Ashley."

"Antoine gave me a copy of the ledger," Phin said to Cora. "Only the first payment was listed. Maybe your father was killed before he could enter the second payment."

Or maybe he was double-crossed by his partner.

Cora nodded, a small frown creasing her forehead. "Maybe." She returned her attention to the Caulfields. "Is there a reason you didn't adopt through an agency? I'm not judging and I'm trying not to pry, but this is important. My father was an eraser. He made people disappear out of abusive homes, relocating them with new IDs. That he brought you a baby isn't what we expected to hear."

Timothy's jaw tightened. "I was in my late forties when we started the adoption process. I'd had cancer when I was younger, but I'd been cancer-free for ten years by the time we got on the lists. I was disqualified because of my medical history and my age."

"Timothy, no." Beatrice lifted her chin. "That's not true. We started trying to adopt when we were still young, but I'm bipolar and that was a major issue back then. I was disqualified, not Tim. We were desperate for a child and one day we met this man in a chat room. It was for infertile couples and I just . . . let it all out in the chat. A few weeks later, I got an email from John Robertson asking how badly we wanted a child. From there we filled out paperwork and he gave us the price. Like Tim said, we paid the money and they handed us an infant with all the paperwork we needed to prove she was legally ours."

"She's a sweet young woman," Cora said. "Clearly loved."

Beatrice relaxed a fraction. "Thank you. We've done our best."

"She has a cognitive disability," Cora observed carefully. "When did you find out?"

Timothy looked at the closed door between the two rooms. "When she was about two. She hadn't learned to talk and there were some mobility issues. We got her the help she needed."

"Because she's yours," Cora said, and Timothy also relaxed a little bit.

"One hundred percent," Timothy said fiercely. "I'd do anything to keep her safe."

Phin wondered what "anything" included. Timothy Caulfield could have been the one to kill Jack that night, to cover up that they'd basically bought a child, but Phin doubted it. The Caulfields had come with them, had trusted them, and the couple had far more to lose than Phin and the rest of them did.

"Tell us about this threat," Val said. "Have you been threatened before? Or just today?"

"Just today," Beatrice said. "We've lived in peace for twenty-three years, just raising Ashley. And then today a man came to our house and told us to run. That someone was coming to kill us."

"Who was the man?" Phin asked, expecting a description of Patrick.

"He said his name was Alan Beauchamp," Beatrice said.

Cora sucked in a shocked breath. "What?"

She wasn't alone in her surprise. Burke muttered a curse, so Phin figured Antoine hadn't had a chance to tell him what he'd learned about the alleged sexual assault, but Val exchanged a look with Phin and he saw they were on the same page.

Beauchamp had deliberately misled them when they'd interviewed Medford Hughes's sister-in-law. Had deliberately set them on a fruitless search. He'd lied. Although the reason for his lie still wasn't clear.

"Beauchamp, the minister?" Phin asked, just to be certain.

Beatrice shrugged. "We don't know about a minister. He seemed young for that."

Burke stepped forward from the wall where he'd been leaning. "How old was he? Because we recently met a man named Beauchamp and he was in his sixties."

The couple exchanged another confused glance. "He was in his twenties," Timothy said slowly, then sighed. "Tell them, Bea. Just tell them."

Beatrice's eyes filled with weary resignation. "I recognized him. Not by his name. By his features. His eyes. His dimple. He looked like my Ashley."

Phin exhaled slowly, the puzzle a little clearer. "Oh. A relative."

"A close one," Beatrice confirmed. "I asked who he was and he said his name was Alan Beauchamp. Then he told me that he'd been sent to kill us, but that he couldn't do it. That someone else would eventually be sent and we needed to run before that happened. Then he left."

There was a long moment of stunned silence.

"You believed him," Cora finally murmured.

"Yes," Beatrice said. "We did."

"Why?" Burke asked.

"Tell them the rest," Timothy said wearily.

Beatrice cleared her throat. "You asked about Ashley's cognitive issues. We wanted to see if there was anything genetic in her makeup, anything that would explain her condition or help us get her the right treatment." She lifted her chin again. "We weren't trying to fix her. She's not broken. She's perfect just as she is."

"That you love her is crystal clear," Delores said from where she sat at the motel room's desk. "We don't think you wanted to fix her."

"Thank you," Beatrice said. "Our doctor suggested we give her up when we found out the truth."

Phin had a very bad feeling about what Beatrice was about to say. "What did the test results say, ma'am?"

"That her DNA was . . . muddled. She had overlaps. Far too many overlaps. Her biological parents were . . . related. Closely related."

Cora flinched as Beatrice's meaning became clear. "Incest."

Beatrice inclined her head. "Yes. Our doctor said the results appeared to be a brother-sister pairing, but it might have been father-daughter. We tried to get in touch with John Robertson again, but the email he gave us came back as non-deliverable. We weren't trying to give Ash back. We wanted him to know that the baby's family had issues. There might even be legal issues if there was no consent to the conception."

"Rape," Cora said quietly.

Timothy's skin had grown a rather alarming shade of gray. "That's what we thought. We love our daughter, but if Ash was a product of rape, someone needed to be punished."

Cora blew out a breath. "That's a secret someone would kill to keep."

"Then and now," Beatrice said quietly. "I'm sorry your father was killed, Cora. I liked him. I don't know if he knew."

Cora shook her head. "I don't, either. I don't want to think that he did."

But Patrick might have known, Phin thought. PN was

the one who created the documents, who interfaced with the clients online. Had he tried to hide behind his more visible partner? The one who showed up at the clients' houses to extract them? Or deliver babies to them?

Had the person who'd hired Jack to place infant Ashley known that Jack had a partner? Who was that person? What was their relationship to Ashley?

And why had the young man today given his name as Alan Beauchamp?

Phin brought up Beauchamp's church's website and found a photo of the minister. "Is this the man you saw today?"

Both Caulfields shook their heads.

"Absolutely not," Beatrice said. "He's far too old."

Phin scrolled through the "About Us" page of the website and stopped cold. There was a photo of a man who looked enough like Ashley to have been her brother. Same golden hair, same smile. Same dimple.

He turned the phone to the Caulfields. "Is this him?"

Beatrice reached for the phone, enlarging the picture. "He had dark hair and glasses, but his eyes and dimple are the same."

"Wig and glasses," Timothy muttered. "Classic."

"Well, he *had* been sent to kill us," Beatrice said logically. "It makes sense that he'd disguise himself." She returned Phin's phone to him. "I think that's him."

"That's Sage Beauchamp, Alan's grandson," Phin said, passing the phone to Val and Burke with a sigh. "That explains why Beauchamp tried to pin blame on Medford Hughes. He was trying to distract us so that we wouldn't keep looking for your father's clients."

So that he could kill them. Or send his grandson to do the dirty work.

"He is a very bad man," Cora whispered.

Phin rested his cheek on the top of her head. "He is." He straightened. "Can we help hide these folks, Burke?"

"Of course. If you'll trust us, we will hide you in a very

safe place until Beauchamp is in police custody. I have a big house in New Orleans. You'll be safe there. I also have a camp on the bayou, but it's a little chilly to go there."

"We can give you references," Val offered. "We're the good guys."

The Caulfields whispered to each other before nodding. "We're going to agree," Beatrice said, "for Ashley. Thank you."

Burke's smile was grim. "You're welcome. If we leave now, we can get to my house by suppertime. I'll follow you in my truck and keep watch for anyone who might get too close."

"I'll get Ash," Beatrice said. She got off the bed and offered a hand to Cora. "Thank you for finding us. I hate that you lost your father. He talked about his family, how much he loved his kids. Said we seemed like nice people with a lot of love to give. He gave us the gift of Ashley. I'll say a prayer for him every night for the rest of my life."

When the older woman had gone to get her daughter, Cora turned to look up at Phin. "Who killed my father? Patrick? The guy who sold them a baby?"

"I don't know," Phin said. "But we need to find out if Alan Beauchamp is Ashley's father."

"And if he has a sister," Val said.

"Or children of his own," Phin said, not wanting to think about Alan raping his own daughter, but he had accused Medford Hughes of pedophilia, so it was possible that he'd been projecting. "We're going to have to figure out how to tell the police what's going on without compromising the Caulfields, but we can do that. We've done it before."

Burke clapped Phin on the shoulder. "We have. Get Cora back to New Orleans safely, okay?"

"As soon as I can."

And then he'd work with the others to figure out exactly what the hell had happened that night twenty-three years ago.

Who had killed Jack and hidden his body in the foundation? Phin's money was still on Patrick because of the paint.

Who had written the letters to Cora? Again, his money was on Patrick.

Who had killed Medford Hughes and Minnie Edwards? That was probably Patrick, but Phin wasn't sure. There wasn't a connection between Patrick and Medford and Minnie. Not yet, anyway.

And who were Ashley's parents? Alan Beauchamp? One of his children?

The more they learned, the more questions they had. But they were getting closer.

24

Baton Rouge, Louisiana
FRIDAY, DECEMBER 16, 4:00 P.M.

VAL PULLED OUT of the fast-food parking lot, heading back to New Orleans. They'd missed lunch, and Cora had been starving. Stone and Delores had stuck behind them like glue, Stone sending Phin a flurry of texts as they'd sat in the drive-through line.

Delores had apparently brought him up to speed with what had been shared inside the motel room, and Stone had questions. From all the texts pinging Phin's phone, the man had a lot of questions. Cora had wanted to ask Phin what those questions were, especially when, in the middle of the drive-through line, Delores and Stone had changed places in their minivan, Delores taking the wheel.

Stone was up to something. Cora could wait to learn what it was. Right now, she was mentally exhausted.

At least the food had helped. Her headache was gone.

Listening to the Caulfields' story had been hard. Knowing her father had trafficked a baby was even harder. Ashley had gotten lucky. The Caulfields were good people.

Another couple might not have treated her so well.

Val eyed Cora and Phin in the rearview mirror. "We need to figure out what we're going to tell Detective Clancy."

Cora had been thinking the same thing. "I don't know

how to tell him anything without revealing what my father was doing. People like Alice VanPatten just wanted to be safe. And the Caulfields thought they were doing a legal private adoption."

"Maybe," Phin said. "They might have wanted to believe that it was an ordinary private adoption, but they got the baby delivered to them in the wee hours of the morning. And what if the mother of the baby didn't give her up willingly? That would be kidnapping."

"Then whoever wanted to place the child needs to be punished. How can we find out if the mother was willing?"

"We find the mother," Phin said. "And then we ask her."

"Wait," Val said. "No, we *don't* find the mother. We let Detective Clancy take it from here."

"And tell him what?" Cora demanded. "Arrest Alan Beauchamp because a couple we aren't supposed to know about, who basically bought a baby, said that his grandson told them that someone was coming to kill them?"

"We can tell him to arrest Patrick for murder," Val said. "Old paint, guys. Old freaking paint."

Cora's headache was coming back. "Look, Detective Goddard in Houma knows about the paint. He's shared the lab results with Clancy. Clancy knows he's looking for an art restorer who has some connection to me. If he comes up with Patrick's name on his own, fine. But if we tell him now, we're going to have to tell him about the partnership and the eraser stuff. Which leads them to Alice VanPatten and the others who legitimately needed help."

Val huffed out a frustrated breath. "Goddammit. I hate that you're right. Let's find the mother of that baby, then."

"We might have some leads," Phin said, showing his phone. There, on his screen, was a photo of Reverend Alan Beauchamp. He was smiling and congenial, his arm around a much younger woman. The caption said that she was his wife, Lexy.

"Unlike you, Cora," he said, "Alan Beauchamp has a *lot* of personal information on the internet. First of all, he has no siblings. He's an only child. So Ashley's biological mother was not his sister. He has three children, though, from his first marriage. Wife number one—Anna—died in a car accident. Their oldest son, Alan Jr., is deceased. He also died in a car accident. He was Sage's father. Alan's middle child is Walton Beauchamp, a decorated colonel in the army. He's served several tours and is currently stationed in Colorado. Alan's youngest child is a daughter, Jennifer. She's most likely Ashley's mother. She would have been fifteen at the time of Ashley's birth." He swiped on his phone. "Here's an article about her from—surprise, surprise—twenty-three years ago, a few weeks after Ashley was born. There's no mention of a pregnancy or birth. The article says that Jennifer took an overdose of drugs. They found her in time to save her life, but she didn't fully recover. She was hospitalized for schizophrenia shortly after the overdose. Her father blamed the schizophrenia on the overdose."

Cora frowned. "But a drug overdose doesn't cause schizophrenia. It can make schizophrenia worse if it already exists, but there's no causal relationship."

Phin shrugged. "Facts apparently didn't matter to Alan. He used the overdose to bring attention to the issue of teenagers and drugs. He raised money off the cautionary tale of his daughter's 'sin' and funded a new drug rehab ministry. His church still runs it to this day."

"What happened to Jennifer?" Val asked.

"Stone's checking it out," Phin said. "He's got contacts."

Cora raised her brows. "What kinds of contacts?"

"Probably the kind we don't ask about," Val said. "Like Antoine's computer searches. Just say please and thank you, and don't ask the details. It's like not asking what goes into sausage."

"Exactly," Phin said. "He's checking the psychiatric hospitals now to see where she might have been admitted. It'll take him some time, but he'll figure out where she is."

"He should pair up with Antoine," Val said.

"He already has." Phin shook his head. "They've worked together in the past."

"I keep forgetting they were friends first," Val said, "before you came into the picture, Phin. I think we should be afraid if those two have joined forces."

"Very afraid," Phin agreed.

"We need to call Joy," Cora said unexpectedly.

"She's good," Val said. "I visited her this morning. They're going to keep her another few days, but she's mending well."

"No. I mean, good that she's better, but that's not what I wanted to ask her. She heard the voice of the man who shot her, remember? Phin found Sage Beauchamp on the church's website and I've seen him on TV commercials for the church. He's about the same size as the man who chased me—and the man who shot Joy."

"Cora," Val breathed. "Burke really does need to hire you."

"He really does," Phin agreed.

"We should get a clip of him speaking," Cora said, pleased at the praise, but she'd be happy when she could go back to the library. This PI life was not for her. "Maybe Joy can ID his voice."

"Find one and send it to Joy's kids," Val directed. "One of them will get her to listen to it. If Sage was the intruder who shot Joy, he is an important connection to Alan Beauchamp. Alan knew Medford Hughes. He lied about him to get us to investigate Medford for a crime he likely didn't do, if what André told Antoine is correct. And André is usually right about these things."

"Reverend Beauchamp specifically asked if Sara Morton had her brother-in-law's laptop." Cora thought about that moment the night before. "Why would he lie about something that the police might be able to challenge—if they had the laptop, of course."

"But they *don't* have the laptop," Val said. "Clancy said

they didn't collect Hughes's computers, only the laptops that were stolen from us, which struck him as odd. That a guy who did network stuff for a living didn't have a single computer in his house."

Cora forced her brain to focus on Medford Hughes's laptop. "Is it too huge a leap to assume that Beauchamp had the computer himself or he knew where it was?"

"I don't know," Val said. "Keep going."

"Well, if he was so confident to make a claim that could be disproven if the police had Medford's computer, I think it makes sense that he knows that the police *don't* have it. He'd be certain of this if he had it himself. If he does have Medford's computer, he had to have taken it from Medford Hughes or from his house. Is it possible that he killed Medford Hughes and took whatever was in the trunk of Hughes's car?"

"I think that's very possible," Val said. "That would mean that our computers that were found in the back of Hughes's car were put there by Beauchamp. Maybe he asked Hughes to break into them. And, if Beauchamp had our laptops, he might have gotten them from Sage, which means he's the one who shot Joy and chased you. We really need a video clip for Joy."

"Found it while you were weaving in the loose threads," Phin said. "Sage's job on Sundays is to welcome visitors from the pulpit, deliver the church announcements, and then introduce his grandfather for the sermon. Listen. He's recorded every week." He hit play.

Cora leaned over his arm to watch the video he'd found. Sage stood in front of the pulpit in a massively large auditorium, his golden hair shining under the lights. He was smiling and joking. He had the audience laughing and turning to welcome the person standing next to them.

Sage was engaging and charismatic.

He'd also warned the Caulfields to run.

But he might have shot Joy. *And chased me through the Quarter.*

"He was only two years old when my father was killed."

"True," Phin said, "but his grandfather keeps him close. Who better to send out for information than a family member who you trust?"

"Could he have been the one following us?" she asked. "Maybe watching us from his car down the street from my house? Maybe even involved with Vincent Ray breaking in to burn my house down?"

"We'd have to see how Sage Beauchamp and Vincent Ray might connect," Val said logically. "We do know that it's possible for Patrick and Vincent to have crossed paths."

Cora pressed her fingers to her temples. "Could Patrick, Alan, and Sage be working together?"

Phin gently tugged her fingers from her brow and began massaging her temples with a pressure that was just right. Cora nearly moaned with relief.

"They might be," he said. "But let's focus on one connection at a time. Sage and Joy. Let's get Joy to listen to this clip. You call one of her kids and tell me who to text the clip to."

He stopped rubbing her forehead and Cora wanted to pout. But he was right. One connection at a time.

Cora called Nala, Joy's oldest. "Hey, it's Cora. Are you with your mother?"

"I am," Nala said. "What's up?"

"Phin's going to text you a video clip. Don't show it to your mother. Just have her listen to the man's voice. Ask her if it's familiar."

Phin fired off a text with a link to the video and then they waited.

"Cora," Nala said warily. "This clip is of a preacher's grandson."

"I know. Just have her listen."

"Okay, fine. I'll call you right back."

Phin held Cora's hand while they waited. And waited. And waited some more. Finally, Nala called them back.

"That's the guy, which is wild, Cora Jane. He's the one

who shot her. Mama's absolutely sure. She said that he sounded familiar at the time and now she knows why. She's seen him on the TV ads for his grandfather's church. How the hell did you arrive at this?"

"Long story," Cora said. "I'll tell you later. Can you let Detective Clancy know that your mother ID'd Sage Beauchamp as her attacker? Don't tell them it came from us. Just say she saw him on TV."

"I can do that. I'll call the detective right now. Mama says you two better come back to visit her or you'll be sorry."

Cora smiled. "Tell her that we'll come as soon as we get a chance to breathe."

"Keep breathing," Nala said, with all seriousness. "Do not do anything dangerous."

"I won't. I promise. Bye now." Cora ended the call and wanted to crow. "Now we just need to find Jennifer Beauchamp. I wonder if her remaining brother knows where she is." She grimaced. "I wonder who's the father of her child—one of her brothers or her father."

"If it's the oldest brother, he's dead," Phin said. "At this point, we wait for Antoine and Stone to come up with a location for Jennifer Beauchamp. Now, I think you should rest. You've had a hard few days."

Cora wasn't even going to argue. "Wake me up if something happens."

Phin kissed her, slow and sweet. "I will."

Ponchatoula, Louisiana
FRIDAY, DECEMBER 16, 5:50 P.M.

"You should wake her up," Val told Phin from the driver's seat. "We'll be there in ten minutes."

"I know." But Phin hated to wake Cora. She'd been sleeping so peacefully in the back seat of the company

SUV, her head on his thigh. He ran his fingers through her hair before giving her shoulder a gentle shake.

"Cora, honey, wake up," he said quietly. "We're almost there."

She'd slept so soundly, not even Phin's phone calls to Stone or Val's to Antoine had disturbed her. She slowly blinked awake, staring at him for a moment before her vision seemed to focus.

"Almost where?" she asked sleepily, and Phin wished they were in her bed. He loved sleepy Cora.

"The Glendale Psychiatric Hospital," he said, and her eyes blinked wide open.

"What?" She sat up, her hair falling in her face. "Why?"

Phin brushed her hair back. "Antoine found the police report from Jennifer Beauchamp's drug overdose. He asked André to contact the cop who'd filed the report. The guy is retired now but remembered that Jennifer was admitted to Glendale. Stone and Antoine did some more digging and found out that she never left."

Cora's mouth bent in a sad frown. "She's been there for twenty-three years?"

"Seems like," Phin said. "And I called one of my old army contacts to track down the middle brother's military record. Guess when Walton Beauchamp enlisted?"

Cora sighed. "Twenty-three years ago?"

"Bingo," Phin said. "Six months before Ashley's birth date. He was only seventeen, so he needed parental permission to join. It was an odd arrangement. He dropped out of high school, got his GED, then joined up. There was no waiting period. He entered boot camp the following week."

"They got rid of him," Cora said. "That's one way to keep him from his sister. Unless it was the older brother?"

"It's possible," Phin allowed. "That brother was Sage's father. He was married at the time and living in Mobile. He and his wife divorced—guess when?"

"Twenty-three years ago," Cora said wearily.

"Yep. I found the record of the divorce decree—irreconcilable differences—and the timing was just too convenient. It's possible that she found out that her husband had fathered the child. We may not be allowed to see Jennifer. But we can try. Best case we find out who fathered her child and if she surrendered her child willingly. That's something we can give to Detective Clancy. If the Caulfields did participate in an illegal adoption, it's unlikely that they'll be prosecuted because the statute of limitations ran out long ago. They're the best case to present to the police because their adoption of Ashley is directly linked to your father's death. You wouldn't have to reveal any of his other clients like Alice VanPatten."

Val's GPS directed her to turn into the psychiatric hospital and Phin's gut tightened. It looked like the VA hospital he'd spent too much time in.

Cora noticed his sudden stress. So did SodaPop. The dog shoved her muzzle into his hand. Cora cupped his face in her palms.

"You don't have to go inside. Val can go in with me."

Val parked the car, saying nothing. It would be Phin's choice.

"I'll go in. If I have to leave, I know where the SUV is parked. I don't want you to do this alone."

Cora pulled his head down and kissed him. "Thank you."

He kissed her back, losing himself in the moment until Val cleared her throat. "Guys, please."

Phin rolled his eyes. "Like you and Kaj didn't do this all the time."

"And you said, 'Guys, please,'" Val shot back.

Phin didn't remember that happening, but he wasn't going to argue. "Let me walk SodaPop. She's been cooped up most of the day."

"She's probably hungry and thirsty, too," Cora said as she slid out of the SUV behind him.

"I fed and watered her while you were sleeping." He took SodaPop to a patch of grass. "Potty time."

It was her signal to go. She was exceptionally well trained.

When his good girl was finished, they joined Cora and Val, who were waiting at the SUV. Val gave him the keys. "In case you need a break."

He hated that he might actually need to take her up on it, but he took the keys nonetheless and together they entered the hospital's front doors.

Phin hated hospitals, but he was calmer than he'd expected to be. Cora had one of his hands and SodaPop was pressed to his leg on the opposite side.

Thank you, Delores. Her gift had given him a freedom he'd only dreamed of.

A woman in scrubs looked up when they approached the front desk. "Can I help you?"

"We'd like to visit Jennifer Beauchamp," Cora said with a smile. "I hope we're still in time for visiting hours."

"You are," the woman said. "Are you family?"

"No, ma'am, but we are friends of her family."

Not a lie, Phin thought. Ashley was Jennifer's family, whether Jennifer wished it to be so or not. He hoped that surrendering her child for a private adoption had been her idea. Or at least that she'd agreed.

"You have good timing. She's pretty lucid today. But if you upset her, you'll have to leave."

"We understand," Cora said. "We just want to drop in and say hey."

Hey and a lot of other things. But again, Cora hadn't lied.

They were given directions to Jennifer's room, where they found a gray-haired woman sitting on a sofa, watching television with a nurse's aide. The woman looked far older than the thirty-eight years old that Jennifer would be by now.

The aide, a young woman of about twenty, looked up in stunned surprise.

"Visitors?" she said. "We don't get visitors."

Jennifer stared at them for a long moment before returning her attention to the television.

Cora smiled at them. "Just not often or ever?"

"Ever," the aide said. "Or at least since I've been Jenny's aide. That's been two years. The aide before me said the same thing."

So this really was Jennifer. She looked like she was sixty years old.

Phin really hated Alan Beauchamp. Not only had the man lied to distract them into investigating a fake lead, he'd ignored his daughter for years.

Like you ignored your family for years?

Phin inwardly winced. It was a different situation, true. But, yeah, he'd ignored his family, too. When this was over, he was going straight home. He was going to make this right if it was the last thing he did.

Maybe Cora would come with him. Her hand in his was a comfort.

And his mother would love her.

Cora squeezed his hand before releasing him and sitting next to Jennifer on the sofa. "Hi, Jenny. I'm Cora."

Jennifer didn't look away from the television. "You have a dog."

"We do. Her name's SodaPop. She's my friend Phin's service dog."

"Why?" Jennifer asked.

Cora tilted her head. "What do you mean, why?"

"Why does Phin have a service dog?"

"Because I get anxious," Phin said. "I can't stop it, and it's not fun."

Jenny nodded. "Dogs are good."

"They are," he agreed.

They were quiet for a few heartbeats, waiting. For what, Phin wasn't sure.

Finally, Cora said, "Jenny, we wanted to talk to you about something that happened to you a long time ago. Right before you came here."

The aide's eyes widened, but she held her tongue. For the moment anyway. Phin was expecting her to call for security any minute, but she didn't.

"Long time," Jenny agreed. She sighed quietly. "Such a long time."

Cora's expression was pained before she regained her composure, her lips curving in a kind smile. "I met your daughter today," she said softly.

Jenny's head swung around, her eyes narrowed. "You see ghosts?"

Cora, to her credit, didn't flinch at the sudden movement. "No, Jenny. She's real. Not a ghost."

Jenny shook her head. "She can't be," she said flatly. "She's dead."

Cora took a little longer to wipe the pain from her face this time. "Who told you that?"

Jenny turned back to the television. "Father. He said she died." She held her chin high, but two tears rolled down her cheeks. "My baby died."

Cora met Phin's eyes, hers sad and uncertain.

Phin went down on one knee in front of Jenny. He knew that the woman was aware of his presence. Her jaw clenched as she gazed steadfastly ahead.

The aide was watching in fascination.

Phin hoped they were doing the right thing.

"Your father didn't tell you the truth," Phin said quietly. "I'm sorry."

Jenny shook her head, her eyes fixed on the television. "No."

SodaPop squeezed between them, one side pressed into Phin's bent knee, the other into Jenny's legs. Phin stroked her back. "Good girl," he murmured.

"She is a good girl," Jenny said, but she made no move to touch SodaPop. "I like dogs. She's working, though."

"She is. Thank you for not distracting her from her job."

"She's warm," Jenny whispered.

"She is." Phin hesitated, then sighed. "Jenny, I'm sorry to have to ask you this, but . . . do you remember the father of your baby?"

Jenny froze, her only movement the shallow rise and fall of her chest as she breathed. She closed her eyes as two more tears slid down her cheeks.

After what seemed like a lifetime, she nodded. "He's gone."

"Dead?" Phin asked, because "gone" could mean different things.

"No. Sent away. Like me."

So she knew she'd been sent away. New rage bubbled in Phin's gut, but he kept his voice gentle. Kept his fingers in SodaPop's coat. "Why, Jenny? Why was he sent away?"

A slight shrug. "Father said Walton sinned. Like me."

Not Alan or Alan Jr., then. It had been the younger brother, who was now an army colonel. *Sonofabitch.*

Alan Beauchamp had known. He'd sent the brother into the army and his daughter to a psychiatric hospital.

Phin drew a breath. "But you didn't sin, did you, Jenny?"

Her thin shoulders lifted in a shrug. "Father said I did."

The aide's face crumpled. "Oh, Jenny. I'm sorry."

Another shrug. "Why? I sinned, not you. I don't like this show. Turn the channel, please."

The aide scrambled to comply. "How about the dog show, the one with puppies?"

"Yes. I like that one." One side of her mouth lifted in what might have been an attempt at a smile. "SodaPop likes it, too."

Phin chuckled softly. "She does. She was raised with dogs in a shelter, so she likes other dogs."

Jenny lowered her gaze to study SodaPop. "Why?"

"Why was she raised in a shelter?" Phin asked.

"Yes. Why?"

"My friend runs the shelter. She takes care of the dogs.

She said that SodaPop was left at the dog pound as a puppy. Her old owner didn't want her."

Jenny's expression softened. "Poor SodaPop. Nobody wanted her."

"But my friend Delores wanted her," Phin said. "*I* want her. I love her."

Jenny splayed her hand over her stomach. "I wanted her. But she died."

Phin wanted to correct her, but Jenny seemed so fragile that he was afraid to. "I'm sorry, Jenny," he whispered instead. Because he was. So damned sorry for this woman who'd been locked away, abandoned by her family, by the very people who were supposed to love her no matter what.

The way your family loves you. They'd loved him even when he'd been too messed up to understand why.

But it didn't matter why they loved him. They just did.

His eyes burned and he had to draw in a breath. "Thank you for visiting with us, Jenny."

Jenny nodded once before turning to Cora, who still sat on the sofa beside her. "He's your friend?"

"Yes," Cora said. "He's a good friend. A good man."

Jenny's gaze was intensely focused. "Keep him."

Cora smiled gently. "I plan to. Would you like me to come back? Visit with you again?"

Jenny turned back to the television. "Do you have a dog?"

Cora laughed. "I do. His name is Blue. But he's pretty old. Do I have to bring a dog to come back to see you?"

Jenny did that little half smile again. "Yes."

"I have a dog," the nurse's aide said. "His name's Trouble, because he's always getting into trouble."

"Bring him," Jenny instructed. "Please."

The aide grinned. "I will. I promise."

"Excuse me?" A woman stood in the doorway, her neat pantsuit marking her as administration versus a nurse or an aide. "What are you doing here?"

"Visiting," Cora said calmly.

"They are friends," Jenny said, focused again on the

television where puppies cavorted. "Go away, Mrs. Collinsworth."

"I'm afraid visiting hours are over," Mrs. Collinsworth said with a painfully fake smile. "Your friends will have to come back later."

"With a dog," Jenny said.

"With a dog," Cora promised.

Phin held his hand out to Jenny. "Thank you."

She took his hand without looking at him. "You're welcome. I hope your dog helps you for a long time."

Phin gave SodaPop an affectionate stroke down her back. "I hope so, too."

The three of them started to leave, Val slipping the aide her business card. The aide's eyes widened at *Broussard Investigations*, and she pocketed it with a slight nod.

They were to the door when Jenny's voice stopped them in their tracks. "She cried, Phin."

Phin turned, ignoring the Collinsworth woman who was ordering them to get out. He went back to the sofa, kneeling in front of Jenny once again, the woman's gaze fixed straight ahead. She was looking at the television, but Phin didn't think she was seeing it. "She cried?"

"My baby. She cried. My father said she was born dead, but I heard her cry." She dropped her gaze to Phin's, her expression steely. "He said I was wrong, but I know I heard her. I told everyone that I heard her and they said I was crazy."

Phin didn't look away. "They lied," he whispered. "You're not crazy."

Jenny nodded soberly. "Thank you."

"You need to leave now," Mrs. Collinsworth said loudly. "Or I'm calling the police."

Jenny rolled her eyes, surprising him. "Come back. Please."

"I will," Phin promised, then briefly squeezed Jenny's hand. "Enjoy the puppies."

"I will."

Phin rose and met Cora and Val at the door. "We'll go," he said to Collinsworth. "No need to call the police."

The woman's eyes were angry. "You are not allowed to be here. The family wishes Jenny to have her privacy and now you've upset her. Do not come back. I'll escort you to the door."

She did just that, making a grand gesture as she waved them out.

Phin stopped walking once he was outside. His stomach hurt. His heart hurt.

"Her brother," he said.

Val sighed. "Yes. I recorded the whole thing. I think Reverend Beauchamp has quite a few things to explain." She rubbed Phin's upper arm comfortingly. "You were so good with her, Phin. So patient."

"She's all alone," Phin said. "I know how she feels. Except she was forced and I chose it."

Cora stepped in front of him, giving his shirt collar a little yank so that he looked down at her. "That is not true. Your brain lied to you, Phin. Told you that you weren't good enough. It's normal to believe your brain. You weren't in the right place mentally or emotionally to make those choices. Now you are, so what you do now is important. Your family will understand that. They will respect that. Or they will answer to me."

Phin could only stare at her. Then her words sank in and his chest filled with warmth and he could breathe again. He leaned in and kissed her and she smiled against his lips.

"Good answer," she said when he pulled away. "Are you ready to talk to Detective Clancy?"

"Yeah. Let's give the man a collar."

"Let's go to his office. I'd prefer not to have him in my house again. Not until I have a chance to make sure that my father's client list is properly hidden."

"He's going to want to know about it," Phin said. "He's going to want to know how we found the Caulfields."

Cora shrugged. "We'll tell him the truth. We'll tell him that we found my father's notes about his side business and a note on his final job that he left for my mother to find because he didn't trust his partner. We'll give him access to my father's old computer after Antoine makes sure the client list is no longer accessible."

Phin kissed the tip of her nose. "You really do fit in with this crowd, telling a lie without actually telling a lie."

Cora looked pleased with herself. "Thank you."

Val laughed as she unlocked the SUV. "Get in and buckle up."

25

R EVEREND BEAUCHAMP, ARE you *listening*
to me?"

Alan winced at Mrs. Gregory's shrill tone. "Yes,
ma'am. I've been listening to you." For hours, it seemed.

"No, you're not," she snapped. "You've been watching
your phone. What could possibly be more important than
the Christmas cantata? It's next week, Reverend, and the
choir is not ready. The sets are not ready. We need another
camera for broadcasting and the sound system is not working. I repeat—what could be more important than this?"

What could be more important? *Just about everything.*

Mainly the fact that he hadn't heard from Sage in hours.
Sage should have finished off the Caulfields by now and
checked in, but he hadn't called.

Nor had Dave Reavey, Alan's PI. He'd sent the man to
shadow Sage, just to make sure Sage did what he was supposed to do. He'd told Reavey that he was worried about
Sage's state of mind, that his grandson might be planning
something terrible. His PI had bought the story, hook, line,
and sinker. Reavey was one of Alan's most faithful parishioners and Alan had never questioned his loyalty.

But the PI hadn't checked in, either. Not by phone, text,
or email, and that was unusual. Alan was anxious about

Reavey's call, because that would trigger the in-person meeting with the PI to hand over any photos that might prove Sage's guilt. At which time, Alan would have to kill the PI. He'd shoot him in the head, making it painless, of course. He wasn't a monster.

And then he'd have to find a new PI, but that was a task for tomorrow. Eliminating the Caulfields was the task for today.

But there hadn't been any news reports about a fire in Merrydale. Alan had been surreptitiously watching the Baton Rouge local news on his phone, although not as surreptitiously as he'd thought, because Mrs. Gregory was still yammering about him not paying enough attention.

"Enough," Alan snapped. "That is enough."

Mrs. Gregory fell silent, her mouth open. "What?"

"I said that is enough. I'm very busy and you are the choir director. If the cantata isn't ready, then make it ready. Recruit friends. I don't care."

She straightened in her chair, expression indignant. "You don't care?"

He stared at her, refusing to allow her to further fray his nerves. "I do not care. I have a headache and I'm behind in nearly everything. Please. Go find someone to help you." He made a shooing motion with his hand, cognizant that he'd pay for his flippancy later.

Maybe he should shoot Mrs. Gregory in the head, too. It was very tempting.

But he couldn't do that. Could he?

No. He could not.

She stood, vibrating with anger. "I will pray for you, Reverend Beauchamp. I'll ask *everyone* to pray, because you are clearly going through a trial."

Wonderful. She was going to tell everyone that he was in an ugly mood.

She left his office with an indignant flounce, closing the door hard enough to make him wince. He exhaled, shaking out a few aspirin from the bottle in his desk drawer. It was nearly empty. His head had hurt a lot the past few weeks.

But he was almost on the other side of things. Sage would do what he needed to do and, even if Cora Winslow discovered her father's other clients, there would be no way to link the Caulfields to him. Therefore, no way to link the murder of Jack Elliot to him.

And if Sage doesn't do as he's told? Then what?

Alan couldn't think about that. He just couldn't. Once again he cursed the disease that was slowly robbing him of his eyesight. A year ago he would have driven to Merrydale himself.

The job would already have been done.

He'd be—

His cell phone buzzed and he immediately picked it up. Then frowned. There was no name on the caller ID, just the number. But Alan would know that number in his sleep. Glendale Psychiatric Hospital.

Maybe she was dead. It was a gruesome thought that should shame him, but it didn't. Jenny's existence there was hardly living.

"Yes?" he answered.

"This is Mrs. Collinsworth. I wanted you to know that your daughter had three visitors this afternoon."

Visitors? Alan was suddenly on his feet, his headache now excruciating. "Which visitors? What happened?"

"Names are Val Sorensen, Phin Bishop, and Cora Winslow."

Alan's knees gave out and he fell into his desk chair. He knew all three of those names. He'd told them incredible lies when they'd visited Sara Morton the night before.

He'd thought they'd believed him. That they'd go after Medford Hughes for pedophilia. But they hadn't.

Because they knew.

But *how* did they know?

"Reverend Beauchamp?" Collinsworth sounded concerned. "Are you all right? Should I have detained them?"

Yes. You should have killed them. Which was ludicrous.
He couldn't ask for such a thing.

I'm going to ask Sage to do it.

Because they knew.

"It's fine. Thank you. Good day." He ended the call,
feeling sick.

Just calm down. Breathe. It might not be that bad. He
might not need to ask Sage to kill anyone else.

If the Caulfields were dead, Cora knowing about Jenny
wasn't a big deal. Even if Cora had found out about Jenny's
child, it would be his word against that of a woman who'd
been hospitalized for mental illness for twenty-three years.

It would still be all right. *If* the Caulfields were dead.

Alan called Sage's cell phone, his gut twisting anx-
iously.

"Grandfather. Hello."

Sage sounded . . . all right. "Did you do it?"

"Of course." The boy sounded affronted. "I did what
you told me to do. The house went up like a box of match-
sticks. No one could have survived the blaze."

Alan wanted to be relieved, he wanted to believe that
Sage had killed the Caulfields. But something was off.
Something is wrong.

Sage might have just lied to him. He knew the boy's
every vocal inflection.

But he didn't want to believe it. He needed to be certain. He needed to see the boy's eyes when he promised
he'd completed his assignment. "Thank you. Where are
you?"

"I'm at my place, cleaning up. I smell like a bonfire."

"Please report to me in thirty minutes. It's urgent."

"Absolutely," Sage said, the word a clash of discordant
notes. "I'll be there."

Alan stared at the phone when the line went dead. Sage
had hung up on him.

Something was very wrong.

He'd lost control of his grandson.

Unfortunately, Alan would have to end the boy very soon. A staged break-in. A thwarted robbery. A bullet between the boy's pretty blue eyes.

I'll do it myself. A sleeping pill in a cup of coffee to knock him out and Alan wouldn't need to be able to see to aim. He'd put the gun up against Sage's head and kill him like he'd done Medford Hughes.

He'd leave Sage's body to be discovered by a cleaning lady. Alan would be shocked. He'd be out of his mind with grief.

The congregation would grieve with him. They'd mourn.

And Alan would finally be free of this whole nightmare. *Because two can share a secret if one of them is dead.*

His phone buzzed in his hand.

His PI. *Finally.*

"Yes?" he answered hoarsely.

"Your grandson is a motherfucker," Reavey snarled. "He hit me. Knocked me out. Tied me up in the back of my own car. Two cops had to free me. I had to tell them that my date had tied me up for kink and then left. They hauled me downtown."

"Did you tell them about me? About Sage?"

"You really are a selfish asshole. No, I didn't, even when I almost got arrested. If I find your grandson, I'm going to kill him."

Alan closed his eyes, so tired. "What exactly happened?"

"I went to the address you gave me and waited for him. He arrived, talked to some girl and an old lady, then drove away. I followed him out."

So Sage had lied. He hadn't killed them.

Why hadn't he killed them?

"Did he say anything when he hit you?"

"Oh yes. He said to tell you that you're a sonofabitch and he's not doing your dirty work ever again. Oh, and that your granddaughter is very sweet and he told them to run. Look,

Reverend Beauchamp, I don't care what you're up to. I don't
want to know any more. I'm out. You're not worth it."

And then, once again, Alan was staring at his phone
after being hung up on.

Sage had turned on him. Sage knew that Ashley was
Alan's granddaughter.

His stomach roiled. Sage hadn't killed the Caulfields.
And Cora Winslow knew about Jenny. How could she have
found out?

And then Alan knew. Cora Winslow had found Ashley.
She'd found the Caulfields.

She knows everything.

I need to run.

He closed his eyes and concentrated. Twenty-three
years ago, he'd had a brilliant escape plan. He'd leave New
Orleans by boat for Mexico.

He could do that now. Even more easily because now he
had more money.

"I need a boat." Surely a member of his congregation
had a boat. He'd ask to be taken to a village in Mexico.
He'd say that he was preaching there, helping them start a
church. But not to worry, he'd be home in time for the
Christmas cantata.

He nearly laughed. He was getting hysterical, and he
needed to calm down.

Maybe he shouldn't ask a congregation member. He
needed someone who didn't know him.

Or he could get on a cruise ship. Plenty of them left out
of New Orleans every day. That hadn't been the case twenty-
three years ago. He'd still have to use his own passport, but
he could get off at the first port and never look back.

He brought up a cruise reservation website. He didn't
care which cruise line. He didn't care how much it cost.
He'd pick whichever one left the soonest.

His heart sank. The earliest departure was tomorrow
afternoon. If Cora was telling the police about Jenny, tomorrow might be too late.

Panic rose, making his head hurt even more. He needed to fly out now. If the police tracked him, he'd just have to lose them later.

He opened a new browser and found an airline website.

Better. He could fly out in two hours. He clicked on the fare and typed in his credit card number.

Declined.

What? No. Not possible. He typed the number in again.

Declined. He ground his teeth. Not a good time for the credit card to glitch on him.

He chose another card and typed it in.

Declined.

He chose his bank cash card and typed it in.

Declined.

A sense of dread rose to choke him. Hands trembling, he dialed his credit card company.

"How can I help you?" the cheerful customer service agent asked.

He cleared his throat. "My card was declined, but I'm certain I have a sizable available balance." He gave her the number and waited, his skin becoming clammy with sweat.

"Let me check for you, sir." She was gone for a moment, then came back sounding less cheerful. "Your credit card was canceled, sir. Mrs. Beauchamp called to say the card had been stolen. We're sending new cards to your house by FedEx. They should arrive on Monday."

Monday. Monday was too late. He needed his money now.

Wait. "Hold on. Did you say my *wife* canceled the card?"

"She did, sir."

"Um . . . thank you." He ended the call and quickly typed in his bank password. She couldn't have canceled all their cards. The decline of their bank cash card must have been a mistake.

He stared at his computer screen.

Zero. His bank balance was zero. That was not possible.

His whole body shook now and he knew he was seconds away from being sick. He called the bank.

"How can we help you, sir?"

"I'm looking at my account online and all of my money is gone." All of it. Every penny.

"Let me check." There was the sound of typing in the background. "Well, sir, it appears that your wife came in at three o'clock and withdrew everything from your joint account. She said she was opening an account elsewhere."

Your wife.

Your joint account.

Lexy, what have you done? And why? The PI's reports showed a godly, submissive wife who didn't cheat.

What's happening?

"Sir? Are you all right?"

"I'm fine, thank you." He ended the call.

He was not fine.

He called Lexy, breathing angrily as he waited for her to pick up. "What the hell have you done?" he shouted when she answered.

"I'm leaving you, Alan. You shouldn't have hired a PI to follow me. For *years*. I'm so *angry*. You haven't trusted me since *day one*. You've had me followed to make sure I'm not cheating, yet *you* have a secret family. Another child, Alan. How dare you!" She was shouting, too.

He'd never heard Lexy shout.

"Secret child? What are you talking about?"

"I'm talking about the photos of a girl in your secret safe behind your secret bookshelf, Alan. I'm talking about stacks of PI reports detailing every move I've made for years. Don't you even try to be the aggrieved party here. I'm leaving. And I'm telling everyone what a fraud you are."

My secret safe? Behind my secret bookshelf?

How . . . ?

Then he knew. *Sage.*

He ended the call with Lexy and redialed Sage.

"Grandfather. How are you?"

There was a lot of noise in the background. Car doors slamming and traffic. "Are you coming in or not?"

"I said I would," Sage said, but there was a hint of mocking in his tone.

"What have you done, Sage?"

"Become like you, Grandfather," Sage said coldly. "Are you satisfied now?"

The call abruptly ended and Alan closed his eyes. What was happening?

This couldn't be real. None of this could be real.

Cora Winslow knew about Jenny. Which meant that she knew about him, too. And somehow had found out about Ashley.

She'd probably already told the police.

Then again, maybe she hadn't. That would mean telling the cops that her precious father's business was on the wrong side of legal.

Maybe they could come to an agreement. She'd keep her mouth shut and he'd pay her . . .

What? He couldn't pay her anything. Lexy had taken his money. The only money left was in the church's treasury, and he didn't have access to that account. Not for lack of trying, but the board of deacons had created a system of checks and balances that allowed no one person to have control of church funds. So money was not going to help him deal with Cora Winslow.

She would have to be silenced. He should have done so two weeks ago. *I was soft. I was afraid.*

He wasn't soft or afraid now.

It's her or me. I choose me. She could drive him to Mexico. He would end her there and he'd be free.

I hope her heart is right with the Lord. Otherwise she'd be going straight to hell.

Alan feared that was his fate as well.

At this point, he'd take as many people with him as he needed to.

The Garden District, New Orleans, Louisiana
FRIDAY, DECEMBER 16, 8:45 P.M.

"I'm starving again," Val said as they left the police station. "Being careful what you say is hard work."

It really was, and Cora found that she could eat again, too.

The detective had listened to them with wide eyes that grew wider with every revelation. Cora had decided—with input from Phin, Val, Antoine, and Burke—to tell the detective as much as they possibly could without exposing the people like Alice VanPatten who'd turned to Jack Elliot for help.

Alice hadn't done anything wrong, except to claim a false alibi. At a minimum, she'd perjured herself with the authorities at the time. Worst case, she could be held for conspiracy to commit murder, since she'd known that Jack had killed her husband but had hidden the truth, and she could still be prosecuted for that.

So Cora had asked that the team have a conference call as Val had driven from the psychiatric hospital back to the city. Timothy and Beatrice Caulfield had joined them as well, agreeing that their story needed to be part of what was shared with NOPD.

The Caulfields were anxious about the possible fallout but agreed that the benefit of taking Alan Beauchamp down was worth the risk of any legal ramifications of admitting to the private adoption. Ashley and her parents wouldn't be safe until Alan was in custody.

Technically, the couple had done nothing wrong. They'd thought they were participating in a legitimate transaction.

At least that's what they kept insisting aloud. Cora had heard the doubt in their voices.

They'd known what they'd been doing twenty-three years ago. But confirmation that Jennifer Beauchamp had been unwilling to part with her child had shaken them soundly.

As it should have, Cora thought sadly. But that was water under the bridge now. Ashley had had two good parents whose care for her had likely been much better than she would have received at the hands of Alan Beauchamp.

Cora really hated that man.

So she'd told Clancy everything she could and he'd said he'd bring Alan Beauchamp in for questioning right away. He'd already been investigating Patrick Napier. The detective had pieced together much of what they already knew—the Renaissance-era paint, the gallery owned by Patrick, the connection between Patrick and Vincent Ray through the mentoring program.

Vincent had admitted that Patrick had paid him to set Cora's attic on fire.

That had been a blow.

Then Clancy had shared that they'd found the black Camry that had followed her—and that there had been a body in the trunk. The victim was Sanjay Prakash, twenty-five years old, a clerk at one of the rental car companies at the airport. Both the Camry and the minivan seen in Cora's driveway had been rented in his name.

They were still looking for the white van that had been in front of Medford Hughes's house the night the man had been murdered. The white van that had killed a carful of college kids as it had fled the scene.

Clancy wasn't sure who'd killed the man found in the trunk of the Camry. At the moment, he had eight bodies in the morgue—Medford Hughes and his wife, the four college kids, Sanjay Prakash, and Minnie Edwards—and three suspects—Alan, Sage, and Patrick. Clancy wasn't sure who'd done what, but he was now looking for all three of them.

That Patrick might have killed so recently left her numb.

But not so numb that she shared everything with Clancy. If Patrick chose to share his and Jack Elliot's client list to get a plea deal, then the police would find out. Cora wouldn't help them with that, though. Clancy had asked for the documentation they'd found on her father's old computer, and Cora had promised to get it to him when she got back home.

Antoine had been busily creating the documentation while she, Phin, and Val had been in Clancy's office. He said it would be simple to craft a note from Jack Elliot to his wife saying that he was doing a favor for an old college friend, helping transport an infant to her newly adoptive parents. The note would look like it had been created twenty-three years ago.

It wasn't a perfect scenario and didn't explain the Swiss bank account, but it protected the people who her father had risked his life for. Who he'd ultimately lost his life because of.

Maybe she wasn't so hungry after all.

But she was hot and itchy. "I'll just be happy to get this Kevlar off. Can we go to my house, Val?"

"That's the plan, Cora Jane," Val said as she merged onto Rampart Street. "I'll be glad to have Molly relieve me tonight, not gonna lie. This has been one long-ass day."

"It really has." Cora turned to Phin, who'd been quiet throughout their interview with Clancy, only speaking when spoken to. His hand had never left SodaPop's back, the dog plastered to his side.

But he'd made it through with no major mishaps. At least none that Cora could see.

"You okay?" she murmured, and he turned to meet her eyes.

"Yeah. Just can't stop thinking about Jenny. How her father dumped her in that place and never came to visit."

"Your family would never have done that."

He nodded. "I know that. Kind of had an epiphany, there in Jenny's room."

"I figured. I could see the moment it hit you." He'd physically reeled in shock but had rallied quickly. He'd been so good with Jenny. So sweet and calm. "What was the epiphany?"

"That my family's always loved me unconditionally. I knew it in my head, y'know? But I think I finally got it today."

Cora smiled at him, cupping his cheek in her palm. "Good."

"You still going to see them for Christmas, Phin?" Val asked.

He nodded. "I am. Scared to death over it, but I'm going."

Cora took his hand. "I'll go with you if you want me to."

His shoulders seemed to uncoil. "Yes. I'd like that."

"I usually spend Christmas with Tandy and her father," she said sadly. "Guess that's over forever."

"I'm sorry," Phin said. "So sorry."

She got that he was sorrowful, not apologizing. "Thanks. So . . . new traditions have to begin, right? What does your family do, Phin?"

He started to tell her, lulling her with the deep rumble of his voice while Val drove them through the darkened streets of the Garden District.

Her home for her whole life. She didn't want to leave, ever. And now that Clancy had what he needed to arrest Alan, Sage, and Patrick, she could start thinking about her plans for the house that was far too big for one person. She could start planning for the way to best help Phin's people.

Vets who needed housing security, who needed a fresh start. A hand up.

She selfishly hoped Phin would come back to New Orleans with her after reuniting with his family. She didn't want to start such a huge endeavor on her own. She could do it alone. She was sure of that.

She just didn't want to.

"What the hell?" Val muttered as they approached her house.

There was a car parked in the driveway, blocking access to the gate.

Cora sat up straighter. "That's Tandy's car."

Tandy was here. She'd come back.

For what purpose, Cora didn't know. Right now, she was just happy to see her friend's car.

Val parked behind Tandy, and Phin got out to look in her car, returning a moment later with a frown on his handsome face.

"She's not in her car, Cora."

But the lights weren't on in the house. It was totally dark.

"She gave me back the key, so she can't have gotten in," Cora said, remembering the sound of the key clanking on her kitchen table when Tandy had tossed it away. "She probably went for a walk until we got back. I'll text her to meet me."

Cora did so, then got out of the SUV. "I want this Kevlar off my body."

"Cora, wait," Val snapped, grabbing her arm. "Me first, remember?"

"Sorry," Cora muttered. Val was right, of course.

Phin fell into step beside her, his arm around her shoulders. "Let her do her job, okay?"

"I know. I guess I'm feeling relieved because this is finally over."

Clancy had everything he needed to charge Alan, Sage, and Patrick.

But Cora still didn't know which one had killed her father. Both Alan and Patrick had had motive. *Please don't be Patrick. Please.*

Val entered the house first, Phin holding Cora back on the porch as Val headed up the stairs to clear each room. But then Cora saw someone sitting at her kitchen table in the dark, barely visible past the foyer archway. Someone with a familiar ponytail.

"Tandy?" She pulled free of Phin's hold and ran to her friend.

Realizing too late that Tandy's hands were tied and her mouth was covered in tape.

Even in the semidarkness, Cora could see the helpless fear in Tandy's eyes.

Cora went still as something cold and hard pressed against her head.

"You couldn't let it go," Alan Beauchamp whispered. "You just couldn't let it go. I tried to help you. To give you something safer to investigate. But you didn't take my help."

Cora didn't move a muscle. Phin was behind her somewhere, as was Val. *They're going to be so mad at me*, she thought.

They'd be right. *I'm so stupid.*

Without moving her head, she looked to her right. A key sat on the table, shining in the dim light from the streetlamps coming in the kitchen window. That explained how Tandy had gotten in, but not how she'd gotten the key.

She'd sworn she'd made no copies, and Cora had believed her.

"What do you want?" Cora asked, her voice shaking.

"I wanted you to stop poking into things that weren't your business. Now I want you to get me out of here."

"Out of my house?" Cora asked.

Alan laughed, an unpleasant sound. "No, out of the country. You're coming with me, Cora."

"And then you'll let me go?" she asked, knowing that he wouldn't.

"Of course. I don't want to hurt you. I just want out."

Lies. All lies. "Did you kill my father?" The question was out of her mouth before she'd even planned to ask it. She winced when he shoved the gun harder into her temple.

"You have one job. That's to get me out of town. You're going to drive me to Mexico."

"Why would I do that?" she asked quietly.

"Because I will kill your friend here if you don't. Believe me."

Tandy made a noise, muffled by the tape over her mouth.

"I believe you," Cora said. "You've killed already. Medford Hughes and his wife. Minnie Edwards. Sanjay Prakash. The college kids who wrecked when you were running from Medford's murder. How do you sleep at night?"

There was a slight hesitation before the gun shoved into her head again. "Let's go. You there, in the chair. Get up or Cora dies."

Tandy struggled to her feet, tears streaming down her cheeks.

Phin, please be there. Please be ready to do something.

Because she knew that Alan wouldn't hesitate to kill her. He'd ordered the murder of his own grandchild today. The man had no soul. And he had nothing to lose.

"Why can't you buy your way out of the country?" Cora asked. "You're richer than God." She winced when he dug the fingers of his free hand into her arm.

"Do not blaspheme," he snapped.

Cora wanted to laugh at the irony, but she didn't dare.

Keeping the gun to her head, Alan urged her forward. "Move. We're going out the back, through the gate. I have your friend's car keys. You'll drive. If you scream, you both die. I'm one hundred percent serious."

Cora didn't doubt that. But his plan wasn't going to work. Val had parked their company SUV behind Tandy's car. She was surprised that Alan didn't know that. Hadn't he looked out a window?

She took a careful step forward, breathing a sigh of relief at the shadow she could see through the window in the door. Phin. Phin was there waiting.

Thank God.

26

CORA WAS SO focused on both the gun at her head and that shadow at her kitchen door that she didn't hear anyone behind her until Alan made a strangled cry of pain. The pressure disappeared from her head, and she dropped to the floor, grabbing Tandy and dragging her under the table.

A thud shook the room and she peered through the legs of the chairs to see Alan sliding down the opposite wall. He still held the gun, but he was blinking hard.

Phin. Phin had thrown him across the room.

Phin had placed himself between Cora and Alan. Phin, who didn't have a gun. He was standing there, making himself a target.

"Don't come closer," Alan said, his arm extended, the gun now pointed at Phin's chest. "I will kill you."

No. No, no, no. Not Phin. Alan would kill him and Cora couldn't let that happen.

"Stop!" Cora crawled out from under the table. "I'll go with you. Just . . . don't hurt him. Don't hurt Tandy, either. I'll take you to Mexico."

"Cora," Phin said, his voice so very calm. "Get out. Go through the back door. Take Tandy with you. Call 911, then Burke. Now."

A shot cracked the air and Phin staggered backward, falling on his ass. Cora didn't think. She just threw herself over him.

"I said I'd go with you!" she cried. "Why did you have to shoot him?"

Alan struggled to his feet. "He wasn't going to let me take you out of here. Now move. You and the other girl. *Go.* I just want to get out of here."

Cora looked up at the man, tears blurring her vision. "No. You want to kill me, too. Because I know who you are. I know what you did. To my father. To your own daughter. To your granddaughter." She blinked hard to clear her eyes. "You're a monster."

Alan strode forward, grabbing a handful of her hair and yanking her away from Phin. She clutched Phin harder, even though her scalp burned and her eyes teared even more. Phin moved beneath her, one of his legs swinging wide.

For a moment, Cora was stunned into immobility. Phin wasn't hurt.

Kevlar, she thought. They were all still wearing their vests. Everyone except for Tandy.

Then the floor shook because Alan had fallen. The gun in his hand discharged, and Tandy screamed from under the table, the sound muffled.

Tandy. Oh God. Tandy.

Phin pushed Cora off him, rolling to his feet as he lurched toward Alan, grunting in pain when Alan fired again. "Get out, Cora!" Phin thundered. "Take Tandy and get out."

Phin dropped to his knees, crawling a few feet forward, his gaze fixed on Alan, one arm hanging limply at his side. Cora watched blood hit the floor around him in a steady flow. She looked up, following the path of the flowing blood.

It was pouring from Phin's arm. *Pouring.*

Cora stared in shock for a few hard beats.

Do something. Help him.

She'd pushed to her knees when the back door flew

open and Patrick appeared, his hair flying every which direction.

"Tandy!" He ran inside, reached under the table, and grabbed Tandy under her arms, dragging her backward toward the kitchen door.

Another shot rang out and Patrick dropped Tandy to the floor, clutching his own chest, his face blank with shock.

No.

But it was true. The front of Patrick's white shirt was becoming dark, the blood looking black in the light from the streetlamps.

Patrick staggered backward, grabbing onto the kitchen counter. He slid to the floor, one hand still pressed to his chest while he shoved the other hand into his jacket pocket.

Cora saw the gun in Patrick's hand an instant before he fired.

Alan cried out, but he didn't slump to the floor. His shirt was also stained red, but not like Patrick's.

Not like Phin's.

Alan was looking around, wild-eyed, the gun in his hand sweeping back and forth as he grimaced in pain. He pointed his gun at Phin again.

Phin, who was crawling toward the older man. While blood still poured from his arm.

No more.

Cora flung herself forward, landing on Alan, grabbing onto his arm, trying to take the gun from his hand, but he was strong and he fought her. Hard.

Knowing that she fought not only for her own life, but for Phin's and Tandy's—and maybe even Patrick's—she put all her strength into bending Alan's wrist so that his gun pointed at his own chest. Not Phin's. Not Tandy's. *Not mine.*

A pair of strong hands—bloody hands—landed on hers, shoving at the gun in Alan's hand. *Phin.* Together they got the weapon pointed at Alan and Cora slid her finger over the older man's. Right over the trigger.

"Let it go," Cora ordered, her words choppy, her breath coming in pants. "Drop the gun, Beauchamp. Or I'll kill you myself."

He met her eyes, his burning with rage. "You won't," he gritted out. "You can't."

One pull of her finger would do it. One little pull.

But he was right. She couldn't do it.

Tears blurred her vision once again. *I have to. I have to. Or he'll kill Phin. He'll kill Tandy.* He might have already killed Patrick. And Val. Where was she? Had he killed her, too?

Do something.

Her mental self-talk shattered into a million pieces when another shot fired. Cora stared at the hole in Alan's forehead.

She fell backward when Alan suddenly stopped fighting for his gun. He hadn't fired, and neither had she. Slowly she looked across the kitchen at Patrick, who lay in a pool of his own blood, his gun lowering to the floor.

Alan was dead.

Cora dropped Alan's gun and scooted away from his body, turning to Phin. He'd crawled over to another wall and was attempting to lift his arm over his heart. Because he was still bleeding.

So much blood.

Cora looked around frantically for something to use as a tourniquet. Anything to stop his bleeding. "Why don't you wear a belt?" she cried, because he was pale and shaking.

He could die.

No. No, no, no.

"Sorry," he whispered.

Call 911.

Do something.

She had no idea where her phone was, so she grabbed Phin's from his shirt pocket. It had miraculously survived the gunfire without even a scratch. She dialed 911 and put the phone on speaker, begging for help as soon as the operator answered.

She pushed to her feet and began opening drawers, trying to find something to stop his bleeding. *Ah.* Cloth napkins and . . .

A wooden spoon. She grabbed the spoon and a handful of napkins.

She could do this. She'd read about it while helping one of her library patrons study for a first-aid exam.

Suddenly calm, she dropped to her knees next to Phin and tied one of the napkins around his arm, above the wound, then inserted the spoon and began to twist it until the tourniquet was tight. She tucked one end of the spoon under his shirt sleeve before pressing another napkin to the wound itself, trying to stop the bleeding.

Phin's other hand came up to clasp the second napkin, putting pressure on the wound himself. "Go to Patrick. I'm good."

"You're not, but I'll see to him. Don't die. I just found you."

Phin's smile was lopsided. "Okay."

She kissed him hard, then crawled across the floor to where Patrick lay, struggling for each breath.

Tandy sat staring at him, her eyes glazed in shock. Blood seeped from a wound in her leg, but it didn't look urgent, so Cora wiped her hands on her jeans before grabbing the tape and pulling it from her friend's mouth as gently as she could. "Tandy?"

Tandy just stared at her.

Cora spun around on her knees, pressing the remaining napkins to Patrick's chest. "Why?" she whispered.

"He hurt . . . my Tandy."

"You were outside the door."

Patrick coughed and blood bubbled from his mouth.

Oh no. Oh no.

"Did you kill my father?" She had to know before he breathed his last.

"No. Just . . . followed him. Needed to make sure he . . . did the job."

"He did. He delivered that baby to the Caulfields."

Patrick made a gurgling sound and reached for Tandy, but all he got was air. Tandy was frozen. Cora wasn't even sure she could hear them right now.

Across the kitchen, the 911 operator was loudly calling for her, telling her that help was on the way.

"Ambulances," Cora shouted. "Three. Maybe four." Because Val was still MIA. She hoped the operator heard her because she needed to focus on Patrick. The napkins were already soaking-wet with his blood.

"Did you put his body in the Damper Building?"

"Yes. Had to . . . keep anyone . . . from finding him. Afraid . . . would lead . . . to me."

Cora barely restrained her fury. "Did you write the letters?"

"Yessss." He slurred the word, more blood bubbling from his mouth. "To distract you. Then . . . to help you. So you'd think he loved you. Sorry. So sorry. Never meant . . . to hurt you."

"You don't get to apologize," Cora snarled. His actions had hurt her mother for years. Had kept the police from finding her father's murderer. "You're not forgiven, Patrick. I'm sorry for that."

"Fair," he whispered. "Tried. To be your father."

"But you weren't. My father was dead." She reached up on the counter and grabbed a towel, pressing it to his wound because the cloth napkins were now too wet. Useless.

"Tandy . . . didn't know."

"I know." Cora glanced over at her oldest friend, whose expression had changed from dazed and numb to full of sorrow. "I'll take care of her, Patrick. You have my word."

"Th-thank you." He tried to reach for Tandy again and this time she scooted forward. Her hands were still tied, but she could speak.

"Daddy?" The word came out a sob. "I love you."

"Love you, too." More blood bubbled up. Cora gave up trying to save his life. She rose and grabbed a paring knife from the butcher block and began to saw at the ropes tying Tandy's hands.

Patrick was going to die. At least Tandy could hold his hand.

The moment Tandy was free she grabbed her father's hands, sobbing uncontrollably.

At least Tandy would get to say goodbye.

Which was more than Cora had been allowed.

Bitter. You're bitter.

I'm angry. I'm allowed.

She returned to Phin's side. "Where's SodaPop?"

"Left her outside. Didn't want her . . . to get hurt."

"And Val?"

"Don't know. Find her."

Cora kissed him again. "The ambulance will be here soon. Do not die."

He smiled weakly. "Yes sir, Cora, sir."

Cora was exhausted, staggering as she ran from the kitchen. She opened the front door first, hoping SodaPop hadn't run away.

She should have known better. The dog was sitting on the welcome mat and ran past her to the kitchen the moment the door was opened wide enough.

SodaPop would keep Phin calm until the medics arrived. That was important.

She made herself run up the stairs, holding on to the handrail for support. Covering the shiny wood with blood.

It'll clean.

She checked all the rooms for Val but found no one, so she ran back down and out the front door. Her back gate was open. It had been closed before.

Running through it, Cora found Val on the ground in the back garden, rolling from her stomach to her back, blinking slowly up at the night sky. She saw Cora and flinched.

"What happened? Whose blood is that?"

Cora dropped to her knees, wiping as much blood from her hands to her jeans as she could. "Not mine. Alan was here. He shot Patrick, who shot him back. Alan is dead, Patrick is dying. Phin is hurt bad, but I think I've stopped his bleeding and an ambulance is on the way. Where are you hurt?"

Val touched her head gingerly, wincing. "I'm okay."

"You lost consciousness for several minutes. You're not okay. Where are you hurt?"

"He stabbed me in the leg, then hit me with something. That shit hurts."

Cora's hands started searching for a knife wound. *I need more napkins.* She found the wound and looked around for something to bandage it with. "Who stabbed you?"

"Patrick. I was clearing the house and saw him from the attic window, creeping through the back gate. Didn't know Alan was here, too. I ran back down to stop Patrick, but he lunged for me. Got me in the leg with his knife. Then he hit me with a goddamn rock. Took my gun."

"He shot Alan with it. May have saved my and Phin's lives."

That should count for something. Someday, when everything stopped hurting, it might.

Sirens came blaring down the street and Cora could see the flashing lights through the open gate. Help was here.

"I'll be right back. Don't move."

Val's laugh bordered on hysterical. "I don't know if I can."

Cora ran to the front yard. "I need one medic back here and two in the kitchen." The ME could come for Alan later.

She hoped he was already burning in hell.

Tulane Medical Center, New Orleans, Louisiana
MONDAY, DECEMBER 19, 10:30 A.M.

"He looks better," Val said, lowering herself into one of the chairs near Phin's bed. She was limping, but, like Phin, she'd make a full recovery. Patrick's knife hadn't hit anything critical. The doctors had been more worried about the concussion. But they'd assured her that she'd recover from that, as well.

Val was more embarrassed than anything else, which wasn't fatal, so Cora wasn't worrying about her anymore.

Phin, on the other hand . . . Cora had come too close to losing him.

She ran her eyes over Phin's sleeping form. "More color in his cheeks. He's been sleeping a lot, which is what he needs right now."

"How about you, Cora Jane?" Val asked. "Are you okay?"

Cora knew full well that Val wasn't talking about being physically okay. "No. I haven't seen Tandy since she left with her father's body on Friday. I still don't even know why she was there in my kitchen."

"I don't know, either," Val said. "I dropped by her condo to check on her. Her cousin was there."

"Maura, her cousin on her mother's side. She's the only family Tandy has left now."

"She said that Tandy was resting. Said she'd call you when she was ready."

Cora sighed. "I think I know how Phin's sister has felt all these years. Waiting for someone to be ready."

Val commiserated with her for a few moments, then brightened. "Oh, we got news you'll want to hear. Sage Beauchamp was picked up by police in a village outside Madrid. He's being escorted back to the U.S. to face charges of murder in the death of your boss and Sanjay Prakash."

"Good. Sage spared Ashley, but he killed Minnie for no good reason at all. Just covering his ass."

A knock at the door had them both looking up. Burke came in and pulled up a chair. "He looks better."

"I feel better," Phin said grumpily. "I'd feel even better if you guys didn't talk so loud."

Cora winced. "How much did you hear?"

"All of it." He clumsily patted Cora's hand. "It's okay. I know waiting for me has been hard on Scar."

Phin knew that his family had been informed that he'd been hurt and that he was okay. He didn't know that Scarlett and Cora had spoken for a long time on the phone. Cora hoped Phin wouldn't be too upset that Cora had contacted the Cincinnati detective, but she couldn't stand to let the woman go another hour without knowing her brother was coming home.

"Tandy will come around," Phin went on, then turned to Burke. "Did Patrick have any files like Jack kept?"

"Not that NOPD's been able to find," Burke said. "Antoine and I have been checking through the initials on your father's client list, Cora, putting old property records with names. Not including the Caulfields and the two clients who were actually guilty men running from the law, all of Jack's clients had filed restraining orders against their abusers and had filed multiple police reports citing the abuse. Jack mostly helped people who really needed it. It doesn't appear that anyone except for Alice's first husband died while the clients were being extracted and relocated. Payment for the new IDs seems to have come from family members. Not the mob."

Cora felt the weight roll off her shoulders. "Thank you."

Burke gave her a gentle smile. "You're welcome. Some of those people had already returned to their old homes and identities after their abusers were out of the picture. Usually the abusers died of natural causes, nothing to do with Jack. About half of his clients are still living under the new names. We can't find some of them, so they're likely still in hiding. The ones we did find said that your father was kind and supportive and they credit him with saving them. It's a good legacy to leave behind, I think."

Cora thought so, too. "I got a call from that Swiss bank this morning. They're releasing my father's account to me." She drew a breath. "It had nearly two hundred thousand dollars in it."

"Wow," Val said. "I didn't expect that much."

"It wasn't at the beginning. There's twenty-three years of interest in there, too."

"What are you going to do with the money, Cora?" Burke asked.

Cora glanced at Phin. His mouth curved in a slow smile of approval that warmed her soul. "Well," she said, "assuming the police let me keep it and if there's any left after the back taxes and fines, I'm going to use it to start transitional housing for military vets. That money, plus the necklace Phin found, will fund the program for a few years at least. The necklace will be worth far more than the Swiss bank account. There are grants, too, so I'll be working to secure those."

Both Burke and Val looked stunned, and then their smiles mirrored Phin's.

"That's perfect," Val said.

"I want to donate," Burke said simply. "Tell me when and how much. I've got an inheritance I barely touch from a crazy old uncle who had more money than sense."

"We'll all want to help," Val said. "We've all served and we all know a vet who could use a hand up."

"At least one," Burke said. "I can't believe we didn't think to do this already."

"You did," Phin said. "You helped me."

That stopped Burke in his tracks. "I guess we did. Best decision ever, Phin."

Phin's cheeks pinked up. He didn't say anything, but he looked pleased.

Val patted his hand. "They also found the white van

that was parked outside Medford Hughes's house the night he was killed. Clancy said that they were able to track it to a storage unit near Xavier University. The storage unit and van, along with another car, were registered in Jenny Beauchamp's name."

"Sonofabitch," Phin snarled.

Cora had to agree.

"Um, excuse me?"

Cora spun in her chair at the familiar voice. "Tandy."

Tandy stepped into Phin's room, looking uncertain. "I hoped we could talk."

Val and Burke started to stand, but Tandy waved them back to their chairs.

"You can stay. I won't take long."

Cora frowned when Tandy pulled up a chair. "You haven't been sleeping, Tandy." There were dark circles under Tandy's eyes and her spirit was gone. She'd been bouncy and irrepressible, but now she looked gray.

Tandy touched the bags under her eyes self-consciously. "I'm leaving New Orleans."

Cora gasped. "Tandy, no."

"For a while. I don't know what I'll do with the gallery, but I'll figure it out. I can't stay here, Cora."

"Where will you go?" Cora asked, her voice small.

"To Seattle. That's where Maura's been living and she likes it." Tandy's smile was wan. "Lots of coffee shops up there. I could use the caffeine."

Cora wanted to beg her to stay, but she could see Tandy's point. Everyone knew about the shoot-out in the Garden District, as it was being called. There would be reporters and memories everywhere she turned. "Will you come back?"

"Someday. Maybe." Tandy blew out a breath. "I need to explain a few things. I owe you that much."

"You don't owe me anything," Cora said fiercely.

"I do. So hush. I lied to you that night in your kitchen. My father had been traveling a lot in the years before we moved, and always to New Orleans. After I left your house

Thursday night, I asked him if he'd ever done any art restoration. I told him that I had an overload of clients and might need his help. He said that he did, back in Thibodaux, when I was little, but he'd lost his love for it." She bowed her head. "He said he was restoring a painting when a friend of his died. Every time he picked up a brush, he was reminded of that man and he couldn't stand it. I . . . I didn't want to believe that the paint found on Jack's clothes could have been my father's."

"But you did believe it," Burke said. "What made you?"

"Two things. Cora mentioned that the letter writer had a wobbly *r*. I checked the last note Dad left me and . . . wobbly *r*'s all over the place. Then I found a little envelope of keys in his coat pocket. They matched the key you gave me, Cora. I didn't make even one copy. He must have taken my key and made copies. So I took one of those keys and went to your house. I wanted to be sure they really were keys to your place, y'know?"

"I know," Cora said quietly. She hadn't wanted to believe it about Patrick, either.

"I unlocked the door and it was . . . devastating. The key fit. But I didn't have time to think about it because that man was behind me, pushing me into the house."

"Alan Beauchamp?" Cora asked.

Tandy nodded, her face haunted. "He made me turn off the alarm and told me we were going to wait for you, and then you were going to take him far away. I was leverage."

"I'm glad he's dead," Cora said, not sorry in the least.

"Me too. There, at the end, Dad said that Detective Clancy had already asked him who might have that kind of paint stain, so he was already a suspect. He used his last breaths to tell me that. When I asked about the restoration work on Thursday night, he was afraid I knew about the stain, too. On Friday, in your kitchen, he said that he'd found that one of the keys he'd made was missing and was afraid I'd gone to tell you. But when he got there, you and Val and Phin had already come back. He thought he'd go around the back, listen in to find out what we were saying. When Val came through the gate, he panicked because he figured that she knew, so he . . ." She shrugged. "I'm sorry, Val. He shouldn't have hurt you."

Val smiled graciously. "Not your fault, hon."

"We saw all of that later, on the camera feed we set up for Cora," Burke said. "We got a notification from the alarm system that someone had entered the house on Friday, but at the time we thought it was Cora, Val, and Phin coming back from talking to Clancy. We didn't look at the camera feed right away and that's on us. We would have known you were in danger, but we were busy settling some visitors in at my house and . . ."

"Alan still would have been inside," Phin said. "Your cameras would have given us warning, but he still would have had Tandy. Your father came to save you, Tandy."

"Well, I think he originally came to stop me from talking. But once he saw I was in trouble, he was going to help. Anyway, I thought you should know. I'm sorry, Cora. I didn't listen to you and it nearly cost us both of our lives. Can you forgive me?"

"Oh, Tandy. There's nothing to forgive. I couldn't believe it, either."

Tandy's lips quivered, then pursed firmly. "Nevertheless, thank you for trying to help him." She pulled a thick envelope from her handbag and set it on the foot of Phin's bed. "The other thing he told me, right before he died, was that he had a safe-deposit box in a different bank than the one we use for the gallery. I retrieved his papers this morning. He kept records, too, it seems. It's all there, Cora. Information on their partnership and their clients. All of his emails to and from clients are in there, too, all signed John Robertson. There were a few clients that he wasn't so proud of, but I think you might already know about them. Your father and the other guy—Tom Rodgers, a cop—were in it to help people, and my father was, too, at first. Then he met a guy in a chat room who needed passage out of the country and, from what Dad wrote, the money was just too hard to pass up. He was a schoolteacher back then, making no money, and he wanted better for us." She took a moment to breathe, then squared her shoulders. "He lied to your dad and Tom about how much those two clients paid them. He kept most of it. I think you'll find that the money he made from their side business funded the purchase of the gallery and the house we lived in when we first came to New Orleans. There was no aunt who left him an inheritance. You were right about everything."

"I didn't want to be," Cora whispered.

"I know," Tandy whispered back. "There's a letter in my father's things. It's from your father to your mother. I . . . I think my father took it from your house."

Cora looked at the thick envelope, considered pulling the letter out to read, but her heart hurt and she didn't think she could bear it. "What did he say?"

Tandy swallowed. "He told her that he'd left her a puzzle, the most important of their lives. That she should remember the night they met and all the nights thereafter, to look at all the beautiful photos they'd taken of their family. Of 'just us.' Then he told her to 'roll the dice' and 'use the key.' That part didn't make any sense to me."

"It does to me," Cora murmured.

"Good. He also said that he loved her and that he's sorry if he's dead. That he was trying to do the right thing. He never stopped loving your mother, Cora. When I said he probably deserved what he got, I was wrong. I was wrong about so many things. And I'm sorry." Tandy rose, gripping her handbag tightly. "Give the papers to the police or don't. I'm too tired to care anymore." She met Cora's gaze. "I'll write you from Seattle, I promise. I'm leaving tomorrow."

Cora jumped from her chair. "*Tomorrow?*"

Tandy swallowed. "I'm running. I know that. But I can't look at anything around here without thinking of my father. I need a fresh start."

Cora took a step forward. Tandy took a step back. "Bye, Cora Jane. Be happy, okay?" Then she was gone.

Cora stared after her, openmouthed. Then she sank into the chair, numb once again. A warm hand covered hers. Phin.

A pair of arms hugged her from behind. Val.

A hand stroked her hair. Burke.

"You're ours now," Phin said. "It'll be all right."

Cora nodded. And let the tears come.

Tulane Medical Center, New Orleans, Louisiana
MONDAY, DECEMBER 19, 12:30 P.M.

"I'm fine," Phin insisted, but Cora plumped his pillows anyway.

Why was he fighting this? Every time she leaned over him, her breasts brushed over his chest and he could inhale the scent of strawberries.

"Actually, I'm not fine," he said, and she looked down at him, surprised.

"What's wrong?"

He smiled up at her. "Just want you to plump my pillow again. Come really close."

Cora laughed. "You bad boy." She sat in the chair next to his bed. She'd barely left since he'd been admitted, and it had meant the world to see her there every time he'd opened his eyes. To know she'd be there when he opened them again. And then she sighed. "Um, I have a confession to make."

She'd sobered, and he felt his smile fade away. "What happened?"

"I . . . Well, I called your sister."

Phin's eyes widened. "What? Why?"

But he wasn't as upset as he once might have been.

"She called you Saturday morning, on your cell phone. Left you a voicemail." She shrugged. "I listened to it and it broke my heart. You should hear what she said."

He didn't want to listen. He hated that his sister was once again worried about him after he'd landed his ass in the hospital. At least this time he was being hailed as a hero, unlike last time when he'd just been in a bar fight. But still.

No, you're going to listen.

"How did she know to call me?"

"You've been on the news, Phin," Cora said matter-of-factly. "You were even trending online for a few hours. This story has gotten a lot of press. Burke told your family that you were here in the hospital and that you would be all right. We figured we owed them that much."

He'd seen a few of the reports on TV, had read a few online. They'd managed to keep everything related to Alice VanPatten and the others secret, but everything else was widely known.

Alan Beauchamp's church was mourning their minister. Phin didn't know what to make of that. They knew he'd killed people, had sent his daughter to a psychiatric hospital after lying to her about her baby being dead, and then paid someone to place that child elsewhere.

The identity of Ashley's father had not been shared, pending DNA confirmation. Phin hoped he never met Colonel Walton Beauchamp. He hoped the cops were able to use the DNA to put the raping bastard away for a long time.

You're stalling. He really was.

"What does Scarlett want?"

Cora pressed his phone into his hand that wasn't hooked up to an IV. "Listen."

Scarlett loves you unconditionally. Remember that. Even if she's mad.

He took a breath and hit play.

"Phin, it's Scarlett." Phin winced because Scarlett had been crying. "I've respected your need for space, but I can't do it anymore. It's killing me inside. I love you and you're hurt and I just want you to come home. Please, Phin. Come home."

That was it. Short and sweet. So sweet that his heart hurt as he listened a second time and then a third.

Cora pushed a tissue into his hand and he realized he'd been crying. "Call her, Phin. You know you want to."

"What did you tell her when you called?"

"That the doctors said you'd make a full recovery and that you'd been shot saving my life."

"Oh. Okay." But she was wincing. "What else, Cora Jane?"

"We talked for a while. I told her that you'd been planning to come home for Christmas. That you might have to wait until New Year's if the doctor didn't release you, but that you were coming home if I had to drive you myself." She winced again. "I'm sorry."

"It's okay." And it really was. "It probably kept them from jumping in their cars and driving down here to see me."

Cora nodded. "I think it did. But now you have to go back because I promised."

"I would have gone even if you hadn't, but I'm glad you were able to make them feel better for now."

He didn't even realize he'd tensed until SodaPop whined from beside him in the hospital bed. He petted her head, was so glad that SodaPop was a trained service dog. She hadn't been allowed in the ICU after his surgery, but they'd allowed her to stay by his side once he'd gotten into a regular room. Delores had been on standby to walk, feed, and water his dog so that she could stay close.

Phin was so lucky to have such amazing friends. He didn't deserve them, but he wasn't going to give them back. As if they'd go.

As luck would have it, Joy's room was only four doors down. She'd come to visit for a while the night before.

You're stalling again.

"Can you dial for me and then put it on speaker?" he asked. "I only have one free hand and that one needs to pet SodaPop."

Cora nodded, her expression softening. "Of course. Do you want me to leave?"

"No." The very thought seemed wrong. *She belongs with me.* "Stay. Please."

"Okay." Cora dialed the number Scarlett had called from and sat back in her chair, the picture of patience.

Phin was not patient. Now that he'd committed to this endeavor, he wanted it to happen now. He waited through four rings and was resigned to leaving a voicemail of his own when someone picked up.

For a long moment, no one said a word, but Phin could hear breathing. "Scarlett?" he whispered.

Cora moved his phone from his lap, setting it on his collarbone so that his whisper could be heard.

"Scarlett?" he said again.

A sob tore through the line. "Phin? It's you? Really you?"

He ran his fingers through SodaPop's coat. She gave his hand a gentle lick. At least he couldn't run, even if he wanted to. "Yeah. It's me."

"Give me a minute." She was still crying, but the sobs had slowed to hiccups. "Are you all right? I talked to your girlfriend. She said you were going to be all right, but I've worried every moment."

He wondered how many moments she'd worried about him, and guilt hit him hard.

"Stop," Cora murmured. "I can see the guilt written all over your face."

"Who's there?" Scarlett asked. "Is that you, Cora?"

"It is. I can leave if you want me to, but Phin asked me to stay."

"Stay. You got him to call me. You can stay forever."

Phin choked on a laugh, then moaned. "That hurt."

"You deserve it," Scarlett said crisply, and then her voice gentled. "I've missed you."

All the laughter was gone. All he felt now was a profound sadness for the years he'd stayed away. Cora took the fingers of his IV hand.

"Be here," she said quietly. "In this moment."

He nodded, his throat thick. "I've missed you, too, Scar. So much. All of you."

"I have a lot to tell you. I'm going to need hours and hours. You're an uncle."

"I know. I look at every photo you send me. I kept that phone number just so I could see the pictures you kept sending. She's beautiful, Scar."

There was a moment of silence. "Will she get to meet you?"

"Yes." The word flew from his mouth, sure and certain. "I was going to come for Christmas. I don't know if I still can come then, but as soon as I can travel, I'm coming."

"Should . . . should I tell Mom?"

"Will she be . . ."

"Will she be mad? Oh yes. Will she want to smack you? Yes. Will she love you and hug you and never let you go? Also yes."

He heard the conviction in his sister's voice, but still he worried. "If she doesn't want me to come, I'll stay away. I don't want to cause a commotion."

"Phineas Butler Bishop. Don't make me come down there and smack you for her. You *will* come home. We *will* fuss over you. There *will* be commotion. Good commotion," she added, her voice breaking. "I can't believe I'm finally talking to you again."

"I'm sorry, Scar," he whispered, closing his eyes and concentrating on the deep, even breathing of his dog.

"I know," she whispered back. "You can tell me about it when you're ready." She cleared her throat. "We're proud of you, Phin."

"I'm not perfect," he blurted out. "I have . . . issues."

"I know," she said again. "I'm not perfect, either. None of us are. We'll work with your issues. You're really coming home?"

"For Christmas, yes. Or maybe New Year's, if I have to wait to drive."

"But you'll go back to New Orleans, after." He could hear the smile in her voice. "That's okay, Phin. We know you've built a life there, but you will always have a place here. In our house. In our hearts."

Phin shuddered out a breath. "Love you, Scarlett."

"Love you, Phineas. I'll see you soon, okay?"

"Okay. Tell Mom . . . I don't know."

"Tell her yourself," she said softly. "Recite a poem, tell a joke. It won't matter what you tell her. Only that it's you doing the telling."

Phin had to breathe through the tightness in his chest. "Bye, Scar."

"Bye, Phin."

She ended the call and Phin lay there, unable to stop the tears that kept running down his face. Cora leaned over him, dabbing his cheeks dry, and he breathed her in.

"You've been here for three days," he said. "How do you still smell so good?"

Cora laughed. "I used the shower in your bathroom. The nurses said I could." She sobered. "I had to go home and shower while you were in surgery. Fastest shower ever in the history of the world. But I was covered in other people's blood."

Phin nodded. It had been on his hands. But it had been his own blood. No trigger. No spiral. Or maybe that was due to SodaPop.

And Cora.

"You were amazing, you know," he said, suddenly so tired. "Fixing me up with a napkin and a wooden spoon. How did you know how to do that?"

"I'm a librarian," she said with a grin. "I know many things."

"Super-Librarian," he murmured. "I'm sleepy. You'll stay?"

"Yes. I'll be here when you wake up."

EPILOGUE

Cincinnati, Ohio
SUNDAY, DECEMBER 25, 8:30 A.M.

"BREATHE, PHIN," CORA murmured as Stone deftly maneuvered their borrowed RV along his parents' narrow street. "It's all going to be fine. Better than fine. It's going to be wonderful."

Wonderful. It would be. Phin would make sure of it.

He owed his family nothing less after all he'd put them through.

No pressure.

His fingers threaded through SodaPop's coat, and he smiled when she delicately licked his cheek. "Good girl."

He was better prepared to face his family than he'd been the last time he was home. Right out of the army hospital, his body still broken and his head a mess. He'd managed to keep a lid on the episodes, up until that night in the bar.

Afterward, as he'd lain in the hospital, he'd had to look into the worried eyes of his twin. He'd rather she'd have yelled at him back then, but she never had.

He hoped she wouldn't yell at him today, but she'd certainly be entitled.

They all would.

This time, though, he had support. He had Stone and Delores, who'd supported him since the day he'd met them.

He had SodaPop, who'd more than proven her worth in the two months he'd owned her.

And he had Cora Winslow, who hadn't left his side.

He was a lucky man.

"I know," he said. "It will be wonderful."

Cora's expression said that he hadn't been as convincing as he'd hoped.

He shrugged. "And if it's not, we can go home." He'd still have his New Orleans family.

"Last stop!" Stone called back cheerfully. "Everybody out."

"I'm impressed, Stone," Cora said. "I didn't know you could drive an RV this big."

Stone got out of the driver's seat and stretched. He had to be exhausted. He'd driven nearly straight through, only taking a few short breaks.

"Me either. I never did before yesterday."

Phin gaped at him. "You'd never driven one of these things before? But you said you could."

"I said I could. I never said I had. Come on, Phineas. Time to get up." Stone offered a hand to Phin, who was lying on the RV's sofa.

Not having to sit up in a car for fifteen hours had been a relief to his throbbing arm, even though Phin hadn't wanted to even guess how much gasoline had cost for the trip. Burke had told him not to worry about it, that the firm had it covered. That he'd fly up himself after the holidays and drive them back, since Stone and Delores had a life—and a dog shelter—to return to.

Had Phin known that Stone had no experience driving a full-sized RV, he wouldn't have slept nearly so peacefully the past fifteen hours.

But they were here, and Stone hadn't wrecked their borrowed vehicle.

He gripped Stone's hand, wincing as he came to his feet, aware of Cora hovering in the background. Like she'd catch him if he fell.

Knowing Cora, she probably could. Wasn't much the woman couldn't do.

His family was going to love her.

Phin glanced out the RV window at his parents' house, surprised that no one waited on the front porch. But it was cold. Maybe they were all inside drinking hot cocoa. That had always been one of their Christmas morning traditions.

Or maybe they'd all fled, not wanting him to come home after all.

Cora lightly smacked his ass. "Stop thinking negative thoughts. It's all over your face. It's going to be fine."

"Fine," Delores repeated, but her tone was less sure. She was concerned that the family would be angry that they'd kept Phin's secret for two whole years.

Phin would take the blame. Delores had no family and he'd be damned if she was going to miss out on his.

"Out we go." Stone helped him down the stairs, forgoing the wheelchair that they'd brought just in case.

Phin was going to walk up to his parents' front door on his own two feet.

"You're ridiculous," Cora muttered, pushing the empty wheelchair that had been a source of disagreement every time they'd stopped.

"You're pretty," he replied, earning him Cora's narrow-eyed glare.

"Don't think you can distract me."

Phin pointed to the front window of the house. "Oh, look. The Christmas tree!"

"Ooh." Cora sucked in a breath. "I know what you did there, but the tree's still pretty."

Too soon they were at the front door, Stone and Delores stepping back behind them. Cora parked the wheelchair on the front porch, then took Phin's hand. He touched the top of SodaPop's head.

I've got this. It's going to be wonderful.

He knocked, then twisted the doorknob, unsurprised

when it opened. For a cop's family, the Bishops were remarkably lackadaisical about locking their front door.

"Um . . . hello?" Phin called when no one came forward to meet them.

"In the kitchen! Come on back."

Phin's throat closed at the sound of his mother's voice. Slowly, he and his small entourage made their way to the back of the house, where something smelled amazing.

Cinnamon rolls. Another Bishop tradition. His mother would have been up at dawn prepping the dough to rise.

His mother stood at the stove, stirring something in a pot. An enormous turkey sat in the roasting pan, a bowl of stuffing next to it.

Scarlett sat at the kitchen table, feeding a beautiful toddler sitting in a highchair. Other than the two women and the baby, the room was empty.

Jackie Bishop looked up and smiled. "Phineas. You made it."

Phin blinked. He'd expected a frenzied welcome of hugs and voices talking over each other. But the kitchen was quiet. Only his mother, sister, and niece.

"I . . . I did. Hi, Mom."

Jackie swallowed hard and it was then that he saw the tears in her eyes, the way her hand shook as she stirred. "I'm . . ." She shook her head, unable to continue.

"We're glad you're home," Scarlett said quietly. "So very glad. But we didn't want to overwhelm you right away. Everyone was here, but we made them go home for a little while."

Phin released a relieved breath. "I thought . . ."

Jackie abandoned the stovetop with a small sob. "I can't, Scarlett. I can't be quiet." She ran to Phin, throwing her arms around him.

Phin swallowed back a small grunt of pain as Cora let go of his hand and stepped back, giving him this moment with his mother. He wrapped his good arm around her, cradling the injured arm at his side.

His mother was crying, and Phin felt worse than shit. "I'm sorry," he whispered.

"Don't be," Jackie said brokenly. "I knew you'd come home when you were ready."

Phin's eyes burned. "You did?"

"Of course I did." She sniffled and pulled back, flinching when she saw his bandaged arm. "I forgot. Did I hurt you?"

"No." It wasn't really a lie. "And if you did, I hurt you first. I am sorry, Mama."

She gripped his chin gently, forcing him to look at her. "I don't want to hear you apologize again. I've been a cop's wife for a lot of years, Phineas Bishop. I know what PTSD is. Do I wish that you'd let us help you? Yes, of course. But you're here. You're staying for a little while, right?"

"As long as I can," he promised. "At least a week. Maybe two. But Cora has to get back to work."

Jackie sniffled again, wiping her eyes on her apron as she turned to greet Cora. "Welcome, Cora Jane."

Cora laughed. "I guess that's my whole name now."

"It suits you," Jackie said, then hugged Cora hard. Cora rolled with it, hugging his mother back. "Thank you, child. Thank you for bringing him home."

"He was coming back anyway," Cora told her. "I was just his escort."

Scarlett wiped her daughter's messy mouth and slowly rose. "We had a plan. We were going to be suave and chill. We were going to behave like you never left, like this was just another visit. We weren't going to make you feel bad for staying away." She came to stand in front of him, her long dark hair in a braid down her back, just as he remembered. She stared at him, her dark eyes intense. "But it's not just another visit. You were gone for five long years. *Five years*, Phin. And I'm so pissed off at you for staying gone so long. But I'm still so damn glad that you're finally home. I missed you."

Carefully she embraced him, and he breathed her in, his heart seeming to settle in his chest. "I'm sorry."

"I know." She clung to him, as if afraid he'd disappear again. Which he supposed was fair. "Just . . . don't do it again, okay? Not for five years."

"I won't. I . . . wanted to be . . . fixed when I came home. Not so messed up."

She glared up at him. "Like we cared that you were messed up. You don't need to be fixed. You just need to be *here*." Then she softened, understanding flickering in her eyes. "It's hard to feel like you're not measuring up. I get that. Just don't leave again, okay?"

"I won't." It felt like a vow. It *was* a vow.

She patted his good arm. "Good. That's all I have to say on that. Now . . ." She turned to Stone and Delores, who still waited in the doorway. "Don't think I haven't noticed the service dog, Delores. The one you've been training for the past eighteen months."

Delores drew a breath and lifted her chin. "We gave Phin a safe place to come when he needed to decompress."

"I know," Scarlett said with a shrug.

Both Stone and Delores stared at her. "You knew?" Stone asked. "How long?"

Scarlett rolled her eyes. "For two years. Ever since he met you. Do you think I don't know what goes on in my own town, Stone O'Bannion? What goes on with my brother and sister-in-law?" She crossed the distance to Delores, bending down to give the smaller woman a gentle hug. "Thank you for watching Phin's back. For giving him SodaPop. Cora's told me how much she's helped him." She straightened and hugged Stone. "I intended to stay mad at you for a little while, but I'm too happy that he's home. Thank you, brother."

Stone only nodded, still looking poleaxed. "I can't believe you knew all this time. We were so afraid you'd find out."

"I know," Scarlett said, just a touch evilly, and Phin felt a rush of love for his sister. "I figured you could stew a while."

Stone huffed. "Now, *that* I believe."

Scarlett returned to Phin, linking her arm through his. "Come on. Meet your niece."

But the front door slammed, breaking the moment. "Jackie," a male voice boomed.

Dad. Jonas Bishop was home.

"There's a big-ass RV taking up the entire cul-de-sac," Jonas continued, still at the front door. There was stomping, and Phin pictured his father kicking off his shoes, just like he always had on entering the house. "There won't be any room for Phin to park when he gets here."

A moment later, Jonas's bulk filled the doorway and his expression froze. "Phin," he whispered. Like a prayer. "You're home."

And then his father was crying. Phin had only seen his father cry once before in his life and it had shaken him. It shook him harder now.

"Dad." And then they were hugging and Phin was crying, too.

"You're home, you're home," Jonas kept whispering, holding him so tight.

"I'm home," Phin said, holding his father as hard as he could with one arm.

Finally, Jonas let him go, but not far. He cupped Phin's face in his big hands, staring at him with a wonder that nearly made Phin break down again. Then his father shocked him by kissing Phin's forehead and both cheeks before letting out a satisfied sigh.

"Now it's Christmas," Jonas said, then turned to Cora. "Cora Jane?"

Cora just smiled. "That's me."

"Welcome. And thank you. Scarlett told us how you made a tourniquet out of cloth napkins and a wooden spoon. You saved our son's life."

Cora's smile didn't falter. "He's important. Plus he saved mine first. He's a hero."

Jonas's smile was sweeter than Phin remembered. "I'm glad someone besides us sees that. We have things to talk about, Cora Jane. Many, many things. Starting with your transitional housing for vets. I want to invest."

Phin stared at Cora. "How . . . ?"

Cora shrugged. "Scarlett and I have been talking on the phone every day."

Scarlett nodded. "We're besties now."

Behind him, Stone groaned. "We're all in trouble."

Jonas laughed. "Jackie, let's have that hot chocolate. The others will be here soon."

Cincinnati, Ohio
SUNDAY, DECEMBER 25, 9:00 P.M.

Cora found Phin in his parents' living room, dozing on the sofa. A fire danced in the fireplace and there were several trash bags stacked along one wall, all filled with wrapping paper, the children having been tasked with cleanup after the presents had been opened.

So many presents. Jonas had played Santa Claus and even Cora had received gifts. She'd been so touched.

It had been a long time since she'd had a real family Christmas. Not since her mother was alive. But the Bishops had folded her into their family with hardly a blink.

It was nice.

Cora sat on the edge of the sofa, carefully checking Phin's bandage. He hadn't wanted to wear his sling today. The man was ridiculous about wanting to appear unhurt in front of his family.

She hadn't fought him on it today. He'd been so anxious about the reunion, she hadn't wanted to make things worse. But the reunion had gone far better than she could have imagined, so he would be wearing the sling tomorrow.

"I'm fine, Cora Jane," he murmured.

She stroked his hair, enjoying a moment of quiet after a day of celebration. "You're exceptionally fine."

He laughed. "You're biased."

"I am." She sighed, content. "It's been a good day."

"It has." Grimacing, he sat up, making room for her beside him. "It's even better now," he said, putting his good arm around her shoulders. "Thank you. You made things easier. And my parents love you, just like I said they would."

"They're going to help me prepare the house for residents once I get all the permits signed, so they'll be visiting a lot."

"I figured they would. I like the thought of it, of them visiting us."

Us. It had a nice sound.

"So . . . have you thought about Burke's offer?" she asked.

They hadn't mentioned it to his family, but Burke had offered Phin a job as an investigator once he got his PI license. Not a bodyguard, but an investigator.

"I have."

He didn't say any more, so she pulled back enough to look up at him. "And?"

"I think I'm going to say no."

Cora stared. "But that's all you've wanted since you came to New Orleans, to be a full member of Burke's team."

"I know." His jaw tightened and he looked away, his gaze settling on the flames in the fireplace. "But I also know that I have to respect my limitations. High-stress situations can make me spiral. I can't avoid all high-stress situations, but . . ." He swallowed hard. "I want to be there for you, Cora Jane. I want to be there for my friends. For my parents and my sister and brothers. My nieces and nephews. I never want to feel like I have to hide for five years again."

Pride warmed her from the inside out. "Look at me?" she asked in a murmur, waiting until he finally did so.

As she expected, there was shame in his eyes. She wasn't having that.

"I'm actually relieved," she confessed, and his eyes widened.

"Really?"

"Really. You are an amazing man and you could do the work Burke wants you to do. But just because you can, doesn't mean you should. I think stepping back from a dream because you want to be present for me and everyone else makes you even more of a hero." She leaned up, brushing a kiss over his lips. "You can still consult for Burke. Help them brainstorm when Molly gets out her whiteboard. You don't have to be in the thick of things."

His relief was clear. "I feel like I'm taking the easy way out."

She shrugged. "So? I think you deserve some peace, Phin. There's no shame in that. And I'm relieved because I won't have to worry that you're getting shot again. That took ten years off my life, I swear."

He rested his cheek on top of her head. "I wasn't happy about it, either."

"Do you know what you want to do instead?" she asked.

"I was thinking about getting my general contractor's license. Maybe get some experience doing electrical work. Just in case a certain house needs it."

Cora winced. "And by a certain house, do you mean a Garden District house that I happen to live in?"

"Yeah," he said ruefully. "You're gonna need a full re-wire eventually."

"And by eventually, do you mean soon?"

"Yeah. Sorry."

"Well, then, I think a GC's license makes a lot of sense. We can fix up my house and then we can train the vets we help. Give them a marketable skill."

"*We*. I like that."

She smiled. "Me too."

"Can we come to Cincinnati every so often? I've missed so much of my nieces and nephews growing up. I don't want to miss any more."

"We absolutely can. Besides, Scarlett and I are besties now. She'll be visiting a lot."

He groaned quietly. "I'm glad you're friends, but you two being besties makes me very afraid."

"It should. It really should." She laid her head on his shoulder. "Thank you for sharing your family. I've missed having one." Cora had been enchanted with Phin's mom, the retired English teacher, and Jackie had been ecstatic that Phin's girlfriend was a librarian.

He kissed her temple. "They've adopted you, like it or not."

She liked it very much indeed. She'd always miss her mother, her grandmother. John Robert. Her father, who really had been trying to help people, even if he'd gone about it badly.

She'd mourn the loss of Tandy's friendship, but hoped her oldest friend would someday return to New Orleans.

And someday Cora might even be able to mourn the loss of Patrick. Or, at least, who she'd thought he'd been.

But she'd found new family—Burke's people and the Bishops had welcomed her with open arms. She wasn't alone.

"Merry Christmas, Phin."

"Merry Christmas, Cora Jane."

ACKNOWLEDGMENTS

The Starfish—Christine, Sheila, Brian, Kathie, and Cheryl. Thank you for the plotting!

Robin Bradford for all the information on librarians. Cora thanks you! As do I!

Andrew Grey for being my word count buddy. And for adding that little twist to the plot I'd been missing.

Sarah Hafer for the editing. Your keen eye catches so many of my mistakes before anyone else can see them.

James Lee for the computer know-how.

Beth Miller for the proofing.

Robin Rue, Liz Sellers, and Jen Doyle for your continued support. Thank you.

As always, all mistakes are my own.

Keep reading for a preview of

DEAD MAN'S LIST

Book three of the San Diego Case Files

IT WAS, KIT thought as she drew her jacket tighter, too cold to be sitting out in the barn. But McKittrick House, despite its homey warmth and delicious smells of apple pie and clean laundry, was not where she needed to be right now.

There were too many people in the big house. She loved them all. Her parents, her brothers and sisters—foster kids, all fifteen of them. It was the first Friday of the new year, and they'd gathered to celebrate.

They were one big truly happy family.

They were one big truly *nosy* family. Everyone wanted to know if she'd had her date with Sam Reeves yet.

She had not. And she might not. Their second date, which had been hanging over her head for more than a month, was now upon her. She'd spent six months during the spring and summer avoiding the police psychologist. *Because I was scared.*

She'd known that she'd hurt him eventually because she was shit with relationships. And Sam deserved better. But then she'd agreed to go on one date and, in a moment of weakness, asked him on a second. That had been over a month ago and life had interfered. But now it was time to face the music. *And I'm still scared.*

"Cold feet," she muttered to herself. "It's just cold feet."

She shifted on the hay bale, glad she'd had the presence of mind to throw a saddle blanket over it before she'd sat down. Hay bales looked like perfect seats but they were prickly as hell.

Like me, she thought with a sigh.

Her sigh echoed back to her, and Kit stiffened. She'd thought she was alone.

"Hello?" she called. "Come on out, whoever you are."

One of the stall doors opened, revealing a teenage girl with pink and blue streaks through her sandy blond hair.

"Rita? What are you doing out here?"

Her foster sister—soon to be legally adopted sister—stepped into the dim light. "I needed some quiet."

"Wanna sit and be quiet with me? Or I can leave."

Rita's smile was wobbly. "I'd like to sit and be quiet with you."

She sat on the bale, Kit's arm wrapping around Rita's thin shoulders. "You're not wearing a coat. You're going to freeze out here."

"I'm *fine*," Rita said with a condescending huff. "It's not that cold."

But Rita was trembling, so Kit tightened her hold. "Mom and Pop know where you are?"

Rita nodded. "I didn't want them to worry."

"Thank you." Kit would say no more, giving Rita the quiet she'd requested. If the girl wanted to talk, Kit would listen.

Rita sighed again, long and loud. "Cold feet, huh?"

Kit frowned. "Did you hear me say that?"

"Yep. You're going on that date tomorrow, Kit."

Kit's frown became a scowl. "Says who?"

"Says me. And Mom and Pop and all the others back at the house. You're meeting Sam tomorrow for your date in the desert if we have to tie you up and drive you there ourselves."

"That's kidnapping," Kit said lightly, wishing she were

certain the family wouldn't do such a thing. But they just might. They liked the psychologist who, for some reason, still seemed to want to date Kit. "I could arrest you."

"It would be worth it."

Kit let go of Rita's shoulders to cross her arms tightly over her chest. "Damn, girl," she grumbled.

Rita laughed, a sweet sound that they were all hearing more often these days. "You will go, right?"

Kit shot Rita a sour look. "I don't know."

Rita shook her head. "Kit, what are you afraid of?"

Kit exhaled quietly. "I don't know."

Rita put her arm around Kit's shoulders, and Kit's heart cracked a little. She loved Rita so very much, even though the girl could be a little shit when it came to Kit dating Sam.

"You wanna know what I think?" Rita murmured.

"I don't know," Kit said again.

"Too bad. I'm going to tell you anyway. I think you're scared you'll like him too much. That you'll have too good a time and he'll want a third date. Am I close?"

Yes. "Maybe."

"I also think you've had too much time to build this up in your mind. You were supposed to have this date over a month ago, but things happened and it got drawn out and out and out."

Defensiveness coiled in Kit's gut. "Not my fault."

It really hadn't been.

"No," Rita said, speaking carefully now. "You had a case and Sam understood that. He had an emergency with one of the teens at the shelter, and you understood that. Then you had another case—which, by the way, I don't think you *had* to work that weekend. I think that was you having cold feet."

She was right again, Kit thought. It rankled, being called out by a fourteen-year-old. "How would you even know that?"

"I asked Connor when he came last week to bring Christmas presents for Mom and Pop. He said the case was important but not so much that you couldn't have investigated the next day. He was peeved that he had to cancel his date with CeCe because you got scared of your date with Sam."

Kit blew out an irritated breath. Her partner in the homicide department had a big mouth. "Connor Robinson told you that?"

"He did." Rita chuckled. "Then he begged me not to tell you he'd said that because he was afraid you'd get even with him."

"He'd be right," Kit said darkly. "Besides, Sam canceled most of the dates. Not me."

"Well, yeah. His father went into the hospital."

Sam's father had had a small stroke and, while he'd be okay, Sam had spent most of December in Scottsdale. Kit had meant to drive to Arizona, to be there for Sam, but she'd lost her nerve.

She hated herself for that. But Sam's father's stroke had made her paranoid about leaving Harlan and Betsy. They were about the same age as Sam's dad. That something could happen to them was terrifying.

"You know too damn much, kid," she said, sounding petulant to her own ears.

Rita tightened her hold on Kit's shoulders. "Kit. You like Sam. I know you do. What's the worst that can happen?"

That I'll fall for him. That I'll come to need him.

That he'll come to need me.

And *that* was too much responsibility. "Since when are you a therapist?" Kit asked, a little more nastily than she'd intended.

"Since you needed one," Rita shot back, unfazed. "Look. You can talk to me or not. But don't cancel your date. Please. I think you need him."

Kit's chin came up. "I don't need anyone."

"That's a lie," Rita said softly. "And you promised that you'd never lie to me."

Kit sighed. Once again, the kid was right. "Why are you doing this to me?"

"Why are you doing this to yourself?"

Kit's lips twitched. "You've been picking up techniques from Dr. Carlisle."

Rita's therapist was Sam's boss, and the woman made Kit nervous. She—and Rita—saw far too much.

"Yes, I have. I'm thinking about being a therapist, too."

"I thought you wanted to be a cop."

"Maybe I do. I'm fourteen. I've got time to decide."

Time. That was the one thing Kit wasn't sure that she had. She *did* want this date with Sam and she *was* scared. But time was passing and, as so many helpful people had reminded her, someone else might snap Sam up.

Because he was a good man.

Too good for me.

"Why are you out here?" Kit asked, desperate to refocus their conversation. "What's bothering you?"

Rita studied her, her gaze cagey. "I'll tell you if you promise to go on that date and not stand Dr. Sam up."

Kit closed her eyes. "Why is this so important to you?"

"Because I love you," Rita said, so softly that Kit nearly missed it.

"Shit." Kit's eyes burned. "No fair."

Rita shrugged. "I calls 'em like I sees 'em."

Which was one of Kit's favorite phrases. *Using my words against me.*

"Brat."

"Promise me," Rita murmured.

"*Fine.* I promise. I will go. I will try to have fun. I just . . ." She trailed off, swallowing back the words.

Rita met her gaze. "You what?"

"I don't want to hurt him," she confessed. "I'm shit with relationships. And why am I getting dating advice from a fourteen-year-old?"

"Because I'm wise beyond my years," Rita said dryly. "You said so yourself, just last week."

"Brat."

"Just . . . breathe, Kit. It's what you always tell me to do."

"You have thrown way too many of my own words back at me tonight. *Fine*. I promise I will go on the date. Now you spill. Why are you here?"

Rita bit her lip. "Drummond's trial is in two weeks."

Kit brushed a lock of hair from Rita's forehead. "I know, honey."

Christopher Drummond had been arrested for murdering Rita's mother. Rita had found the body and had known her mother's employer had killed her, but no one had listened because the man was richer than God and, in San Diego, nearly as powerful.

Kit had gotten the case reopened, recusing herself because of her relationship with Rita. Connor Robinson had investigated the case and made the arrest. And, while it wasn't a slam dunk, the prosecutor was confident he could get a conviction.

But Rita would have to testify. And Christopher Drummond would be there, staring at her.

The worst part was that Drummond had sexually assaulted Rita as well. None of the family knew the details, and Rita wouldn't talk about it. They knew only that it had been one of the times her mother had brought Rita to work with her, cleaning Drummond's house. Rita had refused to press charges, and they'd respected her decision. But that assault had to be dealt with at some point.

Rita's apprehension about Drummond's trial made perfect sense.

"I'm scared," Rita confessed. "What if he gets off, Kit? What if he goes free?"

"Joel isn't going to let that happen." Joel Haley was the prosecutor, a friend of Kit's, and Sam's best friend. He knew what he was doing in a courtroom.

"You can't promise that," Rita said, staring at their feet.

"You're right. I can't. But I can promise Joel will do everything in his power to see Drummond put in a prison cell for the rest of his life."

Rita lifted her gaze to Kit's, her fear clear to see. "If he goes free, he'll come after me. I'm the one who accused him. Even if I didn't press charges on the . . . on the other thing."

Kit's jaw tightened, fury burning in her chest. "He may try, but to get to you he will have to go through me. And Mom and Pop and every single McKittrick. And we are formidable."

Rita smiled, but it was forced. "We are."

"I'll be with you in the courtroom. Mom and Pop, too."

"Promise?" Rita asked, sounding like a very young child.

"I promise. I've already told my boss, and he knows I'm taking vacation days for the trial."

Rita's eyes widened. "You're taking *vacation*? You never take vacation."

"I am this time." Kit booped Rita's nose. "For you."

Rita's eyes filled with tears. "I do love you," she whispered.

Kit couldn't stop her own tears. The words were hard to say back, even though she felt them keenly. She'd only just learned to tell Harlan and Betsy that she loved them. But Rita needed the words.

"And I love you. I will keep you safe, Rita. Always."

"I know. Thank you."

"You never have to thank me," Kit said fiercely. "You deserve to be protected."

"Because you couldn't protect Wren?"

Kit flinched, because Rita was right once again. Kit's sister Wren had been murdered when they were only fifteen, and Kit had never recovered. They'd never found the doer, either. It was a bitter pill to swallow, knowing Wren's killer was out there somewhere, walking free.

Kit didn't want Rita to live her life knowing that the

monster who'd assaulted her and who'd killed her mother hadn't paid for his crime.

"Partly because of Wren," Kit admitted. "But mostly because of you. You are good and kind and you deserve the best life. A safe life."

Rita smiled, and this time it was real. "You really do love me."

Kit rested her forehead on Rita's. "Even when you're a brat who's wise beyond her years."

"Thank you." Rita straightened. "We should get back in there. There won't be any food left." She rose and pointed a finger at Kit. "Tomorrow. You and Snickerdoodle are meeting Sam and Siggy."

"Dogs and desert," Kit said dutifully. "I promised. I won't back out."

Sam loved the desert, and Kit let herself remember that she'd wanted to know why. She let herself remember that Sam was good and kind and deserved a fun date.

Maybe I do, too.

"Thanks, Kit." Rita hugged her, then skipped out of the barn before Kit could react.

Before she could hug her back. Kit wasn't great at giving hugs.

Kit wasn't great at too many things.

Sam was good at everything. He was a caring therapist, he volunteered his time with teens and the elderly, and he had the patience of a saint. He'd never pushed her or made her feel bad for needing her space or for being prickly. Sam was a good man, plain and simple.

With a big sigh, she folded the saddle blanket, putting it away. Then she walked out of the barn, only to see two glowing lights off to the side. Two lights that illuminated a man's big hands as he carved a block of wood.

"Pop? What are you doing out here? You'll catch cold."

He looked up from where he sat on a bench, a flexible flashlight hanging from his neck. Kit had gotten the light for him for Christmas, and she didn't think she'd seen him without it since he'd opened the box. It provided enough light for him to get all the details right on whatever he was creating.

"I wanted to make sure you two were okay. I didn't listen in."

Kit settled next to him on the bench. "Rita was making me promise not to cancel my date with Sam."

Harlan smiled. "Good for Rita. That girl is somethin' else."

"She is. She's also nervous about the trial."

Harlan's smile faded. "I know. We'll stand with her."

"She's afraid if Drummond gets off, he'll come after her."

Harlan's jaw tightened. "I'm getting better security."

There was something in his tone that gave Kit pause. "What's going on, Pop?"

Harlan exhaled quietly. "Someone sent a letter to Rita. Unsigned."

Kit tensed. "Tell me."

Wordlessly, he pulled a folded paper from his pocket and handed it to her.

Kit unfolded the single page with trembling fingers. "'I see your school is doing *Alice in Wonderland* this spring. Have fun being in the ensemble. It's not a huge role, but I know you'll do it brilliantly. I'll be in the front row.'" New rage bubbled up. *Son of a fucking bitch. Drummond.* But there was no signature. No evidence it had come from the disgraced former city council member. The man had been released on two million dollars bail and was freely walking the streets until his upcoming trial. Now Rita's fear made even more sense. "When did this arrive?"

"Right before Christmas."

Kit drew a breath, trying not to sound angry with her father. "Why didn't you tell me?"

"I'm telling you now," Harlan said. "Rita didn't want you to know. She was afraid you'd go after Drummond. Get yourself in trouble."

How Kit wanted to do just that. *Get Drummond. Not*

get into trouble. But they'd be one and the same if she allowed herself the vengeance she craved on Rita's behalf. "Do you think this is from him?"

"Don't you?"

"Yes, but I imagine he's smart enough not to have left any evidence. Did you report this?"

"Joel knows. That letter's a copy. He has the original."

"Okay." The prosecutor on Rita's case would do the right thing. "That has to be enough for now. And it shows that Drummond is scared. That's positive."

"Yeah." Harlan's throat worked as he tried to swallow. "I hate him," he whispered.

"Me too. What security are you having installed?"

"Cameras along the property line and around the house. An alarm system on doors and windows. Cartridges for my shotgun."

"Anson?" Kit ignored that last one.

"Of course."

Anson was one of the fosters who'd passed through McKittrick House the year before Kit had arrived. He owned a security firm up in Anaheim. He'd do an excellent job.

"You might also consider a dog for Rita and the other girls." Emma and Tiffany were the newest foster children at McKittrick House, and they and Rita had become best friends. She lightened her tone, needing to lessen the tension on her father's kind face. "They might feel safer with a dog. And then they won't always be 'borrowing' Snickerdoodle from me."

Harlan lifted a bushy eyebrow. "Did the girls put you up to this?"

"Nope." Kit forced a grin. "All my idea. Every girl needs a dog, Pop."

He chuckled, but it was also forced. Still, it was a chuckle. "I'll take the kids to the animal shelter this weekend. We'll see if we can find a dog who'll suit."

Kit rested her head on his broad shoulder. He was the

strongest, safest person she knew. He'd been her rock since she and Wren had snuck into this very barn as twelve-year-old runaways. Harlan and Betsy McKittrick had found them hiding and given them shelter. And so much love.

"Thanks, Pop. For everything. For me and for Rita and all the others. Love you."

"Love you, too, Kitty-Cat." He kissed the top of her head. "Have fun on your date."

She sighed, letting the Rita problem go for now. "I'll try. But if there's a murder, I'll have to cancel."

Harlan snorted quietly. "You sound almost hopeful."

She kind of was. But wishing for a murder was wrong, and Sam deserved better. "I'm not hopeful. I'm just . . ."

"Scared," he supplied gently.

"Yeah."

"It's okay to be scared, Kit. But other things scare you and you push through. You'll be okay. I know it."

Kit wished she were as confident.

And she still wished for a murder. Just a small one.